WAKE UP
HAPPY
EVERY DAY

Stephen May

Typeset by Hewer Text UK Ltd, Edinburgh
Printed in Great Britain by CPI Group (UK) Ltd, Croydon CR0 4YY

B L O O M S B U R Y

LONDON · NEW DELHI · NEW YORK · SYDNEY

First published in Great Britain 2014
This paperback edition published 2015

Copyright © 2014 by Stephen May

The moral right of the author has been asserted

Bloomsbury Publishing plc
50 Bedford Square
London
WC1B 3DP

www.bloomsbury.com

Bloomsbury Publishing, London, New Delhi, New York and Sydney

Bloomsbury is a trademark of Bloomsbury Publishing Plc

A CIP catalogue record for this book is available from the British Library

ISBN 978 1 4088 4076 4

Printed and b CR0 4YY

A NOTE ON THE AUTHOR

STEPHEN MAY's first novel, *Tag*, won the Reader's Choice Award at the 2009 Welsh Book of the Year. His second, *Life! Death! Prizes!*, was published by Bloomsbury in 2012 and was shortlisted for the Costa Novel Award, and the *Guardian*'s 'Not the Booker Prize'. Originally from Bedford, Stephen now lives and works in West Yorkshire.

www.sdmay.com
@RealStephenMay

000000747653

For Charles Ockelford
and in memory of
Edward May
27 May 1935 – 8 May 1998

A few honest men are better than numbers

Those who hope for no other life are dead even for this
Johann Wolfgang von Goethe

*Whoever said that money can't buy happiness simply
didn't know where to go shopping*
Bo Derek

One

NICKY

Fifty is not the new forty. No. Fifty is the new nineteen. A time when the world is full of limitless possibility. That's what Russell says.

I am in San Francisco. In Russian Hill. In a house that once belonged to Fanny Osborn-Stevenson, widow of Robert Louis. I am drinking 1963 vintage malt and sitting in a fine leather armchair. There is the smoky crackle of vintage blues in the background. On vinyl. Bessie Smith. Good booze, good blues and nothing to do tomorrow. This is actually all anyone needs to be happy. Only I can't concentrate because Russell is still talking in his horrible mid-Atlantic drawl. The voice I'll never get used to.

Some people would say it was better than the mockney whine he used to have. Not me.

'I'm giving it all up, Nicky-boy. Getting out while I can.'

Russell is turning his back on everything. Not the money, obviously. Just the work. Just the life. Just the people. He's fifty tomorrow and he's worked long enough – now is the time for adventure, travel. He's going to see everything. He's going to Marrakesh, Ulan Bator, Spitzbergen. He's going to Easter Island, Dahomey, Kaliningrad. The Antarctic. He's going to Everywhere. And then he's going to Anywhere.

And he's not just going to see these places, oh no – he's going to develop relationships with them. He's going to get under their skin. He's going to pull them apart to see how they work. Maybe he'll write about them. Proper books too. Not just bloody blogs.

And then he's going where they don't even have Starbucks. Where he can't be emailed or poked or skyped or dream-tabbed or sat-phoned.

1

Places where the long needy arms of Facebook friends can't tap him on the shoulder to suggest he like something they've done, made, seen. Or, worse, like things their kids have done, made, seen. He's going where he's beyond the reach of what's trending.

I wonder if there even are such places any more, but Russell's too intoxicated by his plan to listen.

Maybe he'll help set up schools, hospitals. Maybe he'll adopt a few kids. Bright kids. Kids who can talk. Kids who can walk properly. I let it go, don't say anything.

Maybe he'll build his own city. The perfect city. A place where you'll find everything you need. I believe him. He always liked to do elaborate things in Lego when we were kids.

On and on he goes, while Bessie struggles to make herself heard. He says that, then again, maybe he won't help the street kids of South Sudan or wherever. Maybe he won't create Knoxville. Maybe he'll – at last – just have fun. See what happens. He's going to be open to whatever comes along. He's going to have the gap year he denied himself all those years ago. The gratification he deferred then he's going to have now with compound interest. From now on he is going to have a gap life.

His eyes are blazing bright in his lean and sculpted face. This is his renaissance. He is leaving behind the crocodile swamps of commerce. He's terminated all his relationships with anyone connected with his old life.

'Except you and Sarah, Nicky-boy. I hope you feel flattered.'

I take a sip. Bessie has got the Empty Bed Blues. I take another sip.

Russell's liquidated all his interests and he names the figure he's got for them. The numbers make my skin itch.

It's a staggering sum.

Turns out Russell is richer than the Queen, richer than Madonna. Vatican rich. Biblically rich. Richer.

What a waste.

*   *   *

I close my eyes. Listen to the music reaching its fingers out from all the ghosts of the great depression: from the soup kitchens, from all the brothers sparing dimes. And, hey, listen up fellas, Bessie Smith wants a little more sugar in her bowl. The minx.

And then Russell feels the need to tell me why he can afford to do this gap-life thing and I can't. And so the very last words he says to me, like so many other words over the years, are about success, failure and the line between them.

People say it's a fine line, like the one between love and hate. Russell, bless him, has never seen it like this. For Russell it's always been more of an unnavigable ocean. His continent of hard-won achievement on one side – all fifteen million dollar houses once owned by the widows of famous wordsmiths – and the scrubby, barely inhabitable landscape of my failure on the other. It's a subject he finds endlessly fascinating. One he can return to again and again, always finding something new to say.

And now, on this last night, he says, 'Thing is, Nicky-boy, I know that it is partly genetic. And it might be a little bit environment but mainly – mainly' – here he wags a stiff finger for emphasis – 'it simply has to be character. I have it. Sarah has it. You don't.'

He says that, or something very like it, and then he goes to one of the six luxury bathrooms recently restored by Joe Farrell, architect to the stars.

Russell's view is that he's done better because he *is* better. I've done crap because I *am* crap. And, truthfully, I don't mind this talk. Not really. I can't be arsed to even pretend to mind. I'm used to it. It's an old, old routine, easily bearable. It's not like I even really listen any more. Sarah gets annoyed about it, but I don't. And Sarah, my beautiful, loyal, kind-hearted life partner, is upstairs, lying next to Scarlett, my funny-faced newish daughter. Where is Russell's loyal, kind-hearted life partner? Where is Russell's funny-faced newish daughter?

Where is the love?

Exactomundo, my friend. It is nowhere.

I stand looking out into the diamond-studded purple of the San Francisco night until Bessie Smith finishes asking all mankind to do our duty – she's insatiable that girl – and it's the sudden silence that coaxes me out of my fugue state. Where is Russell anyway? Unlike him to nod out. That's one of the things about Russell: he's always awake – thinking, planning, scheming, making calculations on wee slips of paper long after everyone else has finally slid into unconsciousness. Always closing in on something.

Most likely he's taking a sudden conference call with Brazzaville or São Paulo. Because I don't actually buy the giving-up thing. Even if it's for real, it's still going to be a fad, a fling. Russell can't give up whatever it is he actually does. It's who he is. Russell is addicted to getting people to dance for him. Always has been ever since he was buying mint imperials on the way to school at 10p a bag, and selling them individually in lessons at 1p each. He must have been eight when he started doing that.

And now I need to pay a visit too. I know every bedroom – sorry, every *guest suite* – in this place comes with its own wet room but I don't want to risk stumbling into Russell's lair. If he really has crashed then let him stay that way. I don't need a resumption of the never-ending lecture on my own inadequacies. And if he's awake, I don't want to interrupt the soft murmuring of insane strings of numbers into the ears of some minion on the other side of the world. The issuing of orders that might mean the end of a rain forest, the slow death of a language. And I don't want to find our room. I don't really want to wake Sarah, she's a girl who needs her sleep. And I don't want to wake Scarlett either, because she's a girl who doesn't need her sleep. She'll want the telly on and there'll be a scene.

She's got stamina our daughter. When she wants something she doesn't give up until she gets it, so we mostly cut out the middleman and give her what she wants straight away. Just saves a whole lot of time. And, yes, I know: a rod for our own backs. Possibly. But we'll cross that bridge etc. Consistency – I think that's what kids need. And we're consistently push-overs, so everyone knows where they stand, don't they?

I creep into the cloakroom off the cavernous, parqueted, tackily chandeliered hallway. Go into the little slice of England with the vintage Giles cartoons on the wall and the copies of *Private Eye* stacked up. And that's where I find him, kneeling on the floor in a parody of prayer, and already cold to the bone and rigid.

I've seen a dead body before, of course – by the time you get to the age of forty-nine who hasn't? – but that was my mum safe home after a year thrashing on the end of the hook and line that is stomach cancer. Laid out in the scented parlour of a proper funeral home with her face smoothed as bland as the moon. As annihilating as icing on a store-bought cake. She had been moved from the raw, upsetting twitch and flex of death to the still ranks of the dear departed. She'd been properly processed.

Russell hasn't been processed and he doesn't look like anyone's dear departed. And he doesn't look at peace. He looks enraged. Cheated.

There is, I'm certain, a medical explanation for the mottled framboise of his face – something boringly scientific – but at this moment he just looks bloody furious, engorged with murderous intent. The seething victim of a juvenile practical joke who is going to properly fuck someone up when he catches up with them. A paranoid home-owner who has glimpsed an intruder he intends to shoot.

Russell doesn't respond to my voice, or to my hand when I shake his shoulder. He doesn't tell me to sod off. He doesn't ask that if a man can't pass out in his own bathroom, where the fuck can he pass out? He's chill and stiff through his Oakland Raiders sweatshirt. I know it then.

Russell Albert Knox, my friend since 1968 when we were both four years old and both living in Plover Way, Brickhill, Bedford,

Bedfordshire, England, the United Kingdom, Europe, The World, The Universe – is dead. Russell is dead and I feel . . .

What do I feel?

I feel tired.

I've never been a hard man. Never even pretended to be. I'm a softy. Everyone says so. Sarah says it's one of the main things she liked about me. I've even ended up with a reasonably girlie version of my own name. It's always been Nicky, never the curt manliness of a simple Nick, or the formal bow of a Nicholas. So I don't want anyone thinking I take Russell's death in my stride. I'm properly shocked, just as you're meant to be. And shock must account for at least some of the stuff I do later on.

I don't puke or anything – in real life people don't. It's only in films that people routinely throw up on encountering a dead body. No, I'm not sick – but I do need to sit down for a while.

I sit and I finish my drink and listen to the blood thrum in my ears and my heart two-stepping away in my chest and God knows how long that takes, but eventually I recover enough to get up and do something practical. Something useful.

I change the record.

Sounds bad, doesn't it? Callous. But it's not. Not really.

See, I remember the house seeming to get smaller, the walls encroaching on me and I get the notion to honour my dead friend by finishing the bottle and playing something with heft. Something with weight. Which means something with cellos. John Taverner, *The Protecting Veil*. It's one of the few classical pieces I know, and it was Russell who introduced me to it. So it is entirely apt. I absolutely need to hear it. I need that, and, suddenly, weirdly, I need a cheese sandwich. And crisps.

Shock, see. Grief. Makes us mad. Makes us hungry. Makes us do strange and wonderful things.

Pretty soon this place, this luxury faux-castle with unrivalled views over the world's coolest city, is certain to become a venue for difficult phone calls, tricksy questions and form filling. All the dispiriting stuff of clerking. The wee wee hours aren't suitable for all that. Far better, I think, to use the time till morning proper in reflection on Russell's life and work. To ponder in sombre fashion what a fragile, ill-made piece of crap is Man. To acknowledge that we're born astride a grave etc. Russell deserves some modest period of grace before the various civil services of two sick and criminal nations put him through their rendering machinery. He's owed that.

I'm drunk remember. Shocked remember. And in Hyde Street, Russian Hill. Hyde Street. In a house once owned by the widow of Robert Louis Stevenson, where there is a stained-glass window that shows the *Hispaniola* in full sail, through which, on a good day, you can see Treasure Island. And Alcatraz.

I am lost. I'm adrift. I'm drunk. I'm grieving. Maybe I've even gone a little crazy. Let's not forget any of that.

Two

LORNA

And in those same early hours way across town in the Tenderloin, Lorna Dawson holds Jez's cock gently but securely between her thumb and forefinger. She strokes him. She bends and puts the bruised hibiscus of him between her lips, then she unrolls the condom down him while he inhales deeply and raises his hips. It's a smooth, practised movement and she wonders if you can get too expert at something like this. Does it say something about her that isn't so great actually? And then she wonders if Jez's erections are less strong these days, whether there is just a little more give in them. A little more plasticity. She won't mention it, but maybe it means age is catching up with him. Just a bit. He is nearly thirty-five after all.

As she clambers above him, ready for what Jez likes to call docking procedure, she makes the mistake of catching his eye. He winks, and something inside her shrivels and dies.

She closes her eyes and sinks down onto him, settles her weight onto her calves and the backs of her thighs. This is the last time. Please make this the last time. She rocks her hips a few times. Experimental. Tentative. Now that he's inside her, he feels as hard as ever. Maybe she's mistaken about the ageing thing.

She opens her eyes. He's staring right at her. Concentrating, unblinking now, frowning like he's invigilating an exam. He holds her around the hips, moves her gently. 'Baby, that's beautiful,' he says. 'You look so fucking beautiful.' She rocks slowly, forwards and back, up and down. He is such a plonker sometimes.

8

But afterwards, she lies with her head on his skinny hairless chest, listening to the distant gurglings going on somewhere deep inside him. Like a faulty heating system. Like there are bits of him coming loose, and it makes her feel fond of him in a way she never does when they're fucking.

'Here we are again,' she says. Then she says, 'This isn't love.' And is surprised to find she's said it out loud.

'Hush,' he says. 'We said we'd never use that word.'

She's genuinely shocked. Did they agree that? And he must have noticed her quiver because he says, 'You're right. This isn't love. This is something better than that.'

'What's better than love?'

'Almost anything,' he says. 'Almost everything.'

She wants to smack him right in the mouth. It's so like him. Sums him up. Glib and lazy. Clever and meaningless. And, actually, thinking about it, not even all that clever.

She sits up, flicks her hair back out of her eyes. He loves it long and wild and dirty-blonde like this. Idiot man, he thinks dirty-blonde hair means a dirty-blonde soul. Which in her case it maybe does, a bit. But only a bit. Whatever, she's definitely getting it cut. Maybe dyed too. She could be a gamine brunette. She could be that.

She rubs her arms, they're goose-pimply and the friction feels good. Jez looks up at her, smiling. He's like some kind of pale snake. Not a lightning-quick venomous one, not a cobra or anything like that. More like an albino anaconda that's recently swallowed a guinea pig. Smug, sated, sleek, and ready to sleep. Is he even a good shag? She can't tell any more.

Jez's eyes are closing, he's drifting off. She pulls his nose. 'Come on, Jezza, you can do better than that.'

His eyes snap open. He's annoyed. Good. Lorna feels her heart begin to race a little. Good good good. He's pissed off. Excellent.

Jez frowns. 'Desire is better than love. Friendship is better than love. Understanding, tolerance, warmth, self-knowledge. They're all better than love.'

9

'They *are* love, you idiot. All those things – they are love.' She keeps a smile in her voice. Even so, Jez tightens his lips. He doesn't like conflict. He especially doesn't like post-coital conflict.

'No they're not. They all *last*. Love doesn't. Love is like an infection. It's a fever, a nasty little rash. It's a few days of heat and sweat and panic. A few weeks maybe.'

She wonders if he believes this. Maybe he does. 'No,' she says at last, still careful to keep her tone light. 'You're describing something else. Flu maybe. Or syphilis.' Or the early stages of pregnancy. But she isn't going to say that. Jez still doesn't need to know about that. He won't ever need to know about that.

Jez shrugs his shoulders.

And he's not even handsome. Not really. His skin is getting rough, his teeth are going sort of yellowy. Off-white anyway. There are tiny flecks of crud on his eyelids. And he's too bony to be a proper man. He's thirty-five for chrissakes, or nearly, and still a hairless streak of piss. It's not natural.

'I can't come here again.'

'You always say that.'

'This time I mean it.'

'You always say that too.'

She sits up. 'Jez, I do mean it. Next time you call, I'm going to be out, my cell will be off and I'll be out of state. I'll be skiing, or diving or . . .' She stops, unable to think of anything else she wants to do that might sound suitably exotic or playful or adventurous.

'Or what?' says Jez.

'Or dead.' She holds her breath.

'OK,' he says. OK? OK? What does he mean by that?

He pulls her back down on top of him. 'I'm not going to be allowed to sleep am I?' He smiles and his face looms into hers, too close for her to see it properly. There is just a sense of teeth and lips and nose and hot breath and a sweaty lump of hair. But he sounds happy now, and she knows he can look beautiful when he's happy. Her heart cracks.

10

It's Friday. She knows already that he won't call her again until Wednesday at the earliest. She'll be out. She'll be away.

Jez moves his hands over shoulders, her back, her arse, her thighs. She kisses his neck. She feels him twitch beneath her, stir against the fuzz between her legs. The fuzz he's been trying to get her to get rid of actually.

She kisses him again. 'I don't come here for warmth, or friendship, or any of that. I come here because I'm a bit bored and a bit lonely.' And as soon as she says it, she knows that it is true and she knows she has to leave California as soon as. It just isn't her friend any more.

'Hush now,' Jez says.

Three

NICKY

Some time later – who knows how long? – I have the big idea. An idea that could be good for us but one that, miraculously, hurts no one else. Because ideas often do, don't they? Hurt people, I mean.

And it's just taking vague shape when Sarah appears, red hair excitingly disordered, the constellations of freckles standing out against the Celtic pale of her skin. Skin made still more ghostly by her being abruptly shaken from sleep. She is Celtic-eyed too, and right now her sharp blue stare flashes dangerous flames as she stumbles in wondering what – exactly – I think I'm doing. We have a child trying to sleep upstairs. And what is this dreadful, churchy music anyway?

And I'm too dazed to say anything so I put my finger to my lips and take her by the hand and show her Russell on the floor of the bathroom. And when she runs for her phone to call 911, I follow and spill out my idea to her hunched and hurrying dressing-gowned back.

It's important that you know this about Sarah. She's not just loyal and kind-hearted, she's also almost pathologically law-abiding. Even getting a parking ticket or a library fine panics her. Uniquely among the people I know, she never had a shoplifting phase as a kid. She's never even nicked pens or stationery from work. Never jumped a red light, never dropped a sweetie wrapper in the park. She claims she never even tried to buy booze or fags under age. She's a phenomenon. So when I explain my idea I guess I'm almost certain that she'll reject it out of hand. In fact, if I'd genuinely thought she'd go for it, I probably would never have said it. Does that make sense? I think at this stage it is just a theoretical plan. An abstract thing.

A phantasm conjured by grief and whisky. And cellos. Don't forget those cellos.

She stops. She turns around, those eyes as blue and as wide as the bay itself. I think I'm really in the shit.

'What? What did you just say?'

'Nothing. Just an idea. Forget it.'

But she makes me say it all again, slowly, and I do and this time it doesn't sound like a big idea. It sounds a bit rubbish.

Deep breath.

It doesn't have to be Russell there, dead in the bathroom. It could be me. This story doesn't have to be rich bloke collapses in his toilet. Instead it could so easily be the story of an old friend flown over – with his family – by his generous buddy. An old friend who then – tragically – collapses and dies in a foreign land. A simple story and a beautifully sad one. And it has a kind of truth too. It's *more* truthful in a way. It should have been me, not him. It makes more sense that way.

She says nothing. Looks at me agog, scared-looking. I'm in too deep to stop now. I'm aware that what I'm saying is outrageous. Wrong on so many levels, but still on I go.

We have all the passwords. And we have the passports, the utility bills and all the other necessary chip and pin fabric of a life. Two lives. And wasn't Russell planning to vanish anyway? And he's dead. That's nature. It's not like we killed him. And our life? Due for taking to the recycling centre. It's a basement life, full of damp plans and mottled schemes. It's a rusty, grimy, grubby life that needs disinfecting, spring-cleaning, converting into something useful and you, Sarah, you've been saying that for years. And we have our girl to think of now too, don't we? And we won't have been the first to do this. If you can imagine it, then someone has done it. That's something my dad always used to say. One of his many wise observations, along with never a borrower or a lender be and early to bed, early to rise makes a man healthy, wealthy and wise.

I think Sarah's going to slap me. I even flinch as she raises her hands, but she puts her arms around me. She's warm and the dressing gown smells of biscuits and sleep. She kisses me full on the lips. She pulls back, looks me right in the eyes. I can see all the freckles around her perfect nose. Across her forehead, her cheeks, her neck. My father used to call her the dot-to-dot girl.

'Now that is sort of genius,' she breathes. 'It really is.'

'Is it?'

'Shush a minute. Let me think.'

The cellos seem to stab with controlled violence. I love Taverner I decide. Bloody love him. Classical music – it's the new rock and roll, that's what Russell used to say. And tosser that he often was, he was also quite often right about things. Right on the economy, right about music.

At last Sarah says, 'What about our families? What about our friends?'

Which is nice of her because I don't really have family or friends. Not as such. She has both. Averagely irritating mum, two averagely irritating sisters, and lots of friends. Really. Lots of them. She's good at friends and they accept me as part of the package. She shares them. I'm not good at friends. Russell was the height of my success in that area. There are people I can share time with over a sandwich in the council canteen, but they're not friends as such. And my dad might not even notice to be frank. I say all this and she's quiet again.

Those cellos. They're the sound of whole nations bleeding.

She says, 'You better not wimp out of this, Nicky Fisher. You better not let me down.'

And she says she's proud of me. Says she always knew I was probably a late bloomer. Says that's the hope she's been clinging to all these years. She says it with a smile, but I think she probably means it.

And then later, it's actually Sarah that panics and tries to backtrack. And that's another thing that never happens. She's usually resolute. Makes a plan and sticks to it.

*　　*　　*

14

I sober up under the power shower and emerge to find Sarah full of fears, doubts, scruples. While I've been scrubbing the terror of the night away, the water so hot it hurts, relentless jets of hot needles, Sarah has come up with one big new impediment to success in the plan.

And it's this: we'll get caught. We'll definitely get caught. All it'll take is bad luck or bad intelligence or a careless word while pissed – any of that could trip us up. That's what she says. But, confident now, sparked up by Russell's special tea tree and starfruit revitalising gel I have an answer.

'Of course we might get caught,' I say. 'I know that. I'm not an idiot.'

'So what's the point then?'

'The point is that it will be worth it.' And I explain everything gently, quietly, using a voice that actually Sarah is usually master of, expert lecturer and line manager that she is.

I explain that for the months, or, hopefully, the years that we do get away with it, we'll live the way kings and queens do. Or the way they could do if they had any imagination. We'd see and do things that we never could otherwise. We'd be like gods. All of us, even Scarlett. We won't walk, we'll bestride. We'll live in HiDef 3D. And when we do, finally, get caught – well, it won't be so bad.

'Sorry. You've lost me now,' she says.

So I explain that too. Still going slowly, still trying hard, if perhaps not quite successfully, to avoid any hint of lecturing, of line-managering. This, Sarah, my love, this is a white-collar crime without victims. Russell has – had – no family, few friends.

'Anyway,' I say, 'by supporting some well-chosen charities or something, we could construct a decent mitigation. We could say that we were motivated by doing good.'

'A sort of Robin Hood defence.'

'If you like.'

Taking from the rich to give to the poor. Not so much thieves as Mr and Mrs Santa Claus. Mr and Mrs Saint Theresa. Bonnie and Clyde without the random killing. It's a very decent mitigation indeed if you ask me.

The thing is that yeah, we might go to jail. But for how long really? A year? Two? Three years tops. Three years in Ford Open Prison. Or the American equivalent. Three years watching TV in a low-security facility. Or we could use that time to do important work on ourselves. We could learn useful new skills, or just take time to think.

'They'll kill us,' she says. 'They'll lock us up and throw away the key. They'll turn us into monsters.'

'I don't think so, Sarah. We'll be heroes. Kind of. Think about it.'

I watch her face grow serious and still while she thinks about it.

They say it takes 10,000 hours of practice to get to genius level at anything. If that's true then three years in prison would give us both the exact time needed to come out as concert pianists, human rights lawyers, philosophers, or chess grandmasters. We could get PhDs in criminology. Ten thousand hours of study and thought. That's something that honest money can't buy. That's something only crime can buy.

'You're a crazy man.'

But there's a faint hint of a smile now, and I can detect at least a hint of weakening here, just the quick, heady whiff of it. And so I follow up by explaining that of course we would make sure most of the money is secreted in places where the IRS and HMRC can't get hold of it.

'Sarah we could do our time and come out loaded.'

'And what about Scarlett, Nicky? What will she be doing while we do our ten thousand hours? It'll be a big deal for her. Especially since she's only about ten thousand hours old.'

There's an easy answer to this.

'She could stay with your mum. She did all right with you. And she loves Scarlett. Anyway, they might not even send you to jail. In fact I'm sure they won't.' And I look at her carefully again. To see if she gets it. And yes, I can see her working out how that might go.

Hitherto blameless mother of a small child – a child with special challenges no less – clearly led astray by a feckless chancer of a husband. Misplaced loyalty. The judge's summing up practically writes itself, doesn't it?

I press home. 'It's Scarlett I'm thinking of really. That's what the money will be for. It'll be for her. To give her a chance. Think of the shit she's been through.'

'It's completely bonkers,' she says. But she's lost. I know it and Sarah knows it – though, because she's nice, loyal, kind-hearted – because I love her – I'm not going to crow or rub it in. Instead I point out, still gentle, that the real crime would be not to have the courage to act on our convictions. Not to open the door when opportunity is not only knocking on it but trying to break it down. Who dares wins. The only thing to fear is fear itself – all that. She's properly smiling now. OK, OK, enough already that smile says.

'Come here, Pog,' she says, and wraps herself around me, folds me into that biscuity warmth. 'You're right. It's all going to be fine.'

And so, by the time the San Francisco morning is pulling on her hipster threads, putting on her vintage, floaty, cobwebby dress of dust and sunshine – the city's slutty summer wardrobe – we have a battle plan. We're thinking together as a couple, as a proper team and – as a team – we're cooking up breakfast. And Taverner's off and KOIT is on. Classic hits on FM.

I know. Sick isn't it? There's the body of my oldest friend in the bog and we're putting together the fullest of full Englishes to a soundtrack of Jefferson Starship. Russell has all the necessary in that giant double-sized fridge-freezer. Bacon, eggs, mushrooms, toms, 'English-style' sausages. Even baked beans. Even ketchup. These are things he must have had some assistant scouring all the delis of the Mission or Castro for. He even has black pudding. Black pudding. It makes us laugh.

I know, I know, but grief. Shock. Like I say, it does weird things to the appetite.

And so does love.

So does seeing Sarah dance around the kitchen, hearing her sing along to the radio. Because she hasn't had much to sing about in the last few years. There's not been much call for dancing.

Four

POLLY

Daniel is showing Polly how to make a kite. He asked her yesterday what her favourite animal was and she'd said an octopus – she can't think why because she's all about the horses, anyone who knows her knows that – and now, here on the heavy table in the library, is a smiling octopus face on a large circle of some special green plastic with eight legs dangling down beneath it. To be honest, it looks more like a psychotic jellyfish than an octopus. It's cartoonish, but not in a way a child would like. Polly thinks an actual child would be scared of it. But then this is not a kite for a child.

Now Daniel cuts the wood to the right lengths with a Stanley knife. Daniel's hands usually shake quite a lot but today they are firm and steady. He's quick with the knife and even the splodges of liver spots on the backs of his hands seem to have faded so that they could almost be freckles. So quick with that knife, his old hands a blur. It's like watching a top chef chop spring onions on TV. Quite something to see.

And he shows her where to place the struts and how to fix them in place. And he shows her how to tie the string. It's simple really, but he explains that you have to get everything in exactly the right place or it won't fly and, like Daniel says, there's nothing sadder than a kite that won't fly. It's like a dog that won't bark or a canary that can't sing. A woman that can't have a baby. Polly thinks that's a strange and horrible thing to say. She shakes her head.

As he works, his hands as clever with his needle and the special plastic string as they were with the box-cutter, Daniel tells Polly the story of his time in India and how he became a kitemaker. He's told her before several times, but she doesn't mind. It's interesting. She likes hearing about what they do in far-away places. Polly has never even lived outside the Anglia TV region.

He was in India working as an engineer, laying pipelines, away from his family back home in England and he was bored. He was probably lonely too but men never admit to that. Anyway, his manservant – they all had manservants then, even junior engineers like Daniel – took him up into the hills to watch a kite contest. Daniel tells Polly again about all the huge fighting kites swooping and attacking each other while the crowds cheered and hooted. It's like a football match for the people there. And they're all gambling of course. Thousands of rupees changing hands on the result of some wrestling match way up in the air. The idea is to control your kite so well that you can cut the strings of your opponent's and send it sailing off on the wind, or send it crashing to the crowd. Only Daniel says that it's more vicious than that even.

'See Polly, the idea is actually to castrate your enemy. To catch him, rape him, kill him. And then take money off all his friends.' He says that to the players that is what it feels like when someone cuts the strings of their kite.

'You mean it's like having your dangly bits ripped off,' and Polly laughs that big infectious laugh that all the residents of Sunny Bank love to hear. And Daniel chuckles along too.

'Exactly,' he says as his chuckle turns into a phlegmy cough. Exactly.

Polly's big laugh can be heard in the office of the manager, Irina, even though it's all the way down the corridor from the library. Irina pauses in her tapping at her keyboard for a minute and half-smiles, and thinks again how lucky they are to have found Polly. And to think she doesn't even get paid. She volunteers for this. Because Polly is actually here for the good of her own health, not that of the residents. She had a bit of a depression thing last winter after her dad sold the stud farm, and her doctor prescribed being around others less fortunate than herself. Though it is actually quite hard to imagine a depressed Polly.

At her Sunny Bank interview Polly had said, 'To be honest I had been hoping for mega-powerful anti-depressants but getting doctors to prescribe actual drugs is pretty difficult these days I find. They really don't like it. I guess it makes them feel like failures or something.'

So she'd made Irina smile then too. Irina knows what doctors are like. Oh yes. And everyone agrees that Polly is a tonic for the residents. Even the staff who don't like her, who find her relentless cheerfulness incomprehensible and annoying, even they admit that she's good for the old people. Especially the difficult ones like Daniel.

And so Daniel carries on with his story, and Polly smiles and nods encouragingly and murmurs in the right places and generally gives no sign that she's heard all this before. About how when Daniel got back from the fighting-kite festival he got his manservant to find a kite-maker that he could apprentice himself to. In the day he's organising the laying of pipelines – shouting, giving orders, sacking the lazy and the dishonest. Hectoring, cajoling, coaxing the workers while at the same time fending off nonsensical questions from the bean-counters in head office in London who know nothing about the realities of working in a place like India. Doing all that and then three evenings a week he goes and sits at the feet of the kite guru and learns about flight patterns, about paper, about design, about the discipline you need if you really want to castrate, fuck, kill.

Daniel says that he's sure it helped him in business. Polly says that she can believe that. And then she smiles and says that she doesn't really want to castrate, fuck, kill if it's all right with him.

And Daniel says neither does he any more, that he's a bit embarrassed by the man he used to be. And then he asks what Polly does want and she can't believe her own reply. Her own reply is the absolute God's honest truth and it's a thing she's never told anyone before.

'A baby. I want a baby.' And she puts a hand over her mouth. And Daniel looks at her calmly and says, 'Well, that doesn't sound impossible. Easier than making a kite that flies anyway.'

Five

NICKY

The next bit – the beginning proper – is all much, much easier than we expect, but then beginnings are, aren't they? In love, in work, in life: beginnings are always the easy bit. It's endings that are hard.

I've told myself, promised myself, that if there are any problems at all, then we'll get out immediately. And Sarah agrees. Yeah, she says, no unnecessary risks. We can always bail.

At 8 a.m. that morning – five hours after I've found him – I phone 911, tell them my guest over from England has collapsed in my bathroom and that he isn't breathing. It's no problem to sound panicky. The minute I give his name – my name – I feel asthmatic with terror. But it's done now. No way back. The operator is steely as she tells me that she really needs me to stay calm right now. I take a breath. Try to concentrate on her questions.

No, I'm not sure when exactly, some time ago. Last thing I remember is him getting up to go to the bathroom. I'd fallen asleep in my chair. We'd been having a catch-up, see. Drink, smoke, what have you. We're old friends and it's my birthday. Fifty. A proper milestone. So yes, he's been drinking. Wine, beer, whisky. Proper whisky. Glenmorangie. A nice single malt. No drugs. At least I don't think so. He'd just gone to the bathroom which is where I've found him. Just now. Not the one in his bedroom, but in the guest bathroom. Yes, the bathroom. The Bath Room. I'm pretty sure he's, you know, gone – but please hurry. His wife's here.

And the voice stays cool. Unsympathetic I think. Stern. She's saying that she understands that I'm feeling a little shaken up right now, but it's important that I stay focused. Sir.

Do I imagine that or is it real? A tiny disrespectful pause before she says Sir?

But I don't have time to dwell on it, because she's talking again. Where is he now, sir? And I have to take another breath, count to five just so I don't scream out that I've told her already. He's in the frigging bathroom. Bent over. On the floor. Like he's praying. Or about to get shafted. One of the two.

She tells me to go to him and check his pulse again, explains how to do CPR, the kiss of life, all that stuff. I say, yeah I'll do it, but actually I go to join Sarah at the window again. And together we take a long look at the city stretching and yawning. I take advantage of the brief silence the operator allows to concentrate on the vapour trail of a passing jet. Sarah squeezes my hand. It's still bloody early, the heat in the city not fierce as yet, but I'm sweating. Shaking. I sit down as the voice makes me go through everything again. Where is he now, sir? The bathroom the bathroom the bathroom. The can, the john, the restroom, the loo, the lavatory, the fucking bog. Christ, how many more times? Stay with me, sir. Stay calm.

Why is she saying that? Am I gabbling? Does she struggle with the accent? Is it a trick? Is she trying to catch me out, expose some inconsistencies which an attorney could use to put me away at some future court date? Is she retarded? Or is it just procedure? No, it's fine. We're fine. Relax. Breathe. Just breathe.

I'm careful to go slowly now. To speak clearly and distinctly, biting out my Ts and my Ds, to get as close to the voice of Hugh Grant as I can, and, by the time I'm finished, I can hear sirens and I break off mid-sentence.

I look at Sarah. She pulls her oversized, over-fluffy towelling robe tighter around her. She's looking even paler than usual today, the skin on her face thinner, faint lines appearing like invisible ink beginning to give up secret codes in the lemony morning light. Still, you can't ever say she looks bad exactly. Still catches me out after all this time, just how fine she looks.

23

She frowns and tells me she'll be upstairs if I need her. I nod and go to open the door and two tough-looking black women in neon-yellow hi-vis tabards over acid-green jumpsuits hold up lanyards, introduce themselves as Claudette and Soraya, and bustle their way inside. Just before I close the door I see some early morning jogger standing practically in the driveway, gawping at the ambulance. She sees I've spotted her and stoops to pretend to fiddle with the mini iThing on her wrist, clearly embarrassed to be caught in such a blatant piece of rubbernecking. And so she should be. Bloody ghoul.

I take the paramedics straight to Russell and they tell me they can take it from here and that the best thing I can do is to go back into the living room and let them do their thing. Their whole unhurried manner tells me they've seen he's dead at a glance. As far as they're concerned this is no longer an emergency. Instead it's an unexpectedly gentle and unhurried part of their day. A moment of reprieve.

They come into the living room after five minutes and suggest that I sit down and Soraya disappears into the kitchen and does some clonking around that suggests the making of tea, while Claudette takes my hand, looks me in the eye very seriously and says that she's sorry but that my friend has been called home. There's a pause to make sure that I take in this information. It's all in some manual somewhere no doubt. Some online training programme. Managing the newly bereaved: a new vision for field practitioners. Something like that.

Called home.

I resist the impulse to say, 'What? He's been called back to Bedford? Summoned back to Plover Way?'

She goes on.

She understands that this is a difficult time for me but they do need some information. And so, yes, there are forms, just as I'd known there must be. There is also an explanation of the need for an inquest which is nothing to worry about – the state of California does that for any sudden death however straightforward – and Mr Fisher was

British right? Like yourself? And so Claudette thinks that I might need to inform the embassy or at least the consular officials. And I say of course, I get that. Totally.

And Claudette is already moving forward through the programme. Is there anyone who could come over, sit with me awhile? His wife's here I say. Upstairs. And they nod. That's good. Neither of us should be alone right now.

'You should get some sleep, sir,' Claudette says. 'Let Nature start the healing process.'

'Sleep that knits up the ravelled sleeve of care,' I say. She looks confused. So then I'm apologetic.

'English major. It's Shakespeare. Sorry.'

Claudette doesn't say anything. Almost certainly puts this fresh weirdness down to a combination of shock and being foreign.

And it's easy to give them all the details they want, plus some background that they don't ask for, like the fact he was only over here because I'd paid for his flight. I tell Claudette's kindly face how I've spent more or less every birthday with Nicky since we were both kids, though for some reason we've missed the last couple. 'Because of business stuff, you know how it is.' And she is looking at me with those nice brown eyes and I feel like crying but I can't because I have other, more pressing concerns. Like whether I got the name right. Did I say Nicky or Russell? I'm pretty sure I said Nicky. I must have done. Surely? Fuck. Fuck. And now I'm shaking again. And Claudette strokes my arm and I turn it into a hug and I feel the doughy warmth, the soft rise and fall of her breasts beneath the plastic crackle of her tabard, and I want to kiss her. But I don't. I don't. Thank Christ.

And then Soraya is back with tea which is way too milky because Americans never get that right, and Claudette pats me on the back as if to say enough already and I disengage and try for a watery smile. And I sit and Claudette sits, and she squeezes my knee and asks again if there is anyone they can call, but they are relieved when I decline. No, I say, you're busy professionals. And they swell up a little, look at each other and smile. Yes, we are. Look at us. Professionals. And busy. You betcha.

Everyone thrives on praise. Everyone needs recognition for what they do.

Soraya murmurs that Mr Fisher died quickly – brain aneurysm she thinks, though she can't say definitively of course. Claudette says he died without too much suffering or panic or pain. I wonder, but not out loud, just how much suffering, panic or pain is too much. I'm of the opinion that any suffering, panic or pain is too much. But Soraya is talking now, saying that Mr Fisher died among friends, on holiday and in America too. And the unspoken assumption is that there is no better place to die than the land of the free, home of the brave. And I think what she's really saying is that Mr Fisher should be sorta grateful for his good luck. Lots of worse places to die. And a lot of worse ways to do it. It's not something to get too hung up on. And I find myself getting angry. And it's an effort to keep my voice level as I explain about the promise unfulfilled. The waste.

Nicky Fisher was not even fifty, I tell them. He still had time to Do Something. To Be Someone. To be the best that he could be. It wasn't too late. He was a great writer. He could play guitar. And he was so quick-witted. He could have been a stand-up. I take huge offence on behalf of my discarded self. And Claudette sees that emotion is getting the better of me and offers to pray with me and I say no, Nicky wasn't religious. And when they ask about my own faith I find myself babbling stuff about thinking that there might be some spirit, some force, and I catch Soraya blinking in a way that seems meaningful while Claudette seems to try, unsuccessfully, to hide a sudden smirk as if I've said some really stupid thing. But she gives me a card with a number of someone people often find helpful 'even if they aren't conventionally religious'. And then Claudette and Soraya go back into the bathroom, and there's that fucking terrible zipping sound.

And when they come back with Russell he's all bagged and tagged.

It's a surreal scene. Horrible too. It's like Claudette and Soraya are, for some reason, carrying a newly purchased M&S suit on a stretcher. The body bag looks as neatly synthetic, as grimly cheap as that. Russell doesn't look human. Which I know is the point. But I didn't expect him to look like so much packaging. So much rubbish. He looks like nothing anyone could care about. He looks like he's never been. And clearly, Russell, lean from the gym, the cycling, all those triathalons is no weight to carry. No bother to anyone. Claudette and Soraya don't even get out of breath.

I see them out to the ambulance and that is pretty much that. We all shake hands and I promise to take care now and there's more sad smiling. Everyone manages to refrain from saying have a nice day. And they drive off with both the old Russell and the old Nick sharing the one body bag in the back of a shiny California Crusader. The new force in the type-two ambulance market. No turning back now.

Fifteen minutes tops. That's all it takes to move from one dream of life to another. Unless you count the interview with a diffident cop, which happens twenty-five minutes later and takes another quarter of an hour. And that's an interview Sarah sits in on holding my hand, exuding sorrowful dignity, and I think it's that which makes the cop so nervous that he can't wait to leave.

And that's it. All that's needed. Almost all. We have to email work – mine and Sarah's – and, more importantly, someone will have to let the people at Sunny Bank know so they can break the news of my death to my dad. And we still have to work out the details of what to tell Scarlett but it's a big bold start. We've begun.

Sarah can see I'm suffering with the strain of it all and so she makes me a proper cup of English builders' tea, as richly brown as autumn leaves piling up on a London street. Then she gets me to speak about our hopes, dreams, all the things we could do, the things we could see, or own even. The First Folio, the Aramaic Bibles, Paul Weller's guitars, handscrawled first drafts of Dylan songs. We could put Tracey Emin's infamous bed in our second-best spare room if we wanted. There's beautiful stuff out there, all of it waiting for a man and a woman of taste and discernment. Plus, she reminds me, there's the good we can do. Yes, there's that too. She strokes my cheek. And I feel the tension slowly leave my face, neck, shoulders, back – all the places it collects.

It's the tranquillised afternoon British time, and the heavily accented Eastern European girl who picks up is clearly grateful for any interruption. She clucks briefly at the news that nature has gone wrong again. That a man in his summer years has died while his poppa hangs on and on disgracefully through the epic ice age of decrepitude. She tells me that in her opinion Mr Fisher is too out of it to be reached by anything, even the death of his son, but that nevertheless someone will tell him. Or at least, someone will speak the necessary words in his general direction. Probably Polly will do it when she comes on shift. Polly is good at things like that. And I wonder about Polly and how you get to be good at things like that and what good at things like that even means. And I wonder if it is too early to drink.

Sarah comes back into the room. She's been checking on Scarlett.

'Still asleep?'

'Yeah.'

'Probably jet lag.'

'Probably. Everything all right at Sunny Bank?'

'I think so.'

'You haven't seen him for ages anyway, Nicky.'

'I know.'

'He wasn't such a great father, Nicky.'

She comes over, stands close to me and presses my head against her chest.

'I know, I know.'

'It'll all be fine, Nicky.'

'Yeah. I know. I know.' And I make the decision not to be irritated by the way she keeps using my name like this. I wonder if it's an old HR trick. Something they teach on courses about managing difficult conversations. There's probably research somewhere that shows people are comforted by hearing their name spoken aloud.

But who cares if I'm being ever so slightly line-managed here? It's probably what I need. I put my arms around her. Sarah and Scarlett – the family I never expected to have. All the family I need.

Six

CATHERINE

Catherine Baker despises joggers but there's no better way of moving around the city and staying invisible. Especially if you're middle-aged. Women joggers in their perimenopausal years are everywhere and so no one notices them. You can go anywhere and not be seen. It's important you keep your pace sedate of course, it wouldn't do to actually run properly. That would attract attention for sure. Catherine Baker can do a half-marathon in one hour eleven and keeping herself to the wobbly tippy-toe stumble of the average evening jogger is irritating to say the least.

And just how has running become so popular a pastime with middle-aged, middle-class ladies? Catherine Baker is forty-four years old and can't remember there being joggers when she was a little kid. If you did ever see anyone out running in Ipswich in the 1970s then they were serious, tiny, bony men in old T-shirts and shorts – not chubby book-group types in designer shades.

The book group. They are meeting in three days and Catherine hasn't even started this month's yet. Still, there is a long plane journey ahead tonight, she'll probably get through most of it then, though she's also meant to be writing a book of her own. She's had this great idea for a kid's story. A young girl accidentally stumbles into the cave where King Arthur is having his enchanted lie down with all his knights, and she wakes them up and they go on to save England from various menaces. At the same time of course the young girl – Heidi – has to guide them through all the complexities of the modern world. It's a good idea she thinks. Funny, exciting, quirky, and could easily stretch to a series. It isn't a J.K. Rowling kind of idea, it's not on that scale, but she thinks it might have legs.

Maybe she can do both. Some writing and some reading. It's twelve hours back to the UK after all. She just hopes she isn't stuck next to a baby. On the flight over the baby next to her had alternated between vomiting and crying. And her screen had been broken so she couldn't even distract herself with some mindless action movie. She's going to write and complain, not that it will do much good but she just might get a £100 discount off her next flight and that'll be something. She's going to Abkhazia in a couple of months and those flights aren't cheap.

And that's another thing, when Catherine was growing up air travel had been glamorous. Catherine had even wanted to be an air hostess. When she went to Spain with her family the stewardesses had seemed impossibly beautiful. Sleek, gracious, like people from some future where stress, hustle and ugliness had been outlawed. They had been these exquisite angels, dispensing inner peace along with crisps and light refreshments. Now they were just snotty waitresses. And she's sure the planes had been bigger then too, the seats wider, the toilets cleaner, and the airline meals not only edible but tasty. And you could get from London to the States in ninety minutes on Concorde. Hard to believe now. When Catherine was growing up, anything was possible. People played golf on the moon in the seventies. Bloody golf. On the moon. And the music was better too; then there was Abba and the Bee Gees. Now there is, well, that's the thing, Catherine doesn't even know what's around now. K-pop? Is that a thing? Pimba? She's fairly sure she's heard someone talking about that on her travels. Where's that from? Angola? Thing is, she doesn't care that she doesn't know. Who can be bothered with keeping up with music now?

The world is going to shit. What we need is a real King Arthur or someone like him to sort the mess out, to bring some pride and ambition back to the world. Only these days it wouldn't be a man. The new hero would be a woman. A bloody angry woman. A new Joan of Arc.

No one in their right mind would want to be an air hostess now would they? Not with the lowlife who travel by air these days – the crying, vomiting babies and their crying, vomiting parents. And the crying, vomiting students. And the crying, vomiting pilots. She's heard the stories. Stag parties probably go to Abkhazia now. Club 18–30 probably have an office there.

Catherine is approaching the glass block of the Mercury hotel – just four hundred yards to go, surely she can risk a sprint? She glances about her. Hard to be sure with these shades on but there doesn't seem to be anyone around. Some traffic obviously, but no people. Bugger it. She's going to go for it anyway.

Christ, it's good to open out full throttle, feel her lungs begin to burn, feel the power in her legs. She's like a Ferrari she thinks, a Ferrari that is being used to trundle to Lidl and back. It's a disgrace.

In her room, after her shower, Catherine Baker examines herself. Her sturdy compact body; the thick, dark forest of her hair. The sharp planes and angles of her face. Her body is in good nick, no doubt about that. Yes. A classic Ferrari of a body, and it should be, it's well maintained. She gives it the right fuel. Lean protein, lots of leafy green vegetables, fibre, pulses, good carbs, water, lots of water.

Moving closer she inspects the crow's feet and the deeper lines beginning to carve themselves each side of her mouth. The mouth that is perhaps getting a little thin. A little flinty. She smiles. Her teeth are OK. She was going to get them properly fixed up after that thing in Sierra Leone left them a bit of a mess, but in the end she'd been gripped by tightness. All that dosh on a luxury like straight teeth. She just couldn't bring herself to do it. Just as well she made it a policy these days not to smile much.

She remembers now her first week at Sandhurst. The drill sergeant, the one that had a bit more about him than the others, the Welsh one, the one that wasn't just about shouting VERY VERY LOUDLY – she remembers him saying, 'Don't smile Miss Baker, ma'am. It'll make people think you're stupid. Or up for sex. Or both.' And it had made sense, so she has trained herself not to smile. Even when she feels stupid. Even when she's up for sex.

And now when she does smile it maybe looks a bit weird.

She crosses to the wooden table that, apart from the bed, constitutes the entire furniture in this hotel room. This hotel is, she decides, pretty much on the low side of mid-range. She picks up the cell she'd bought when she arrived in California. She thinks for a minute, then texts. It takes her almost no time at all. Best to keep things simple. Then another few fumbling seconds to remove the sim and to carefully snip that into four with her nail scissors. The phone itself she places in the full sink in her bathroom. It can steep there for a couple of hours and then she'll bin it on the way to the airport. That's the thing about this job, people don't realise that it's mostly housekeeping and keeping things tidy.

Housekeeping done, she stretches out on the floor in the narrow space between the bed and the wall, and begins to go through her stretching routine. It is, she decides for maybe the ten thousandth time, her favourite part of the day.

Seven

NICKY

An hour later and we go into Russell's office. Everything is run from this room. An empire commanded from the second-smallest room in the house. There's also an office somewhere downtown, a place for the mail to be picked up from, but really the whole operation is controlled by clicks on a wafer-thin iThing in metallic purple and a printer. There isn't even a desk, just a worn armchair, though the room is crammed with the paraphernalia of art, music, film. A screen way too big for comfortable viewing in that pressured space, an electric guitar, an acoustic guitar, an amp, a box of obscure percussion instruments, vintage seventies hi-fi system, shelves of DVDs along one wall, shelves of vinyl along another. No books. There's Pre-Raphaelite art on the walls. Beautiful pale-skinned, large-breasted, full-lipped beauties swooning in lakes or forests. They all look a bit like melancholy Victorian versions of Sarah actually. If Millais were alive today he'd definitely want to get off with my wife, no question. So, anyway, it's not a traditional home office, more a den for an adolescent of refined sensibilities. A cave to hide in. Or a tomb. The tomb of the Unknown Sixth Former perhaps. Definitely Russell's room.

I flick up the lid of the iThing. Type in the password. SgtB1lko. As long as there had been PCs in our lives, Russell's password had been SgtB1lko. Sergeant Bilko was one of our shared passions, affectations, whatever. There were whole episodes we could both recite from memory. At uni me and Russell would have Bilkofests. The two of us in my fetid room chortling our way through classic eps. It would screw things up totally if he'd changed tack in the three years or so since we spent time with him. Since the night when he was dancing half-heartedly at our wedding. It'd be crap if he's now encrypted his vital info in Sanskrit or something.

But he hasn't. SgtB1lko does the biz, and there it is: all laid out for us The good stuff. The honey. The money. Ten minutes of patient clicking to find accounts in Switzerland, Swaziland, Jersey, Guernsey, The Virgin Islands, Turks and Caicos, the Seychelles, the Maldives, Bhutan, Liechtenstein and Monaco. All the most secret safes in the world in the very same places that had the grooviest stamps when we were both briefly collectors back in the day. None of them real countries, more like PO boxes for white-collar rapists and the grandchildren of the SS.

As passwords go, SgtB1lko isn't such a bad one actually. What East End crack baron or psychotic Rumanian people trafficker is going to connect Russell Knox with anything as mundane as a cosy teatime US sitcom from the distant mouldering past?

I know the kind of people that Russell schlepped around with in his old day-to-day working life would definitely have tried to rob him blind. I see them employing relays of kids to do the job too, in the manner of modern Fagins. Teams of teenage Asperger types, obsessed from infancy with hacking through Pentagon firewalls, recruited now to burrow into Russell's electronic counting houses. But those kids would have never heard of the wiles of Sergeant Bilko.

Nostalgia. Sentiment. Those were Russell's weak spots and neither autistic hacker nor murderous gangster would have those qualities in anything like the right amounts.

It really is a lunatic amount of money. Written down as a dizzying, paragraph-long string of zeros, it doesn't even look like a number. It looks like a page from an avant-garde text-art project.

And the property. For his new super gap life, Russell hasn't just rented out rooms in hotels. It's not like when we went InterRailing in 1985. For this trip there's to be no sharing Deutschebahn seats with

New Zealander backpackers called Kev. For this trip he's bought houses, villas, riads, barns, high-spec yurts, castles, compounds in the desert with helipads. Farms complete with llamas, goats and petting zoos. Narrowboats in Birmingham and stilt houses in Papua New Guinea. He's bought rivers, lakes, Southwold beach huts and Icelandic turf longhouses. He's bought yachts with armour plating and sea-to-air missiles.

He's spunked over all the top property totty of every continent. If anything remotely desres has caught his eye in even the most glancing of ways, then he's gone for it. He's been playing supermarket sweep in a top-end realtors. No collection of bricks and mortar anywhere has been safe. No stretch of heather, heath or moorland too wild to escape consideration as a future domicile.

I'm exaggerating obviously – but not by much.

And it isn't just bricks and mortar. Not just beaches and moors. Not just canvas, keels, decks, hulls and rockets. There's the whole gamut of RVs too. Magic buses of every kind are part of the portfolio – ancient psychedelic veedub campers that might well have seen action at Woodstock or Altamont. Caravan-club veterans of the B roads of 1950s England, all the way up to the Fleetwood Providence 3000, the ultimate chromium monster designed to glide across the American prairies. A kind of mobile motel complete with its own bar and gymnasium.

Russell, we begin to realise now, was probably clinically insane. Depressed certainly. He was like that old guy we'd lived next to in my second year at uni, when we'd had that house in Wimpole Street. The chap who couldn't stop ordering from the Littlewoods catalogue. The chap who, when he died, was only found by the emergency services after they had tunnelled a way through a Bauhaus maze of unopened boxes containing kettles, toasters, microwaves, breadmakers, radios and fondue sets. At the end of an epic trek from the front porch, down the hallway to the kitchen, they found the source of the stench the neighbours had reported. There, at the end of the trail was Mr Harry

Sigman. A liquefying corpse, still sitting at the kitchen table amid a nest of more boxes – juicers, electric carving knives, outdoor Christmas lights – still with one dripping finger pointed at page 197 – foot spas.

Since he saw us last, Russell seems to have got just like old Harry. Pretty soon he would have needed saving from himself. He would surely have been sectioned before he went completely Howard Hughes.

But the important thing for us is that everything is in order. We have the money, we have the addresses. Another click and we have all the tickets. Tickets to ride that entitle us to travel whenever we like. These are super-first tickets. Tickets that allow us to bump people out of first class should our chosen flight be full. Tickets that mean homeland security come to us and check our passports in the comfort of our VIP lounge. Tickets that mean no queuing ever, for anything.

I check Russell's personal emails. There are fifteen. That's all. Even I get more than that on an average day. And his are begging messages mostly. Even the cheery notes from people who might just be mates. Even the ones wishing him safe travels and bon chance. All of them have a sneaky sleeve-tugging quality. *Don't forget us* they seem to wheedle. *Feed us. Look out for us. Help us, we're dying here.* Like so many hands stretching out through the bars of some camp, some pen, some cage. Well, fuck that. Fuck them. I feel a pang for him then, but it's not like we killed him. The worst you can accuse us of really is opportunism and hell, in the modern world that's actually one of the highest arts, is it not? They teach it in schools now, don't they? It's what they do instead of Citizenship or History.

Russell has already set up a curt out-of-office message saying he's going to be out of circulation. That he is going to find himself and that it might take a while. No one will think it odd when he doesn't call. They'll forget him soon enough. And the PAs and the flunkies and the cleaners and the drivers are all gone, all paid off. So it's just us now baby. Just us and the money. Alone together at last.

I look at Sarah and she's frowning.

'All right, oh queen?' I say. 'The world is our bivalve mollusc. Where shall we go first?'

My tone's all wrong though. I feel foolish.

Sarah smiles but tuts, exasperated.

'How like a man,' she says. 'We can't just go. There are things to do first.'

'What? Packing and shit?'

'Packing and shit,' she says. And she then laughs. And then she kisses me on the nose. 'I love you, Pog,' says Sarah. 'Can't think why.'

Eight

LORNA

Lorna has stopped crying by the time she picks up her bike from Macarthur. More or less anyway. He's so not worth it. Not that she's really crying over Jez. She's crying over all the unspeakable shits she's been drawn to all her life. All the good-looking, self-absorbed bastards she's wasted precious time on while ignoring all the nice sweet boys.

Twenty minutes later she is letting herself into the Emeryville apartment where she can hear some shameless movie starlet coaxing Megan into stretching and flexing, into reaching out just that little bit further than she did yesterday.

'Tell the bitch to fuck off and die!' Lorna shouts this from the hallway as she kicks off her boots. Megan enforces a very strict exclusion zone on outdoor footwear.

When Lorna gets to the living room both Megan and the starlet are doing the downward-facing dog, the starlet with a serenity that makes Lorna want to put her fist through the TV. Megan looks up and Lorna knows that she can tell she's been crying. Her roomie's welcoming grin fades. She rolls herself up into a standing position. She frowns at Lorna, hands on hips. Megan has a long, lean, straight-backed dancer's body with broad swimmer's shoulders. She keeps fit doing all that boxing training and lacrosse and shit, and Lorna wonders again why she wastes her time on the floor of their lounge copying bullying instructions from a dime-store hoofer on a DVD.

Megan bends at the waist, plucks the remote off the carpet and zaps the bitch into oblivion.

'The Fuckweasel,' she says. It's a statement not a question. Lorna shrugs. Megan's mouth, normally full and wide and laughing, thins to a hard straight line. Lorna says, 'Uh-oh, it's the boyfriend police.' She tries her best Marilyn voice. 'Was I doing something wrong, Officer?' She sticks her little finger in her mouth. 'Is there anything I can do to make you go easy on me?'

Megan isn't playing. Just stands there waiting. She'll make a great mum some day. Her kids are going to get away with fuck all. Lorna can see explanations are needed.

'Oh nothing really. Jez has just been . . .' Lorna stops.

'Been busy being Jez,' Megan finishes the sentence for her. 'What a wanker.'

Lorna sometimes feels that one of the attractions she has for Megan is in providing her with an exotic vocabulary. Her room-mate enjoys Anglicisms. Collects them. Wanker is possibly her favourite, though she is also very fond of blimey, bin bag, arse, spot-on, cashpoint and snog.

She makes a point of rarely referring to Jez by name. He is usually simply The Fuckweasel. While Lorna is thinking about this, Megan crosses over to her and wraps sinewy arms around her. Lorna closes her eyes and breathes in the mixture of fruity soap and heat. Megan always smells delicious.

'Megan,' she chokes and swallows. 'Megan. I love you. I love you, I love your face and all your funny little ways. And I love Armitage Shanks. But I've got to go home. And soon.'

Armitage Shanks is their cat, and on hearing his name, he pads into the living room to have his belly rubbed.

And later that same evening, after pasta and during Ben and Jerry's Chunky Monkey, Lorna explains that Jez is only part of the problem and she shows Megan the Things I Miss About England list she'd scribbled down on the BART. Megan takes her time studying it. There are thirty-two separate items on that list.

'What are Hoglumps?' Megan asks at last. 'What the fuck is Mucky Fat?'

'Oh, pork scratchings and dripping.' And then Lorna tries to explain their appeal, but she can see that Megan doesn't really get it. 'And lads?' says Megan. 'We have lads.'

'No you don't. You have guys. A lad is different. Bigger, louder, cheekier. More boastful. More fun if you don't take them too seriously.'

And Lorna thinks now about Yorkshire lads with their big shiny faces and their hair inefficiently spiked and their noisy shirts loose over wobbly ale bellies. Their efforts to impress. Their clumsiness. She thinks about the bloke she saw at Huddersfield station the day she left. A fat boy with a T-shirt that proclaimed REMEMBER MY NAME – YOU'LL BE SCREAMING IT LATER. Cocky but insecure Yorkshire lads, she really does miss them. She even sort of likes the dirty carelessness of the way they can go to the bog and come back with suspiciously dry hands but she can see why Megan looks so unconvinced.

'Mm OK. What about drizzle? That's like rain, right? Why would you miss that?'

Lorna looks down at the quarried tub of ice cream in her hand. Doesn't an Inuit miss snow? Doesn't a monkey miss the green sweat of the jungle? But Megan, clearly thinking the undesirability of drizzle is evident now that she's pointed it out, is demolishing another item on the list. 'And Liberal-Democrat newletters?' Megan takes a dainty sip of her wine while she waits for an answer. Oh God. Lorna knows now is not really the time for a discussion about the British system of local government.

'The Liberal Democrats are a political party,' she begins.

'I know that,' Megan cuts in. 'They're the guys that come third right? But I thought you were a Green Socialist?' Lorna blushes. She remembers a party – possibly more than one – where she had waved a bottle and berated the Americans present about how right wing they all were, about their absence of a socialist tradition. It was something guaranteed to upset any Democrats in the room, which, this close to Berkeley and to Pixar, meant practically everyone.

'I'm not a Lib Dem, no.' The syllables feel awkward in her mouth, like a sweet you want to crunch but can't. Megan arches an eyebrow. 'Stop it. I'm not a Lib Dem but they're so *keen* about local politics. It's like as long as they keep producing their newsletters telling us about how they have managed to get the council to repair the kids playground or improve street lighting or whatever, then it's like we can sort of rest easy. Like England's safe, you know?'

Megan shakes her head. It's clear that, no, she doesn't really know. She waggles Lorna's notebook in the air. 'I think this is actually a list of reasons why you left England in the first place.' Lorna pauses, teaspoon of Chunky Monkey halfway to her mouth. Meg has said it casually but it has the weight of elemental truth. Lorna puts the spoon back in the tub. Megan grins happily. She knows she's hit home. 'Go me.' She chuckles. And then, 'I think you need a new list. A list of things you'd miss about here. And she makes Lorna get out her pen and write Great Things About the US of A on a fresh page.

Lorna writes SUNSHINE in capitals and then MEGAN and then ARMITAGE SHANKS and then pauses, sucking her pen. Seeing she is struggling Megan says, 'You've got to factor in the exchange rate. This isn't a one for one currency conversion. Our sunshine has got to be worth quite a lot of your English Liberal newspapers or whatever.'

Lorna smiles. 'I never thought I'd say it, but sunshine gets boring after a while. I think I've been brought up to expect variety from my weather. Four seasons in one day that kind of thing. Am I spoilt?'

'Totally. Jesus, girl, you're some kind of princess.'

In the end the American list reads sunshine, Megan, Armitage Shanks, surf, hipsters, HBO, Ethiopian food, NFL, service, portion sizes, Michelle Obama and 'a general attitude to life'. Lorna has been adamant in ruling out anything that was American but that she could get just as well in Yorkshire, and that turns out to be quite a lot of things. 'You guys get proper squeezy mustard in England now? It's not just tiny-weeny jars of that Colman's crap? I'm impressed.'

When she was sixteen, Megan had toured Europe with her parents. England had been a blur of red buses, palaces, Shakespeare, surly desk clerks and shitty food served in tiny portions. And she'd loved everything except the food. Even the surly workers had had their olde worlde charm.

It is finally, as Megan says, a small list but full of high-quality big ticket items. Then there's more wine and music that only they love. Music they can only play when it's just them, when there are no guys around. The Carpenters. Grimes. Kate Bush. And then they trawl the net looking at random stuff. Megan shows her a gay porn site she's found that specialises in very fat, very hairy men. Bears. It is as compelling as it is gross.

'Do you have bears in England?' asks Megan. 'Because if not, you should add them to your list.'

And then they talk their way through a Woody Allen movie. One of the not so good ones. And just before bed they take a quick peek at some dating sites. It is very depressing. On one site six different men have described themselves as jazz-loving vegans. Megan puts her head in her hands. And then they count over thirty boys who somehow think it's acceptable to say that the thing they most enjoy doing is 'chilling with my xBox'.

'Blooming heck, matey – we're going to be single for ever.'

Lorna laughs. 'Meg, no one in England has said blooming heck since 1955 or something.'

At some point Megan gets around to asking Lorna about her dad, about the whole reason she'd come out to America originally. And Lorna replies that it's pretty hopeless, isn't it? There's hardly ever anyone in that bleeding office and when there is they won't let her in. And in any case, even if she did see him it would probably end badly. The guy hadn't given a shit about her for nearly thirty years, he's hardly likely to come over all doting now, is he? Best thing is to go home and forget him, live her own life. And in any case she'll have to go home soon when her visa runs out.

And, in the morning, when Lorna has to stagger from her bed to the living room to answer the insistent goddamn nagging of her cell-phone, which, it turns out, she'd left under her notebook, she finds that Megan has scrawled some things onto the end of her best of the US list. In the wonky scribble of someone who has consumed way too much pinot grigio, she's written Bears, Dentists, Jazz-loving Vegans and, finally – in capitals – she's put MEGAN'S FUNNY LITTLE WAYS underlining it many times for good measure. She's also drawn rather a good cartoon of her own face. It's way better than the sketches Jez does, and he fancies himself as a pro artist.

Whatever, it means that despite her hangover, Lorna is smiling as she says hello into her phone.

'You sound cheerful,' says her mum. And then does her unthinking best to put a stop to that.

They chat about this and that. It's raining in Yorkshire. And the train drivers are on strike. And somebody they know has breast cancer. And they are trying to close the library. God, she misses England.

'Mum are you sure you're all right? You don't normally call like this. In the morning, out of the blue.'

They usually make Skype appointments where they never quite judge the time delay, and so either speak over each other or leave unnaturally long pauses between sentences. Awkward. And also entirely fitting for the way her relationship with her mother has evolved.

'Oh I'm fine . . . I'm just . . . you know, keeping on keeping on. But listen, are you still serious about getting in touch with your dad?' Oh God. 'Only I think I've found his address. His home address. It's in somewhere called Russian Hill and I've street-viewed it and it looks very swish. Quite close to Nob Hill which might have suited him better. But not too far from where you're staying. Lorna? Are you still there?'

'Yes, Mum, I'm still here.'

Nine

POLLY

Irina calls Polly into the office. It's a bit like she's been called in to see the head teacher at school, though Polly was never one of those girls. Polly's a good girl, but she's pretty sure Irina wasn't. Isn't. You can tell by the way she looks, by the mean look in her eye. By the permanent frown mark above her nose. Her clenched bumface. She's never said much about her life in Poland, but you can just tell she was more of a Rizzo than a Sandra Dee. Polly reminds herself that Irina isn't a headteacher, a school bully or her boss. Polly tries to remind herself she's just a volunteer. They can't do anything to her.

Irina sits behind the desk and doodles for a while leaving Polly to stand, getting more and more nervous, until she's sure she must have done something proper terrible. It's probably only a minute, but a minute without any noise feels like ages. Polly likes to have noise around her. When she's on her own, she likes to have both the radio and the TV on. Silence scares Polly and it's like Irina knows that, so by the time she looks up and tells Polly that Mr Fisher's son has died out in America and could she let him know, she's relieved. Of course, she says, it'll be fine, and she comes out of the office smiling because it's turned out she's not in any trouble. And she bumps into Daniel straight away because he's seen her go into the office and has been waiting outside to show her this new thing he's made.

It's a really, really horrid experience actually.

He smiles because he sees Polly smile and he's showing her this horse he's carved out of wood which is a bit rubbish to be honest, looks like a deformed bear, or a dog, but he's done it out of love. And probably because carving an octopus would be just too hard with all the legs and everything.

'Very much a botch job, I'm afraid. They wouldn't let me have a sharp enough chisel,' he says. 'Look all right when I've sanded it down.'

And Polly is so flustered she just comes right out with it.

'Oh, Mr Fisher. Nicky's dead.'

And she puts her hand over her mouth because she can't believe it's just popped out like that. And it gets worse because then he says, 'Who?' And she has to explain that his son, Nicky, has died on holiday in California, but he won't take it in. Actually, he won't even listen to her, keeps wanting to talk about the bloody chisel, so Polly ends up almost shouting. She's like, 'It's true, Daniel! Nicky's dead!' And the door of the office opens and there's Irina and she gives Polly a stinging look and she takes Daniel's arm, leads him away and she's murmuring into his ear, and Daniel is shaking his head. And then he starts crying, and even though they're at the end of the corridor by now and just about to go into the library, Polly can hear his sobs and coughs and she's just left there with this stupid wooden animal in her hands, and she feels all hot and dizzy and needs to run to the bathroom.

When she comes out, she goes straight to see Irina who's back on reception and she's quite casual, like it's all no big deal, like she's over it all. Polly asks her about Mr Fisher and Irina just waves her hand like she does. She tosses her viciously blonde curls.

'Oh, we gave him a pill. He'll be OK. Forget it.'

Polly tries to apologise and explain, but Irina just gets snippy. 'I said, don't worry about it. Really.' And then she asks Polly to cover reception while she pops out, and, even though she's a volunteer and doesn't actually work at Sunny Bank, Polly says she will because she feels so bad about making a mess of telling Daniel about his son.

And so she's on reception when a Russell Knox calls to ask how Mr Fisher had taken the news about Nicky. He explains that he is Nicky Fisher's oldest friend, the person Nicky was staying with in California.

'I feel responsible,' he says.

Polly starts to say how it went, but she starts crying so Russell has to comfort her and tell her not to worry and he thanks her for doing something so difficult, which just makes Polly feel even worse. But this Russell, he's great on the phone. He's like a top counsellor and he laughs and says that Polly is the first person to say that. He's interested in Polly, asks lots of questions about her life. And by the time the conversation is over she's smiling, plus she's given him her mobile number and her email just so he can check in with her about Mr Fisher from time to time. She wonders about asking if he wants to be friends on Facebook, but maybe that's too much, though at least she's talked to him. Polly has quite a few FB friends that she's never had an actual conversation with, and some of those people are the nicest people she knows. And sometimes they have really funny status updates which she always comments on, and then they comment on her comments and all that.

Polly has to ring off quick when Irina comes back because she's making a face and hurry-up noises, but she's OK after Polly says she'll make her a coffee. Polly finds nearly everyone's OK if you fetch them a cookie and a brew, or a bit of cake maybe. People are easy to make happy. Little treats, that's what people need to get through the working day.

Polly finds Daniel sitting at the piano. He's not really playing it, not a song or anything, just odd notes and funny chords. Polly doesn't think it's a real piece at first, it sounds like a soundtrack to a moody horror film, one of those where not much happens but there's loads of tension and suspense. She asks him if he can actually play.

'Bartok,' he says.

And she says, 'There's no need to be rude.'

This is just a joke though. Polly knows who Bartok is, but then she remembers about his son, Nicky, and she feels her cheeks go hot. She says, 'I'm sorry, Mr Fisher, I can't get anything right today. I don't know what's wrong with me.'

He just says, 'Please, Polly, call me Daniel.'

'Sorry, I forgot.'

'I'm meant to be the one with a hole in his head.'

'I know. Sorry, Mr . . . Daniel.'

And he laughs at her, but not unkindly. And then he starts on the piano again and Polly doesn't know whether to stay or go. She's just decided to go when he starts to talk.

'I didn't see Nicholas until he was nearly a year old. I was in India, you see, and it was a big job, you know, laying the—' He stops. Polly waits. But he doesn't carry on.

'Laying the?' she asks. He looks straight at her. His eyes all glittery and wet.

'I can't remember the damned word.'

'Pipelines?' Polly says.

He is delighted. 'Yes! That's it! Pipelines! Huzzah!' He's grinning all over his face now. It's scary the way his mind bungee jumps. Down and up, down and up, his moods on a great big piece of elastic. And now his face suddenly changes again. He frowns and his mouth goes wobbly. Polly thinks maybe he's going to cry again and she's not sure she can handle that.

Now Polly rescues him for a second time. 'You were talking about not seeing your son? Because you were in India?'

'In India? Yes, India, right. Yes, I was in India . . .'

'Laying pipelines . . .'

'I know, I know. I was in India laying pipelines . . .' He tails off again. Prods at the piano. It needs tuning Polly thinks.

'And you didn't see your son?'

'My son?'

Gosh this is hard, Polly thinks. Mr Fisher – Daniel – is not having a good day. She takes a breath and counts to ten, tries to be understanding. She reminds herself that he has just been given some kind of medication and God knows what that was – could be anything in this place.

'Nicky?' she prompts.

'Nicky? Oh, yes, right.'

And somehow he gets the story out in the end. How the job was too big and too important for him to travel all the way back to England just to see his first-born son, his only child as it turned out. Things kept going wrong. Strikes and protests and bombs and murders and corruption, and Daniel was the only man who could keep everyone doing what they were meant to. He knew who to bribe and how much to pay. He knew who to threaten or blackmail. And he knew the most about pipes and pipelines, even though that was actually the easy bit. He had to keep the whole thing on schedule and there was no one else the company could trust.

'Sounds amazing,' Polly says. 'Not much time for kite-flying though.'

'Kites?' he says, lost. And so she has to remind him about being a kite apprentice and even when she's finished she's not too sure he really remembers. She thinks he might be pretending just to get her to stop going on.

'I've got a hole in my head, you know.'

'I know, Daniel.'

'Really. I have.'

'I know, Daniel.'

'I could show you the X-rays.'

'I've seen the X-rays.'

'You've seen the X-rays? But they're meant to be private. Confidential.'

'You showed them to me, Daniel. On my first day here.'

'Oh, yes. So I did. Sorry.'

You have to get used to this sort of thing in Sunny Bank. It's still upsetting though, it's always upsetting, and kind of worse this time because it's Daniel who Polly really likes. She likes him so much that the fulltime members of staff sometimes tease her about it; they call him her boyfriend and tell Daniel, as a joke, to watch out, she might be after his money, and if it's a good day he says that no, it's his body she's after. And they all have a good laugh about it.

Now there's a pause, and Polly thinks that now she really should go because she doesn't seem to be helping much today. They're both having bad days, Daniel and her. Then he says something that people are never meant to say.

'I never really liked him, you know.'

At first Polly is confused. 'Who?' she says.

'My son. Nicky. I just never really liked him. As a person. I feel bad about it. But there it is.'

And she's not shocked. Some people would be. Some people would be all, he didn't like his own kid? Even when he was a little boy? Even when he was a *baby*? And they'd think it was an outrage and get themselves all riled up. But Polly knows about horses and she's seen mares reject their foals. Happens a lot. They had one mare that was basically raped by a stud Paso Fino that got out from Mr Barker's farm next door. He kicked down their fence to get at the mares and later the mare he did get to, Angelina, just wouldn't have anything to do with her foal. Five of them – Polly, her mum, her dad, Mr Barker and his son Gerry – managed to restrain her and tie her up and get milk and colostrum from her, and they fed the foal from a bucket for a while but it – she – still died.

Quite often mares don't just ignore their foals, they kill them – kick them right to death – and there doesn't have to be a reason. People say that it might be because the mare was disturbed by people in the pasture when she was giving birth, or by other horses getting between her and the foal when she should be bonding. Or it might be that it was a difficult birth, or because her teats are sore and she associates the foal with the discomfort. But it could just be that the mare simply has an unpleasant personality – too dominant or something. Sometimes they say that a mare can sense if a foal is retarded or sickly and so just wants rid. And studs, well they never really care about their foals anyway.

So it doesn't shock Polly that some people can't get on with their kids. She reckons quite a lot don't, they just don't feel they can admit it. She knows she won't be like that though.

Daniel Fisher says, 'I did try, but he just seemed annoying. Whiny, demanding, boastful. Generally petulant. Priggish too, as he got older.'

Polly's not even sure what priggish means but it's close enough to pig and to prick for her to get some idea.

'Were you jealous maybe? I mean, he had your wife's attention.'

'I'm not sure Susan liked him that much either. He just wasn't a likeable child. And later on he wasn't a likeable adult either.'

Polly considers telling him about her horse experience but Daniel seems like he's off into a dream and just sits there at the piano. And the silence goes on and on and Polly hates silence, but she tries not to panic or laugh or say something totally crap. Instead she thinks about sperm. Human sperm. She's been looking at the internet and it turns out it's pretty much as easy to order as horse sperm. There are even price-comparison websites to help you get the best value. She's going to do some more research tonight. Daniel was right. Having a baby is very possible indeed. Who needs a boyfriend? Who needs a man?

She's not sure how long they sit there. At one point Irina opens the door, gives her a sour-face stare, and goes again even though Polly is begging with her own eyes for her to come in and take over.

Later, at home, Polly googles Russell Knox but there are loads of them, more than you'd think. She's only interested in Russell Knoxs who live in America, of course, but there are quite a lot of these too. There's the real-estate agent in Fort Lauderdale, the Christian Science fiction writer from Arizona, an actor that used to be in *Dynasty*, a professional trombonist, and a Russell Knox who has a blog about derelict buildings. There's a Russell Knox who breeds horses in Kentucky and wouldn't it be great if it turned out that he was the right Russell Knox? But she doesn't get her hopes up and two clicks later it turns out that Russell Knox Kentucky horse breeder is seventy-four, way too old to be a schoolfriend of Mr Fisher's son. And why is she trying to find out about this Russell Knox anyway? It's not like she's ever going to meet him, is it? Myownbaby.com, that's the site she should be on. It's got lots of good reviews. That's the site.

Ten

NICKY

One dirty night, one night rolling in the sewer of all the bad-good, good-bad things money can get you. We've promised ourselves one wild night of decadence. One night of fun.

Thing is, nothing is harder than the quest for fun. On a Tuesday at any rate.

Even in the world's coolest city. Even with unlimited gelt. Even with Jesus as your guide and Mary as your babysitter – it still takes work.

We get Mary from an agency that says they are 'Proud to give the second-best kind of love'. The very best presumably coming from mom and pop themselves. And Mary herself seems up for fun. She's all about the pigtails, the lilac knitwear, the glittery nail polish, the unnaturally clean white sneakers, the white jeans, the socks with tiny red love hearts on them and a truly grisly bouncy, day-glo vivacity.

And she arrives with two ukuleles – one for her, one for our little princess. I wish her good luck with that. Scarlett is only three after all and – lovely though she is – even I must admit she's shown few signs of prodigious musical talent. She certainly doesn't do much singing. And she might find the fingering more than usually difficult with not really being able to use her left arm and everything.

'Oh, everyone loves learning to play music, Mr ... sorry, I've forgotten ...'

'Knox. Russell Knox.'

'We're going to have the best time, Scarlett and I. The Best Time.'

'Not second best?' I want to say, but I don't.

'She's adorable. I can tell we're going to be friends already.'

I wonder if Mary is on some kind of medication. Prozac maybe, or one of its stronger successors. You hear these stories about how the whole of American youth is junked to the eyeballs. Probably right now, somewhere out in a mid-west kindergarten, the next president but three is getting his daily Ritalin jab. Quite frightening really when you think about it.

Our last babysitter back in the UK was a student of Sarah's called Noel who was fired when we came home at ten one night to find him asleep in our bed and Scarlett roaming free around the top of our house covered in her own faeces. All the bedroom windows were open and there was the gory finale of a zombie flick on the TV screen. Noel was apologetic – hard few days working on an essay, plus he was a bit hung over from celebrating finishing said essay and sorry it won't happen again. Etcetera, etcetera.

I was all for punching his lights out. And it takes a lot to turn me violent. Sarah was cooler. Calmer. Kinder. Understanding. More rational. Like she always is. She held me back. Calmed me down.

She simply shook her head sorrowfully. She even paid him. All of which Noel was grateful for at the time. Though a few weeks later he somehow failed all his exams quite spectacularly. He couldn't under-stand it, he'd put lots of revision in. He'd thought he'd done well. But he lost his appeal to the dean, and now he works in a kebab shop and can never go home again. Not with both his parents being doctors who prize academic success above all else.

That's what Sarah heard on the uni grapevine.

She looks kind. She is kind. But you really don't want to cross Sarah. I wouldn't risk it anyway.

I don't think we'll have a Noel kind of problem with Mary. She has completed numerous courses in childcare and her whole gleaming, glowing, creamy-faced perkiness does not suggest that she's a zombie film fan. So what if she's on the happy pills?

Mary leaps straight in with the songs and the dancing and Scarlett hides her face in Sarah's shoulder, grunting wetly until I tell Mary that we don't mind if she lets our baby stay up and watch as much telly as she wants. And she can even eat her own weight in ice cream. Mary doesn't have to live up to the agency's mission statement. This second-best kind of love absolutely doesn't have to *combine the best traditional and contemporary childcare thinking in a way that means your most precious possession is being nurtured and helped to grow into the person she deserves to be with every minute she's in our care* . This Best Time she mentioned can be just slobbing out in front of the multi-plex-sized screen watching Spongebob and eating stuff that's spun out of sugar, emulsifiers and air. That's just how we roll in this family, Mary. Mary's perky popsicle face loses just a little of its iridescent pep.

'Er, I think I'll just stick to agency guidelines, if that's all right with you, Mr Knox.'

We show her round the house and she nods and murmurs and doesn't look overawed or anything, and we show her the room where she can crash if she wants because we're planning to be home very late. It's the deal we've agreed with the agency, anything after 1 a.m. and we have to provide bed and breakfast for the sitter of a quality equivalent to at least that of a four-star hotel.

'OK for you, Mary?' I say as I show her one of Russell's ridiculously well-appointed guest suites.

'It's fine,' she says.

Well, don't sound so impressed. What can she have been expecting? I think about telling her something of the history of the house.

'Do you know *Treasure Island*?' I say.

She nods enthusiastically.

'I basically adore all the Muppet movies,' she says. 'I even have a favourite Muppet – Animal. He's so cute, so big and hairy and all.' And she does the Muppet's voice. 'Mah na mah na.'

What can you say to that?

*   *   *

Our first child-free evening in months starts with a stretch limo. Not just any limo either – no, it's a classic Cadillac from the days when limos were the sole preserve of the ruling class rather than something Joe Drone hired to take his daughter to the high school prom. This is a vehicle from back when cars said something. And that something was 'Fuck you, peasant.' This is a car a president would be proud to have his brains blown out in.

We're talking a limo whose innards resemble the smoking room of some nineteenth-century London gentleman's club. We're talking a limo with leather armchairs that might have been transplanted from the Athenaeum in the same way that the original London Bridge somehow ended up in Nevada. And these are chairs that may well have gone from having their seats buffed by Gladstone or Disraeli, to having those same seats glossed by the arses of William Randolph Hearst and all his rosebuds.

We're talking Jazz Age champagne flutes whose elegant super-model thin lines might have been twirled in the gas-effect lamplight by a young Zelda Fitzgerald. We're talking a limo with its own gun cabinet containing antebellum Winchesters used to scare marauding Cheyenne in the distant past, but still kept oiled and ready for action today.

We're talking a car kitted out with a vintage Dansette and classic 45s. A car with soul where modern cars just have the tinny functionality of an iPod dock.

And fuck ashtrays. This car has handcrafted spittoons. It also does fewer mpg than your average airliner. A modern limo is an eco-friendly dickless geek using swanky design to cover embarrassment at its very existence. Modern cars – all modern cars, not just limos – have shame as standard. This car, on the other hand, is a living embodiment of an older, better, more sensual, less craven time. Yup. The only thing green and good and wholesome about this car is the driver's livery.

Ah yes. The driver.

Jesus Rodriguez. A twenty-three-year-old Guatemalan business studies grad student earning some extra Yankee dollars driving for the masters of the universe. Jesus is a chauffeur; he wears a chauffeur's cap but he somehow makes his uniform look like a creation from the fashion avant-garde – he has a catwalk strut. Really we should close the partition between driver and the car's stateroom and not even glance at him. He's no one. A random civilian in our new world order. But we are new to wealth. Don't know the rules. Haven't begun to speak the elevated body language of the billionaire tribe. We don't know about the shields and force fields that money can give you.

We are babes lost in the dark woods of money and looking to kindly strangers for help. And of course, there are no kindly strangers anywhere ever. And certainly not in the woods, as any fairy tale will tell you.

We should just tell Jesus to shut up and drive, to give us a thousand bucks' worth of Bay Area trunk road. We should draw the drapes, dim the lights and make out in the back like teenagers. We should rub and fumble, tug and stroke, lick, nibble and suck. I'm being buried in a week or so after all.

We should set the tone for our new wealth in that way. By properly enjoying the fun anyone can have – rich or poor.

Instead we leave the itinerary to Jesus. We put ourselves in his hands and let his power move us.

'You English?' Jesus says.

'Yeah,' Sarah says.

'My cousin is in England. London. Place called Plumstead. Do you know it? Martina's her name.'

'Martina from Plumstead, right. I'll look out for her.'

'She's hot. I mean I know she's my cousin and all, but I'm telling you, I wouldn't mind.'

'Hot Martina from Plumstead,' I say. 'Got it. I'm sure our paths will cross one day. Bound to in a tiny place like London, England.'

And he probably starts hating us right then. And where did it come from that weary sarcasm? The proper rich would never stoop to it. But then, as I say, they wouldn't ever be suckered into actual small talk with the help.

We try to row back from it of course. But rowing back from it is actually the worst thing to do. Once you've chosen assholery as your route of choice you have to stick with it all the way. You have to stay committed. Retreat looks like weakness. Looks like weakness, because it is weakness.

'I'm sorry,' Sarah says. 'We're a bit stressed. An old friend has just died. Very suddenly. No offence.'

'No problem, ma'am.'

But there is a problem. We just don't know it yet. And maybe it wouldn't have made any difference if we had been super-nice to him from the start.

'Just take us to the places the rich, the beautiful and the damned hang out,' I say.

He doesn't even have to think.

'You got it.'

So it's Krug in the car, dirty Martinis at Romans in Castro, back through Nob Hill for a 1945 Mouton-Rothschild with dinner at Fleur de Lys. Brazilian chicken for Sarah. Fillet of sea bass for me. Roasted quail with Swiss chard and pine nuts with a red wine and thyme reduction for our driver.

Then back in the limo for Aberlour scotch while gawking at the trannies on Lower Polk and then, suddenly, somehow, we are in Oakland blinking in the strobes of somewhere called the Starlight disco, watching dead-eyed waifs gyrate to the European piano-house music of twenty-odd years ago. We don't dance. Not even to 'Ride on Time' by Black Box, though I think Sarah would like to. We sit in the VIP chill-out zone and listen to Jesus talk business.

'My philosophy is this,' Jesus says. 'In business you can either be the cheapest or the best. Everyone else fails in the end, but the cheapest and the best survive. And it's helluva lot easier to be the best, my friend. See, the big guys can always be cheaper than you are, they can cut their margins to the bone to fuck you over. But if you're the best – hey, you can put whatever premium you like on your product and people will pay it. There are always people who will pay top dollar for the best.' He licks his lips, sniffs. There's a better than even chance he's on drugs too. And not Prozac or Ritalin either. I wonder if he's bought the cheapest or the best.

'The trouble is,' Sarah says, 'lots of people can't tell the difference between the cheapest and the best.'

'Those folks don't deserve to have dough. Fuck them,' Jesus says.

'But also,' she says, 'sometimes the cheapest *is* the best.'

But Jesus isn't listening to her. Most men don't listen to women about business, like they don't listen to women about films, or music or drugs, or sex or money. They sometimes listen to women about food or furniture. But even then not all that often, and not for long. Their loss frankly, as they sometimes come to realise. When it's too late usually. Not me of course. I'm not like that. But then I'm not most men. I do listen to women. I listen to Sarah anyway.

We watch the rising dawn from Marin Headlands. Sun coming up like a fiery baseball, and that bridge. That bridge. Pretty stunning. Pretty gold. We shiver and shake and say nothing much. There is nothing much to say. Then back into our oak-panelled mobile clubroom for the trip back to the house. We thank Jesus for showing us a real wild time. We pay him for the dints and scratches and bumps in the Cadillac – by the time we get home it looks like it has been in a Mogadishu firefight – promising to hook up with him real soon. We watch him attempt a 27-point turn, before giving up and reversing at speed. Him, his hidden hate and the dozen cellphone numbers of blonde wraiths that he'd somehow managed to harvest during the evening between business lectures. Oh, and Mary, because he promises to drop her off on his way home. She gets in without much of a backward glance. She seems way more excited by riding in Jesus's limo than she is by the house. And I do kind of get it. A house – however nice – is just a house, but a good car, well that's something else.

'You have a lovely kid,' Mary says as she clambers in the back. 'Very sweet. Good ear too.' She almost certainly says that to all the parents – it's probably strict company policy – and we know this, Sarah and I, but still it gives us a small glow. There's no flattery so seductive as flattery about your kids, I find, and we look at each other and smile. How the hell would she know if Scarlett has a good ear or not?

Inside the house we go and look at our lovely kid twitching amid whatever crazy dreams three-year-olds have. We hold hands. I wonder for the ten thousandth time just what will become of her.

'Do you think Jesus enjoyed himself?' Sarah says. It's like he's a lovely kid himself and we're grandparents who have taken him out to the museum for the day. I don't reply. I don't give a shit about Jesus.

Back downstairs we undress slowly in the living room. We do it in silence, looking carefully at each other the whole time. We haven't done that in years. I see Sarah taking in my incipient breasts, my swelling second-trimester belly, my greying chest hair, the shy snail of my penis. The weary sag of my shoulders. I'm not in good shape, I know it. I see it reflected in Sarah's eyes, in her sad smile, as she takes in all the vandalism time has done to me since the last time she really looked. I see her thinking that something radical needs to be done. You know, when I was younger people used to mistake me for Bono from U2. Well, it happened once or twice. And Bono – he still looks like Bono, doesn't he? I, on the other hand, look like Baldrick from the *Blackadder* TV series. Or at least that's who I'm mistaken for these days. Sarah says she doesn't mind. She says, 'I like Baldrick, he's my favourite.'

Sarah looks OK, of course. More than OK. If you were being picky you might say legs are a bit varicosed, breasts slightly less pillowy than they once were – we both blame Scarlett for that – but generally she's looking good. Forty-two and she could be, oh, thirty-eight, easy.

'Russell kept himself in trim,' she says finally.

'Look what happened to him,' I say, and I smile at the accidental rhyme which is like something from Hilaire Belloc.

'What's so funny?'

'Nothing. I don't really know.'

And we pull all the blinds but this house is fifteen million dollars' worth of too damn airy, too damn spacious, too damn everything, and we can't keep the light out. Not really. That goddamn light gets everywhere. We lie awkwardly under a duvet on the sofa and hold each other and listen to the freeform music of the city. And Sarah talks about how the search for real fun is going to need imagination, planning, and organised thinking. What we need is proper project management.

'Targets, goals, objectives,' I say.

'Absolutely,' she says.

'Milestones,' I say. She nods.

She goes on about how we are going to need smart objectives to make the best of our new situation, our new lives. We are going to need goals that are specific and stretching, measurable and motivating, achievable and agreed, relevant and reinforced, timed and trackable. SMART in other words. Or SSMMAARRTT I suppose, strictly speaking. She gets quite excited. Quite passionate. There's heat in her voice. A flush across her neck. My shy snail stirs a little. Not too much, but a little. She talks about storming, forming, norming – which are, apparently, the three necessary stages of change for any organisation, even a small one like our little family.

I tell her not to bring her filthy performance-management talk into the bedroom, not unless she's prepared to take the consequences, and she giggles and we cuddle for a while. I don't know about Sarah but I certainly feel unusual. Sleepy and buzzy at the same time. I guess I feel all moneyed up.

I'm in this foggy twilight world for a while – a short time? A long time? I have no idea – and then Scarlett wanders in and squirms her way between us.

'Hello, lovely,' I say.

And Sarah gets up, makes tea and comes back and explains to Scarlett about the game. The game that means I'm going to be called Russell from now on, rather than Daddy. If we keep it up we get to win a massive prize. Scarlett nods and gurgles. She has an extensive repertoire of nods and gurgles as you might imagine, and I'm pretty fluent in them. This, I reckon, is a *yes, I get it* kind of nod. It's a *Daddy's called Russell, now can we get on with breakfast and Nickelodeon please?* kind of gurgle. It's a nod and a gurgle that says that Scarlett is impatient for some of the best kind of love.

None of this second-best shit.

Eleven

LORNA

Lorna has never really done sweat. She avoided sports at high school, her mum wearily colluding in the skiving by agreeing to pen the necessary notes until, in the end, everyone quietly accepted that during PE Lorna would just make her way to the library or the textile room.

It's textiles she's doing now, she supposes. Crocheting what will become a cuddly mouse for Armitage Shanks to play with while Megan does her rough games. Her silly PE. Funny how life could change so much, and also hardly at all at the same time. She can easily imagine that if she ever has a child she'll be sitting in sports halls all over the country reading or knitting, while little Marley or little Dinah takes part in judo or Irish dancing or whatever. She could be doing what she's doing now for years. And then there might be grandchildren. Wherever she goes, whatever she does, it might always be a simple twist on what she's doing now.

Sitting with her wool and her thoughts Lorna is able to tune out most of the class. Despite this she's aware that Megan is the best. Not just the fastest in the sprints, but she has the quickest reflexes in the various games they play. There's this one game where everyone is wearing boxing gloves but instead of fighting each other, they have to slap the elbows or the shoulders or the arses of a partner without getting slapped themselves. Megan is terrific at it. She is lightning fast – in – *slap* – and out, like an otter gulping fish in a rushing stream.

She is also the most elegant. Some of the other women are quick and strong, but with them there is always a sense of effort, of labour.

Everyone else in the group is plum-faced and soaked after a few minutes. Megan is merely slicked, glistening, tinged with just enough of a hint of colour to make a spectator think of apricots or peaches. And she keeps control of herself too. She stays nimble on her toes and her back stays straight where others begin to hunch and shuffle slightly as the class goes on – like they are becoming old in front of everyone.

And when they hit the pads or the bags the class is encouraged to vocalise, and most grunt formlessly, but Megan restricts herself to a controlled percussive *pa pa pa-pa*. Or, when jabbing, a quicker, aspirated rhythm *pha-pha-pha*. Long and short of it, Megan is good. And for a nicely brought up middle-class white girl from Berkeley, she is aces. Lorna gets that.

When the class starts sparring, Lorna puts down her needles and her wool. People trying to hit each other is always fascinating. It is gruesomely compelling outside the Ginger Goose in Bradford on a Saturday night, and it is still very watchable here now.

The way it works is that the class do two-minute circuits. Ten stations: skipping, squat thrusts, press-ups, bag work, step-ups and oh, loads of things, and one station is the ring where Linwood, the instructor, defends himself against each girl in turn. He doesn't really fight back, though he sometimes taps the women on the forehead – gently, so gently – if he thinks they are leaving themselves too open.

It is clear to Lorna that this is what the women pay for. Ten dollars for the chance to hit a guy in the face? A total bargain. However tired the women are when they come off the bag work, they perk up significantly once they are in the ring and loosing off shots for real. And it is for real. While even an amateur onlooker like Lorna can see that not one of these try-hard soccer moms would last a minute in a real fight, and probably not survive even one decent counter-punch from Linwood – in their heads they are fighting for their lives.

Just how good Megan is can be gauged by the fact that Linwood does genuinely bop her on the nose a couple of times. Hard enough to make the watching Lorna wince. Hard enough to bring a proper flush to Megan's face for the first time. And when Megs comes out of the ring she doesn't go to her next station but goes straight to the showers saying, 'I guess we better get going Lorna, my dear,' and she's trying to sound breezy and doing OK but Lorna can still hear angry tears in her voice. And Megan can tell that her roomie knows she's not so blasé because she gives a wibbly-wobbly smile and says, 'I'm OK – just need to work on my defence. Can't be going forward all the time. Give me five minutes, 'kay?'

While she is in the shower Linwood comes over to Lorna.

'You know, I'm hard on her because that's how she'll get better.'

Lorna just looks at him. Keeps right on crocheting. Linwood looks at the floor. He is handsome, sort of. A fine, well-built black man with that big-gunned, xylophone-abbed, even-featured look men aspire to over here. He has a face so sternly symmetrical, so coolly contemporary, it could win design awards. To tone this down he is wearing heavy black-rimmed specs, a transparent effort to soften the jockness.

Linwood smiles and Lorna flinches at the sudden gleam of the wall of teeth. Like the sun shining off a row of riot shields.

'You should have joined in. The class I mean. Gotta be better than knitting.'

'Crocheting.'

There is silence again.

'You're pissed at me. A little. Admit it. You are. For hitting your friend.'

'She's a big girl.'

Linwood is delighted. It seems he feels this meant he is exonerated in the court of Megan's friends. It isn't the impression Lorna means to give. Not at all.

'That's it.' He nods so vigorously his head actually seems to bounce. 'Right. She's an adult. And she's the best. Totally. She's just got to learn to keep her hands up. To defend herself at all times. Come on, stand up.'

'What?'

Linwood reaches down. He's very tall. Like a big, black tree, only supple. A black willow maybe. He very deliberately moves the wool and the hook from Lorna's hands and lap. Then he pulls her up to her feet. 'You'll like boxing,' he says as he moulds her hands and feet into a fighting stance.

'I don't think so. I don't do PE. Sorry.' But she doesn't attempt to move away or change position while Linwood pulls his gloves back on. Lorna feels ridiculous but also hypnotised somehow. It's because she is so many miles from her comfort zone. When had she last been in a gym? Year ten was it? So that would be 1997. Empires have risen and fallen since then. The world has boomed and bust twice at least. There have been wars. Some of them have even finished. More or less.

'Now try and hit me.'

'What?'

'Hit me. Hard as you can.'

'Hit you?'

'Hit me. Give me your best shot.'

'Oh, fuck it.'

Linwood purses his lips. 'No need to curse.'

'I think you'll find that there is usually every need.'

And then she swings at him, and he bats her away easily with his gloved right hand. He laughs. 'It goes best when you don't shut your eyes when you throw one.'

'I didn't.'

'It doesn't matter, but you so did. Come on, again.'

So she throws a few bare-knuckle punches, painfully conscious of how flappy and girlish they seem, even to her, and Linwood catches them all with no trouble. And he corrects her stance and teaches her about snapping out the jab and the difference between a hook and an uppercut, and shows her to swing her hips with the punch, and he more or less ignores the other women calling out their exhausted goodbyes to him.

And after a few minutes he says, 'You're actually a natural.'

To which she replies, 'And you're actually a bullshitter.' And Linwood purses his lips again at the cursing. It makes her smile that this big tough guy is so prim. And she also can't help feeling pleased at the praise, and then she notices Megan standing watching, hands on hips, eyes narrowed.

'Ready to go, babes?'

Megan just inclines her head slightly, then turns and strides away towards the stairs that lead to the car park and, feeling weirdly caught out, obscurely naughty, Lorna trots after those big shoulders, that narrow waist, those dancers thighs – the whole package, it seems to Lorna, transmitting a disapproving haughtiness.

'Hey, Megan!' Linwood is calling. Megan turns. 'Nice work today. Fast hands.'

Megan nods gravely but says nothing, just raises the hand that isn't carrying her gym bag. She looks at him coolly for a long second. Flicks her wet hair away from her face.

There are no words in the car for ages. Megan has the radio up too loud to talk comfortably and is concentrating on the traffic in any case. It's building up now. She is doing the thin-lip thing again. She can make it go like razor-wire when she wants. It's such an obvious sulk that Lorna wants to laugh. It's funny though, because she wouldn't have thought Linwood was her usual type. Altogether too jock, despite the glasses. Maybe we're both getting desperate, she thinks. Or maybe it is just that they had been in Megan's space, the gym being her domain. If it's that, well, it's unfair because it was Megan who had insisted she should drive her to Russian Hill after class, be there to provide back-up. It wasn't like Lorna was begging to hang at the boxing club. And she hadn't wanted the attention from Linwood, hadn't encouraged it. She had, in fact, been fairly abrupt with him, a bit off. Rude even.

She supposes now that the best thing would be to clear the air with a few light remarks, to make Megan laugh. It is usually easy to josh her out of a mood, but Lorna is starting to feel a bit tired and head-achy and anyway, maybe Megan isn't even thinking about Lorna's accidental flirtation with Linwood at all, maybe she is just stressed about the traffic. Maybe she is genuinely and simply concerned about flyovers and intersections and freeways. Whether or not to take the FAIR lane, the one where you can pay ten dollars and ensure a queue-free ride. The stuff Lorna, as a permanent passenger – as one of the fourteen or so people in the state who doesn't drive – never has to worry about.

She had already formed the impression from her mum that her father had done well in business, but even so this neighbourhood is still a bit intimidating. These have to be the most expensive houses in the city. Huge, surrounded by electronic gates and walls and looking down on everyone else. Each one like a castle busy getting on with its own fairy tale.

Uncertain of where the house is exactly, they park up to consult the scrap of paper on which Lorna has scrawled the address. The gran-deur of the area makes Lorna feel drab and shy in contrast. Megan conversely seems to brighten now the drive is over. Yeah, maybe it really had been the traffic making her do the tight mouth thing. Lorna hopes so. She doesn't want a ridiculous spat over some idiot boy to spoil what could be her last few weeks in the States.

'I think it's that one,' Megan says as she points at a particularly film-setty palace painted the colour of manuka honey. 'And do you think that's him?'

Lorna follows Megan's imperious finger with its short athlete's nail. She sees a plumpish, balding, rosy-cheeked man in a dark suit come out of the gate that belongs to the golden house. They watch as he points elaborately at the line of parked cars. It's a gesture that seems overdone, more like a G-man taking a bead on a mobster with a handgun than a man opening the doors to his car. It does the job though, the lights on an anonymous, grey Lexus-Volvo-Audi-SUV thing blink twice.

The guy is about the right age, and he looks anxiously uncomfortable. Meaning that, yes, he looks English. Is there any creature less built for elegance in the sun and heat, than the middle-aged English bloke in a suit? So it could be her dad, it really could. Yet she feels no exhilaration. Instead she feels flat and frumpy and her headache is worse.

Megan is already out of the car. 'Come on, sister, look alive.' And yes, of course, this bloke, this possible dad, might be driving off any second. There isn't time to sit around plucking up courage and rehearsing what she is going to say and whatnot. She clambers out of Megan's battered Focus feeling hot, ungainly, sticky, sweaty and nauseous. Perhaps it is just as well her dad – if that's who he is – doesn't look like a glamorous movie exec.

Megan links arms with her and hurries her along. 'Exciting, huh?' she says, and she doesn't sound satirical or anything. She sounds like she means it.

They are about 100 metres from the house now, and the silver Lexus-Volvo-Audi or whatever is maybe another 50 metres beyond that. The man, her dad, whoever, hasn't got in yet – he is leaning against it waiting for someone. Waiting in fact for this small, thoughtful woman coming out of the gate now. A woman with a kind face wearing a funky mod-inspired black–and–white dress that almost fits, but somehow doesn't quite.

'Balenciaga,' whispers Lorna to Megan, 'four thousand dollars. At least.' And then she notices that both the woman and the man are now standing together, silent, motionless, looking at them oddly. Megan and Lorna come to a halt too. There is an uncomfortable gap of thick swampy air between them. Lorna feels panicky now. There's nothing to say. Nothing at all.

It is the woman in the ill-fitting Balenciaga dress who speaks first.

'Can we help you?' A kind voice. Soft. Pleasant. Cautiously friendly, with warm brown tones to it. It's also definitely English. Southern but

69

not London, maybe just a hint of the M4. Reading? Bristol? Bath? Not as far west as that. Swindon? A careful voice anyway, one that doesn't want to draw attention to itself.

'Um,' says Lorna. The thick dead air sucks at her tongue. Next to her Megan coughs.

'Excuse me, sir.' This uncomfortable bloke turns his worried frown towards her. 'My friend was wondering if maybe, by any chance, you were, kinda her father?'

Uncomfortable bloke opens the car door, making ready to leave.

'I don't think so.'

He is also English though. Southern again, with more of a London thing going on. That 't' on 'don't' almost disappeared. Her dad was from the south-east originally. Lorna swallows hard and steps forward. She puts out her hand.

'I'm Lorna. Lorna Dawson.'

He looks at her hard now, lets a few long moments pass, and then, briefly, touches her fingers with his.

'I'm not your dad,' he says quietly. He sounds tired. Lorna looks at his face and, true, she can't see herself there. She just sees some randomer's ordinary middle-aged face, pouchy with weariness, pink on the cheeks and nose where the sun has caught him.

'So. Tell the poor girl your name.' The woman sounds like she's smiling, but her eyes are glittery. She suddenly has the look of the women in the gym, thinks Lorna. She looks like she proper wants to belt something, someone. And to belt them very hard. Not so soft, pleasant or cautiously friendly now.

'Nigel,' says the bloke at last. 'Nigel Smith.'

'Oh right.'

'Nigel,' repeats the woman heavily. Then she says, 'He – *Nigel* – works for Russell Knox. Is that who you were looking for?'

'Yes. Yes it was, ma'am.'

'He's gone travelling.'

'Oh.'

There is silence.

'He's not expected back for months. If at all. Sorry.'

And she actually does sound a bit sorry.

Megan ignores the woman, directs her whole attention to Nigel, gives him the steady force of her peachy, apricotty light. She says, 'Sir, perhaps you have a number? Or an email address? My friend has been trying to find Mr Knox for a long time. I'm sure you understand.'

'Well, I . . .' The bloke – Nigel – looks confused. He glances towards the woman who makes a face, shakes her head slightly. 'Well, I . . .' Nigel begins again. The woman cuts in briskly. Sharp.

'We can't give out contact details, dear. Nigel would get fired. As I'm sure you understand.'

'Oh right.' Lorna just wants to be gone now. This is all excruciating.

'But maybe you could give us your details and that way Mr Knox can get in touch with you if he wishes.'

'I never knew he had a daughter.' Nigel seems to be announcing this to the world at large. There is a silence. The world at large doesn't seem to be listening. Doesn't seem to care much.

'Have you worked for Mr Knox long?' This is Megan again.

'We've known him years, haven't we, darling?'

'Quite a while.' Nigel seems to be recovering his composure now, thinks Lorna. Perhaps he senses the whole conversation, confrontation, whatever, coming to an end.

Lorna gets her pen and notebook out of her bag. She starts to scribble her email and phone number. The pen goes dead after the first three letters. She scratches furiously at the page, but it has really had it. Lorna can feel herself blushing. It shouldn't matter – one of the others is bound to have a pen – but, somehow, it does. A competent person, a person with a proper father, would have a pen that worked.

Silently Megan hands her another Biro.

'Thanks.' Lorna feels like crying.

She finishes scrawling all her details, not just cellphone and email, but her address in Emeryville and her mum's in England. Nigel takes the page from her and examines it carefully.

'You're from Saltaire in Yorkshire?'

'Yeah.'

'The town Sir Titus Salt originally built for his mill workers?'

Lorna is startled. She rarely meets people who know her hometown.

'Yeah, the very same. They let ordinary people live there now.' And then in a rush she says, 'They don't do that these days, do they? Modern millionaires, I mean. Where's Billgatesville? Where's Tetrapack City?'

The man smiles. 'Who'd want to live in those places?'

'You're right. Billgatesville. Imagine, everyone rocking the double denim and getting themselves all stressy about recycling.'

The man's smile broadens. He looks nice now. Shy. Decent. Ordinary.

'Nigel,' the woman prompts.

'Oh right, yeah. We better get going.' Nigel's smile vanishes, replaced by the worried frown again. She can see black fillings in his mouth. Russell Knox – her dad – clearly doesn't pay enough for proper dental care. Who has black fillings these days?

'We're going to a funeral,' says the woman.

'Oh, I'm sorry,' says Megan.

'It's OK. It's not—' she stops, looks over at Nigel.

His face is twisted in an odd little grin. He finishes the sentence for her. 'It's not anyone close.'

'That's right,' says the woman, and she's also strangely twinkly. 'It's only my husband.'

Afterwards, when the couple have driven off in their Lexus-Volvo-Audi thing, after Lorna has sat in the sticky passenger seat and wept for a while, without knowing why, and after she's kissed Megan and told her

72

how much she loves her for coming with her, and how much she admires her for always knowing what to do and say. For always having a Biro when one is needed. And told her how great it has been to see her do her thing at boxing and how ace she is at that and at everything else actually, and after Megan has told her to shut up, but in a way that tells Lorna she's pleased and that the whole business with Linwood is forgotten about. After all that, and when they are driving back through the city, something occurs to Lorna.

'She never told us her name.'

'What?' Megan has her grim traffic-face on again.

'The woman who was with Nigel. She never told us her name.'

'Do we need to know her name?'

'I guess not. It's a bit weird though.'

'They were both weird. They were freaks.'

'He was OK. Anyway, I bet they think the same about us.'

'I bet you're right. I bet they do think that. But that's because they're freaks.' She clicks the radio on, a kooky girl is singing a funny little song over a scratchy guitar about wanting to be a bumble-bee. College folk. Kinda twee, but kinda fun. '*Honest-ly . . . I'd be quite hap-py . . . Yellow and black is where it's at . . .*'

Lorna finds herself idly curious about what Jez is up to. Next to her Megan shifts in her seat.

'Don't,' she says.

'What?'

'I know you've had a stressful day, but don't do it.'

'Don't what?'

'Don't call the Fuckweasel.'

Spooky. Sometimes Lorna wonders whether Megan is actually a qualified witch.

And on the radio the girl sings: '*. . . made out of fluff . . . life wouldn't be tough . . . I wouldn't need no clothes or go to fancy shows . . . all I want to be is . . .*' Lorna thinks that if she ever had a coat of arms it would feature a bumble-bee. The creature that

Twelve

CATHERINE

She is in the kitchen making scrambled eggs and getting wound up by the radio. The presenter is quizzing some cabinet minister on the *Today* programme and not giving him anything like enough of a hard time. It makes her cross. They are reducing troop numbers again and the wars are not actually won yet. Imagine if budgetary constraints had led to the allied forces being cut in half three weeks after D-day. The liberation of Europe would have been a lot more tricky then. A war isn't over just because an accountant in Whitehall says it is.

And it is stupid because soldiers are cheap. You can get a fully trained up squaddie for £25K a year. Peanuts – about the same as a teaching assistant, or some call-centre kid in a shiny Top Man suit. And all those laid-off soldiers, fit and knowing how to fight, are going to be hitting the streets angry and broke. Most of them suffering from PTSD. It's a recipe for a shit-storm, anyone can see that, and here is this soft-bodied desk-jockey mumbling on about tough decisions and hard choices. Leave him alone on an Helmand hillside for twenty-four hours and then let him talk about tough decisions and hard choices.

And then it's time for the bloody sport. Football and Rugby. Bread and flipping circuses more like. Spectacles to keep the population entertained so they won't notice the mess they're in. And this bread and these circuses are not even trying to entertain the whole population. Just the men. And how much do those players get paid? A million a week? And none of them would last a day in Afghanistan either.

She beats the eggs carefully, adds them to the pan where the shallots and chopped green-finger chillies have been frying in butter. She puts the bread in the toaster.

Catherine thinks that politicians shouldn't run armies, it should be the other way round. Look at Greece – the economy was fine when the generals were in charge and turned to shit when the politicians took over. Same in Spain. Not that she would necessarily trust British generals, most of them are like politicians anyway. And that's not surprising given that most of them have been to the same schools as the bloody cabinet. They're probably all related, or have touched each other up in the dorms after lights out.

Catherine had been in the Army ten years when she went to Afghanistan. Ten years of having to prove to everyone, including herself, that she was better than the blokes. Better at everything. Better at running. Better at the assault course. Better at shooting. Better with a bayonet. Better at swearing even. Proving that she could carry more, further, faster, than anyone else could. Ten years to progress from hoisting arseholed grunts out of dodgy clubs in places like Colchester and Aldershot as part of the military police, all the way to getting her commission in 2001. By that time she could fly helicopters and gliders, she was an accomplished sniper and she could kill with her bare hands. She knew she could because she'd done it, more than once. In Iraq and in Bosnia.

And then, in Afghanistan, months after 9/11, the rules of engagement changed and female officers like her weren't allowed to give orders to men in public. The idea was that a woman ordering men around would infuriate the local population and so encourage resistance, which was debatable but it meant that when out on patrol even the most Neanderthal private had more status than she did. It was crazy. Can any other army in history ever have taken the sensibilities of their enemies on board in this way? Could you imagine the Red Army doing it? Or Genghis Khan? Or the Spartans? And just as well the Iceni didn't worry about such things when they put Boudicca in charge. And what about Queen Elizabeth I at the time of the Armada? What about Joan of frigging Arc?

She'd argued – ranted even – to anyone who would listen, regardless of rank or gender and, in the end, she took a Hercules home. She had to. When the head of land operations asks whether it's the time of the month just because you've expressed some disquiet about the way the war is being fought, then you really do have to get out. And yes, she bloody well knew that Joan of Arc and Boudicca both lost in the end, but that is hardly the bloody point. They didn't lose because they were on the blob, did they? They lost because the bloody men did everything they could to shut them up. They bloody burned Joan of Arc. Burned her. That's how much some men hate a stroppy woman.

She folds the eggs gently and turns the heat off. That's the way with scrambled eggs, they should still be quite runny when you take them off the gas. If you do that then they are cooked to perfection as the heat disperses. They don't go rubbery. Scrambled eggs should retain a hint of warm egg-nog about them. She folds in a little cream. Just a drizzle. She adds grated double Gloucester.

The toast pings up.

She puts both slices on a plate, scrapes a thin layer of Marmite over them, tips the perfect eggs on top and sprinkles on a pinch of cayenne. Superb. She is, she thinks, very possibly the queen of scrambled eggs. She gets herself some juice. Catherine long ago decided that grapefruit is the only proper breakfast juice. It is wake-up juice. Orange juice is acceptable as an alternative but really it's for the slack, for people who don't really want to wake up. As for those who like apple or cranberry juice in the morning, you just know they are weak. Masturbators and adulterers. People unlikely to last a minute under interrogation. No, a fast early morning run in hard country in the rain, a scalding shower followed by eggs, grapefruit juice and fine strong black coffee – Rwandan if poss – that's the best way to come alive. Catherine feels her mood begin to lift. And then she thinks about how she has to go back to America and her spirits droop again.

Catherine is a conscientious professional and she hates making mistakes. The news that this latest trip was a screw-up really pissed her off. Now she is going to have to go back to the States. She's going to have to squeeze it in before heading off to Abkhazia, and that means the usual stressful hassle that goes with flying and with hotels.

But it isn't just the hassle, there's something else. There is a word in the Army – Snafu. Means 'situation normal all fucked up'. Only things getting fucked up isn't normal for Catherine. For Catherine things don't go wrong. And if they do they are not her fault. And yet yesterday she'd had to endure being mildly bollocked by Madam, with her sanctimonious jolly-hockey-sticks voice. Oh, she'd kept it all very light, all very don't-worry-these-things-happen, but Catherine knew she thought it was her mistake. And that's why she'd sounded so cheerful. Madam's wanted to catch Catherine out for years, feels threatened by her or something. God knows why. Catherine isn't after her job. She doesn't want to sit in an office pushing paper, counting pencils. And they are both women in a world of men, so Catherine feels they should stick together somehow, however naïve that sounds.

And there was the sneaky way she'd mentioned a forthcoming organisational review right at the end of the conversation, just to unsettle Catherine a little more.

But, as she eats her eggs and drinks her juice, Catherine knows it is more than hurt pride and office politics affecting her here. There's grief too.

She knows bad things happen in wars, of course she does. Sometimes it turns out that you don't zap the bad guys but their nice neighbours instead. Sometimes those vicious fighters who pop up in your sights running for their RPGs, turn out to be farmers, or a wedding party or a bunch of kids playing whatever the Afghan version of Knock Down Ginger is called. Sometimes the vicious Pathan with a sniper rifle turns out to be a boy with a stick playing cowboys.

So she knows these things are bound to happen. One of the things that makes the bad guys bad is the way they hide their badness among the skirts of their wives and daughters and obedient servants. All of which means that it is even more important, in her kind of struggle, to try not to make those kinds of mistakes. To check. But it seems she has fucked it up this time. Some ordinary Joe has paid the price for somebody else's crime.

Of course, he was probably still a bad guy. Or at least an accessory. And even if he wasn't, people die all the time. They die crossing the road, they die falling off things or under things or into things. They die because there's no antibiotics or no water or no food. They die of overwork and they die of broken hearts.

And sometimes they die young. And even a long, full life is only an instant looked at in the proper historical scheme of things. A human being dying isn't a big deal. The wrong person died in the wrong place at the wrong time: boo fucking hoo. It happens. And this civilian, whoever he was and whoever he was working for, he died painlessly, quickly, and without fear. And these are things of real value. He was lucky in that way. Catherine knows all this and yet still it bugs her. It especially bugs her when Madam tells her to put it behind her and move on.

And now, right on cue, the radio moves on to *Thought For The Day*. It's the earnest Sikh guy and so Catherine stops to listen. She likes him. He has a nice voice. Deep and rich. It's the Christian speakers that annoy her, they remind her too much of school assemblies. Their voices always sounding like those of deputy head teachers.

The guru is talking about the problem of living Chakar Vati, that is how to live in the modern industrial world without being a slave. He is talking too about how big business often makes its profits from stirring up the five evils – by which he means ego, anger, greed, attachment and lust. The fate of those vulnerable to the five evils is, he says, separation from God. This separation can only be cured by devotion and study. But it is possible, he said, for all of us to come to union with God. That is, to live a life free from illusion, free from oppression.

And this is where Catherine and the guru part company. In Catherine's view once the five evils have really begun their work, then

79

no amount of study or devotion is going to cure it. And also, she doesn't believe most people are anything like ready for a life without illusion. Illusion is pretty much the only thing that keeps them going.

Thought For The Day gives way to the weather. Easterly winds. Rain for most of the country for most of the day. At least California will be warm.

Catherine finishes her breakfast, wonders briefly whether to have another slice of toast, but that's how the five evils get you. It begins with extra toast at breakfast when you don't really need it. And anyway there is, for Catherine, a sixth evil – procrastination. The thief of time. We've got so little of the stuff over the course of a life that to waste it really is the ultimate crime.

With a sigh, Catherine begins to clear up her breakfast things. She'll get her flat properly and completely cleaned the way she always does before a trip, then she'll work on her story for an hour, then she'll do all the tiresome flight stuff – the printing off and so forth – then she'll pack. Then she'll meditate.

Catherine is a big believer in meditation. It's another thing she and the Sikhs have in common. She always makes time for it, wherever she is. Catherine discovered meditation early on in her career and that and yoga are two of the things that keep her sane. In fact Catherine has five virtues of her own to counteract the five evils: meditation, yoga, reading, writing and exercise. And they are all linked too. Do one well and all the rest go better. And they are all things that let you bend time. Get lost in any one of these things and you can disappear into a long journey, come back and find you've only been away for an hour or so. Each of these things does more than just help you relax, they take you to a little personal Narnia.

Of course, if you just want to chill then decent wine will do the job, but fine wine is Tough's way really, not hers – he's a connoisseur – but the problem with booze is that it speeds time up, puts the days and nights on fast forward, and Catherine is very much in favour of having more time not less.

Thirteen

NICKY

My favourite fictional funeral is in *Richard III*. King Richard has had his rival murdered and uses his funeral to get off with the guy's widow, Lady Anne. And not only does Lady Anne know he's the killer – and also the killer of her father by the way – but Shakespeare's Richard is not some good-looking brooding hunk. No, he's disabled, his body as twisted as his mind. In fact his mind is, in Shakespeare, twisted because his body is all messed up. Given his disadvantages it's quite a big ask for Richard to get the girl, but he does it. A combination of traditional bad boy I-don't-give-a-fuckness, plus bambi-eyed vulnerability and, crucially, a nice line in chat. These are what do the business. We all know the nice girls love that particular combination. It's a hard lesson we nice, shy boys have to learn on the first day of puberty.

Actually, maybe it's even earlier than this – doesn't the tousle-haired kid who chases the girls in the first year of infants, the tyke who pulls their hair and then cheeks the teacher – doesn't he get an undue amount of attention? Don't the teachers – most of them women – work hardest with him? Every little terror of the infants gets a queue of Lady Annes in the end. And if they're good with words too, why that queue can stretch round the block.

Russell was popular in this way. Always a monstrous platoon of squealing pinafore dresses after him in playground kiss-chase. Always a big-bosomed matriarch smiling indulgently as she told him she'd swing for him one of these days.

It wasn't like that for me. And it won't be like that for Scarlett. It's just not like that for little girls. They can wrap their dads around their little fingers but they can't do that with their primary school teachers. And especially not the little girls who can't speak, who can't walk normally. Girls who may never be able to stand up straight. Do we think Scarlett will ever have boys queuing up to take her out? Do we think she'll ever be asked to the prom by the football captain? We do not. But hey, that could be a good thing even if she never sees it that way.

Anyway, bollocks to all that. That's the difficult unknowable, unforeseeable future. What about now? What about this solemn laying to rest of that unlucky kiss-chase loser Nicky Fisher?

This funeral is boring in every way, but that means success of course. It's what we've hoped for. It's what we've planned. Boring is absolutely the theme here. We're definitely not about to put the fun in funeral.

In your average real-life burial, you get all these people together, people that for very good reasons haven't seen each other in years, you put them and all their grief and, more importantly, all their seething resentments, jealousies, rivalries and bitter memories into one room and then stir in unlimited alcohol. No surprise then that sometimes it kicks off.

And there's usually sexual tension too. After all, everyone at a funeral has had to come face-to-face with mortality. And – reflexively self-absorbed species that we are – this means someone else's death goes straight to our own loins. In the midst of death we want to create some new life. Everyone is kind of on heat, at least a little. And I do mean everyone, not just the nubile and the virile. Every grandad and every spinster aunt feels it too. In real-life funerals even the most unbending of people are more tactile than usual, less buttoned up. Sometimes quite literally. Conversations are saturated with sex talk, the way a good trifle is laced with cheap sherry. You can smell it. Taste it.

But this is not real life. It's not real death. And it sure as hell ain't Shakespeare.

Sarah and I have planned a drab funeral of convenience. A consommé of a ceremony. Chill and thin and pointless. There are no Lady Annes and no King Richards here. Instead there's just Psalm 23 and a poem which we choose because it is, according to Wikipedia, the most popular poem at the contemporary funeral, the undisputed number one in the funeral hit parade. A poem which ends with the line 'Do not stand at my grave and cry/I am not there; I did not die', which is a joke just for us. Oh, what cards we are. What merry pranksters.

There are flowers. And not all of them are ones we've bought ourselves. Sarah gets quite a few from England to express sympathy for her loss. I'm touched to see a handsome wreath from my colleagues in the cultural services department, even though most of my closest colleagues were despatched in the last restructure. And I mean closest in its most literal sense. The people who sit near me. Those who take turns with me in getting the tea round at eleven and again at three. I don't mean close as in shared confidences. Shared pain.

And we have a song too. 'There Is A Light Which Never Goes Out'. One of Russell's favourites. The song he'd always said he'd have at his wedding.

Morrissey begins his thing and Sarah composes her carefully made-up Dignified Widow face. She pauses to put her lips to my ear.

'How does it feel to be dead?'

I hear the bubbling smile in her voice and it annoys me somehow.

'Oh, I've known how that feels for years.'

'Well, that makes me feel just great.' She turns back to face the front. And I feel crap. I'm such an idiot sometimes. What is wrong with me?

Besides us there are just four people here. Two of them were found for us by the funeral home we employed on the recommendation of the coroner's office. The office who had signed the death off as being premature but entirely natural, undeserving of further investigation by a hard-pressed public service.

83

There's the milky-faced minister. An Episcopalian of gentle manners, with all the charisma of a wet tissue, which suits us. There's the man who presses the buttons to start the music and conveyor belt to the furnace. What would you call him? The AV technician maybe? He's a cheerful, ruddy, tubby man who looks like he should be sitting on a barstool with other cheerful, ruddy, tubby men talking ball games – or taking his cheerful, ruddy, tubby children bowling. Or taking his cheerful, ruddy, tubby dogs to chase more slender girl dogs in the park.

There's an unattached old lady in an inappropriate pink jogging suit. All funeral audiences, however small, feature at least one unattached old lady. It is a law I think. And she must have been found by the funeral directors too, because she certainly doesn't belong to us.

There's also a depressed-looking chap in a charcoal three-piece shiny with wear, and we are a bit concerned about him.

Other people wanted to come of course, Sarah's mum and sisters, some of her friends, they wanted to be here to lend supportive shoulders for weeping on. We put them off. No, no need. Sarah doesn't want to see anyone at the moment. Can't face it. She'd rather be alone with her memories for a while. And of course it would have been way too much for my dad.

Russell's body trundles on its final trip. If he looked like an anonymous package when he left the house with Soraya and Claudette, now he looks like a piece of baggage going through the scanner at a very provincial airport. There are faded grey curtains instead of those flappy rubber bits you get in baggage check, but it's still the same bumpy journey along humming rollers. There's no poetry in it. Not even the Purple Ronnie kind. Not even the number one on Wikipedia kind. No comfort. And for the first time since Russell's death I get a spasm of grief. A real, gut-twisting physical pain deep in my guts.

This parcel of meat and bones we're gathered here today to dispose of was a little boy once. A boy I knew. A boy I played Subbuteo with. Went on bike rides with. Played tig in the playground with. Kicked endless balls around with. A boy who loved making Airfix models and doing jigsaws. And, later, this was a boy I had my first drinks with, went to my first gigs with. We even went to the same college, shared a terrible squalid house together. Argued about who ate the last can of baked beans, who stole the leftover sausage from the fridge. Even when I no longer liked him all that much, he'd been the natural choice for best man at my wedding.

And now I have to stand and watch while the coffin moves towards the incinerator, and 'There Is A Light' plays. I have to stand and think about what a terrible person I am. And I think about The Smiths. We both rated them too. Saw them three times on their first big tour in 1983. Loughborough, Leicester, Luton. Hitch-hiked to all the places beginning with L, because it amused us. The L and Back tour. Except for London, we didn't go there. We were scared of London. Yes, Russell as well as me, though he'd never admit it. London was too big, too wild. Too loud with a capital L.

But the theme song should really be 'This Joke Isn't Funny Anymore'.

Next to me Sarah finds my hand and squeezes it, and I find I'm sniffling, then sobbing. And then weeping noisily, messily, my nose blocked and my eyes streaming, there's a weird kind of lowing and it goes on for several seconds before I realise it's me. I take a breath, try and get some control.

And then it's the end. The final curtains. The boxed-up Russell rumbles unsteadily up to the gateway to the fiery furnace, those final curtains fail to part properly and they stroke the lid of the coffin as it makes its way through. It seems to stick halfway for a second or two and I have to swallow hard, but then the material comes free, swinging gently. The milky vicar rises to do his soggy homily and I try and remember that yeah, Russell was my playmate that lifetime ago in Bedford, yes he was best man, but he could also be a bit of a cunt. Quite a lot of one actually. Even before he'd made any money. Even when he was very young.

I find myself thinking about the day in 1974 when he'd got his cycling proficiency certificate. He'd been especially insufferable that day. A mark of what he would become. What he would allow to happen to him.

To be honest, it hadn't been passing the cycling test that had fired Russell up, as much as the fact that I had failed it. I'd been the only one in our year to stuff it up. Well, not quite. Tanya Lyons had failed too. But Tanya Lyons was widely recognised as a mong, a joey, and being lumped in with her just made things worse. It would have actually been better to have been the solitary failure. It would have looked willed. Could have been passed off as deliberate. Part of an insurgency against dull conformity. Impossible to do that when yoked together with Tanya fucking Lyons. Anyway, it was something Russell brought up occasionally, even right up to the end. I'm sure he mentioned it on our last night. In fact, I'm positive he did.

Maybe I wouldn't have been any different if I had passed and he had failed. In fact it would have been nice to have got the chance to find out how we'd both respond to my winning and him losing, but I never did. In sports Russell was in the football teams, while I was sub. And sometimes not even that. He got As and Bs in his exams and I got Bs and Cs. He got a 2:1 degree. I got what we called a Desmond – a 2:2. And he would win at all those board games – Risk, Monopoly, Buccaneer, Scrabble, whatever. And when we played tennis or badminton and later, pool, snooker, poker, he would scrap for everything. And cheat. And yet I know he wasn't any cleverer than me, he just wanted it all much more than I did. And I guess I thought: oh, go on, Russell, if it means so much to you then just have the bloody point, have Mayfair, have that triple word score. Yes, you're the winner – big deal.

And that person who had that last can of beans? The leftover sausage. Him. It was always him.

I come to. The preacher is finishing up – every man's death diminishes us etc., which isn't true, is it? Some people's life diminishes us a whole lot more than their death. Pol Pot for example. Lived on for thirty years after the killing fields. That was quite diminishing for the human race, I would say. Sarah squeezes my hand again. I squeeze hers back. I'm being forgiven for the crass been dead for years comment.

I take another breath. Because I can. Russell can't, but I can. So I'm the winner this time, aren't I? When it really counts. In a way. And am I diminished? Maybe. Time will tell.

After Psalm 23 we retire to a meeting room next to the chapel to drink warm white wine and to eat some beige food. We've tried not to over-order but there's still too much, though the unattached old lady makes impressive inroads into the sandwiches and the Doritos. I speak to the man in the three-piece. It turns out he is Mr Jones, the man from the British government.

'I come to the funerals of as many UK citizens as possible.'

'That's your actual job?' I say. 'Being the Queen's representative at funerals?'

'Well, no. I'm also a businessman. Import. Export. You know. Fruit. Computer chips. Things like that. But I do also provide a number of small services to Her Majesty's government from time to time.'

'A sort of consul.'

'Well, an unofficial one, yes.'

'You're a spy.'

'Good heavens, no. I'm more of a consultant.'

'Ah,' I say. 'More proof the world's going down the toilet. We used to call our spies honorary consuls, now they're honorary consultants. Just four added letters but a whole world of difference, my friend.'

I'm a little drunk by this time but it's understandable. It's my funeral after all.

The honorary consultant flushes. 'Well, nice to meet you, Mr Knox. I wish it could have been under better circumstances but, if you'll excuse me, I have a meeting.'

'About fruit? Computer chips? Things like that?'

Mr Jones smiles wearily. 'Things like that,' he says. And he presents his card, shakes hands and is gone.

'Why the fuck have we got spies in California?' I say to Sarah.

'I don't know, Nigel.'

'Will you stop calling me Nigel? Please? Someone might hear.'

Sarah has been calling me Nigel ever since we left Russell's daughter and her mate outside the Russian Hill house. It tickles her. She thinks it's funny. Me? Well, not so much.

I look around. I'm going to talk ball games with the tubby AV man. And then I'm going to find out what the deal is with the old lady. As I look about me I notice the honorary consultant taking a couple of vol-au-vents on the way out. That clinches it for me. He's definitely MI6. I imagine the British secret service is pretty tight when it comes to the old expenses these days. Not wanting to be pilloried in the tabloids and all that. No purple procurement cards for the spooks in austerity Britain, so free vol-au-vents are not to be sniffed at.

They were mushroom vol-au-vents. I'd insisted on those, despite them being hard to find in the Bay Area.

'It's what I would have wanted,' I'd said. 'And if Russell can organise black pudding then someone out here does frigging vol-au-vents.'

And after it's over, after we pay the milky-faced Episcopalian minister and pour the brazen Dorito-scavenger into her taxi, we go back to Hyde Street where Mary from the agency has been looking after Scarlett.

On the way, Sarah says, 'Did you notice that the businessman and that old biddy seemed very friendly at the end there?'

And I had noticed. There was a definite frisson between the consultant and the jogging suit. So it would seem even a dreary little fake wake like ours can stir up the hormones just a little.

'Sarah?' I say. 'Sorry, for being a git earlier. You know when I said—'

'You know what it's like to be dead? Forget it. You're stressed. High cortisol levels can turn people a bit weird. You're all right. Really.' She gives my arm a squeeze. For some reason I fill up again, but I don't think anyone sees.

We get home. Scarlett greets us like a cheerful terrier. Panting, slobbering, jumping up at us. I always think she's half small child, half small dog, half excitable Shetland pony. And yes I know that's three halves. Who's counting? There's something of the giddy pet about her definitely. Though you couldn't ever say her bark was worse than her bite. It's so great to see her.

'She been OK?' Sarah asks.

'She's been an angel,' says Mary, her wide smile showing all the complicated Meccano of her braces. Braces and she must be in her twenties. Americans and their orthodontistry, honestly, you'd think the right to a brilliant smile was enshrined in the constitution. Now Mary's pigtails swing, her dimples seem to bob on her skin as she grins, pebbles being skimmed across placid water. Her pert nose twitches and wrinkles prettily. She is a right little Anne of Green Gables.

'It's nice to have a quiet one sometimes.'

Is it? Because actually we find it quite a strain. Quite a worry. I think this but I don't say it, and Sarah surprises me by laughing. Maybe she's a bit drunk too.

'Yes, I suppose it must be,' she says.

'I'm praying for her,' Mary says.

Well, that's all right then. Because we'd never thought of that, had we? Praying. But I try and keep the irritation out of my voice as I ask Mary if she needs a ride home, and she smiles shyly and says no, it's OK her boyfriend is coming to get her.

'Your boyfriend?'

'You know, Jesus,' she says.

Jesus and Mary.

89

Sarah looks concerned. 'Jesus? The limo guy? Well, you go careful, yeah?'

Mary looks a bit puzzled. 'Well, gee, yes . . . I will, I guess. But you have to be careful with all guys, don't you?'

Maybe she's not Anne of Green Gables, maybe just one of the flirtier Waltons. Wholesome anyway, raised on Nancy Drew, peanut butter and the Bible. Sarah laughs again.

'That is so true. Beware of all blokes always and forever.'

Jesus isn't driving the limo today. Rather he's in an old but immaculate Subaru.

'Is my own car. So of course I look after her. She is like my home.' He's friendly but, I feel, a little distant given that we have, in the recent past, spent the whole night carousing together.

When they drive away, Scarlett starts crying and won't be comforted. It's like the time we left Spot the Dog in a thrift shop last year. Scarlett may not be able to talk, but boy can she tear the arse out of crying. The operatic sobbing went on for an entire miserable week then until Argos got a new batch of Spots in. I bought them all. I wasn't going through that again. Ten Spots at £6.99 each. A sound investment. Only seventy notes, I'd have paid twice that.

If you knew how Scarlett could tantrum. The whole thrashing, low-budget horror flick violence of it. Tantruming is definitely her thing. Like something from a gorier remake of *The Exorcist*. The body going rigid, the uncontrolled hitting, clawing, kicking. The wet mouth attempting to saw through your wrist. The face so purple it's nearly black. The breath-holding. The nuclear rage of it all. It's a sinister, unnatural thing. I can't bear the thought of it, and neither can Sarah, and we find ourselves promising that Mary will be back real, real soon.

Fourteen

POLLY

'Hello, doll, I've been waiting for you. Let's celebrate.'

Daniel meets Polly before she even gets to the entrance of Sunny Bank. He's there on the gravel practically hopping from foot to foot in his excitement. And when she asks what's the occasion, he grins all over his face and whips something out of his pocket and holds it up with a flourish. A bit like a referee sending someone off in a big match. He looks puffed up with pride. Honestly, when he's happy Daniel could pass for a teenager. And because he's happy, Polly feels happy too.

She still can't work out what he's got in his hand though.

'This, Polly my love, this is freedom.'

'Is it?' She says as he waves it about in her face. 'It looks like a piece of plastic to me.'

'And that is how freedom comes these days!' he yells. He's got the volume turned up to eleven again. But it's early and they're outside and it's chilly, so Irina and the rest aren't around to shush him. Sometimes you'd think shushing the residents is what they were actually paid to do. Whereas Polly, she's at Sunny Bank to unshush them, kind of.

'It's a key,' Daniel says finally. 'It's a car key.'

Five minutes later they're off out in Daniel's new Alfa Romeo Giulietta. It's bright red and Polly's trying to remember if she's ever been in a brand-new car, and she doesn't think she has. Her dad always had old Land Rovers because of the horses, and the boys she's been out with have only ever had bangers.

It's exciting, or it would be if she wasn't so terrified. Daniel is an old man! He has a hole in his head!

What Daniel actually has is vascular dementia. This means that every so often he has a little stroke and the veins in his brain leak a bit. It's like there's some bad weather in there which damages the vein wall and then there are some days of confusion, of getting things wrong. Things like his own name.

Daniel says it is funny that he should be suffering because of badly put together pipework – ironic. You know, given what his job used to be. Polly doesn't think it's funny.

The progression with vascular dementia is stepwise, rather than the steady slippage downhill like it is with Alzheimer's. With vascular dementia after a stroke the hole widens some more, the patient steps down to the next level and then there's a plateau for a few days, weeks, months, until the next bit of proper turbulence in the pipework of the brain.

What's amazing is that sometimes Daniel can step back up a level. It's like the brain finds new ways around this hole in his head. The temporary traffic lights go up, those yellow diversion signs are put in place and all the pulses and messages and memories find clever new ways to work. Smart new rat runs to get to where they need to go. It can't last though. Some day there'll be a massive brain hurricane and he'll be dead or as cabbage-like as the worst of them in Sunny Bank, but for now he's got enough marbles to get by.

'Don't worry about me,' he says now, 'I've been driving sixty-two years.' Which doesn't actually make Polly feel better.

Truthfully, he does seem to be a decent driver. He gives it plenty of mirror-signal-manoeuvre when they're in town anyway. In fact he's very, very careful, almost a bit old ladyish, which is surprising. It's only when they get into the countryside that he gets more calm and confident. He whistles a bit.

He tells Polly that it was Nicky dying that made him want a new car. Made him realise that life was short. And he tells her that he loves cars, that he did the Paris to Dakar rally once, that he used to race Minis in some special league, that he even collected Dinky cars as a kid and still has them all back in his room at Sunny Bank under his bed.

'What? You've still got all those toy cars? Not in boxes?'

'No, of course not still in their boxes. I was just a nipper, what sort of lunatic child would keep their toys in their boxes? But they're in very good condition for their age. Not like their owner. Ha ha.' And he chuckles to himself. Then he starts talking about the car they're in, this red Alfa Giulietta. He says it's got good handling, plenty of welly and that he's pleased that he went for the limited-edition one with wood-veneer dashboard and leather-veneer steering wheel. 'It's the details that count, isn't it?' he says. And Polly is thinking yes, details like having a licence because it's only just occurred to her that Daniel might not have one. Surely the hole in the head thing must disqualify him from driving? Surely they've taken his licence off him?

Apparently not though. They stop in a village out of town that Polly's never been to before, at a pub called The Old English Gentleman. It's a typical country pub with a Yorkshire terrier sleeping before a blazing coal-effect gas fire and lamb rogan josh with naan for just £6.99. Daniel says he's going to treat her. And then it's like he's a mind-reader.

'Amazing that I've still got my licence, isn't it? Bureaucratic cock-up I'm sure, but I'm damn well going to make the most of it.' And he sips his dark beer. Daniel is a real-ale man. He always has a bottle of London Pride with his lunch at the home, and then another at six o' clock on the dot. Actually lots of residents have a drink at six. It's like the last normal habit that a lot of them stick with. Even when they're totally gaga in other ways, they'll still demand wine, beer or sherry at six. They say that music is the last thing the demented can appreciate, that even when everything else has pretty much faded away they can still hum along with 'In The Mood' or whatever. Polly thinks that's wrong though – the very last thing to go is the desire for a drink before dinner.

So they have lunch and then Daniel beats Polly at pool, and at darts, and wins £24 on the SmartAss quiz machine, and he has two more pints. If it was any other resident Polly would have been very strict and told him that he couldn't have more than one if he was driving, but Daniel is completely in charge. He does banter with the woman behind the bar, he talks about football with some lads near the pool table. He's so at home here. No one is ever really at home in a home.

Polly only remembers about drink driving when they're back in the car park. Daniel blanks her when she tries to bring it up, and she thinks they're only a few miles from home so it will probably be all right.

When they're in the car it reeks of London Pride and she gets all nervous again, but she doesn't have to say anything because suddenly Daniel goes, 'Tell you what, my lovely, why don't you drive us back?' And she immediately sees why. There's a police Astra in the car park with them. So Daniel gets out and strides round to the passenger side while Polly fumbles to find the seat-belt releasing thingy.

So now Polly feels properly scared. This is a fast, powerful, brand-new car – of course she's going to crash it. She's going to put them both in a ditch, or wrap them both around a tree. She can picture it very clearly. A stew of crumpled metal, squashed body parts, two different kinds of veneer and a mashed-up elm tree. Even walking to the driver's side feels like the start of *Casualty*.

But she doesn't actually ever get in the driver's seat. She's about to when she sees the policeman walking over. They always make you feel guilty, don't they, the police? Whenever the police want to talk to her she always thinks she's somehow shoplifted a sandwich or accidentally manslaughtered someone. And actually it doesn't even have to be a policeman. Community support officers, security guards in the shopping centre, traffic wardens, anyone in any kind of uniform really, they all make her somehow want to confess to stuff.

But this policeman isn't interested in talking to Polly. He wants Daniel. So Daniel has to get out again and it's a bit of a struggle. He's still a tall, powerful man, which is something Polly hadn't really noticed till today. Everyone in the home seems small to her, frail, but here now, in this pub car park, Daniel seems strong. He towers over the policeman in a way that makes Polly wonder if they've got rid of the height requirement in the police force now. She wouldn't be surprised. And she remembers that she actually thought about joining the police after her GCSEs – she thought it would be a good way to ride horses and get paid for it – but her dad just laughed and that pretty much killed the idea.

Daniel is smiling. It's a wide welcoming smile showing all of his teeth. And they're all in good nick for his age. They're pretty white and pretty even. Not perfect obviously and the smile is actually too big. Just a bit much. It looks desperate. The policeman is smiling too but it's a tight, fake smile and it doesn't reach his eyes, which are small and hard and starey like a birds. A starling maybe, or a seagull.

'Hello, sir,' he says, and he asks if it's Daniel's vehicle and then he asks if Daniel has had a drink.

'Yes, it's my car and of course I've had a drink,' says Daniel. 'We've just come out of the pub. I've had three pints.'

The policeman says in that case he'd like Daniel to take a breathalyser test. Daniel huffs and puffs.

'But I'm not the driver.'

The policeman keeps his cool as he explains that he and his colleague had noticed them leave the pub and get into the red Alfa Romeo Giulietta, registration XL12YY. He explains that they both formed the impression that Daniel had been drinking, this was because of his unsteady gait.

'I'm seventy-seven. I have a dodgy knee. And in any case, let me repeat: I'm not the driver.'

The policeman ignores him and carries on about how he now requires Daniel to take a breath test to determine whether he has a level of alcohol in his blood which would be deemed unlawful under the terms of the Dangerous Driving Act of 1979. Something like that anyway. Polly doesn't catch the exact details because she's watching Daniel's face. It's gone a scary purply red colour. He moves forward so he is in really close to the policeman. He leans down into his face and yells.

'But I'm not the fucking driver!' Little bits of spit zoom out and over the policeman. It can't be very nice. There's little flecks of rogan josh in there for a start. The policeman blinks twice very quickly. It's the first time he's looked properly human. He steps back and keeps his voice very calm as he explains that Daniel was in charge of the vehicle while he was behind the wheel and being in charge of a car while intoxicated is, under the terms of whichever Act it was, an offence.

'Even when it's not moving? Balls!'

Polly thinks Daniel is going to hit him, but he makes a big visible effort, takes a breath and decides to try and be reasonable. 'Look, Officer, I'll be honest. I was going to drive, but then I noticed you and your colleague and saw sense. Your presence in this car park did the trick. It acted as a deterrent. It prevented a crime being committed. So that's a good thing, isn't it? I saw you and decided that my wife should drive instead.'

Wife? Wife? Polly sees the policeman's eyes widen a little. Wife. Cripes. Polly wonders how old this police guy is. It's hard to tell, but he has a smooth well-moisturised face. Not too many lines and no bags under his eyes. She reckons he's twenty-eight or so. Just a bit younger than her. She shakes her head but she doesn't think he notices. He must know that her being Daniel's wife is bollocks though, mustn't he? I mean it's not like she's Asian or anything. Not like she could be a mail-order bride. Maybe she could be Russian or Bulgarian or something, but even so.

The policeman explains all over again that being in charge of a vehicle while being intoxicated is unlawful. Even if that vehicle is stationary.

'Not just fucking stationary! The fucking engine wasn't even turned on! We have just been fucking talking in the fucking car.' Daniel's eyes are red and burning. The copper's eyes just twitch and flicker in that birdy way.

The policeman explains for the third time about the definition of the Act, and then there's silence and again Polly wonders if Daniel is actually going to deck him. There's a long, long moment where this seems the most likely thing. Then Daniel gives up. His shoulders sag. He gets about twenty years older in about half a second. He takes a step back. He says, 'Well, let's just get this bloody charade over with,' and Polly's heart hurts. All the fight has gone out of him and it's hard. He only got that car today and now this nasty little twonk is going to take it off him.

The policeman unwraps the little cylinder and explains the procedure. Polly can tell he's working hard at keeping the triumph out of his voice. Polly thinks how this breathalyser resembles the latest range of predictors you can get in Boots. The new ultra-accurate pregnancy-test sticks.

Daniel puts it between his teeth. He grins at Polly and makes like the breathalyser is a fat cigar. He waggles it and jiggles his eyebrows, which is when she notices that he's trimmed them. They're nowhere near as wild and bushy as they were the other day and it's another sign of how Daniel wanted to look his best for this trip out in his new car. The fact that Daniel is now trying to make a joke of things is making Polly feel physical hurt in her tummy. The policeman tells Daniel to blow into the device properly and Polly finds herself starting to hate him and his stupid smooth plumped-up face. She wants to bite it. Puncture it somehow and watch it deflate.

Now Daniel starts blowing. He blows. And he blows. And he blows. The policeman loses his cool a bit. 'Please blow properly, sir,' he says.

'I am fucking blowing properly,' snaps Daniel.

'Don't swear, Daniel,' Polly says. It's the first thing she's said in the whole incident so far.

Daniel laughs. 'Sorry, dear,' he says. And she laughs too. They do sound exactly like a husband and wife. The policeman is trying hard not to stare at her she can tell.

More seconds pass. The policeman takes the device from Daniel and examines it. He bites his lip. He explains to them that the device appears to be faulty and that he will have to administer the test again and that he will need to return to his vehicle to fetch a new test kit. As he goes and does that Polly asks Daniel why he called her his wife. He doesn't answer, just shrugs.

'Jumped up little Gauleiter,' he says.

And they stand in silence until the policeman is back with his new test which he unwraps. Daniel does his little routine with the kit again, sniffing it, rolling it between his fingers, pretending it's a posh cigar and everything. The policeman sighs. This is all getting too much for him and Polly can't help it – she giggles and Daniel laughs and the policeman sighs again and puts on a serious voice as he tells them that being in charge of a vehicle while intoxicated is a very serious offence, carrying a possible jail sentence as well as a fine of up to £20,000 or something, and a mandatory twelve-month driving ban.

'Yes. But I wasn't fucking driving was I, constable?'

'Come on, darling, just do it,' Polly says and she blushes a bit as she feels the policeman's creepy starling eyes on her.

Daniel smiles at Polly and she smiles back, and then he puts the thing to his lips and blows. He blows. He blows. He blows. The policeman takes it and examines it closely. He puffs out his cheeks.

'Umm,' he says.

So Polly sees it now. She sees that the little light on the tester thing is never ever going to go green, or pink, or blue or whatever. It's just not going to show Daniel over any limit. She can see it from the way the policeman's face goes a bit wobbly somehow, by the way he presses his lips together, by the way he looks like he's going to cry. Her heart doesn't hurt for him though.

Of course the last person to realise the way things are now is Daniel. While the policeman pointlessly twists and turns the little machine in his hands, a delighted grin begins to spread very slowly over Daniel's face. It's like the sun coming up, it really is.

'Oh, my goodness,' he says. And he starts to dance. He actually starts to dance. Slowly, yes, but for real. He lurches in a slow-motion dance. Almost a spazzy mosh really. He looks like a lunatic drunken great-uncle at a wedding. A lunatic drunken great-uncle who loves the Foo Fighters or something.

'Woo-hoo!' he goes. And 'Yeah, man!' It's ridiculous and it's very, very funny and Polly starts giggling again, she just can't help it.

Then Daniel starts coughing and he pulls himself together. 'Phew,' he says. 'Sorry about that. Guess we don't want to have a heart attack, do we?' He means not now, thinks Polly. Not at the moment of victory.

The policeman doesn't know what to say. He looks at the ground. Polly wonders about his life. Does he have a girlfriend? Kids? Probably not. He doesn't look like he has a baby that keeps him awake. Is he gay maybe? It's all right for there to be gay policeman these days.

Daniel is still smiling, beaming like a lottery winner.

'Don't worry, constable,' he says. 'Just doing your job, we know that. Dirty work but someone's got to do it, eh?' There's another long awkward pause before he says, 'Well, we can't stand here chatting all day, can we, darling? Places to go, people to see.'

Polly doesn't join in the husband-and-wife game this time but Daniel doesn't seem to notice as he goes round to the passenger door and opens it.

'Hop in, dear,' he says. The policeman looks at her. His eyes twitch – not a starling, she thinks. Not a seagull. A sparrow. A scared hedgerow bird at the mercy of everything.

Polly ducks under Daniel's arm into the car which, she notices, still smells of beer. Daniel slams the door shut and walks back round to the driver's side. The sounds of outside are muffled now so she doesn't hear any words, but she sees him put a friendly arm on the policeman's shoulder. She imagines him saying something like, 'Keep up the good work,' or 'Chin up, sonny.'

Whatever he says, the policeman doesn't say anything back. He just stands and watches as Daniel drives carefully, so, so carefully, out of the pub car park.

They don't speak for a little while. Daniel puts the radio on. Classic FM. They're playing a tune that Polly recognises from an old advert.

'Maybe you should have let me drive back.'

'No, no, no.' Daniel slaps the leather-veneer steering wheel. 'That was the best bit. His face as he realised that I was going to drive after all. Priceless. Absolutely priceless.'

'You were very lucky,' Polly says.

'Yes,' says Daniel. 'I always am. You can judge the quality of a man by how lucky he is. Napoleon said that you know.' And then he explains how it wasn't just luck, how the whole this-is-a-cigar comedy mucking about had been disguising some effective squeezing and shaking and breaking of government equipment. 'They should invest in the proper stuff,' he says. 'Bloody typical of the British plods to spend hard-earned taxpayers' money on cheap crap.'

Clever man, thinks Polly.

As they stop-start-start-stop through all the traffic in town Polly asks again why Daniel said she was his wife.

Daniel turns to look at her for a long time. Polly stares straight ahead. Behind them there is an angry toot. Funny how you can always tell the difference between an angry get-a-bloody-move-on hoot and a friendly hi-there hoot. They finally start moving.

'I just wanted to put the little Nazi on the back foot. To discombobulate him. You're not offended, are you?'

And she's not, not really, but she wonders if she should be.

'You're a bit old for me, Daniel,' she says.

'Age ain't nothin' but a number,' he says.

And then they bump into the car in front.

Later she puts the whole incident down in an email for Russell Knox. She's been sending him little messages most days, any funny little things Daniel has said, what he's eaten, that kind of thing, and she knows he's going to want to know about today's great big adventure.

And she's right because tonight, for the first time ever, Russell writes back.

He writes: 'This is hilarious. We should meet up when I'm next in England. R.' A short message but an exciting one. She writes back straight away saying that yes they should definitely.

And then while she remembers, she writes an Amazon review of the Alfa Romeo Giulietta. Five stars and she makes sure she mentions the classy wood-veneer dashboard and the leather-veneer steering wheel. And she mentions the bumpers because there was hardly a mark on it, while the back end of the shitty Ford they hit was a right mess. And she wonders if somewhere the scary bird-eyed policeman is writing a one-star review of the breathalyser.

And then she surfs the sperm-donor sites for a bit. She's almost decided on Norwegian. But it's a big decision. She doesn't want to rush it.

Fifteen

LORNA

Saturday brunch in the Lover's Rock Diner. Lorna's last full day in the States. Her visa is on the point of expiring and it's time to go home, see her mum, look for a proper job. A career maybe even. Time to accept that the trip to the States hasn't really worked out and then to put this whole lost decade of assistanting behind her. No more arse-wiping for idiot men in business casual. No more getting too intimately acquainted with a new set of printers, photocopiers and Excel spreadsheets. It is, finally, time to grow up, to think about a mortgage, driving lessons, a teaching qualification perhaps. Christ. She could always kill herself. There is always that.

So lost in the depressing weather of her own thoughts is she that she take ages to notice that Megan is crying. Sluggish twin becks are running from her eyes into her mouth.

'Don't,' Megan says. 'Don't say anything.'

So Lorna doesn't. Instead, she puts her hand out across the plastic table and Megan takes it. Lorna and Megan lock eyes. What a strange impenetrable grey Meg's eyes are. The colour of ancient standing stones on a moor somewhere. Not American at all really.

They stay quiet like that, Lorna stroking Megan's thumb with her own, until a goateed hipster appears at their table and coughs. He looks like Jack Black but also, weirdly, a little like Jack White.

'Shag, marry, dump?' says Lorna after the waiter has taken their order and sauntered back to the kitchen.

'Dump,' says Megan, emphatic.

'It's always dump with you, young lady. It'll heal over if you're not careful.'

'Yeah, I got a problem. But you see, I have these things called standards . . .'

Lorna laughs. 'You like your little luxuries, don't you?' Then she says, 'Here's to us. Here's to the transatlantic special relationship. A love that will never die.'

It's afternoon before they are back in the apartment and Megan clatters around the kitchen fixing snacks while Lorna locates *Some Like It Hot* amid the DVDs scattered like so many giant pennies across the floor of her room. She does this surprisingly quickly and so has time to check her bank balance. Brunch had come to over thirty dollars but Lorna doesn't mind. She's determined to empty her American bank account before leaving and that's only twelve hours away now. As she taps her PIN into her iThing it occurs to Lorna that she is actually going to have to pack at some point.

Ten minutes later she is sitting on the bed, head in her hands, when Megan comes in with hot chocolate.

'Everything OK?' says Megan.

'I'm not sure.'

Megan's eyebrow quivers. She waits.

'There seems to have been a bank error.'

Megan is expressionless. 'I have money,' she says.

'No, no, no, dear heart. You misunderstand me. This bank error is in my favour. Yesterday I had fifty-six dollars and nineteen cents. Now there seems to be over a hundred gees in my account.'

And it's true. Yesterday she was more or less indigent and now she is properly loaded. It is very worrying. Best thing is not to think about it.

'Ready for this movie then?'

But Megan isn't ready for the movie even though *Some Like It Hot* is their favourite film and watching it together one last time is what they had agreed to do today. Megan wants to sort out the mistake. She wants to call people, yell at people, make people wish they'd never been born. Really she wants to *pah-pah pah-pah* their stupid, inefficient, incompetent heads in.

'Just a mistake, babes. Tomorrow it'll all be gone again. I'll be lucky if they don't charge me for the inconvenience. But I really don't want to spend my last afternoon on the phone to some android. Especially when I've been that android and know how shit they feel all day, every day.' Lorna had spent twenty hours a week cold-calling for a windows company while at uni and had felt her soul shrink a little during every second of every minute of each of those hours. The weird thing was that she'd been quite good at it. Employee of the month four times.

But Megan can't settle until this is sorted and so Lorna agrees to send a WTF email expressing her dismay at having her mind messed up by Mr Wells and Mr Fargo.

Which is how she finds out that the cash had been deposited by a nigel@nigelsmith.com overnight. And that means it isn't a mistake. It's worse than that. It's her dad trying to wash his hands of her. Directed by the android at the bank she finds an explanatory email from Nigel lurking in her spam account.

Nigel@nigelsmith's email explains that her dad is sorry but he's planning to be away for an extended period and that he feels it will be too emotionally complicated to begin a relationship now after all these years, but that he – this Nigel – has persuaded Mr Knox that he should at least make a gesture. Hence the cash.

'What a cunt,' says Lorna. Megan nods.

'Gesture my eye,' says Lorna. Megan nods again.

'I'm going to send it back,' says Lorna. Megan doesn't nod this time. She frowns. She does that thing with her eyebrow.

'You could do that,' she says. 'Or you could . . .' She pauses meaningfully. Lorna feels she is missing something.

'What?' says Lorna.

'I don't know,' Megan shrugs. 'You could maybe sorta keep it. Spend it. Invest it. Build a future. You could – and here's a wild and crazy idea – use it to stay here in California. In a nicer apartment maybe.'

'I like this apartment.'

'Whatever.' Megan shrugs again.

'Bollocks. Let's watch the bleedin' film.'

But it turns out that now neither of them can settle and by the time Spats Columbo's men have machine-gunned their rivals, and before Curtis and Lemmon are even into their frocks, Lorna has inwardly acknowledged that Megan maybe had a point, this is the kind of break that people pray for. She shouldn't let pride keep her poor. She zaps the DVD to pause.

'Tell me what I should do, Cap'n.'

It's amazing. It's almost as if Megan has been waiting for this question. She makes a show of stopping to think but it's clear she has it all worked out.

'You should cancel your flights. You should go to grad school – which will allow you a visa to stay as long as the course lasts, and, right now, you should let me make margaritas to celebrate.'

'But won't there be tiresome bureaucracy?'

'In making margaritas?'

'No, you spoon, in cancelling flights, finding a course, registering on it, getting a visa. That all sounds like a major ballache.'

'OK. You do margaritas. I'll do tiresome bureaucracy.'

'Deal. And Megs?'

'Yes?'

'You're very good to me.'

'You got that right, Miss Dawson.'

And so, even though it's late Saturday afternoon, Megan manages to rouse some friendly professor and get a verbal contract off him to accept Lorna on a Masters programme. Nineteenth-century English Literature. A programme that specialises in women novelists.

'Goody,' said Lorna. 'Bustles, corsets, urchins and the evils of drink. Can hardly wait.'

Megan smiles. 'Knew you'd be pleased.'

'Though of course I was really hoping to do a Masters in ventriloquism. Or taxidermy.'

Megan ignores her. She's busy getting stuck into some tetchy email to-ing and fro-ing with United Airlines, punctuated with quick phone shout-outs to various relatives. The end result of which is that Lorna's ticket is given gratis to an Eli Brookbank, an old friend of Megan's father, who has always wanted to visit Duxford, Cambridgeshire, where his poppa had been stationed in the war, but who has never had the wherewithal.

She even manages to get through to a snippy woman at the end of an immigration hotline who is, in the end, forced to agree that getting a new visa is probably going to be a formality given how solvent Lorna now is and the contribution she is therefore going to be making to reducing the US balance of payments deficit.

'Bet immigration still make me cry,' says Lorna.

'Yeah probably,' says Megan. 'But it's just part of the process, right?'

Immigration had managed to make Lorna cry three times on the way over. At Manchester, at Philadelphia and at Oakland she'd been aggressively challenged about her intentions. It had been suggested that she was going to look for work. Even her faithful accordian had been cited as evidence that she might be intending to busk thus depriving good ole American street entertainers of their due.

It's when Megan begins treking around Gumtree, hunting for new places to live 'just to see what's out there', that Lorna starts to feel restive.

While grad-school courses were being organised and immigration gatekeepers sweet-talked, Lorna had had a tense conversation with her mother which had ended with a tired-sounding 'whatever you think best, dear'. This had, naturally, made her feel like shit. Which is what it was supposed to do of course.

And it's now that Jez calls.

She makes him work for it this time at least. Settles into monosyllabic near-silence while he chatters nervously about this and that. She likes that he's uncertain and wrong-footed. This clumsiness on the phone is quite sweet actually. It reminds her that a lot that is irritating about Jez is just because he isn't really a grown-up. Over the last couple of weeks there have been cheery texts which she's been scrupulous in ignoring. There have been a few slurred late-night messages too. But now he sounds both eager to impress and bashful somehow. Still, it comes as a surprise to Lorna when she finds herself agreeing to go over. How, exactly, has that happened?

Knowing that Megan will be a bit parental about it, Lorna chooses not to have that conversation with her. Instead she leaves Megs looking over spacious, light, characterful apartments within walking distance of the UC Berkeley campus, while she showers and tries to decide what to wear. What is the most nonchalant outfit? The one that says effortlessly, casually hot in a language that Jez can understand. In the end it's her reliable midnight-blue, one hundred per cent viscose, spot-print tunic dress, cinched in at the waist with a grosgrain ribbon tie. Yeah, the soft open neckline definitely says feminine, elegant and thoroughly contemporary. It also says come and see what's under here, boy, if you think you're up to it. But says it in a whisper rather than a brazen yell. She teams it with simple back leggings. Perfect.

It's as she's rummaging around the closet for shoes that are also feminine, elegant and contemporary while suggesting – but not screaming – possible wantoness, that Megan comes in.

She's proper pissed. Even from where Lorna is, on her knees rooting through the jumble of footwear – thank Christ she wasn't having to pack after all – even with her back to her, Lorna can tell she's pissed. Pissed drunk and pissed mad. Here we go. Lorna stands, straightens her shoulders, waits for the inevitable lecture. There is a long silence and in the end it's Lorna who feels compelled to break it.

She holds up both her hands. 'I know, mate. I know.'

'You're so fucking dumb sometimes.'

This is too much, but still Lorna tries to keep everything as light as possible. Aims for joshing.

'Well if you haven't got anything nice to say . . .' At which point, she spots them. Victorian-style lace-up boots. Plain black heels, that are high but not too whory. Boots she's had for ever and forgotten all about. The absolute very thing. She bends down to get them and, as she stands up again, Megan crosses the room in two quick steps and slaps her hard across the face.

Lorna staggers to the side with the force of it and then puts her hand up to her stinging cheek. It hurts but it also feels unreal, an impossible thing. Megan has belted her?

She raises her head and looks at her flatmate through eyes that are wet with hot sudden tears. Through her blurry vision she can see that Megan has taken a step backwards and is standing with her mouth now a little o, her hands clasped before her chest in what looks like a prayer. She is breathing hard and shallow. She looks like she is going to have a panic attack. She's bricking it. Absolutely bricking it. Lorna meanwhile feels calm. She feels that how she acts now is going to be pivotal to the future direction of her life. Lorna has never been in a fight. Not even any hair-pulling in the playground at St Thomas Junior and Infants. She sees that Megan is struggling to speak.

'Oh shit. Oh shit. Lorna. I'm really, really sorry. Oh my God.'

'Sssh,' says Lorna. 'Sssh.' And then she hits her as hard as she can with her closed fist.

It is a wild, wide, swinging punch. Later she thinks that Linwood would have been underwhelmed by the technique, but he might have been impressed with the power, the speed and the accuracy. What would have caused him real despair was the way his favourite student left herself wide open.

Lorna's fist connects with Megan right on her cheekbone, just beneath her left eye and she goes down immediately. Poleaxed, thinks Lorna. And she wonders vaguely where the expression comes from.

What, exactly, is a poleaxe? And then she feels a wave of pain begin in her fingers and travel all the way up her right arm. Begin and not stop. She looks at the back of her hand. A red flush is spreading across the knuckles. She thinks about that phrase too, that commonplace. I know it like the back of my hand. But how well do any of us know the backs of our hands? They're not places we examine, or even look at much. Of all the parts of the body, the backs of our hands might be the places we know least of all.

Megan is lying still, half in and half out of the bedroom. Armitage Shanks's anxious little head appears. He puts a tentative paw on Megan's shoulder. Megs doesn't move. What if I've killed her? Lorna thinks. But she doesn't go over and check right away. First she examines her cheek in the mirror. There's no mark any more. Megan's slap has left no imprint at all. And now Lorna discovers she's not angry any longer. Now Lorna can begin to worry about Megan, who still hasn't moved. She turns from the mirror and steps over Megan's legs so that she can get into the hall, and kneels down by her head. She picks Armitage Shanks up and cuddles him. *Oh Christ, what if I really have killed her?*

Just then Megan groans, comes to, turns to the side and quietly, almost delicately, pukes. Lorna releases Armitage and strokes Megan's hair. Megan sits up, Lorna wraps her arms around her. They stay like that for a while, until it gets too awkward and cramped for Lorna. She stands up and holds out her hands. Megan takes them and hauls herself upright. They stand facing each other, hands loosely clasped. Megan's eyes are downcast, her lip trembling. She looks so utterly abject that Lorna wants to laugh. It's just too much. She draws her friend into a hug. Ignores the whiff of vomit and booze and sweat. Ignores Megan's generalised clamminess and holds her tightly to her.

'You dodo,' says Lorna. 'You total loon.'

'You'll be late for Jez,' Megan says after a bit, her voice small. Lorna feels momentarily irritated again. But it passes and Lorna realises that she can't be arsed to go all the way across town just for Jez.

Maybe she's cured? Maybe Jez is sort of like hiccups and she just needed to be surprised out of him.

'Fuck the Fuckweasel,' she says. 'Let's look at those apartments you found.'

Megan says, 'We should talk about this. Properly. Soon.'

And Lorna laughs. 'That's my girl,' she says. 'The old Megan is back. But, you know, we so *don't* have to talk. Talking is not really the English way.' Punching, she thinks. Punching turns out to be the English way. Even for lazy, unathletic pacifists like her. But she doesn't feel any need to say this. Instead she breaks the embrace, finds her phone and texts Jez. 'Not coming. Just don't fancy it. Sorry.'

'Tea,' she says. 'That's what we need.'

'Right. A cup of tea solves everything,' says Megan, drily. The quarter-sized mark under her eye is purpling by the second. That is going to be one heck of a shiner.

'You know it, girl,' says Lorna.

Sixteen

NICKY

Why I don't see my dad. It starts with a row about inheritance tax and ends with me deciding not to have anything to do with the old sod any more. And it's not even my row actually. Sarah's row.

We're at my dad's for the monthly Sunday dinner. Five of us. Sarah and I with Scarlett – who is just three months old then – my dad and one of the apparently endless supply of women who always pop in and out of his life. He's always managed to find ladies to take care of him. Kitty, I think this one was called, but they all tend to be the same type. Well-preserved, well-groomed ladies of indeterminate age. Serious women gone carefully blonde. The widows and divorcees of small town big cheeses. Women who are invariably magistrates.

Women quite like my mum in other words. Or what my mum might have become had she not had the effrontery to widow her own small town big cheese.

On this occasion we have lamb shanks and my dad remarks – mildly enough, but apropos of absolutely fuck all – that he doesn't see why the state should have all his hard-earned pounds sterling after he's gone.

And Sarah replies – also mildly enough – that that's all very well, Daniel, but your pounds sterling aren't really hard earned are they?

And he is genuinely put out and asks her what she means, and Sarah tells him that luck has played a massive part. He was lucky to be born in the time he was, in the place he was.

'Think about it,' she says. 'You were raised by a generation that had been through two world wars and a depression and who were

111

determined that their own children should never suffer like that.' And she lists all my dad's advantages. He was, what, seven, when the 1944 Education Act was passed which gave him the chance to go to grammar school. He was, what, eleven, when the NHS was created. And on it goes. How he benefited from full employment, from final-salary pension schemes, from being able to buy houses cheap and sell them dear. How the cost of the mortgages was eroded by inflation. How his Brookman's Park house was worth getting on for a million, not because he was a shrewd speculator but because of the haphazard vagaries of an economic system that values real estate much higher in the south-east of England than anywhere else.

'I've worked for what I've got. I've worked bloody hard.'

'Yes, I'm sure you have, Daniel,' though she doesn't sound sure. 'But can you really say that you've worked harder than an ex-miner who lives in a council house in Rochdale and so has nothing to leave his kids when he passes on?'

She goes on to say that she thinks inheritance tax should be raised. At the moment it's forty per cent of any estate over £250,000 and in Sarah's opinion it should be more like seventy-five.

'Why not one hundred per cent?' snorts my father.

'Actually, why not one hundred per cent?' muses Sarah. And she goes on to advance other ideas. For example, there's her idea about how to deal with the homeless problem.

'Basically, anyone with more than one house should be asked to choose which one they want to live in, and we – the state – should be able to take the others and redistribute them to people who need them.'

Which is when my dad calls her infantile and says even the Khmer Rouge didn't try anything so stupid and, in any case, we will change our tune when we see how much money we need to support a retarded child.

Kitty – or whoever it is – tuts. And this just seems to enrage my dad further.

'Well, it's true. All children cost a fortune and retarded children cost even more.'

Kitty – or whoever it is – says, 'Daniel.'

And he goes, 'What? Aren't you allowed to call a bloody spade a bloody spade any more?'

And I say something lame about calling a spade a shovel, while Sarah is already getting up and gathering all the paraphernalia of new parenthood. The nappies, the wipes, the creams, the potions, the powders, the bottles, the spare Babygros, the blankets, the plastic jar of cotton buds, the toys designed to sooth, the toys designed to stimulate. The unfathomable tank of the buggy.

'Oh-oh,' says my dad. 'She's losing the game so she's storming off the pitch.'

And Sarah says that she may be infantile and stupid and she may have a retarded kid but at least she's not an ignorant old cunt.

And Kitty – or whoever it is – tuts again, while my dad goes puce and looks like his head is going to explode.

His last words as we leave are, 'Well, I don't think you're going to have to worry about inheritance tax as far as you're concerned. I'm going to make sure there's not a penny left. Not for you anyway. And when you're struggling to buy all the special equipment you'll need just remember that there was an ignorant old cunt who just might have helped you out.'

'Fuck off, Dad,' I say, and he tells me to watch my lip, that I'm not too big to get a clip round the ear. 'Yes I am,' I say.

We go, and there's silence in the car for a good few miles, until I say, 'Well, that was nice,' and Sarah suggests that maybe we don't go and see my dad as a family any more. 'You should go, Nicky. Every now and again, see how he's getting on. But I don't think we should all go. I don't think Scarlett should hear language like that.'

'Cunt? That won't mean anything to her.'

'I meant,' and her voice drops to a whisper, 'retarded. She shouldn't have to hear words like that.' She looks over to the back where Scarlett sleeps in the car seat.

She's right, of course she is, and I think it's then I make the decision not to see my dad either. You don't have to see your family, do you? Being related is an accident. And you don't have to put up with the consequences if you don't want to. You can decide to be free. As far as I can see that's one of the big triumphs of Western civilisation – we have liberated ourselves from our obligations to our blood relatives. We can invent our own extended families, thank you very much, make them out of friends and work colleagues – we don't have to put up with the difficult demented ones. Let the state deal with them. We pay our taxes after all.

And then the weeks and months go past and we hear that Dad has sold the house and moved into this care home place. Sunny Bank. I hadn't realised his condition had got so bad.

I phone him. He sounds OK and I do actually offer to go and see him, but he tells me he doesn't want that, doesn't want me to see him there. He's adamant. And then he tells me that I should know that there really won't be any inheritance, not unless Sarah apologises. We both know that's not going to happen.

'It's a bloody shame,' he says. 'I liked her. Sarah was the best decision you ever made, that's for sure.'

'I know, Dad,' I say. 'I know.'

Seventeen

JESUS

Jesus has no one. Whenever he reads about how the great entrepreneurs got started there is always someone who can lend them the first thousand dollars. Some sap with no business sense but who just wants their homeboy to succeed. Even Zuckerberg who no one has ever liked found a couple of buddies to set him up. But not a single person can lend even a few hundred to Jesus. It's not right.

'You know I'd give you scratch, Jesus.'

This is Mary, and he knows she would. In their short time together he has learned that Mary will do pretty much anything for him. Really, anything. It's scary actually. Awesome and scary. She looks so innocent but on their first date he'd been doing stuff with her that he'd never done with any other girl. And he'd done it because she'd told him to. She likes to give instructions during sex, which is new to Jesus but he finds he likes it.

He looks at her now sitting cross-legged on his bed, naked except for her glasses, taking deep hits from her Beretta. She is wild. He stares, fascinated as always by the tattoos. The green, red and blue birds that flutter across her breasts, the purple snakes that writhe around her thighs, the sunshiny flowers on her shoulders, the carnivores of many colours roaming the burnished prairies of her skin. The trees that climb around her shins and calves. The lifelike red rose petals dancing over her belly as though scattered onto a honeymoon bed by a Valentino.

Most girls Jesus knows have tattoos, but not as many as this and they don't keep them such a secret. Mary never wears tees and she never wears skirts. Her tats are a hidden thing. Something she only shares with him.

'The thing is, I know a lot of people who would, but I don't know anyone that can.'

'You've tried banks yeah?'

Jesus makes a face. Yes, he's tried banks. He's tried every bank. Even the small-time savings and loans like the ones in that dumb black-and-white movie with James Stewart in it. The one his father makes the whole family watch every year on the night before Christmas in Quetzaltenango. Not that many of the family are left in Quetzaltenango now. Everyone gets out as soon as.

For some reason no one is lending to immigrant grad students with no collateral and no resources of their own. And now he doesn't even have a job, not since he'd brought the limo back so trashed after that night out with that crazy English couple. Actually he has been thinking, maybe they would back him. They had been pretty receptive to his business ideas, they might even feel that they owe him.

He says as much to Mary and she lies back on his narrow bed – the bed that she has told him he is going to have to upgrade if he is to be her regular polollo, and he watches her think about it. She parts her legs just a tiny bit, left hand resting on the tattoo of an orchid on her hip bone.

From where Jesus sits on the bedroom's single plastic chair he can see all her shaved papaya, her munch. Does she know what she's doing, he wonders? He thinks she probably does. She takes another drag, closes her eyes, now her hand strays between her legs and idly, absent-mindedly, strokes. Yes, she definitely knows what she's doing. Another thing Jesus knows already is that nothing Mary does is casual, not really.

He stands, strips off the tracksuit pants he only put on minutes before and crosses over to the bed, he lies next to her and covers her munch-stroking hand with his own. Her eyes open, she smiles. His heart kicks hard in his chest.

116

'I don't think Russell will help. I mean he might want to, but she won't let him.'

'She wears the pants, huh?'

'Most definitely.'

It's what he's known all along. Poor people will help you but they can't. Rich people can help you, but won't. It is the way of the world. What you need is someone poor enough to be kind, but rich enough to have some spare centavos. It's the kind of business angel that is hard to find, the piece of the start-up jigsaw that they never mention in the manuals – even though it is absolutely vital. He exhales, blows air towards the dark hair on his lip.

'Cono,' he murmurs into her ear, her neck, her breast.

'What's that?'

He raises his head, looks into her eyes, smiles. 'I said, "Shit. Shit."'

'Potty mouth,' she says.

He bends and kisses her nipple, she strokes his hair, his shoulders, his back. She smiles up at him. Mouth wide. Her breath smells chemical and sweet. It smells of Diet Coke. Mary has a real thing for Diet Coke. Gets through about twelve cans a day. Says it makes her feel good, but also it cleans her braces. If ever Jesus hears someone pop a soda can out on the street these days, he feels a sudden need to go home and see his love.

Now Mary says, 'You do something for me and I'll tell you my idea.'

Jesus thinks that he perhaps already knows what the something is and begins to shift down the bed, kissing and licking as he goes. Taking his time. Breasts, stomach, hip bones. Birds, flowers, snakes. Covering with slow kisses all the life that walks, crawls or flies across her honeyed skin.

Mary really does have a lot of tattoos. From her chest to ankles, she is a gallery of sorts. This close the flowers look wild. The animals fierce. Untameable.

Jesus has no tattoos. Mary was a bit shocked at first. She hadn't been with a boy without tats since high school. She had asked if it was a religious thing, something to do with the Kabbalah maybe? But no, he just liked his body the way it was. Mary told him she admired him for being an individual, so he didn't tell her the real reason, which was that he had promised his mamma he would never get a tat or a piercing.

Jesus explores on past her knees, down the leaves and vines on her calves then around her ankles, feet, toes. Slowly, slowly, slowly. And then back up again. He's in no rush.

'You move to your own beat,' Mary says softly. 'I like that in a guy.'

And, later, softer still, hardly more than a breath. 'I really like that in a guy.'

Eighteen

CATHERINE

Her best chance is when he's out running. She can just put on a bit of a sprint and fire the thing as she passes. He'll feel it like a wasp sting or a mosquito bite and between five and ten days later his heart will stop. Very clean, very simple. This stuff has revolutionised things in the industry. No more poisoned umbrellas. No need to blast people on their doorsteps. No need for the double tap. No need to lock drugged targets naked into their own holdalls to make it look like some weird sex thing. Much, much easier now than when she'd started, but there are still precautions to be taken: a need for basic professionalism.

But he is never on his own these days.

It had been easier with the other guy, the wrong guy. He'd gone out at exactly six each and every morning. Up at 5.45, quick cup of instant coffee and then a reasonably fast jog around the same old route. Around Huntingdon Park, along California past Grace Cathedral, quick sprint up Larkin as far as Pacific. He'd hang a right there and it was down to Powell, back to Sacramento and home. Not that far, but he'd always done it fast and he'd done it easy, watching out for all the dog-walkers. And when he was back, well, he was precise in his routine then too. Shower for nine minutes, porridge made with Quaker oats and Tate and Lyle golden syrup, and then he was on the iThing or working the phones for the rest of the day. Then, when the day's work was done, there was a ready meal for one in front of the TV. Comedies or action thrillers. The wrong guy had been a man of fixed habits. A solitary man with an unchangeable schedule. An easy job.

She'd got him to the stage where he'd been used to her passing him in the opposite direction every day. They'd got as far as smiling and nodding, and then on day six she'd done it. She didn't really know why she'd waited so long. Maybe it was that he was a good-looking chap. Maybe it was that she'd had some sense, some instinct that he might not be the mark. That he might just be a citizen. A civilian. After all, she could remember thinking it was weird that he had no security, no grunts running alongside.

This mark, the right mark, he always has a grunt with him, sometimes two. He also varies his routine. He never does the same thing two days in a row. One day he goes running for three slow miles at nine. The next day he gets himself driven to that poncey gym on 3rd. The day after that he might workout at home with weights and barbells, his trainer standing over him. At other times he will emerge from the house and get a cab downtown and disappear.

It's very frustrating because she doesn't want to be here. She wants to do the thing and hightail it home in time to properly prepare for Abkhazia.

Catherine has been looking forward to Abkhazia because, for once, it isn't just work. The work should actually be done pretty quickly and then she might get to spend a week hiking with Tough, and she always learns things with him.

They'd met in 2003 in a museum in Rutbah, Iraq. She'd gone there on a whim to have a look-see after some Mickey Mouse mission nearby, and she'd arrived to see Tough apparently executing three US marines he'd found pissing on the exhibits. The soldiers were kneeling on the ground, blindfolded, gagged, hands bound behind their backs sobbing, choking, straining at the bonds that held them tight, while Tough stood behind them smoking a small cigar. Nearby a towel-head in the uniform of the museum service stood fidgeting nervously. Not knowing what was going on she had, of course, reached for her own gun, but Tough had turned slowly, seeming quite unconcerned, and he'd just grinned and shaken his head. And she'd been confused. He'd put his finger to his lips. Then he put his gun close to the left ear of each weeping soldier in turn, and fired pointing away from their heads. The shots were painfully loud in that echoing room.

He fired three times and each time the blindfolded GIs must have thought that one of the others was getting whacked.

After the reverberations of the third shot had died away, he'd said to her, 'Now, you. You are bloody gorgeous. Fancy a wet? A proper one?'

And so they'd left the soldiers, still bound, still gagged, still blindfolded, ear-drums ruptured, but alive and, Tough hoped, sadder but wiser grunts. And the two of them had found a tea shop downtown – a place where Tough was welcomed like an old friend. They had retreated to a cosy spot near the back. And, over tea and sticky cakes, they'd clicked.

'This is Mesopotamia, the country where they invented the wheel. This is the land where humanity learned to make bread for fuck's sake. Not to mention wine. And those animals were pissing on it all like dogs on a lamp post.' Plus, he told her, two days earlier, three US marines had carried out mock executions on a group of Iraqi schoolboys.

'So you thought you'd make them see what it felt like?'

'Exactly. And it's not only in the interests of justice. It's good tactics too, isn't it?'

'How do you work that out?'

'Every time some dough-boy intimidates an Iraqi kid, or micturates on a piece of their culture, he simply ensures a thousand other people hate us. He gets his mates killed. He gets our mates killed. If we let it happen we're being bad soldiers.'

Tough should be in a comic book really. They should make films based around him. He was already fiftyish back then, with a permanently amused expression, desert-sky eyes radiantly blue in a lean face the colour and texture of sand. He was like Indiana Jones. And he had that great name.

121

'I know. What else could I do except join the Army? Caused me some grief as a kid though. Everybody wanted to fight the kid called Tough.'

'I bet.'

'Especially when they found out I was gay.'

'Bollocks.'

Tough had raised an eyebrow, blown out a full lungful of poison from one of those stinky cigars he liked. 'You don't think I'm gay?'

'Well, it's hardly likely . . . is it?' But the last part of the sentence was uncertain. Tough had laughed. 'My dear, I'm out and proud and I don't think my colleagues really care. As long as you do what you're paid to do, and do it well, the Army is a very tolerant place. Don't you find?'

'Not if you've got a vagina it isn't.'

Tough had laughed again.

And it was then that the American captain burst through the sequined curtain that separated their little nook from the rest of the tea shop. It appeared that he and Tough knew each other. The captain was tomato-faced and pretty aeriated.

'I should have your fucking balls, Tough.'

Tough had turned to look at him slowly. 'Captain, I believe I have, through my actions today, saved you and your force a great deal of future trouble.' And he'd outlined once again his theory about why it might be a bad idea, tactically, to go around desecrating the sacred works of the people whose hearts and minds were, in his opinion, crucial to the longer term strategic aims of the campaign.

'And I have photos of what your goons were up to before I arrived. So off you jolly well fuck, there's a good captain.' And he had turned back to Catherine and, somewhat to her surprise, the captain had, indeed, fucked off.

And they'd stayed friends since. Tough had been a mentor and a guide. Not just in Army stuff, and not just in getting her this gig after she left, but in everything else as well. Tough was one of those people who knew everything about everything. He knew about history, art, literature, music. He reminded her of the old boys who used to hang out in the library a lifetime ago. And he'd made her want to know those things too – and the old boys in Hildreth library had never done that. He wrote as well. Not books or anything, but letters. As far as she knew he'd never written an email, never sent a text. Instead he sent funny postcards and long, brilliant letters about the places he'd seen, and what he was reading or listening to. And the boys he was paying to bugger him.

They'd known each other eleven years, and now Tough was some kind of special advisor to the government in Abkhazia. A place the size of Hertfordshire that had fairly recently won its freedom from Georgia by the inspired tactic of getting the Russians to bomb the shit out of the men from Tbilisi. Like a little kid getting his bad boy big brother to twat the reception-class bully.

Tough had been very insistent she come over and see him. In daily letters he told her she'd love the people, the landscape, the language. He also said she'd hate the city, that a combination of earthquakes and Soviet planning had done for it, but they could get out of the capital and walk and talk and catch up properly. She was sure he was behind the job she was doing out there, otherwise it was a bit of a coincidence – a contract comes through for a thing in Abkhazia just as her old friend Tough moves out there.

He'd sent her a book called the Nart sagas about mythical heroes of the region, translated into English from the work of a guy called Bagrat Shinkuba and a DVD of the local martial art, a vicious scrappy version of wrestling with few discernible rules. *You like fighting, come and learn this* he'd written on the card that came with the package. Eleven years and he still doesn't get it. She doesn't like fighting. She hates fighting. Hand-to-hand fighting of any kind is primitive and ugly. She never fights unless she has to. She just thinks it's important to be prepared, because you do have to fight in the end. Everyone does sometimes. And if you are small, if you are a woman, then you need to be able to fight harder and dirtier than everyone else.

She likes arguing with Tough. She doesn't really win against him – he's read so damn much – but he is always interested in what she's saying. And he always stays calm. Always stays dry and amusing actually, and this is probably because not a whole lot means anything to Tough. Not really. For Tough everything is interesting but everything is meaningless. He should be a guest on *Thought For The* bloody *Day*.

And now that trip is in danger of being messed up by this Russell Knox and his failure to adhere to a routine, by his inability to ever be on his own. It is beyond irritating, it really is.

Nineteen

NICKY

And now we are into our Grand Design weeks. The weeks where I'm at the mercy of the man we come to call the architect. Because, yes, it was indeed true that Russell had kept himself in good nick right up until the end, and that meant problems to solve. Risks to assess and then to mitigate. More milestones to negotiate.

When we settle our account with the undertaker, he tells us that the pathologist had commented on the fine figure of a corpse Nicholas Fisher was. How he was a real good ad for that British NHS. Said he had been won over to the whole idea of socialised medicine as a result of dissecting this Fisher guy. The pathologist told him that for a guy that was meant to be more or less broke he had great teeth, great skin, great hair, great muscle tone. He even had great nails.

'Hell, he told me this Nicky Fisher even smelt good when he was first brought in. Now that's rare in his line of work. Mine too.'

This admiration has made its mark on the undertaker so that's two potential new votes for pro-universal healthcare democrats. And the undertaker, like nearly all his profession, had been solidly Republican up to that point. Was it Mark Twain who said there's nothing certain in life except for death and taxes? Well, undertakers as a profession are unsurprisingly OK with death. They are, after all, sitting pretty. Death is one of the few businesses that can't migrate to the internet. It's not like books or music or matchmaking. Death demands a physical presence on the high street. You can't do the death business via a portal. Undertakers are far less sanguine about taxes than they are about the web.

It's all an early vindication of our Robin Hood theory. Through our plan – through what we've taken to calling our new business model – we're not just helping ourselves, we're already helping the powerless, the dispossessed. The poor huddled masses of the near future might have cause to celebrate us. Maybe we really could be heroes. It's heart-warming really. Right from the very first moment of his death Russell finds himself taking the opportunities to do good with his wedge that he has so rigorously spurned in life. It's like something out of Dickens, and it is a truth universally acknowledged that there is nothing more heartwarming than that. Unless it's *Toy Story 2*.

It'll all look good in the dock of the future.

But Russell's self-absorption in life has given us a set of problems which definitely need some of Sarah's SMART solutions. How are we going to make me – an averagely crumbling middle-aged wreck – pass for an expensively maintained global oligarch? It's a big ask. This can't be a mere makeover project. This absolutely has to be a Grand Design. You'll remember *Grand Designs*. It was that architectural TV programme where couples would take some public toilet, some church, some water-cooled nuclear reactor or whatever and – after a rollercoaster ride of adventures involving cowboy builders and dodgy plumbers – turn it into a modernist palace.

Sarah has always been a fan of these shows and even a casual study reveals that the switchback of triumph and disaster – the sense of jeopardy and threat essential for ratings – is caused by the hubris of the participants who don't take the advice of the expert presenter. It's clear the producers deliberately select the psychotically headstrong over the sensibly amenable. Sensibly amenable butters few parsnips in the world of reality TV.

But we are neither of us suicidally stubborn, so we are going to follow to the slavish letter the advice of our chosen experts. We are going to demolish the derelict shed that is Nicky Fisher and remake it as a cathedral. I'm going to get reshaped into the image of the man whose passport is essential to our new lives.

To accomplish this we need a skilled and accredited practitioner of the arts of renovation, preservation and tasteful alteration. We need an architect, in other words. A drawer-up of plans, a supervisor of the building process.

And because the final programmes of works are so radical, Sarah also talks of hiring a support team of counsellors, shrinks, lifestyle gurus – what you might call architects of the head – to sandblast my brain. To supervise the repointing and replastering of the cracks in my psyche. To damp-proof my very soul and guard it against rot and worms. But it turns out that because I have Linwood I don't need most of these others. Like pretty much everything else in our new lives we find him through Jesus.

'Linwood is the best trainer on the West Coast. Well, the Bay Area anyway. Everyone knows this.'

'Expensive?'

Jesus shrugs and smiles. 'He is the best.'

And he certainly looks the part. Peak period Denzel Washington in looks, with the grave manner of a Harvard maths professor. A man you can tell it will be hard to say no to.

Nevertheless, I think Sarah's surprised at how compliant I am. I'm not resistant in the way I'm sure she expected me to be. I submit to all the tests, all the treadmills and the charts. And then, when all the assessments have been done I just get on with it. I do the laps, the squats, the lunge-walks, the bench-presses, the pull-ups, the press-ups and all the cardiovascular stuff. I do the yoga – Ashtanga and Hatha – I do the Pilates and eat up my Alexander technique like a good boy. Quite unexpected really, willpower never having been my thing up to that point.

I do the full range of workouts more usually associated with suburban ladies. I do step aerobics, skipping, spinning. I do bloody Zumba for chrissake.

Of course, by necessity, I'm often in a class of one. It's usually just me working out to the sound of Tom Waits rather than a class of sweating MILFs wobbling to glossy, high-BPM pop. This is my only small rebellion and it causes a satisfying amount of pain to Linwood. He's a big Katy Perry fan. Sporty types always have terrible taste in music. This is an iron law.

However, sometimes, to keep things interesting, he allows me to do games too. Squash, badminton, tennis with country-club coaches. Basketball on floodlit courts specially kept open late at night just for me where Linwood teaches me the arcane mysteries of the dunk.

I grapple with Brazilian ju-jitsu masters, chase the ping-pong balls of ex-pat ex-North Korean ex-Olympians who came to the 1996 games just to defect. I scramble over the assault courses of the Navy Seals, play carefully supervised beach volleyball with college girls – all in the cause of keeping the regimen stimulating, to avoid the dreaded plateau – which, according to every single architect whatever their discipline, is the very last place you want to be. In the world of the sports coach a plateau is a kind of hell.

And I give up sugar and dairy and alcohol. Replace them with raw carrots, leafy veg and thin lentil soups. I allow my carbs to be weighed, my every wild rice grain counted. And if ever I feel like I'm going to crack then I have Linwood's soothing tones on speed dial, always ready to talk me down from ordering something dangerous like a pizza, or a fajita. Meanwhile genuinely Scandinavian masseuses – the best, not the cheapest obviously – stretch and sooth mutinous hamstrings and tortured calves, necks, shoulders, ribs.

What anyone who is serious about self-improvement learns is that if it works it hurts. If you're serious about losing flab and gaining muscle then you will always be hungry and you will always be hurting.

And it's because of this that we are required to have Linwood or Jesus or both around more or less 24/7 to prevent me from leaving the house on my own. They accompany me on my runs to ensure there are no opportunities to score illicit Oreos or Hershey bars. And some-times Linwood makes me sit down with him to watch uplifting movies. The kind of movies I've put on for Scarlett in the past, to give myself a respite from childcare. The kind I've never actually watched properly before.

This is how come I see *Watership Down*, *The Sound of Music*. All the *Back To The Future*s and all the *Toy Story*s. Fables of evil overcome. Tales of grace under pressure. Parables of the little guy made great, the nice guy finishing first, ordinary heroes fulfilling their potential. Stories that should be banned for giving average chumps impossible dreams. God, I can't believe we've been filling Scarlett's head with this stuff. Thank fuck the agency doesn't allow Mary to let kids watch DVDs. Not even Pixar ones. It's not part of the Second-Best Kind of Love method.

But I am not a child. I am a grown-up and I think I should be allowed to watch old-school pornography too. Porn is motivational as long as it's not too weird. At least as inspiring as anything from Disney anyway. Modern porn can be scary and odd, but classic is a different story. Classic. Vintage. Retro. These styles in porn – as in clothes, cars, and music – are uplifting.

A buffed youngish teacher gives extra tuition to an entire sorority. A buffed youngish pilot takes care of all the flight attendants while the plane flies itself to Stockholm. A buffed youngish plumber services the needs of a whole gated community of bored housewives.

The moral of your classic porno is broadly the same as *Watership Down*. Follow your dream, stick at it whatever the obstacles, and you'll end up with loads of bunnies. You'll become Bigwig. That sad sack Nicky Fisher wouldn't ever get to share a hot tub with Shyla, Shannon, Shanta, and all their pneumatic friends – but a fully operational lean, clean, sex machine like the all-new Russell Knox surely would. As I say, motivational. Uplifting. Keeps your eye on the prize.

There is a Martin Luther King element to classic porn without a shadow.

But I somehow sense that saying this to Linwood or to Jesus would be to court their disapproval. Conservative sexually as well as tin-eared, that's your average jock for you.

And when I'm not running, wrestling, lifting, stretching, sharing my hurt, then I'm in a clinic being worked over with retinol to peel away the dry tundra of my skin. I'm having vitamin-X enriched unguents worked deep into the baby-soft vulnerabilities revealed beneath the dead surface. Or I'm having my teeth underpinned and then bleached to an unearthly electric white. Oh I'm a Grand Design and no mistake. Not half.

And Linwood never questions why a faceless guy like me might suddenly want to turn myself into a kind of Jimmy Dean at fifty. But I guess part of being the best in any business is knowing when to shut up and simply trouser the fee.

And talking of trousers . . .

One of the things that keeps me going is that of how great I'll look in my suits. Because from now on, or when I've finished this programme anyway, I'm only going to wear handmade bespoke clothes. I'm going to have a suit for every day of the week and a real bobby dazzler for high days and holidays.

Jesus has found me a guy. An old Chinese tailor called Jimmy. The one everyone uses. By everyone I mean those who can afford him. Everyone in this context means about fifty blokes in the whole world. New threads to go with my new architect-designed body.

Almost as tricky to sort as the body, and certainly trickier than the tailoring, are the tattoos. It isn't the pain – I turn out to be more stoic about that than I had expected – no, it's what they say and how they say it. No illuminated Latin tags or beautifully worked copies of great works of art for me to wear. No, when he was fourteen Russell had tattooed himself with Ozzy on the knuckles of both hands. Over the years this leads to dozens of illiterates in bars hassling him in the mistaken belief he is Australian.

He also had a wobbly home-made LUFC on his shoulder. Having these done really hurt my sense of aesthetics – not least because I had mocked Russell for having them for over thirty-five years, even though

I'd encouraged him to have them done in the first place. Back in 1978 it was me who had actually inked the first O and the first Z, before being unable to carry on because of the blood.

I do it though. Get the tats. Hate it but do it and just get over it. Hey, imagine if I'd been like that at school, at work, or in relationships? Imagine what I might have achieved. Funny that it takes the exigencies of committing a major fraud to give me the kind of work ethic and capacity for self-sacrifice that I have never shown before.

And an incredible thing happens while the kid we've hired to scrawl this amateur graffito on my body is doing his thing. He's definitely the cheapest, because for this job cheapest is perfect. And it turns out to be the best sixteen dollars I've ever spent.

He's at OZ on my left hand when Scarlett lopes in wearing a pair of Mary's old sneakers, carrying one of her ukuleles, and tossing her head in imitation of Mary's carefree movement through the world. She canters up to me and stares hard at the blood and ink on my hand. She prods it.

'Ouch,' I say. She giggles.

'Ouch,' she says back. We're gob-smacked. It's a word. Or almost. And then, the unlooked-for miracle. She puts down her instrument and then pokes my gory fingers again with her own tiny hand.

'Ouch,' I say, not because it hurts – which it does – but to encourage her. Which it also does.

'Awesome,' she says. 'Badass.'

Unbelievable. I think we all cry. And we laugh. Our baby can talk. And such a Mary thing to say. Especially as it really isn't awesome. And in no way badass. But that's the moment that makes everything worth it.

Of course, there are other good things. I'm also beginning to feel strong now too. I'm enjoying waking up and feeling alive. The old pains, the old twinges, the old spasms, they are all gone. And they are replaced by new pains, new twinges, new spasms, but the old pains felt like approaching death – these ones feel like life. These ones are accompanied by spontaneous erections. I think that's the difference. That and being able to twist open the lids of jars with barely a flick of the wrist. I'm here to tell you it's true what they say about vegetables, kids. The stuff Linwood calls sport candy.

Six weeks it takes. That's all. Six weeks in which I lose a stone of flab and tighten everything that's left. And in which our baby proves she knows the impact of a surprise announcement.

Twenty

POLLY

This is what Polly learns about sperm. She learns that with sperm – like with everything else – you get what you pay for. Pay a couple of million for your ten centilitres and you get the spunk of one of the better-looking former world leaders or that of a sprightly Nobel prize winner. A few hundred grand will put the juice of a top brain surgeon or an astrophysicist in your turkey baster. Lower down the scale you can expect to pay in the high tens of thousands for that of film directors, or games designers. A lower five-figure sum and you are looking at your soap-opera actor, your retired pro-soccer player, your TV talent-show winner. Your Supreme Court judge.

As with thoroughbred horses, so with men.

And it is all carefully calibrated. Different nationalities attract different premiums and you can expect to pay more for looks too. Put it this way, the DNA of an athletic six-foot Ethiopian with a PhD is going to cost you way more than that of a Birmingham car mechanic. That should be obvious. What is more surprising is that an Ethiopian car mechanic might well cost you more than a Brummie PhD. It depends what you prioritise. Polly has spent a long time thinking about it and knows what she wants. She's a focused and determined shopper. She wants fit, but not too fit. She doesn't want to spend years in draughty sports centres watching her kid win the regional javelin cup or whatever. And she wants brainy but not too brainy. She doesn't want her kid leaving her behind by going off to do something she doesn't understand in a medieval university covered in ivy and privilege. In any case super-genius means super unhappy in Polly's experience. No, Polly wants quite coordinated, quite clever, quite good-looking, a decent ear for music and languages. She wants OK-looking, averagely symmetrical. She's not bothered about hair colour or height. As long as he or she is not a dwarf or a giant then that'll do. And that's another thing, she's not bothered about the sex of the child. Or the colour. On balance she thinks boy babies are cuter than girl babies, black babies better looking than white ones, but they're not deal breakers.

You have to shop around of course, look out for the best value. And these days there are so many flexible payment plans that it can all get very confusing. But Polly quite enjoys this sort of thing. It's always Polly who books the holidays for her and her mum. It's always Polly who gets the quotes on insurance. Polly can compare the market dot com. Polly is not daunted by terms and conditions. Polly is not afraid of small print.

Just at the minute there are those special offers on in Norway and Polly is thinking a clean-limbed Viking might be OK, but she's in a pickle because the offer expires soon. It's all a gamble, isn't it? In the end? However much research you do there's always the fact that your own genes are going to be stirred into the mixture, so maybe she should just fill in the online form, push the button, and get it all over with.

That's what she's thinking when the PC in the office goes ping. It's a message from Russell and it reads: *Hey P – can you tell Mr F that Scarlett said a word!!!!!!! Two words!!!!! (I know he won't care but could you tell him anyway?).* Who, she wonders, is Scarlett? And why all the exclamation marks? She likes the fact that Russell Knox says 'Hey P', it sounds matey, like the way you'd write to a friend. And she thinks she'll worry about the sperm later. Anyway, in Polly's experience the minute you've filled out the online form and pressed send, you find yourself regretting it. Ten minutes later you find the same item for less on a different site. Or you find you've changed your mind and don't want the thing anyway. And all special offers and sales are a con. They say ends soon, but then there's always another sale along in a minute. Maybe she'll miss out on Norway but there are other places that will probably be just as good. Nigeria maybe. Or Indonesia. They look good value too.

Polly finds Daniel in his room having his hair cut by some woman from the council and she's making a right pig's ear of it. All that fabulous newsreader hair piled on the floor around him like a sudden and severe snowfall. She's giving him a number four all over with an electric clipper thing. Polly can't let it happen and she's across the floor in a flash and turning it off at the wall.

The woman from the council is puzzled. 'Excuse me, what are you doing?'

'Get out. Just get out.'

The council woman, moon-faced and slow, doesn't know what to do. She doesn't know what's going on. And neither does Polly really. She's simply enraged and knows that she can't have this woman near Daniel. He looks like he's in prison.

The two women glare at each other and into the jagged silence Daniel suddenly says, 'Polly! It's Polly!' and he sounds so relieved and delighted that Polly knows he's been sitting there trying to remember her name.

'I'm just doing what he asked for, love.' The woman has a soft voice. It makes her sound sad.

'Thought I'd go for something simple and low maintenance. Like myself. Ha ha.'

'Oh, Daniel,' says Polly.

'I can't leave him like this,' says the council hairdresser woman. 'Not half done.'

'I'll do him then. I'll finish him off.'

'Oo-er missus,' says Daniel. Polly and the council woman both ignore him. 'Not appropriate, I see.'

'Sorry, I don't let anyone else use my instruments. Just a rule I have.'

135

'Yes because you're such a professional, aren't you?'

'You've got a problem, dearie.' The soft voice and fat face mask an appetite for battle.

'Now, now, ladies.'

'Come on, Daniel, we'll get you done in town by someone who knows what they're doing. You'll need a hat.'

As they go past the front desk, Irina says, 'Where are you going, Polly? You've only just arrived.'

The council woman huffs up behind them. 'You should sack her. She's a lunatic.'

Polly rounds on her. 'They can't sack me. I don't work here. I'm a volunteer.'

She turns back to Irina. 'And there's loads of mess – hair and shit – in Daniel's room. It'll need clearing up.' Irina's face darkens. 'Not actual shit,' Polly adds hastily, because in Sunny Bank clearing up shit quite often means exactly that. 'Just hair.'

'I was going to ask you to cover reception,' says Irina sulkily.

'Tough,' says Polly as she marches out, and it feels great. But Daniel lingers. 'Awfully sorry,' he says, enveloping both Irina and the council woman in an anxious smile. 'Don't know what's got into her today. I thought you were doing a splendid job,' he says to the hairdresser.

'Daniel!' Polly snaps from the front door.

'Well, I best get along. She who must be obeyed and all that.' And he does a little bow, touches the brim of his battered trilby.

'Coming, dear,' he says.

They are in the Banker's Draft, the cheapest pub in town. It's the pub that used to be the Midland Bank and is always busy because you can still get a pint for less than three quid and a full English breakfast for £4.99. Though for lots of people in here a couple of pints is all the full English they need.

Daniel is at the bar buying the second round of drinks. She looks at him waiting patiently to be noticed. He looks old in a way he didn't in the Old English Gentleman. He passed for middle-aged in there. Here it's different.

Polly thinks that old age is a kind of skin disease, a kind of facial disfigurement. It makes people want to avert their eyes. And some people – like the barmaid – seem to think it's contagious, that if she handles Daniel's crisp new note, withdrawn just an hour ago from the hole in the wall, then she'll catch the weird leprosy called Being Old. And the worst thing is that people – some people anyway – seem to think the victims of Being Old Disease have brought it on themselves, that they could have avoided it somehow. They are in this state because they were careless, or stupid. It makes Polly very angry, you shouldn't be allowed to treat other people like that. There should be a law.

Daniel must realise it too. He watches the barmaid serve absolutely everyone else, including some in the other bar. He watches her go and refill the crisp boxes and when he is finally served he is ridiculously chatty as he gets the drinks. He has Bombardier.

'Best thing to come out of Bedford since Bunyan,' he says, his voice unnaturally loud as if he were some kind of town crier. He orders white wine for Polly. 'Chardonnay? Is that really all you've got? Have to do then, won't it? No strawberries to go with it I suppose?'

'Is that everything?' A flat, sullen voice full of resentment at having to get so close to a guy so clearly riddled with Being Old.

'No, how about some comestibles? A couple of those lovely looking pickled eggs perhaps?'

'You what?'

'Two pickled eggs. They're in that jar over there.' He points over the barmaid's shoulder. Her eyes narrow. Is this old fuck taking the wotsit? No one has ever ordered a pickled egg. Even her most regular regulars avoid them. Even the thought of them makes her ill. 'Pickled eggs?'

'Yes please, madam. They are full of protein and the vinegary tang . . . well it gives them a certain *je ne sais quoi*. Don't you agree?'

She jiggles a couple of the off-white ovals out of the jar with a teaspoon. It's not easy. It's like a sideshow at the fair. She dumps them onto little saucers.

'There you go. £8.12.'

Daniel pays with a fifty-pound note. The barmaid sighs. She may not realise it, but her worst fears are coming true. She is visibly catching Being Old. Maybe she was right all along, because dealing with Daniel seems to be activating that latent oldness germ we all have inside us.

Daniel carefully counts his change. And then weaves back to the table where Polly sits. Then he does the trip again for the eggs.

'Are you really going to eat that?'

'Of course. I'll eat yours too if you don't want it.'

'You need looking after, you do.'

'I thought that was your job.'

'I keep saying, it's not my job. I'm a volunteer.'

'Same difference.'

'Is it? Is it really?' She takes a taste of her wine. It's room temperature and sickly sweet just like the previous glass was. She watches Daniel take a deep swig of his beer. Polly is sure that too much alcohol can't be good for the old vascular dementia.

'Actually, you're wrong. Alcohol is good for those with cardiovascular deficiencies of all kinds. It keeps the blood thin. When I had my first stroke the nurses brought me a double scotch every evening. They had a special bottle labelled NHS blend. Rather tasty too. Satisfyingly peaty. Of course that was ten years ago. You wouldn't get that now unless you paid for it. NHS blend. Imagine that.' He smiles at the memory. 'No, what's bad for you is the drugs they give you. What does you in is the Warfarin. Same stuff that's in rat poison, you know. No chance of an erection when you're on that.'

She wonders if she's heard him right – the pub is quite noisy – and makes the mistake of asking him to say that again. 'I said, no chance of getting an erection when you're on that stuff.' He uses his big booming town-crier voice again and the pub falls silent for a second. A good dozen pairs of eyes fall on the disgusting old perv sitting with the pretty girl. He sounds posh too. What a disgrace. Polly can practically hear the thoughts of the outraged red-faced drinkers all around. Drinkers that haven't had an erection in years. Drinkers who can't even see their cocks beneath their beer guts when they go for a wazz.

She takes another nervous sip of her wine. Daniel seems oblivious to the change in the weather of the pub. Takes a deep pull of his dark beer and exhales noisily and with obvious relish. 'Ah, Bombardier. Best thing to come out of Bedford since Bunyan.'

'Yes, you said.' Why, she wonders, would Daniel ever want an erection? And so, amazed at herself, she asks him. Must be drinking in the daytime she thinks. It's not the sort of thing she'd ever normally ask. And now, suddenly, Daniel seems almost shy.

'Oh, Polly, use your head – the usual reason,' he says.

'But you can't . . .' she begins.

Daniel watches her coolly. 'I wish I still smoked,' he says. 'I wish I still smoked and that you could smoke in pubs. Still seems unnatural to me to have a pint and not to have a fag with it.'

'But who?' she begins again.

'Oh Christ, not anybody in Sunny bloody Bank if that's what you're thinking. I haven't sunk that low yet. There's this marvellous thing called the internet, Polly my love. You should try it. Get to know someone online. Do all the chat there, and then, if they agree to meet, well Robert is your father's brother.' He sits back in his chair grinning. Polly feels suddenly cross.

'I really don't like your hair like that, Daniel. It makes you look like a criminal, like a murderer.' They'd managed to get it tidied up in town but the bloody council woman had done too much damage for it to be properly sorted. 'How many women have you met like that? Through the internet I mean?'

Daniel looks shifty now. 'Not that many.'

'How many?'

'A gentleman never tells.'

'Bollocks. How many, Daniel?'

A long pause. 'One.'

'One?' Polly laughs. 'How did it go?'

'Rubbish actually. We went back to her house and, well, the Warfarin, you know . . .'

'How did she take it?'

'Well, she was very kind. But I felt terrible.'

'I bet you did.'

'I paid her anyway.'

'You paid her?'

'Well she wasn't going to do it for free was she? Not with . . .' He tailed off.

Not with someone with Being Old Disease he means, thinks Polly and she suddenly feels sad. 'This wine tastes like warm wee,' she says.

'The beer's not so great either actually. That's the trouble with these sorts of places, they don't know how to keep it,' he says loudly.

Polly knows that there is something she is meant to tell Daniel, but she can't for the life of her remember what it is. She can't think in this stupid pub. She knows she wants to be out of the Banker's Draft, with its stupid name, with all its stupid men and its stupid barmaid.

'Daniel, let's go and find a quiz machine.'

'There's a quiz machine here.'

Polly takes a breath. 'Well, let's go and find a quiz machine somewhere else.' But wherever they go the pubs are the same, and the people are the same and the drinks are the same and there's always a group of idiots cheering by the quiz machine so they can't get near it.

And then somehow there's a taxi and then they are back at the farm and her mum is making tea and egg and chips while Daniel makes her laugh and Polly goes into the living room, holding on to the wall to keep herself upright. More eggs. It can't be good for a man of Daniel's age to eat so many eggs. Or maybe it is. Maybe Daniel would tell her that the yolks are proven to fill holes in the head or something.

She sinks on to the sofa and she closes her eyes. Everything is spinning. How many drinks did they have? Lots. It must have been lots. And her mum places a plate of eggs and oven chips on the coffee table next to her head. She tells her she should eat. She's always telling her she should eat. She wants to say, 'I know I should, Mum, but I can't. I just can't.' But she's too sleepy and too drunk to speak. And there are lots of calories in wine. Everyone knows that.

She thinks her mum will be cross with Daniel for bringing her back in this state but she doesn't seem to be. She can hear the murmur of chit-chat. Sounds all very civilised. It's all 'Can I get you some ketchup, Daniel? Or brown sauce?' She hasn't ever come back home drunk in the day. And then she remembers something.

She struggles upright. 'A word,' she says.

She tries to focus. Her mum and Daniel are sitting at the table. Have they stopped talking? Have they stopped eating? Yes. Yes they have. She sees Daniel put his knife and fork down carefully. How come he doesn't seem drunk? How come he's got room to eat? He must have had loads of pints. And why isn't he full up? It's disgusting to stuff yourself like that.

'We'll have a word later, dear. I don't think now's the time,' Daniel says. And her mum chuckles.

'No, Scarlett. Scarlett.'

'Scarlett? What about her?'

'She can speak. She said something. Russell Knox. A message. I got a message. Nicky's friend Russell sent a message. Scarlett can speak. That was it.'

'Ah well, that is good news,' says Daniel. And then to Polly's mum, 'My grand-daughter. Handicapped. Never been able to speak.'

'Oh, the poor mite.'

'Russell Knox.' Daniel says it like he's trying to remember where he's heard the name before. 'Russell Knox.' He gives up, turns back to his chips. 'I've got a hole in the head you know.'

Polly sinks back down onto the sofa. She can just sleep now. She's done what she said she would, she's passed on the message. She listens to her mum and Daniel talking.

'I could show you the pictures. Massive black hole right in the centre of my brain.'

'Must be a worry.'

'Well, at least I haven't got Alzheimers.'

'That is good.'

It's like a play, she thinks. She hasn't seen many plays but it sort of sounds like Mum and Daniel are acting. Like they're on stage.

Daniel says, 'Oh yes, Russell Knox. I remember him now. Nice boy. Clever. A bit of get-up-and-go. I used to wish our Nicky could be more like him.'

Polly hears her mum say, 'Looks like Polly's get up and go, got up and went.'

Oh, Mum, thinks Polly. Oh, Mum.

'Ha ha. Very good, Jean. This is delicious by the way. Just what the doctor ordered.'

'Norwegian semen.'

'What, dear?'

'I think she's dreaming about sailors. Foreign sailors.'

Polly's eyes open. Oh shit. She knows she's said something very weird. But she can't worry about that now. There's pain in her stomach. Sudden pressure in her guts. Oh shit. Oh hell. And she's sick everywhere. Oh, oh, oh. She heaves rancid Chardonnay all over egg and chips, all over the coffee table, all over the carpet. The carpet. Oh no. Oh fuck. Oh well. She lies back down on the sofa. She feels better now. She feels her mum's warm hand on her forehead. Polly loves her mum and she thinks she should tell her.

'I know you do love.' Her mum's voice sounds like it comes from a million miles away. From outer space.

Polly sleeps.

Twenty-one

NICKY

Turns out that unlike Scarlett and unlike me, it is actually Sarah that has no stamina. The plan was that while I was getting rebuilt from the floorboards up, Sarah would have her own regime of Prosecco, chocolate and buying stuff.

Sarah has never spent money on clothes before now. Not really. She has her capsule wardrobe, her six quality pieces she can rotate at work, and the rest of the time she rocks the jeans and the jumpers. People think she doesn't care about clothes. And they're wrong; the truth is she's never really been able to afford to care about them. Never been able to allow herself to think about them.

But anyway, while I start the whole process of losing fat and gaining new muscle, new hair, blinding new teeth – Sarah gets herself fawned over by professionally bored-looking girls in hard-to-find boutiques. She makes the transition from boho scruff to fashionista very easily and very quickly. Sarah was, let's face it, a bit of a slattern before, often hanging her clothes up on the floor to be picked up and worn the next day. More than once Sarah has worn jeans for an entire morning only to discover that knickers and tights are still bunched at the foot of one of the legs.

And it's Jesus who is her retail therapist. It is Jesus who negotiates with the gatekeepers of exclusive frock emporia, the places that don't allow ordinary mortals to sully their hushed, softly lit showrooms if they can avoid it. It's also Jesus who finds the make-up artists with copious IMDB credits who'll slum it on Sarah's face between TV gigs.

And Jesus can talk shoes – and not just Manolo Blahniks upon which any averagely metrosexual bloke can discourse these days, but he is conversant with DVF, with Tabatha Simmons, with Jeffrey Campbell. Names Sarah had never heard before she started hanging with him. And he knows where to get a limited-edition Coach Stewardess iThing bag properly monogrammed.

Jesus finds the spas with their nail architects, their renovators of finger and toe. It is Jesus who discovers Austen, a fragrance made up of essences of ancient love potions that retails at nearly $600 per art deco bottle. It is Jesus who leads Sarah to hidden lingerie booths whose names resemble those of old established London solicitors. The more staid the name, the more the products promise tasteful, top-end, bespoke raunch. Grieves and Sanders, Daunt and Co, Malik, Styles and Mills – these are the places to get your basques, your camisoles, your stockings, your garter belts and all the buttons and hooks of a lost age of sexual glamour. Sarah says she likes it in these places, with their smells of lace, leather and the woody essence of desire.

One shopping session lasts from ten in the morning till ten at night and Sarah comes home drunk. She collapses into bed, and an unusually bashful Jesus makes an attempt at a slurred explanation involving the Hyatt and cocktails infused with real whale skin. Mary leads him away, scolding him affectionately and smiling prettily.

And as I undress Sarah she tells me the price of every piece of clothing. For the cost of what she's wearing, you could buy a decent family saloon. The knickers alone are the price of a premier-league season ticket.

And when, finally, she's lying there naked, she giggles. 'And this,' she says, running her hands down across her breasts and over her stomach, 'this is priceless.'

And then she turns over and I stroke her back, kiss the archipelagos of freckles on her shoulders.

'Sleepy,' she says.

And I sit there, every part of me aching, thinking what a privilege it is to be able to watch my naked Sarah sleeping. It is a much bigger piece of outrageous good fortune than the fact I'm now one of the richest people on the planet.

I go back into the living room. Mary is there watching *Millionaire*. It is the $500,000 question.

'What, last year, was the gross domestic product of the European Union?'

'What kind of question is that?' Mary is aghast. She loves *Millionaire*, though she rarely makes it past $64,000.

'Is it a) 16,500 billion US dollars; b) 16,700 US Dollars; c) 17,200 billion US Dollars, or d) 17,600 billion US dollars?'

The lights swirl, the music bleeps, sounds like an ancient ventilator in a provincial operating theatre. The contestant, a pudgy former steel-worker from Detroit called Norm, licks his lips and sweats. He has no lifelines left.

'It's d,' I say firmly, though it's a guess. I've chosen the highest figure and even then I'm surprised how low it is. Only 17,600 billion US dollars for the GDP of the entire European Union? Things are clearly worse than any of us thought.

Norm's eyes flick towards the camera; for a second it's like he's looking right at me. And he looks desperate. He tugs at my heart. The presenter says he'll have to hurry him. Norm's in agony.

'Come on,' snaps the presenter.

Norm goes for a. The presenter relaxes.

'Final answer?' he asks, genial now.

Norm relaxes too. He even smiles. He's taking comfort from the presenter's easy warmth.

'Final answer,' he says. The house lights are up, the music collapses, the presenter slaps his forehead with theatrical relish.

'Norm, Norm, Norm,' the presenter says cheerfully. 'It's d. The answer is d.'

'I nearly said that,' says Norm. He sounds broken.

'Oh, Norm. Oh, you,' says the presenter. It doesn't sound like he believes him.

Mary looks at me with shiny-eyed respect. 'Good work, Mr Knox,' she says. 'You are definitely going to be my phone-a-friend.'

'Where's Jesus?' I say.

'In the blue room, getting himself sober I hope.'

The blue room is where Mary sleeps when she stays over, which she's done a few times now.

Mary's been over a lot in the last couple of weeks, because with me running, skipping, spinning, Zumba-ing and all that, and with Sarah shopping and – it turns out – drinking whale-skin cocktails, we need help with Scarlett.

They seem to get on, though it's always hard to tell with Scarlett. If I had to guess I would say she's generally pleased to see her and Mary keeps up a stream of chatter around her which we are told is a good thing to do. And I find it oddly comforting anyway. It's been helping me, even if Scarlett can take it or leave it.

And now, sitting companionably with Mary, I wonder out loud about these all-day shopping explorations. It does cross my mind that while I am being stripped down, while I am hurting and hungry, maybe it isn't just drinks Sarah's been having in the Hyatt. Maybe the aphrodisiac qualities of all her new buying power, of all her gear, all her stuff, means that in some fancy suite with free Wi-Fi and discreet room service, she's having her $25,000 finery ripped off her by a slightly overweight business studies grad student who is almost certainly in denial about his own sexuality. And come to think of it, it's weird how Jesus stays ten pounds above his best weight when you consider he's often running alongside me. Maybe it's a glandular thing.

Mary thinks hard for a long moment. Then she says, 'Mr Knox, you know what the most important three words in a long-term relationship are?'

'No,' I say, wondering that she can be so confident about this sort of thing at twenty-whatever, while still being the possessor of braces

146

and pigtails. Of course it is actually only the young that are confident about this stuff really.

'It doesn't matter.'

'No, tell me. I'd like to know.'

'No, silly. Those are the three most important words. It. Doesn't. Matter.'

'Ah. I get it. Wise words indeed.'

And she's right, isn't she? Out of the mouths of babes and all that. It doesn't matter. When your partner pisses you off, take a deep breath and say to yourself that it doesn't matter. It doesn't matter. Most things don't. In the end.

Then she says, 'Anyways, Jesus wouldn't cheat on me. And Sarah wouldn't cheat on you.'

'You sound very certain.'

'I am certain. They love us.'

I laugh. 'Of course. How could they not?'

'Exactly. Me and you, Mr Knox, we're catches. I'm hot and you're a total high-baller.'

'You know, Mary, I think you might be my phone-a-friend too.'

And then we hear Scarlett whimpering. I tell Mary to relax, to stay where she is and I go to see my little girl. Though it turns out she's actually asleep again before I get there.

I sit by her bed and watch her dreaming. I wonder if she speaks in her dreams. I wonder if she runs, and skips and climbs trees in her dreams. Maybe she spanks the ukulele like a rock star.

When I go back to the living room Mary has gone to the blue room and the lights are off. And I sit in the warm dark, listening to the house whisper stories to itself. I'm beginning to hate this house. It's like an ill-fitting suit. A second-hand Oxfam suit like the kinds Russell and I used to search for in the eighties. The kind you could pretend looked modish and didn't smell of dead people. This house is loose and flappy, and it smells of dead people. Really. Every now and then I swear I catch a vaguely spermy whiff of Russell. Doesn't

147

matter how many plug-in odor-munchers we use, Russell is still lurking in the air con and in the underfloor heating. And I think this house is beginning to hate me. Sees me as an interloper. Which I am of course, but I don't like the idea that the stories it tells are all spiteful anecdotes about my lack of suitability as a tenant. I fear this house is a snob.

Sarah sits up as I come into the room.

'Hi,' I say.

'Hi,' she says back. And that's when I find out about her lack of stamina because she tells me that she's sick of shopping, sick of clothes, sick of shoes. Sick, even, of Prosecco and chocolate. 'I've had a fun couple of weeks. I've had a holiday. But now I want to use my time properly.'

'You're such a puritan,' I say.

She looks sad. 'I know. I can't help myself.' She pauses. 'I'm going to spend time with Scarlett. If I do buy stuff it'll be for her. And I'm going to learn a language. Really learn it. I'm going to stop shopping with Jesus and start paying him to teach me Spanish. It'll help when we go travelling.'

She tells me that she doesn't want to become one of those wealthy, purposeless women with expressionless faces that you see everywhere.

She says, 'I don't want to become a lady who lunches. Especially since I've no one to lunch with.'

I start to get undressed. It doesn't take long. I'm wearing jogging bottoms, T-shirt and sweatshirt. Total value, maybe thirty dollars. I flex the new muscles on my arm.

'Do you think Jesus is the best Spanish teacher out there? He certainly won't be the cheapest.'

'I know, but he needs the money. And he'll be good enough.' She pauses. 'I think successful learning is more about the learner than the teacher in any case. Don't you?'

I think about Sarah having Jesus as her teacher, having to repeat what he says. Having him correct her. Having him give her new words, new ways of thinking. It's a pretty intimate thing to be doing. I almost say something.

'What?' says Sarah. 'What were you going to say?'

'It doesn't matter,' I say.

Twenty-two

LORNA

The thing about the dinner party is that it's all nightmarishly grown-up.

Lorna has met Megan's boss and her husband a couple of times before. They'd been in the bar when they'd all gone out for Megan's last birthday but there had been loads of people out that night and Megan had – hilariously – been very drunk and very sick. Lorna had spent a lot of time in the bogs of some bar holding her mate's head and stroking her hair while she had upchucked pasta, tiramisu and Sierra Nevada ale. It had been her twenty-ninth after all, and if you can't get wasted on your last birthday of your twenties, when can you? Lorna had been quite pleased to see it actually. She had been beginning to think Megan's self-discipline was a bit unnatural.

Amelia and John had also been part of the group that went to the theatre a few months back, but Lorna hadn't really spoken to them then either. She'd sat next to Amelia but she'd felt oddly shy.

Lorna knows that Megan admires Amelia. She often talks about her calm good sense, how organised she is, how well read, how funny. She tells her about her support for progressive causes – financial and practical. Lorna had always thought that she sounded a bit irritating to be honest. A bit too good to be true. Amelia was still a boss after all. Still a leech. But Megan, well, she always sticks up for her.

'She's a good boss. A good person actually. She listens. She values what I've got to say. She doesn't belittle anyone, or steal their ideas.'

Lorna had to let it lie. Maybe there are decent people in the world of senior management somewhere. It just isn't her experience is all.

Lorna and Megan are in a contented phase. Things are good. They have a much nicer, much bigger flat right on Telegraph. They even have a cleaner – Leslie – who comes on Mondays and Fridays for a couple of hours. They'd argued about this for days. But eventually Megs had caved.

They are both uncomfortable with it, a discomfort they resolve by overpaying her. And by frantically tidying and cleaning before she arrives. They have cable, they have new bikes. And now, apparently, they have dinner parties.

Lorna is also enjoying her course. Her days with minor Victorian women novelists are actually quite congenial. Like spending her time with a gang of eccentric, waspishly gossipy aunts. Mostly they take the genteel piss out of vicars while fantasising about getting off with the landed gentry. They're quite modern really. On balance this course is probably better than taxidermy, though she will definitely do that one day.

They never did talk about the fight, even though Megan's eye had swollen so much and become such a vivid supernova of angry reds and yellows and purples that she hadn't gone out of the house for a week. And even after that she'd felt compelled to tell perfect strangers about this terrible bike accident she'd had after she had been cut up by some city-trader wanker in an SUV downtown.

There has, Lorna feels, been a subtle shift in the balance of power in the home. Megan maybe not quite so parental, not quite so bossy. Perversely this means Lorna working harder at being mischievous, playful. They can't talk about this either. But they are more or less happy.

Happy.

Amazing how much happiness a bit of financial security can bring. Lorna read somewhere that the optimum amount of extra cash a person needs to improve their mental health is £30,000 – enough to have no debts. To have something in the bank. Enough to know that you can quit your job if the boss stops being a good listener, starts stealing ideas or just generally begins to get a bit belittling on yo ass.

It's enough for a long holiday, for new books, for shoes, for funky wooden salad bowls and all the vital little treats that make life worth living. In a proper, decent-ordered Green Socialist society everyone would be able to live like they had at least £30k in the bank all the time.

Yes. Everyone should have enough for a cleaner. Everyone should have enough to host dinner parties to which your room-mate can invite her boss.

And inviting Amelia and John means gin and tonics, olives, spinach with nutmeg soup, lamb-stuffed green peppers with couscous and a spicy tomato sauce, different kinds of salads. And good old apple and blackberry crumble with custard and cream for dessert. Proper home-made custard. Proper thick organic double cream.

This had been Lorna's contribution. Everyone likes a crumble. And custard is England's signature food. *Crème anglaise* they call it in France, don't they?

And there are fine wines. Yeah, since The Money life has become a great deal more like a TV-advert life. A magazine life. Life like it should be.

Lorna's not sure how it happens but instead of books and politics and holidays and funky salad bowls they find they are talking about John's work. He is in insurance. And – luckily – he is surprisingly entertaining about it. It helps that John is handsome in a TV way. In a state senator sort of way. He fills his suit well. Broad shoulders, straight back, laughing brown eyes in a tanned face. He looks well cared for but not fussily overgroomed. And he has a deep, reassuring voice. Lorna likes him. She notices his hands. Strong hands.

And she has to admit that Amelia and he seem to be a decent match. They laugh when they talk over each other. They bicker good-naturedly about the detail of anecdotes that involve them both and she is good-looking too in a pointy way. A tanned lustre to her skin that speaks of some exclusive tennis club. A hungry face that says ambition and no carbs after twelve on weekdays. Big lips. The Victorian lady novelists would have had her down as dangerous straight from the off.

She has interesting eyes, almost lilac in this light, and a runner's body. Only with breasts, which most serious runners don't have. And if it's a puppy job it's a good one. Subtle. And her hands are as delicate as John's are tough. Lorna can picture them both in a deli – her pointing at jars of expensive pickles, him opening them with those big hands when they get back home. They definitely match. Complementary.

Once they've done John's work they talk about films and about HBO box sets. They even talk about minor Victorian lady novelists for a while. And on the whole Lorna likes it all.

She's always been sniffy about middle-class dinner parties but, really, what's not to like? Good food, good conversation with handsome people with nice hands who smell of sandalwood and purposeful days. And if, yes, it does feel like she and Megan are just playing at being adult somehow – that sooner or later a real responsible member of the community will come along and tell them to tidy up and put all their toys away – maybe that's how everyone feels, all the time. Maybe everyone is waiting for Daddy to get home and tell them off. Maybe Amelia and John feel like that too. Maybe she should ask them.

John looks thoughtful as she puts the question. 'I think you might have a point,' he says.

'It would explain the appeal of the Republicans,' Amelia says. 'Daddy knows best so leave all the decision-making to him.'

'Daddy being the military-industrial complex? The elite?'

'Exactly.'

And though Lorna has started this conversation – and though she agrees with this analysis – she's a bit buzzy and doesn't think she has the legs for politics tonight. Especially when they are all sitting stuffed with lamb and fancy salads and crumble, and with Megan heading off to the kitchen to make Irish coffees using single malt Jamesons.

So she goes to the loo and when she comes back she tells some stories about blokes. She gives them some of her finest. The guy who, after a year of not-all-that-casual-actually dating asked her to move in with him. And his wife. The randy old poet she met at a barbeque her mum had, who asked her straight out if she'd like to fuck. And who, when she declined asked plaintively, 'Is it because I'm old?' To which she had to reply that yes, it probably was. At least a bit.

And there were other stories too, some about blokes weirder than this. The boy she accidentally slept with during Freshers' week, who then sent her a poem more or less every day for three years. The freak. What was his name? Peter something? Paul?

She tells the table about deluded boys, mummy's boys, dull boys. The boy who kept carnivorous spiders. The man who offered to sponsor her through college. He'd said he'd pay her £10,000 a year if she'd spend a weekend with him once a term and give him the full girlfriend experience.

'That one was quite tempting actually. Ten grand and all I'd have to do would be to spend a few weekends moaning that he spent too much time on the Xbox. Though I suppose it's just possible he might have had other ideas about what the full girlfriend experience meant.'

And they are funny stories and they all laugh lots, even Megan who has heard them all before and had even been there for some of the choicer incidents. Because, yes, there are stories that involve The Fuckweasel which Lorna tells because, yes, she was so over him. She tells the story of how she'd met him. About how it was her first week in California and she'd been in Vesuvio – the famous beatnik bar, just down from the City Lights bookstore where only tourists go now. Jez had been in there drinking draught Sierra Nevada and looking so crassly like an artist with his Jim Morrison hair. Early sexy Jim Morrison mind, not fat, bearded Jim Morrison. Jez had even been wearing leather strides for fuck's sake.

She tells them how, drunk, she'd gone over to him and harangued him about how ridiculous it was to be doing the beat thang in Vesuvio in 2013. She tells how she'd laughed at him when he'd got huffy and said he was a proper artist actually. The real deal. And then, seeing the way she just smiled harder, how he'd shifted tack with surprising deftness and told her how right now he managed a tattoo shop, but how he was also a qualified horticulturist. And she'd tested him on the Latin names for plants, and at the end of the night when they were getting in the cab to go back to his place, she had told him, 'Just so you know, it's your horticultural Latin that is getting you laid. Not your ridiculous pants.'

And now there is a pause during which Amelia fixes her with those deep lilac eyes.

'Wow. You and Megan. What a great relationship you two have.'

Seems a bit of a conversational swerve, but she'll go with it.

'Yeah, we get on, don't we Megs old bean?'

And Megan smiles briefly too as she says, 'Yep. We're muckers all right,' exactly the way Dick Van Dyke might have said it in *Chitty Chitty Bang Bang*. And Lorna raises her glass and Megan sighs but smiles again and raises hers too and they clink. No, thinks Lorna, it's good to be grown up at last. A good thing definitely.

And Amelia smiles more, showing all the little swords of her teeth.

'I mean if John told those kinds of stories in public about his adventures with all his former lovers . . . I mean, gee whizz. I reckon I'd be pissed.'

'But it's not the same, is it? I mean you and John, you're an item. You're married. We're just . . .'

Lorna stops. Christ. Amelia leans forward. As Lorna remembers it later she actually flicked her tongue over her lips. John and Megan just look into their glasses. Lorna remembers something important about Irish coffee.

'Do you know how Irish coffee was invented? It was made up on the spot by a barman at Shannon Airport when John F Kennedy was delayed there on his way from the States to Berlin. On his way to do

'Ich Bin Ein Berliner'. Guy convinced him it was a local speciality. And so then it became one.'

'Is that right?' says John. 'It's not a traditional thing then? It's not like Guinness?'

'Guinness was brought over to Ireland by the English anyway,' says Lorna. She wonders if she might be on the point of gabbling.

'You're kidding me?'

'No straight up.' Though to be honest, she isn't absolutely sure about this. She knew the Guinness family were loaded and that they'd been loaded in the eighteenth and nineteenth centuries when the real Irish were starving, so that would suggest that they were English, wouldn't it? She meets Amelia's puzzled frown. Or is she laughing? It's hard to tell in this grown-up dinner party light.

'So you guys aren't partners?'

'Christ, no. I mean, Megan, she's beautiful and everything, but all that wetness on my face . . . No, ta.'

'Oh, it's not that bad. Wetness on the face in general I mean. Not Megan's in particular. I wouldn't know about that. Obviously.'

This is John. Lorna feels a surge of gratitude to him. No, not a surge – it wasn't as dramatic as that – but a flow anyway. A flow of gratitude. John trying to keep the situation light. John trying to help them through the embarrassment of this. Sweet really.

'I feel so foolish.' Amelia isn't letting it lie. And she doesn't sound like she thinks she's been all that foolish. She sounds amused. 'It's just that . . . I mean . . . Megan's always talking about you. It's always Lorna thinks and Lorna says, and I remember when Lorna I went to Vegas, or Lorna and I are thinking of going hiking in Yosemite. And then this apartment. The way you are here. I just assumed . . .'

Lorna takes a quick look round the apartment. Tries to see it through Amelia's eyes. It's tidy. Understated. Chic. It comes with a neurotic cat and there are also bits of crocheting around the place, but that isn't enough to make an apartment seem all tipping the muff is it? Perhaps it is.

'No, mate. Megan is my bestest chum in all the world. My pal – but we don't do owt like that. I haven't got a Sapphic bone in my body, worse luck.'

'Why worse luck?' John again, cool, quiet, courteous. He just needs to get his missus under control.

'Oh, you know. Girls. Prettier. Smarter. Nicer than boys. Not as generally rubbish.'

'Sugar and spice and all things nice?'

'Mostly yeah. I guess.' She turns to Megan who is still frowning down at the table. 'When are we going to Yosemite?'

Megan shrugs. 'Just an idea.'

'Well, I think it's a great idea. I'm definitely up for that.' And she pats her on the arm.

And then they talk more about men and women and the differences between them, and Amelia is all women are so bitchy with each other and Lorna is all speak for yourself love, but she doesn't quite put it like that. And John says how all his best friends are women and Amelia agrees a bit too enthusiastically about how he gets on really well with women and how great it is that he can be manly but with like this really open feminine side. And how liberating it is that there were other women he can talk to about emotional stuff, you know?

Yeah, right.

Then they count all the units of alcohol they've drunk and Amelia and John seem very chuffed with themselves when they decide that it comes to something like thirty-two.

'That's like,' Amelia counts on her slim, pointy fingers, 'that's like eight units each. Wow.' And she giggles. And it sounds wrong somehow. Lorna is pretty sure she isn't one of life's natural gigglers. Then she says, 'We'll suffer for this in the morning.'

And Lorna thinks of the time, not that long ago, back in West Yorkshire, when eight units was what they'd have before they started the real drinking. Eight units – which is only just over a bottle of ordinary Chardonnay after all – was just a pre-drink drink then. A livener.

A sharpener or two. What they had just to get the party started. The good old days.

But then there is a taxi downstairs and there are hugs and air-kisses in the hallway and Amelia telling Megan not to be late on Monday and finally – finally – they are gone and Lorna can turn to Megan and say, 'Well, your boss. Do you think she knows John's playing away? Because he so clearly is.'

But Megan just sighs. 'She's all right.'

There is a little debate about whether to leave the clearing up but neither of them wants to face the dishes in the morning, so they carry crockery and glasses from table to sink. They rinse plates. They finish off the crumble, and then rinse those dishes too. They argue gently over how best to load the dishwasher. Megan wins as usual, so she does that while Lorna takes out the trash.

It's still warm in the parking lot and the rumble of distant freeway traffic is comforting. She has a cheeky rollie and thinks about how strange it is that she's standing in California, living with Megan. If her friends from wild, wet West Yorkshire could see her now, standing in a car park in Berkeley. But somehow she can't imagine their voices just at this minute. Just can't conjure up their faces.

When she gets back in the apartment she finds that Megan is still doing stuff with the dishwasher, making minor adjustments that will ensure maximum ergonomic efficiency or something.

Lorna says, 'Christ. No wonder smelly Melly thinks we're pioneers of gay marriage. No one is more married than us.'

Megan doesn't say anything, just carries on moving bowls and plates around. So Lorna adds, 'It's nice though. I like being married to you.' And she goes over to the dishwasher. She puts her arms around Megan from behind and kisses her on her cool cheek, which is how she discovers that Megan is crying. Despite everything Lorna has Megan's wetness on her face after all, but she has the good sense not to say this.

She moves away a couple of steps and Megan turns to face her.

'Don't say anything. I'm just being an idiot.'

'A little bit tired and emotional, huh? The Johns and the Amelias of this world will do that to a person.'

'Something like that. I'll see you in the morning, 'kay.'

'Yeah. And I really am up for Yosemite. Hiking, camping, being eaten by grizzlies. The whole thing.'

Megan smiles weakly. 'Yeah. Well, we'll see.'

Twenty-three

NICKY

The new hair. There is a piece of architecture Linwood can't do for me, something not even Jesus can sort. And that is my hair. Hair has to be a whole separate team.

Imagine a TV ad that is all science bit – that's these guys. They talk like an Open University programme. Three of them, all deftly coiffured, of course, trumpeting their equations with the warm voice of God.

Nate, Valerie and Don. Or, rather, Dr Nate, Dr Valerie and Dr Don because though they are friendly and informal and everything, they do also want us to know that they are doctorates in the follicular sciences. They spend a busy couple of hours with us, not only explaining their pricing structure but CAT-scanning my head with some hand-held implement. They use lasers to measure the nature and speed of the erosion taking place along my hairline. They take DNA swabs, as well as blood and follicle samples in order to form the basis for a considered judgement on the best way forward. They are thorough. They talk through the Norwood scale which is to baldness what the Beaufort scale is to wind speed.

And the report they produce is thorough too. More like an academic monograph than a quote from a tradesman. Eighty closely argued pages suggesting that transplant isn't really an option. Neither is weaving, however hand-loomed. It's the full syrup they recommend for me. And their catalogue – as thick, as lavishly illustrated and as creamily glossy as a high-end cookbook – is there to show how follicle-support technology has changed since the days when an ageing

TV presenter tried to defy time by sticking rough hexagons of roadkill fur on his bonce.

No, the hair-replacement therapy recommended for me is emphatically bespoke and undetectable. It's a modern wonder of the world, up there with Teflon and nicotine patches. It's stealth hair. And, like every other great leap forward of the last seventy years, it's almost certainly a by-product of both Nazi experiments and the space race.

'Are you sure about this, love?' says Sarah.

Sarah's worry is that this might be a humiliation too far for me.

'It's just that there's such a stigma about wigs, isn't there?'

And there is. It's because hair – for men as well as for women – is about sexual display, isn't it? I mean this is obvious. Men are such peacocks really. Even the fat sweating ones you see on the BART wearing cheap suits and comedy ties. Every man is a Samson in his own head and cutting his crowning glory is – as the writers of the Bible knew only too well – like slicing off his penis and mincing it. A bit like it anyway.

And it's not even as if I'm totally bald now. Plenty of men my age are balder. There's no doubt the ranks are thinning, however. My hair is a picket line where the workers, the union rank and file, are gradually being persuaded back to work while the hardcore activists – the ones that are left round the cooling brazier – grow greyer, colder, weaker. My head is a large egg in an increasingly ragged nest. If we're not to be stopped at airports by suspicious homeland security personnel with their armoury of facial-recognition devices, then hair replacement is a necessity. I can see that.

'I mean we don't have to travel. We could stay here.'

'Yeah, but what about your mum?'

'She could come here.'

'Yeah, she could. But she won't.'

Back in England, Sarah's mum came to us once in five years. And she lives in Enfield, all of two hours away. Tops. My limited research on the subject tends me towards the opinion that the average mum likes to be the visitee, rather than the visitor.

'Let's not think about it. Let's just go for it,' I say. I have got quite fatalistic by this time anyway. And people have worse things to wear. Colostomy bags, glass eyes, false legs. Compared to those kinds of accessories a wig is nothing really. No hardship at all.

Dr Don reminds me of some of the proven drawbacks of baldness. The lack of self-esteem, the absence of bald leading men in the movies, the fact that no bald man has been elected president since the dawn of the television age.

'Not all that many women either,' says Sarah.

Dr Don – obviously the most people-pleasing of the trio – tries to make me feel better by hinting that almost every male celeb you've ever heard of has been under their care at some point. Even the really young ones. He won't name them – discretion is his watchword – but I run through a few names and he nods at all of them. Jagger? Nod. McCartney? Nod. I move forward a generation. Morrissey? Nod. Bono? Emphatic nod. I move forward another few decades of pop years. Timberlake? Nod. Forward again. The Jonas Brothers? Justin Bieber? Those insanely hirsute One Direction boys? Nod, nod and nod again.

Blimey. There's a lot less hair around than you'd think. The world is actually a pretty bald place.

So I allow Dr Nate, Dr Valerie and Dr Don to assess my strand type and search their database of donors. When, eleven minutes later, the perfect match is found, Dr Don's phone buzzes. He's thrilled to tell me that my donor is a handsome Icelander called Siggi. They show us a photograph of a young bloke scowling. He looks like he could be a cop in one of those Scandinavian murder shows. He couldn't be the killer because in Nordic noir it's always an angry middle-aged man, usually a top civil servant, often bald, that does the killing. An interesting contrast with American cop shows where it's a hot pneumatic blonde who kills, and with British murder stories, where it is so often

162

an acerbic, well-preserved female member of the upper middle class what done it. A magistrate. You want to know what frightens a society: look at their TV killers.

Dr Nate tells us the process. 'Siggi will be visited at home in Akureyri and given a diet sheet and a lifestyle focus to ensure his own hair stays in the most robust state possible as it grows.'

'Absolutely tip-top condition,' says Dr Valerie.

'And he'll be regularly monitored,' says Dr Don.

'When his hair has reached the required length he will be carefully shorn . . .'

'And then the tresses will be vacuum-packed . . .'

'And couriered over to San Francisco . . .'

'Where our team of specialists will work on it . . .'

'It's a kind of farming basically,' I say.

'Organic though . . .'

'More or less free range . . .' Dr Valerie and Dr Don are smiling. Dr Nate isn't. You can tell he sees all this kind of talk as essentially frivolous. And he makes sure the others don't interrupt any more. He quells them with a look and a stiff, chopping hand gesture and delivers the rest of the spiel in a steady monotone. When he's finished I explain it back to him, just to make sure I've got it.

'So, I remain linked to the donor as long as I keep paying the standing orders?'

'Yes, the payments ensure that Siggi remains a donor just for you.'

Out in Akureyri Siggi Einarsson gets on with living, his hair under contract to me alone. I wonder what he does for a job.

'I think he's a teacher. All our donors are of the highest quality,' says Dr Don.

'Trustworthy and respectable members of the community,' adds Dr Valerie.

'So maybe not a teacher then. You read the news, right?'

Nate just curls his lip. It's the hair that matters – who cares about the donor's lifestyle. He's obviously a loser or he wouldn't be selling his own body parts. Even minor ones like hair. Dr Nate doesn't have time for banter.

In any case the quality of the hair isn't the main thing for Dr Nate. He is all about scalp visibility and he gets almost animated as he explains how chip-controlled micro wizardry ensures that Siggi's hair is punched strand by strand into a layer of polyurethane as thin and as malleable as skin itself, thus allowing for a truly realistic look and feel. Someone – a lover, Dr Val suggests with a twinkle – could pat, ruffle, tug, stroke, pull my new hair and not realise it was all Siggi's cast-offs. I could have my hair washed, shampooed, blow-dried and set, all undetected. I could safely have an Indian head massage. In fact I could have a proper rolling in the dirt street-fight. Urchins and muggers could pull out handfuls and the young guttersnipes would never twig my secret. I could have my hair examined forensically for nits and still not be outed. In fact the nits themselves would be fooled and make themselves right at home.

'OK, Doctor,' I say. 'I get it. It's a damn good wig.'

'The best,' says Dr Nate.

Next to him Dr Valerie and Dr Don smile and produce the paper-work for me to sign.

'You'll need three, of course,' says Dr Nate.

'At least,' says Dr Val.

'So people think your hair is growing,' says Dr Don.

'And you must always have them professionally fitted.' Dr Nate getting the last word, like he got the first word. I bet Dr Val and Dr Don have some splendid bitching sessions about him. Of course they do. He's so clearly the talent. They must hate him. Admin always wants to murder talent.

The hair takes far less time to sort than the suit. I hope it wasn't too much of a shock for Siggi, I hope he didn't have an air-guitar competi-tion he needed his hair for. For some reason I'm really sure Siggi is a full-on head-banging mosher. Teacher or not. Anyhow, a couple of weeks later and I'm sitting in front of a mirror trying to get used to this new bloke, this movie star, staring back at me. Dr Nate, Dr Valerie and Dr Don coo and purr and want to take photographs for their website, which we won't allow them obviously.

I think Dr Nate is about to argue. Dr Nate is the artist of the three, the visionary. He is proud of his craft and, like any artist, any craftsman, he wants to show the world. Dr Valerie and Dr Don, on the other hand, are understanding of my position.

'Discretion . . .' begins Dr Valerie.

'Is our watchword,' finishes Dr Don.

Dr Nate sighs, and to cheer him up I say, 'Damn fine work. Beautiful. Absolutely beautiful.' And, finally, he smiles. Which means the others smile too.

The thing is, it is beautiful. I'd never realised how much I'd hated losing my hair. I mean, I never did anything with it. Short back and sides as a kid, a bit spiky in the late seventies, a bit of Sun In in the 1980s. And that's it. And my hair loss started early as if, depressed by my lack of any sign of tonsorial development, my hair lost interest in our partnership and began to leave the building.

Not like Russell's. When he was a first-year student at the Poly his hair was long and spiked and black on top and the sides and blond with blue streaks at the back. Combine that with his very skinny, very white face with its long sharp nose, and he looked like a parrot. He looked ludicrous, but this was the era of ludicrous. Ludicrous ruled. It was the time of The Cure and The Bunnymen, of Kajagoogoo and A Flock of Seagulls. A time when hair was often worn vertical and Krazy Kolor was big. A time when fashion caught Psitticosis. When all the cool cats wanted to look like parrots.

Later, after uni, Russell seemed to travel back through all the ages of hair, moving from this parrot-gothic, through short punky hedgehog spines, to a brief flirtation with a Beatley moptop, then skipping back further towards rockabilly quiffs and flat-tops, before ending up with an artfully tousled grown-out crop suggestive of special ops forces in World War Two. The raffish look of one of the original SAS officers maybe, and that's how he was wearing it on the day he died and so it's what I have now too.

Thanks to the miracles of modern technology, the artistry of the three doctors and the sacrifice of Siggi of Iceland, my hair is back and better than it ever was. As I tease and twist it in the mirror, I can practically feel my testosterone count rising. Yes it's fake, yes it's absolutely, entirely inauthentic, but what does that mean, really? It means it's even better than the real thing. Nearly everything good in this world is fake and inauthentic. And nearly everything truly horrible is natural. Microwaves good, smallpox bad. Music good, earthquakes a bit shit. Fake hair good, baldness crap.

Scarlett comes over. Tentatively, she pushes her hand through my new rug. Then she pulls. Then she tugs. Hard.

'Ow,' I say. 'Ow, ow, ow.'

'Ow,' she says back. Out loud. This is a game she knows and likes. And then she laughs and almost, but not quite, manages to clap her hands. And then she says a whole sentence. Well, almost. 'Oh, my actual god,' she says.

Twenty-four

CATHERINE

What, Catherine wonders, would life have been like if she'd stayed working in the library? She'd liked it there at first. The Hildreth branch library where she'd worked was small and always packed.

People think that libraries are quiet places, but they're not. They're full all day every day with people looking for jobs, updating their CVs, or just sitting about flicking through the magazines while their children run around tagging each other between the stacks. Sometimes people even glance at the books. A library is the last public space where you can just sit and be without someone insisting you buy a flat white cappucino and a blueberry muffin.

She had quickly got to know all the regulars. Mr Stooks who read a western a day and whose wife read the same number of Mills and Boons. Catherine liked to imagine them side by side in bed, him galloping across the prairie closing in on the bad man in the black hat, while next to him but in another universe his wife swooned in the arms of a swarthy polo player.

Who else? Jade Feasey, all of eighteen, who looked like a right slapper with her microskirts and make-up, but quietly went through all the books relating to starting your own business. Mrs Denby who kept a goat in her garden. Mr Eagleton who was a *Janes Fighting Ships* obsessive and knew everything about the world's navies. You wanted to avoid getting in a conversation with him. Mr Plantagenet who smelt of pot noodles. Mrs Welsummer who smelt of turds.

It was in the library in Hildreth that Catherine had come across her first writers' group, not that she'd wanted to join one then. They'd frightened her a bit with their air of barely concealed competition. They would go into the little meeting room on a Wednesday night like poker players trying to look relaxed in the face of a big pot. They would smile and talk about houses, holidays, schools and grandchildren on the way in but there was the giveaway stiffness that betrayed how nervous and keyed-up they were. Catherine saw the same thing years later in soldiers before they went on patrol. The same little tells. For the squaddies the conversation was fanny and football but the tells were the same, the same tension running down the neck and across the shoulders. The same little twitches.

And the staff in Hildreth library were nice too. Three of them worked there more or less fulltime. Anna Knight who'd been there since the library was built; she'd been at the official unveiling on 5 February 1968 and never left. She was the manager when Catherine was there, sternly efficient but you could have a laugh with her when you got to know her. Nervy Bridget Dunkley with her breathless stories of her two handsome, brave and clever boys. It took Catherine several weeks to realise that her boys weren't boys at all but dogs. Labradors with boys' names: John the eldest and Paul the smartest. They were, Anna told her, named after the songwriters of The Beatles.

And there was the area manager who popped in once or twice a week. Ted Arnold spoke like he'd been to an English public school though he hadn't. All the women in the libraries had a crush on Ted, even Catherine. Looking back, Catherine now thought she'd developed one just to fit in with the other two. He was fortyish, had been handsome once but was now going a bit squishy round the edges; still, there was something about him. Bridget said that it was because he had worried eyes; Catherine thought that yes, the eyes might have had something to do with it – the exact colour of chocolate buttons – but it was maybe that he asked questions. He asked about Bridget's dogs, he asked about Anna's old mother – ninety-two and going blind – and he asked Catherine about everything. Everything except the obvious. He didn't ask about boyfriends, which everyone else she ever met was obsessed by. He used to talk to her about maybe taking the library exams and going to college and making it a career. He took her seriously and that – together with the sad eyes – was probably enough to make you the George Clooney of the Suffolk library service.

Maybe she could have wooed and won Ted Arnold. He would have been too old for her really, there would have been an enjoyable fuss about that. There might have been a honeymoon in Spain or Barbados and maybe a child. Maybe two. There would almost certainly have been a divorce – she was too young for it to last after all – but probably not for ten years or so. And you just knew Ted would have been decent about it. He wouldn't have tried to hide from the CSA or anything.

She knows, however, that the library wouldn't have been enough. Not even if she'd done as Ted suggested and become chartered or whatever – even if she might have finished writing a book. Surrounded by other people's books, she would have been in a better position to finish her own, surely?

These days Catherine looks at other people and wonders what they would say or do if she were to lean into their space, right into their personal bubble, and say, 'Hey, you know I could kill you with my bare hands.' Probably they wouldn't do anything. There were so many nutters around now. Probably they'd just smile uneasily and hope she went away. And now here she is flipping jogging, tailing a rich fuck just so she can cull him. *Think of it as pest control*, Tough's words from back when she'd first started. *Baby rabbits are cute but we kill them. We cull badgers, seals. We fucking eat little baby lambkins and what have they ever done to us?* And this guy is no rabbit, no badger, no seal, no little baby lambkin. The data says this guy is a monster. She just needs one clear shot. Then it's done.

Twenty-five

NICKY

We try but we can't get her to do it again, but we don't mind really. Scarlett has proved that her silence can be overcome, that she might one day climb from the swampy grunts and snorts to the firmer country of 'Yes' and 'No' and 'Can I have a biscuit now?' This is stuff we've hoped for all along, but having actual evidence – well, that's huge. And it's frustrating that for the minute she chooses to go back to the nods and the gurgles, but we're not going to get too hung up on it.

The mood in the house is lighter, happier – pretty goddamn cheerful actually. Though of course from time to time I still seem to feel it watching me, whispering its snide jokes about me, its sly put-downs.

But, you know what? Fuck you house. I'm looking good, Sarah is looking good, and her Spanish accent is coming on leaps and bounds. And my records and my guitar have arrived from England (minus the three most valuable LPs of course). And one day we have sex Sarah and me. In fact we do it twice. Once in the evening and then again the next morning. That hasn't happened for a while. And 'by a while' I mean literally months. And then, when I'm bringing in the post-coital tea, Sarah says we should have a proper chat about where and when we're getting married.

I put the tea down carefully. And tell Sarah that I'm going for a run. I need to think.

'I'm surprised you have the energy. I can hardly move.'

And it's true, we did really go for it. We were like something you might see on RedTube. From nowhere we seemed to find our inner porn-star couple. I was the hard-bodied millionaire playboy, she was the lonely MILF next door. We put the new hair through its paces too. There was a lot of tugging at it from above. It passed the audition.

'Linwood will be disappointed with me if I don't keep up the programme.'

'And we shouldn't disappoint the architect,' she yawns sleepily. 'I've a lot to thank him for. Thanks for the seeing to. And the tea.' And she turns on her side, pulls the covers up.

Yes, I need to think about this getting married business. When would be appropriate, for example? Surely even her mother, her sister and her mates would expect Sarah to wait a decent while before getting hitched to her late husband's best friend?

I think about our last wedding. All our friends came. That is – all Sarah's friends and Russell. And some blokes I sat close to at the council. It was OK I suppose. No one ever had to hold an empty glass. Everyone got shit-faced. Except for Sarah.

I remember other things: the amusing, surprisingly generous best man's speech written for Russell – it turned out – by a former script-writer on *Days Of Our Lives*. Soundtracked by the crying of babies. The first dance. 'Into The Mystic'. My semi-erection firming up romantically against the exciting bulge of Sarah's baby bump. Later, all the men casting aside their thin grey jackets and knitted ties to be videoed by their wives, doing the Gangnam-style dance quite compet-itively to much standard-issue hilarity. Yeah, OK – but there was some Best Western hotel sadness to it all. And then there was the unspeak-able shame of what Russell made me do at the stag night.

Mainly though, the very idea of another wedding makes me nerv-ous, like we're spitting in the eyes of all the gods. And I know this is ludicrous, not just because I don't believe in gods, but because the fact of taking Russell's fortune in the way we have would seem to be enough of an outrage to any godly sensibility already. We're already in so deep, that the odd bit of marrying can't do any further harm, can it? Especially as those non-existent godly eyes would surely think we're still married in any case.

And I run, enjoying doing it on my own for once without feeling that I'm holding Linwood back. I stretch out, feeling my stride lengthen, my lungs open.

It was me that insisted on us getting married before, that lifetime ago when we became Mr and Mrs Fisher; Sarah wasn't that fussed. She certainly wasn't as keen as she is now.

But I get it. Or I think I do. Before, when we didn't have much, then it was just a piece of paper. Purely symbolic. Now, of course, theoretically I'm free. As far as the world is concerned Sarah is merely the widow of Nicky Fisher, a status update which has netted her precisely £125,000 in life assurance (the exact sum I wired to Russell's daughter, not that Sarah knows this), while I'm King of the Universe, able – again in theory – to not worry about the health and well-being of the widow Fisher or her daughter, Scarlett. As far as the world knows they are nothing to do with me. I could just disappear. Be a bachelor again. And one with my pockets full of spending loot.

But in fact that can't happen. We're yoked together for all time by our secret, Sarah and I. We're in a classic state of mutually assured destruction. We have risen together, so we must fall together. If it goes tits up, it goes tits up for both of us.

So I worry that people will talk. And by people I mean the *FT* or *The Wall Street Journal*. Gossip rags like that. I can imagine the water-cooler conversations. And you say he's married his high-school friend's wife? Not a supermodel? Not a Finnish actress or a Vietnamese pop singer? Not the daughter of an oligarch? You're telling me Russell Knox has eschewed the time-honoured right of the highest high-ballers and not gathered to himself the firmest-fleshed representatives of nubility, but instead married a forty-something lecturer in human resources?

Will people buy that? Will they let something as against nature as that go by without comment? Without digging around for the real scoop? Of course they won't. Have you read *Investors Chronicle* lately? It's like the *National Enquirer* or *Chat*. Prurient and obsessed with sex lives of the rich and reclusive.

We all know what the super-rich are like. And what they are like is super-predictable. The more money you have the more predictable you are. When rich men marry they carefully study the market and then select the most appropriate bride. And the most appropriate bride is one almost half their age. Read *The Economist*. They have an equation. The average multi-millionaire marries a women half his age plus seven years. This is a fact. So in real life Russell would be wanting to get hitched to a thirty-two-year-old. Anything else would look a bit weird.

Money buys you a lot of anonymity it's true, but even if we could do it without any fuss, and do it somewhere so remote even the hardiest wedding photographer and most imaginative financial hack wouldn't see us, well there'd still be paperwork. Forms to be filled in. Boxes to tick. If you're going to get married you have to get into a waltz with the state, you can't avoid it. Even the Kings of the Universe have to scrawl a name on a record somewhere, leave a paper trail.

And then there are Sarah's mother and sisters. Her family has become a coven of psychotherapists. These days her mum or one of her sisters is on the phone every couple of hours wanting to know how she's bearing up and when she's coming back to dear old Albion. We're not going to be able to sneak a sudden wedding past their radar.

And I must be beginning to think a little bit like a rich man, because it doesn't take all that long for my thoughts to turn from marriage to divorce.

Being married to Russell Knox seems to really matter to Sarah. And somewhere, in the deepest most insecure part of my mind, I begin to wonder if getting hitched is, for Sarah, simply a necessary first stage on the way to getting divorced. Because that's something else the rich do. They get divorced. A lot. A marriage for the rich is rarely for life. It might just be for Christmas, or a summer, or a long weekend even.

In the country, where the rich hang out, marriage isn't a sacrament, it's an event like Henley or Glyndebourne. Something you go to because it's what everyone does. And just as you might take milk thistle to minimise your post-event hangover, so you vaccinate yourself against the effects of divorce with legally watertight pre-nups. The rich are very keen to promote safe consummation.

During exercise things seem to become clearer. Possibilities you hadn't noticed before take hard shapes in your head. This clarity of thought, as much as the erections and the thrill of the six-pack in the mirror, is what keeps a person going through the hurt. And one of the well-documented effects of sudden wealth is a propensity towards paranoia, even towards those closest to you.

Especially towards them.

This all the more true where money and power are concerned. Think the Borgias, the Roman emperors, the Egyptian pharoahs. Think the Jacksons, think Lacoste. Think about the break up of any major rock band. Think, for that matter, of your own fucked-up kinfolk. Somewhere in your own family right now there are brothers and sisters, uncles and aunts, cousins and step-children scheming or feeling that they are being schemed against.

And so now I find myself thinking: if we were married for a year or two in California, and then Sarah went for a divorce, well, she'd get half of everything. *More* than half because of Scarlett. And she'd have her more than half legitimately. I couldn't expose her, could I? Not without triggering disaster for myself.

I know we've discussed the possibility of getting caught and how sort of OK that would be, but now that it comes to it, I find I don't actually want to do 10,000 hours practising my scales, even if it is in a low-security facility. In any case, I now think I could be wrong about the kind of time I'd serve. I think that maybe these days you do very hard time indeed for financial felonies. You don't spend your time at the baby grand, instead you do ten to fifteen years being buggered senseless in Sing Sing.

And once divorced, she'd be able to go everywhere, do anything with anyone, and even if I wasn't in jail I'd be wearing a wig in a gated community somewhere remote, terrified that every knock on the door was going to be the police or the press. Or both, knowing how inter-dependent they've become these days.

I'd be sitting in the dark, bewigged but alone, brooding. I would, finally, have become Russell. I'd be in a worse place than Russell. Old Knoxy didn't have to worry about the terrible moment when Siggi of Iceland had a heart attack so ending the supply of natural hair.

As I run, this suspicion grows in the aggressively cancerous way that suspicions do, and that's when I notice the woman jogging ahead of me.

She looks pretty good from the back, but I've been fooled like that before when out running, fallen for the old 1861. You know, looks eighteen from behind, but sixty-one face on. You get a lot of that in California.

She's running confidently but at a moderate pace and I'm gaining steadily. I like overtaking people. If you've ever done any running, you know the small but important thrill it gives to pass someone without huffing or puffing, but as though you were simply moving at a natural pace, moving at, what is for you, a very modest speed. As though you were, in fact, taking it pretty easy today.

As I approach her though, something happens. The woman goes sprawling forward with a yelp and face-plants herself on the road. She rolls over whimpering, holding her knees. As I sprint towards her I can see that her wincing face makes her an 1836 or thereabouts. Which is OK. That's a perfectly acceptable year.

'You all right?'

I offer my hand and she grabs it while trying for a watery smile. She has a strong grip and hauling her to her feet is no problem because she's light and moves from a sitting position to standing easily. She's fit all right, there's a bounce to her. She has a guileless, open face. Honest dark eyes. Firm jaw. Long unruly curls of hair the colour of

175

dark chocolate. She has a wonky front tooth. The one on the right is at an angle and slightly crosses its neighbour. This is rare in California. Well, it's uncommon here among people who have any money at all. That is, it's rare among white people.

'I think so. More shocked than anything.' Ah. She's English. Possibly East Anglia, there's a slight but definite agrarian roll to her vowels. She rubs her hands together; they are streaked with blood and grit. She makes a face again. And then rubs her knees. She has good legs I notice. Slender but muscular. Good trainers too. Expensive without being ridiculous. And worn. This is someone who runs regularly at least. Not a dabbler. She's too small to have been a netball whizz, but I could see her jinking down the wing at hockey no trouble.

'Thank you,' she says with an embarrassed smile. I love her teeth. God bless the UK. A cheer for the English heedlessness of their teeth.

'That's quite all right.'

'Hey, you're English.' Her smile grows wider and I catch a glimpse of her exciting dental wonkiness again.

'Guilty as charged I'm afraid. Why are you here? Holiday?'

She frowns, the assumption that she's a tourist is a mistake. 'No, I wish. Work.'

'Oh yes, what business?'

'It's boring my work.' She looks around. Blows on her hands. 'Look, thanks for stopping but . . .'

'I know – you want to get on with your run.'

'Do you mind? It's just that I get grumpy if I don't run in the mornings.'

'No, no, go ahead. I'm the same.'

'But . . .' She stops. 'Oh dear, I feel a bit weird.'

'Look here's a bench.' And she lets me help her to it. She's really shaken up.

So we sit on the bench and she composes herself and after a few minutes we start to chat about stuff – about the UK, about the shitty weather, about work. About what we listen to while running. She's listening to cheesy eighties pop. A-ha, Duran Duran, Spandau Ballet.

She's some kind of systems analyst so she's not wrong about her work being boring. But it's interesting about the big corporations she works for. Among others she works for both Coca-Cola and Pepsi. I ask her which she prefers.

She smiles. 'I can't possibly tell you that.'

'No, of course not. Rude to ask really. Sorry.'

'Anyway, I prefer water.'

She nods gravely in agreement when I tell her how I feel I have to keep running so as not to disappoint my trainer. How it almost feels like he's my boss. We swap stories of aches and pains. It's a fun twenty minutes, more fun than running anyway, and easier on the joints.

There's a pause.

'Are you an actor?' she says. I laugh.

'No, why?'

'It's just . . .' She tails off, looks at the ground again, twists her wild hair. Finally she looks up. She looks embarrassed.

'It's just?'

'It's just you look so . . . so like one. You look like someone who might be in films,' she says in a rush.

'Why thank you, ma'am,' I say. 'But I'm not a film star. I'm just . . .' But what? What am I? 'I'm just a guy,' I finish lamely.

'Well, that's a relief,' she says. And then more shyly. 'Married?'

'Not married,' I say, without a beat. I'm amazed at myself.

'Girlfriend though, right?'

'Yeah. A kind of girlfriend. I suppose.' You Judas, I think. Your girlfriend is the kind that's really a wife. I'm possessed, clearly. Bewitched.

She doesn't let her face fall, I see the effort. She says, 'And I'm going back home in a few weeks anyway.'

Another pause. And then she seems to come to a sudden decision. She stands, stretches and puts out her hand.

'I'm OK now,' she says. 'Thank you and –' She stops and looks at the ground, scuffs at a tuft of grass that is breaking through a crack in the pavement. She is still holding my hand.

'And what?'

'Nothing, really nothing.' She's still holding my hand, which she notices suddenly and drops. I laugh and she grins.

'No, go on,' I say

'Really. It's silly. I can't say.' She looks at the ground. Then looks up and pulls again at the dark thickets of her hair.

'Yeah, you can. In fact you have to now.'

'Oh, well . . .' There's a long pause. She looks at the ground again. And then up again. Catches my eye. She has great eyes, as black as those of any seductive landlord's daughter. Intense with a serious stillness, even when the rest of her is embarrassed and fidgety. 'It's just that . . . Oh look. I'm just going to say it . . . I'd be up for a coffee sometime soon if you wanted.'

OK it's just coffee and there's no firm date, but nevertheless it's only the second time I've been asked out. Getting asked out is not something that happens to me. It didn't happen even when I was looking my best, not even when I was very occasionally being told I had something of the look of Bono. Not like Russell, women were always stopping him, even when he looked his worst. Hungover, unwashed and in the same army combats he'd been wearing for a fortnight, girls were still forever passing him notes in lectures or stopping him in the street to tell him he was a babe. Most of the time Russell would just frown and walk on.

And that's what I should do now, isn't it? Frown, jog on.

It's not what I do.

'Yeah. I'd like that,' I say.

'Really?' She seems surprised and delighted. And she gives me the chance to see the endearing untidiness of her smile again. I smile back.

And she gives me the number and I'm thinking, yes, it would be easy to say I have some architecture appointment downtown. Volleyball, say. Or wrestling something that might account for scratches and bruises. Very easy to spend an afternoon with wonky-smile girl. It would be manageable. My heart twitches. My stomach fizzes. And of course I have nowhere to put the number. I have to hold it folded in my fist.

'I should memorise this number then swallow the paper,' I say, then feel a fool.

'It's what I'd do,' she says, deadpan.

'Oh, wait. I don't even know your name,' I say.

'Ah, right, yes.' She's all bashful again. 'Catherine.'

And I wait because now she's supposed to ask me mine, but shyness has made her ditsy. It's quite cute really. 'And I'm Russell, by the way,' I say.

'Oh good,' she says. She looks relieved. I'm puzzled. There's a beat before she says, 'It's a nice name.'

Is it?

'Listen,' she says. 'You carry on with your run. You're much faster than me. I don't want to hold you up.'

'OK,' I say, 'Bye then.'

'Bye.'

'Bye then.'

'Bye.'

But I don't actually turn around and run off – we keep eye contact the whole time – should I kiss her? Maybe just chastely on the cheek? In the end we hug. She smells of fruit and sweat. Her breasts springy against my chest, her hands strong around my back and shoulders. Her lips press against my neck for a fraction of a second. She smells of cheap hotel soap and sweat. God, I could do it right now. But I turn and begin to run.

Conscious of being watched, no, conscious of being *admired*, I remember everything my architect has said and my stride is long and regular, my back straight, my head up, my arms pumping loose and easy. There's a blue tram up ahead clanking and bumping its way down this wide boulevard that is Hyde Street and I set overtaking that as my target.

And when I'm about a hundred yards away from where I left Catherine, closing in on the tram, I feel the sting. It's sharp and bloody painful. They have some vicious bugs out here in the golden state. I don't stop though. I don't want to look like I'm getting out of puff, so I just rub my arm and keep going. I run faster, move close to a sprint in fact, and after a minute the sting doesn't hurt. When I do finally stop to look there's the tiniest red mark where the bloody insect did his thing. And I wonder briefly if it was a bee that is now lying dead somewhere having ripped himself apart dealing with some non-existent threat to bee-kind, or whether it wasn't a bee but a wasp still flying around all blithe and unconcerned having zapped me out of pure grumpy badness.

Actually, I don't mind wasps, never mind bees. I don't even mind flies or roaches all that much. The insects I hate are butterflies. Yes, they can be beautiful from a distance, but see them close up and they're hideous. Like finding a decomposed corpse under the finest silk bedsheets. Butterflies are liars. The ultimate in 1861 tricks, I don't see how anyone could ooh and ahh over them.

I start to run again past the coffee kiosks, the coffee shops, the hurrying office kids clutching corrugated cups of double expressos and skinny lattes. This place runs on coffee, the way England runs on booze. I remember how Russell was contemptuous of people who bought coffee in Styrofoam cups.

'It's a tax,' he would say. 'A cappuccino tax. You see these minimum-wage suckers spending five dollars on hot water and a muffin and then having to work for two hours to pay for it. One hundred dollars a month. That's twelve hundred dollars a year – that's a holiday. It's a good guitar. It's a motorbike. It's a very decent French wine. It's a long weekend in Mexico with good coke and two imaginative ladies. It is, in fact, all the things that make life worthwhile. All swapped for a milky drink. Pathetic. Shows a lack of backbone.'

*   *   *

I'm deep in the financial district now. The place where San Francisco has been most Manhattanised. Though the truth is the whole world has been Manhattanised. Every city now has iconic statement buildings. Bank-statement buildings you might say. They all have their towers, their shards, their needles, their pins, their fins, their gherkins, their fuck-you middle fingers. Their rigid digits. And after those sky-taunting gestures come all the steel and glass cubes. The galleries housing the same butterfly colours and shapes of the same conceptual art, replicated on the same postcards in the same gift shops. I'm sure Timbuktu will have a museum of modern art by now. I bet Kinshasa has a sculpture park. Cities like to wear what all the other kids have. They all want the fashionable gear.

The sting is already fading and I force myself to pick up the pace even more. The further I get from this Catherine and her shy, crooked smile, the more ridiculous I feel. The more disloyal. 'Just coffee,' I say out loud. 'Just coffee.'

I think about the other time I was asked out. By Sarah. It was she who made the first move on me a lifetime ago in the council and that was just for lunch, and look where that led. And sprinting to overtake that thought is the next one. Yes, I must marry her. As soon as is decent – which will be a while yet after all. We'll find a way to make it work. And I won't even wear the marital condom of a pre-nup.

And, as soon I've finished this run, I'll call this Catherine and tell her even a quick espresso is out. I'll tell her I was dazzled by her. I'll tell her that in the bright smiling light of her I wasn't thinking properly. I'll find a way to let her down that also makes her feel good about herself.

Twenty-six

CATHERINE

It was the right guy this time. She took the trouble to check and all she has to do now is wait. Five to ten days. The stuff has to travel to the brain, or the heart or the lungs, until it finds an important tunnel or valve, where it sits all snug, swelling gently till it blocks it. This has the predictable and deadly result and then, as the blood slows, stops and congeals in the arteries, the stuff dissolves to nothing. Efficient and undetectable and not even that expensive.

She could maybe head home now, start to get ready for Abkhazia – but that's what she did before and there turned out to have been a cock-up, so she resolves to wait. To be really sure. She feels blue though, the way she always does after an action, so she phones home but it doesn't help. It never does. Her mum witters on about her sister's kids – Harry is in the school chess team, Ruby is being a bit of a handful – but she doesn't really even ask about what Catherine is up to. She never does and hasn't really ever since Catherine joined the Army. To be fair, Catherine hasn't encouraged it, but it's still hard sometimes. Sometimes she needs a mum to be there just like everyone else does.

She goes through her yoga routine and her meditation and she does feel better, but she's still sick of this mid-priced room. Maybe she could upgrade for the last few days of her stay. A junior suite maybe, with some space to stretch out properly? She knows she won't though – she doesn't like unnecessary expense – but it feels good to know that she can if she wants.

In the end she decides that there is nothing for it. She'll have to write. She sets up the laptop and after a quick hour of eBay and FB, she gets started. The King Arthur story doesn't seem so great now that it's actually underway but her rule these days is to finish anything she starts; she has too many unfinished pieces of work already. Finally, finally, she gets going and it's hard but after a few false starts and a bit of pacing and swearing she seems to get into some kind of a groove. She gets her young heroine to the cave where she finds Arthur and the other knights sleeping, and she manages – with some difficulty – to wake them up and they are immediately waving their swords and calling for their steeds and all ready to save England from whatever disaster was afoot. War, dragons, sea monsters, ogres or green knights – they are ready to take them all on. Her heroine – now called Harriet because Heidi was too foreign somehow – has explained that she's sorry to disturb them. There is no war, there are no dragons, no green knights, but there is a nasty bully at her school and maybe – now that they are all awake – they could help deal with that if they like. Arthur and his men say they would be delighted.

It takes her about half an hour to get that scene done, and she's pretty pleased with it and so she decides to have a bit of a break, watch some TV, catch up with the news.

It's familiar stuff. Another teenage berserker howling his rage at the world in a hurricane of lead. Mothers bent double with grief, held by cops on whose body armour they then begin pounding, in whose faces they start screaming, choking, drowning in their own tears and snot. Dead children under olive-green army-issue blankets, stretchered in convoy to the ambulances whose futile lights spin feebly like those at the drab lunchtime discos of her youth.

It's Catherine's view that all this could be avoided. Give every teacher a gun to keep in their desk. Regular INSET days to make sure they know how to use it. Killer appears at the door toting his piece and bam, he goes down. Fight fire with fire.

It wouldn't always work. Maybe the whining loser would get the kids and the teacher in the first class he came to, but he'd find a whole militia blocking the corridors when he tried to move on to the next.

Seems simple. Gun control is never going to happen, so work with what's possible. It wouldn't be expensive, needn't cripple any school-authority budgets. A gun is cheaper than one of those Smart Board things they use now. Lots of teachers would probably buy their own weapons anyhow, like they buy their own textbooks.

The phone breaks into sudden spasms on the table next to the bed. Madam. She doesn't do chit or chat. She's straight to business which suits Catherine. She has news about OR. The long-awaited organisational review. She needs to talk about finessing budgets, refreshing priorities and what that will mean in practice.

'We're having to chunk up I'm afraid.'

'What?'

'We're all having to do more work. It'll be just temporary I'm sure, till they get the review sorted. But it means we'll all have to do more plate-spinning. Sorry about that.' And Madam goes on to speak about intelligent investment and redeployment pools and competitive migration, as well as all the stuff that Catherine will have to decode later to find out details of her targets and deadlines and all that.

'OK got it.'

'And we should have a real chat when you're back in London. We haven't ever had a proper one-to-one have we?'

'Look forward to it.' And then she remembers something. 'Oh, I'm taking some extended leave. When this gig is over, I'm going to see Tough. In Abkhazia.'

There is no need to tell her about it being freelance work. Madam will probably want to insist that she get written permission from HR, a signed note from the minister. There would certainly be a form and notification needed for the tax people.

Now Madam says, 'Abkhazia? Is that really a place?' And then she says, 'Tough – he was a character, wasn't he? So old school. Ancient school really.' And the way she says the word 'character' makes it sound a bit like the word wanker. And she makes it sound like Tough is dead. Catherine really doesn't like this woman.

Madam rings off. The whole call has taken two minutes and twenty-four seconds and Catherine lies back on her bed and sighs. Then she plays through her recording of the conversation, makes a mental note of the important details and puts the phone in the full basin ready for binning later.

It isn't good practice to suddenly dump new work on people, but to be honest Catherine doesn't mind. It's always nice to have real stuff to do. Sometimes this life is just too much like the Army, too much waiting around.

Twenty-seven

NICKY

The first time I am asked out: 2008 and it is my annual review. Sarah is my new line manager at the council and is discussing my personal objectives and the development plan that goes with them. I have already decided that Sarah is a big improvement on the previous senior manager in cultural services. She's a looker for a start with her autumnal hair, her translucent, speckled skin, those appraising eyes a cool hydrogen-blue and, even more importantly, she seems to find the whole business as ridiculous as I do.

'I see you've rated yourself as outstanding for every area of your work.' She can't quite keep the smile out of her voice. This is the system at the council. In negotiation with your manager you set yourself objectives and then, a year later, you rate yourself to see how you've done. Meanwhile, management also assess you and together you find a result that you can both live with.

There are only three possible rankings: Outstanding, Good and Developing. As a matter of principle I rank myself Outstanding for everything. Of course I do, because then, when the line manager negotiates me downwards it's hard for her to go all the way to Developing. We'll probably have to stop off at Good. If I think I'm Outstanding and they think I'm Developing and we both stick to our guns, then there's going to be tedious paperwork, additional interviews in the presence of our HR partner. A great big long stretch of precious flexi-time wasted over several weeks. Whereas this way we can all sort things pretty briskly.

Can you tell I've been doing this kind of thing a long time now?

And you'll want a key to the terminology: Outstanding means doing OK, while Developing means doing a bit shit. There's an alternative language in place in local government but the key that unlocks it is a simple one. Nearly everything equals shit. Developing means shit. Challenging means shit. Problematic means utterly, emphatically, impossibly shit. Though Challenging and Problematic are generally words we reserve for the general public and their insane ways.

And I'm a small cog in the council machine so it's not worth spending a lot of time working on my professional development plan with me. I'm the assistant in the cultural services team, which means I'm the one who sends out invites to private views, poetry readings, book launches and the opening nights of concerts to councillors and the local press. I maintain the cuttings file. I do a daily google search for news of any cultural events we might possibly be able to claim credit for for supporting.

And quite often it's me who has to meet the hopeful poets, writers, directors, actors, artists and musicians and explain why we can't support their lunatic projects. We can't even support worthwhile projects really. Cultural services give council-taxpayers' money to the museum and to the football team, no one else really gets much of a look in. Though we might occasionally sling a few quid to the brass band for outreach work.

Most of the time I don't mind doing this saying no business. I've done a lot of boring jobs and in every single one of those menial jobs my co-workers were all experts at something. Everyone could do something brilliantly. It just wasn't what they were paid to be doing. Even in my summer holiday job where I found myself working in the warehouse that just packed greetings cards, even there you found people who knew everything about classic cars; people who coached judo clubs all the way to black belt and beyond; blokes who could grow beautiful cauliflowers on the most unpromising of allotments; women who were champion pedigree dog breeders; men who regularly dug up Roman coins on metal-detecting weekends. You found real-ale connoisseurs. Amateur inventors, amateur astronomers, part-time magicians, Cordon-Bleu standard cooks. There was even an expert on the daughters of Coleridge and Wordsworth.

These were people who dreamt of winning the lottery, not so they could lie on a beach all day, but so they could devote more time to their true calling. One soul-grinding job, in one faceless factory, in one drab industrial zone, in one dead town, and it contained so much varied and wasted human talent. Do the math – as they say here. Multiply that solitary greetings-card warehouse by the number of other similar places. Add all the call centres and offices, all the other hives and nests where human beings toil like termites – and, well, that's a lot of experts putting their joys and expertise on hold. A lot of people kept away from their passions just so that stuff can be packed, filed, boxed, scanned, photocopied or otherwise moved from one place to another. Stuff that is shoved around for a bit, before ending up broken in a landfill somewhere where the poor live.

Work is a shit way to spend your time and everyone knows it.

And as far as I know, not one of these self-taught, self-financing, desperately self-actualising amateur experts ever went to the council to ask for a grant to pursue their dream. And yet poets, actors, novelists, directors, conceptual artists . . . Every week a pale goateed bloke comes to cultural services saying he 'just needs time to write'. Or a woman who looks like she lives on seeds comes in to ask for a grant to buy welding equipment for her sculpture project. No actual welder comes in asking the council to buy his equipment for him.

The sense of entitlement from the arty middle class is breathtaking. It's always a pleasure to PP the letters that say no to these people.

But saying no to poets is only one minor outcome as far as management in cultural services is concerned, so I have also had to come up with some objectives that specify engaging proactively with . . . Taking a hands-on partnership approach to . . . Encouraging ongoing stakeholder input in . . . Challenging myself to exceed expected competencies and organisational behaviours by . . . I can't be sure of the exact wording because I do it on autopilot one lunchtime. But I must be generally okayish at my job, because I have survived no less than five restructures.

And now I'm in Meeting Room Three in a building actually called The Hive, being gently interrogated by my hot new line manager. Who thinks of these names? Who thinks it's a good idea to call a workspace a hive, with its clear mental picture of thousands of sexless drones slaving till death for one idle fatso.

'Nicky, why are you here?'

That's the big question, isn't it? Why are any of us here? And I'm stumped, and in any case I suspect the question is rhetorical and so it proves. 'It seems to me you're a bit overqualified for what you do.'

Everyone at the council is overqualified. Even the receptionists have MAs. What she really means is – you're a bit old for what you do. And I'm sure even hinting at that is explicitly against some employment code here.

'I've got to pay the rent like everyone else.' I'm irritated, so I'm curt. But she's not fazed, she just smiles and says, 'The rent, yes. That can be a bastard, can't it?' And then we talk engagement, proactivity, outputs and outcomes, service delivery and stakeholders for our allotted twenty-five minutes and, in the end, she agrees that my work has, indeed, been outstanding over the last year.

I'm astonished, and I must look it because she laughs as she says, 'And this qualifies you for entry into our employee of the year cash draw.' She's not even joking. It turns out there really is such a thing. Huzzah! First time ever I've qualified for entry into the prize draw, the one I didn't know existed, the one where the lucky winner gets a three-day spa break while ten runners-up get vouchers for seats at the ballet. The poor bastards. And then she asks me if I'd like to grab a bite to eat.

She asks me out.

'I hear you're the office enigma,' she says. 'I want to find out all about you.'

'You mean the office weirdo,' I say and she laughs.

'I prefer enigma,' she says. 'Everyone seems to like you – no one seems to know you.'

She doesn't want to go to Pret because there are too many council people there, so we go to the Golden Fleece, though it is frowned upon for council employees to be seen in the pub at lunchtime. Apparently the taxpayers don't much like it. But not only do we go to the boozer, but she announces she needs a proper drink – 'It's been that kind of day' – so I have a pint and she has a vodka and tonic – a drink I realise can be passed off as sparkling water should any vigilante from the Taxpayer's Alliance take an interest in our order.

And, most startling of all as far as I'm concerned, she orders pie and chips. At lunchtime.

I have lived long enough to assume all girls, all women, have a dodgy relationship with food. Women are almost all semirexic. Forgive me if I generalise a bit here but women, it seems to me, have the same relationship to food that men have to pornography. They want it, they need it, they hate themselves for it and want to do it in secret after everyone else has gone to bed, or when they have the whole house to themselves.

It's as rare to find a woman who is unabashed about her appetite, as it is to find a bloke who announces to his office that he 'watched Amateur Cumshot Compilation 3 on RedTube last night. What a movie that is. A classic.'

You do meet those kinds of blokes from time to time, but not too often thank God.

And I've never understood the fear of food. Because food is not porn. Being embarrassed about eating is being embarrassed about living, isn't it?

And yet, bizarrely, there is one food group that women are not afraid of or embarrassed by. Cake. Take it from me, local government offices are mostly about flexi-time and cake. Cake comes in for birthdays, for house moves, for news of engagements, births, weddings, christenings, driving tests, kids making the cross-country team or passing grade one piano. There is no news too small that it can't be celebrated with chocolate brownies for the whole office.

Obviously though, I'm not such an idiot as to ever say any of this out loud to the women I work with. No, I eat their cakes, I bring in my own cakes. I watch them fill the minutes between slices of cake with crispbreads and low-calorie soups and I say nothing.

Anyway, that lunchtime, Sarah has pie and chips and then she has pudding. Black Forest gateau. And she doesn't apologise once. By the end of that lunch I'm already a little bit in love. And when we come back to the office she looks up at the sign over the automatic doors of our building and says, 'Council business used to go on in Town Halls, now it goes on in Hives. It's depressing really.' And she had me then. Completely.

And over the next few weeks we go out to lunch a few times. And I tell her about accidental drift. How I trained as a teacher but quickly discovered that to be a high-school English teacher in modern Britain is to be a bad comedian in a hostile club. You have to deliver your terrible material six times a day to a crowd that would rather be somewhere else. And the heckling is vicious and it never ever stops. So I left, drifted through offices, shops, factories and warehouses before washing up at the council.

She just nods. 'My sister's a teacher,' she says. 'She's looking to get out.'

And that's something I did learn in my year and a bit of teaching. Teachers – they all want to leave school. No one hates school like a teacher does. No one feels like setting fire to the bogs more than the staff. When I was working in schools a teacher in Hampshire killed a kid, battered him to death with a chair in design technology. When we heard about it my head of department said, 'One for our team.' There was a slightly more cheery atmos in the staffroom that day. It was then I knew I had to leave. The council was a safe haven. Sarah nods. She gets it.

We go to the movies. We go to the theatre. We go to the bleeding ballet. We have dinner. We kiss politely afterwards. I meet some of her many friends. I go to Sunday dinner at her parents.

Then one weekend Russell flies into London to acquire something, or liquidate something. And we go to the dog track. It's the most fashionable night out that year. He bets a ton a race. And mostly wins. He has a system. Of course he does. Russell always has a system. And it works. And he leaves £4K up. Most of which he gives to waitresses as tips. He buys £100 bottles of Krug. He talks brightly, wittily. He's a hurricane of energy and charm. He calls everyone sweetheart. He shines. At least, that's what I think.

When he gets a cab home, Sarah sighs and says, 'Thank God, he's gone. I know he's your oldest friend and everything, but I'm sorry, he is a complete arse.'

I tell her not to be sorry. To think nothing of it.

That's the night we go to bed. We go straight to bed, we don't even pause for drinks. We're both of us more than ready for it. And it's uncomplicated and fun. She sets to with an appetite – as you might expect. You know those things men and women do to and with each other? Turns out she knows them all and she loves them all. And she's happy to wait while I learn them. While I play catch-up. I wasn't exactly a virgin, but there were certainly gaps in my personal development. Gaps which Sarah identifies and makes sure I address. With her support I go from developing to outstanding pretty quickly. I think I do anyway.

She's a laugh. She really is.

On the Monday after that first night I stop off at Greggs and buy every cake in the shop for my delighted co-workers.

And six or seven months on, we're in bed at hers. A lazy Sunday, Adele on the iThing.

Sarah says, 'So . . .'

And I say, 'So . . . what?'

And she says, 'So . . . we're going out now, right? You are my boyfriend?'

And I say, 'It certainly looks like it.'

And she says, 'Good.'

And then, later, at the Shoulder of Mutton where we often go for Sunday lunch, Sarah starts again 'So . . .'

And I laugh and say, 'So . . . what?'

And she says, 'So . . . I want you to move in. And I want a baby.'

I laugh and she laughs. And she says, 'I'm going to have sticky toffee pudding and custard. Oh and, actually, Nicky, I'm not joking.'

And I say, 'Ah.'

And she says, 'Ah? Ah?'

And then she orders pudding. I don't have any dessert. I have a whisky. The house double, which is very good value.

And back at her house she says, 'Nicky, if you have regular sex with a thirty-eight-year-old woman, then you need to expect to have these conversations.'

And she tells me that if I'm not into it I have to let her know right now because she'll have time to get over me, to fall out of love with me. And then she'll need time to meet someone else and fall in love with them, to trust them enough to want to have a baby with them, and then time to get pregnant by them.

But actually I only really hear the bit where she says she'll have to fall out of love with me, because that means she's in love with me now, right? I seek and get clarification. It is, indeed, right. Right. And then she tells me I'm an idiot.

And that afternoon there is more music – Dusty Springfield this time – and there's more whisky and we make a start on a baby. And, eventually, just when we're about to do the calculations about IVF and whether we could re-mortgage the house to pay for it, we make Scarlett.

193

Babies turn out to be more complicated than love. Love is a cinch by comparison.

At first it all seems easy. At first it just seems like a happily endless stream of cake-buying obligations. I'm moving in with Sarah – there's cake. Sarah's pregnant – there's cake. We're getting married. A rush job. But time for cake, naturally.

We've had the first scan – cake. Second scan – cake. Third scan – cake. Maternity leave – cake. And suddenly there's a baby. A real-live girl-child who slides out with ridiculously little trouble or trauma. A girl as pinkly slippery as a young salmon.

We call her Scarlett. Yes, it is a lovely name, thank you. And how is she? She's gorgeous, thank you. Beautiful. Happy. Smiley. Strong-willed though. She's her mother's daughter right enough. Oh and yes, she's hemiplegic. Cerebral palsy. According to our Dr Joshi she has a neuromuscular mobility impairment stemming from an upper motor lesion in the brain as well as the corticospinal tract of the motor cortex. This damage impairs the ability of some nerve receptors in the spine to properly receive gamma amino fluid leading to hypertonia in the muscles signalled by those damaged nerves. Determined googling would seem to confirm Dr Joshi's diagnosis.

No cake.

And then Sarah goes back to work. Should mean cake surely? Then she gets a new job at the uni. That should be cake too, right? Senior Lecturer in Management, which means more money plus she has the holidays and can be at home a lot more. In the normal world, the one we've left behind, this would definitely mean cake. Double cake. Cake overload. Cake frenzy. Cake apocalypse. Only we don't feel much like cake any more.

And Scarlett walks, eventually, though with a pronounced limp – or dynamic equinus as we call it in the trade – but she doesn't start talking and so we stop too. Silence comes into our house like a thief. A professional burglar who knows where all the good stuff is kept and removes it a piece at a time so that it takes us a while to notice.

And meanwhile sympathy waits on us outside like a policeman, ready to escort us everywhere, making sure we don't get into trouble. I think sometimes that the sympathy might be worse than the silence. The policeman worse than the thief. Police and thieves. Neither are good. Neither are anything like cake.

Twenty-eight

JESUS

Jesus is in Lilith with Sarah and she is parading for him in a variety of $5,000 dresses. The best dresses. But don't think of it as a shopping trip, he tells her. Think of it as a school assignment. Today Sarah must speak Spanish only.

He thinks Sarah looks good, he can feel the air fizzing around them. He'll do it today. Today is a good day for it. But the time must be right. He must make sure she's in the right mood. A good salesman must be a psychologist, a storyteller, a lover. He must seduce and he must enchant.

They are cool the English ladies, he's heard that, but after three hours downtown in all the Latino boutiques he is certain that Sarah looks at him with a little extra heat in her eyes. A little more light.

And now here in Lilith the spark between Sarah and Jesus is making all the store clerks smile. And they don't smile easy these chicks. They are in a universe way beyond cool. But this handsome young man, this rich older lady learning Spanish for him, is like a kind of fairy tale maybe. Or a story from the entertainment papers. Even this kind of rinky-dink boutique clerk is warmed up by this. And for Jesus it feels good to be looked at like he's someone.

He makes sure they all know who is boss. No. No. Not this one. Something not quite right – neckline is wrong. And then at last – yes, yes, perfecto – that one, yes. Does you right, does you justice, brings out the azul of your eyes – the azul of your eyes and your beautiful, beautiful chichis. The girls in the shop all cover their mouths and giggle at that. Jesus includes them all in his widest smile.

'Sarah. She has beautiful . . .' He makes a shape with his hands. 'Amazing chichis, yes?' He is outrageous, but Jesus knows that women like that. A salesman must perform. He must captivate. Sarah blushes, but everyone can see she likes the fooling around. Likes to be seen as a sex symbol. Who can resist that? And the chicks in the store, they all agree, yes, she has beautiful breasts. Amazing chichis.

And later, in Latin Grill Express, Jesus makes sure to compliment her accent, her vocabulary, to express admiration for the way her chichis looked in the last dress all over again, then Sarah asks about his plans for work, what he will do when they all leave. She says he must be keen to get back to his studies, and he knows he must tell her about his business plans right now. His heart dances hard in his chest and he knows that the time is right. A salesman must know the exact time to close.

'Tees,' he says

Sarah frowns. 'Tees?'

'Yeh. T-shirts.' And he explains: high-quality American-made tees with a distinctive logo. That is his plan. That is the business to be in. To be the best in. High-grade tees with an awesome logo.

'It's the logo that counts,' Jesus says. 'Look at Superdry.' The riches from rags story of Superdry is a fable to Jesus. A legend about how to get on and get up, but he says the time is right for a new contender. Like Mary says, 'There's always room for a Pepsi.' By which she means any business has room for two giants at any one time.

'The cheapest. And the best,' said Sarah.

'Exact. You get me.'

And he goes on to tell her how maybe some markets even have room for four mega corps. Two trying to be the cheapest. Two trying to be the best.

'And people have to wear clothes. You can't digitise T-shirts.'

He claps his hands together. 'Sí.'

So then he takes a breath, makes his face all serious and asks. And she sits and takes a sip of her drink. She closes her eyes. She makes a

197

show of thinking hard and serious. And he gets that. He knows that she needs to do that, to look like it's a big decision.

And then she says no.

She says no. He can't believe it. After everything.

She says, 'Let me tell you why I'm out.' Like she is from one of those shows where tycoons crap all over the dreams of the little guys. Like she's a dragon in her shitty stinking den. And she asks him if he would have taken a bank manager to Lilith, if he would have told Donald Trump or the manager of the Chase Manhattan Bank that they had amazing chichis? Like that is relevant to anything.

She tells him that she thinks, yes, tees probably are a good business to be in, relatively easy access to the market, fewer barriers to entry for small-time operators than most industries, but she doesn't trust him to run an effective company. She doesn't think he'll take advice. She reminds him of the time they all went out and got ripped that night they first met. How he didn't listen to her.

She goes on to say that she is happy to pay for services, like the Spanish lessons, but she couldn't invest in a business on the scale he's asking. It would make her too anxious and she has too much anxiety in her life already. And she tells him some bullshit story about lending her sister money to pay her divorce lawyer and her sister getting back with her husband and spending the money on a new car. And how her sister and her don't really talk much any more.

Last of all, she tries to say she won't give him the money because she likes him too much. 'It will spoil things between us all. Between me, you, Mary, and Russell. Money and friendship – they just don't work together.'

Jesus is shocked. Does she really think they are all friends now? Just because they've been shopping? Just because Mary looks after their spastic kid? She's saying she won't help him because she likes him? That is fucked up.

And he has to smile and say of course. It's no biggie. It's fine. He understands completely.

198

He spreads his arms wide. Smiles. 'Of course, of course. I get it. Maybe I shouldn't have asked. But I just wanted you to be the first to have the opportunity to invest. Is a sure thing for certain.'

And she laughs and says that she totally got that and it was a kind thought. 'But we should definitely keep business and pleasure separate.'

And so they talk of other things, and she pays the bill and gives him fifty dollars to buy something nice for Mary. And Jesus feels a murderous rage in his stomach. A sickness right in his guts. The bitch will pay, he decides. Her and her freaky geeky dickless man. They are undeserving of their good fortune and some day soon they need to find that out.

There is a silence and Sarah tries to bring a smile back to their table, like it can all be normal again. 'One for the road?' she says, and orders Mojitos in Spanish. 'How was that?' she asks, and for a moment he thinks about telling her it was an epic fail. But this is not the time. Sure, there needs to be a reckoning, but not now.

And she tells him that she and Russell are planning to go back to Europe. 'I'm feeling homesick,' she says. 'I miss my mum. I miss my sisters. Even the one who ripped me off. I miss my friends. And I want my daughter to grow up with an English accent.'

Like that is a thing to be proud of. She wants her daughter to grow up speaking in the voice of the dead, because the UK is so over. Europe is so over. Don't these people even know that?

With Sarah's dollars Jesus buys a bottle of Jim Beam on the way home. She said buy something nice and Jesus doesn't think there are many things nicer than bourbon.

And at home as they drink he tells Mary how things have gone down, and she is as pissed as him. 'That bitch,' she says and she puts her glass down on the little table by the bed where she is lying and crosses over to where he stands in the doorway. She puts her warm arms around him. She smells milky somehow and there is a mark on the shoulder of her sweater. Drool from the goddamn kid for certain.

Jesus is still agitated, still upset. He is pacing as he talks.

He says it again. 'That total bitch.'

'Yeah, but maybe we rushed it, baby. Pushed too hard too soon. But it'll be OK.' Mary takes his hands and looks up at him and smiles that wicked smile that always makes his heart flip. 'So just hush up now. I will get your money, honey.'

'Oh yeah? How?'

'From Russell. I'll sweet-talk him.' And she presses herself against him. Now he begins to grow calm again, made soft by Mary's heart keeping time against his. Soft and hard. He closes his eyes, breathes her in. Candy, milk, smoke, and the vanilla of some discount perfume. They stand like that for a long moment.

'Or I'll do this.' She puts her hand inside his sweatpants and squeezes gently, then not so gently.

'Or I could do this.' She drops to her knees, roughly jerks his pants down over his hips. Jesus opens his eyes, looks down at her shining hair. The hair she brushes at least a hundred times every morning before she puts it into pigtails. The hair she brushes until it is as silkily golden as the sun on the mid-west wheatfields where she comes from. She grins up at him. Licks her lips and puts him in her mouth. She sucks and licks while her hand explores him. She knows what she's doing. She is good at this. She is the best. He can't let her do this with that English faggot. He pulls at her hair. And pulls harder. 'Hey,' she says. 'Hey.' She stands up rubbing at her scalp.

'You big meathead,' she says, but she is still smiling and she keeps her hand around him. 'Does it make you angry, thinking of me blowing another man?'

'Of course it does. You're my girl.'

'I'm going to do it though.'

'You think so, huh babe?'

'I do think so. Babe.' She imitates his accent. She is smirking. She is still stroking him slowly.

'You are not.'

'It'll be for you.'

'I don't care. Is a bullshit idea.'

'Makes you mad, huh?

'Of course.'

'Show me.'

'What?'

'Show me how mad it makes you.'

Afterwards she rolls a fat one and makes cups of some herbal shit. Fag's tea he calls it, though he is getting used to it now. Still, he adds a shot of Jimmy Beam to his. She tells him she loves him and that she'd never really do any of those things with Russell. He needs to know that. The guy wears a freakin' wig for a start. And she shudders. And then she smiles wickedly again and smokes and strokes his leg, and says that he should just trust in the Lord and wait. Eventually they – Russell and Sarah – will need them so much that they'll do anything they ask. Fact is, she thinks pretty soon they won't even need to ask. That kid is loving her so much right now and that if they just keep right on with what they do – just being around smiling, helpful, kind – then they will get his start-up centavos no problemo.

'Babe, is not going to work.'

'Why not? We just need to be patient is all.'

'I'm telling you. We don' have time to be patient. They're leaving. Going away. Going back to Europe.'

Mary is quiet. He can feel the gathering weight of her anger.

'Do you wanna do something? Go out somewheres maybe?'

She ignores him.

'When are they going?'

'I don't know, babe. Soon I think.'

201

'OK.' Her voice is hard. He doesn't like it. For a minute there is quiet. He can hear laughter from a TV show in another apartment. He can hear voices from the sidewalk outside. Some bullshit argument.

'So you want to hear my new big idea?' she says. He thinks maybe he does, but also that maybe he doesn't.

She kisses his chest. 'Hey, don't be like that. It'll be OK. No one will die. No one will even get hurt.' Her voice is soft again now. He relaxes. The storm has passed without breaking. She is over it. And so then she tells him her idea.

'Worth thinking about, huh?' she says. And when he doesn't say anything she takes her beautiful ass out of bed. His eyes follow her. The butterflies, the birds, the flowers, that perfect eagle that spreads majestic wings across her golden back. He can't help himself. He is lost to her. She bends and picks a pink tee off the floor. He feels a tightness in his chest. She turns to face him and holds it up in front of her. Hides those perfect breasts. It's a Superdry tee of course. And he sees all over again that it is all about the logo. He'll need an absolutely, totally awesome logo. Who does he know who could come up with something like that? But there will be someone. The world is full of artists.

'Well, what do you think?'

'Yes, pequeña. Yes.'

'Cool.' She throws the tee to him and walks to the bed slow and easy. She leans over him, so his face is inside a golden tent of her hair. She laughs. 'We are going to so kill these fuckers. Superdry, you are so over. Superdry you are toast.'

Twenty-nine

SARAH

Nicky knows most things about Russell's life, but he doesn't know this. He doesn't know about Russell standing in Sarah's office, shivering and almost naked, bottom lip stuck out like a petulant child.

He doesn't know about the gramophone. He doesn't know about the walk. He doesn't know about 'Smoke Gets In Your Eyes'.

Just after the wedding, nearly four years ago, Scarlett unfurling inside her, Sarah looked up from marking essays to see Russell already in the overheated, airless grey refuge of her office. Her private space. The place where even Nicky had only been a couple of times. Russell closing the door behind him, putting one long finger to his lips and then running a hand through his spiky crop, making it look just that little bit more roguishly tousled. It was ridiculous.

'Come for a walk,' he said.

'Russell. Bog off,' she said.

And he clapped his hands, delighted at how matter-of-fact she sounded, how unfazed she was at his being there even though he was meant to be busy stroking the lovely face of the yuan, cosying up to the voluptuous bosom of the rouble. Stomping with his bespoke shoes all over the tired face of the euro. Or vice versa.

He was very keen to get her to go for a walk and eventually, even though she was busy, even though she didn't like him much, she agreed to step outside with him. She was intrigued despite herself. She said she'd go for a bite down by the river. It's a nice day after all and they should take advantage of that.

'I have something to show you,' he said.

They walked out of the office down the careful beige of the corridor with its splashes of Manet prints on the wall. It could, she thinks, be an institution anywhere. This university corridor could just as easily be one in a hotel or a hospital or a prison. They passed some students and some staff, all of them carrying documents on drab recycled paper. Everyone nodded, everyone said hello. No one stopped for a chat.

It was five minutes to the river and they went there in silence. Russell was lugging a huge black rucksack. He was sweating beneath the weight of it, he had no breath for conversation and in any case Sarah wasn't going to ask what was inside. She was pretty sure he'd tell her when he was ready to. And she was also pretty sure she was expected to be impressed, and the thought already made her a bit tired.

As they walked alongside the embankment, the prettiest bit of town as it followed the lazy curves of the Ouse, Russell seemed to be looking for the perfect spot to stop. Quite clearly not any bench would do.

They walked for about fifteen minutes in the end, before Sarah refused to go any further. It looked for a moment like Russell would argue, but he didn't. It was nice here after all. There were willow trees and this bench was dedicated to someone's darling Jo who always liked this view.

But they didn't have to sit side by side on Jo's bench, seeing her view, because from the rucksack Russell produced a plaid rug. And he also produced plates and cutlery. Proper stuff, not plastic. He brought out rolls and pâté and ham and Belgian beer and fine French cheeses. Roquefort and Camembert. It was like a scene from *Wind in the Willows*. And he's Ratty, Sarah thought, because she knew where this was going, though of course in the book Ratty prefers boats to girls.

But Russell had another thing in his rucksack. His best thing. With both hands he hoisted out an old wind-up gramophone and he placed it on the grass. And then he fetched out records too. Brittle shellac 78s in battered sleeves. Sarah took one from him. It was hard and heavy and smelled of antique-shop dust. It was already growing warm in the sun. 'Smoke Gets in Your Eyes'.

Now he placed another record on the turntable. The air was filled with the scratchy waltz of clarinettists and the very proper RP croon of a long dead singer telling the world he'd fallen for the charms of a sweet young thing. She'd captured him magically, wonderfully, utterly. She was a jewel.

Now Russell held out his hands and Sarah sighed at the nonsense of it all, but she climbed to her feet and there, by the indifferent Ouse, in that small town on a Wednesday lunchtime, they danced. It was quite romantic, she supposed. The sort of memory that might keep you warm on winter nights in your cot in the care village when you were old. Man flies all the way to see her for a picnic and a smooch. But no.

And when he asked her – as she'd known he would – to come back to the States with him to be his girl, she looked him in the eyes for a long, long second. He closed his. Was he really expecting her to kiss him? Did he really think it was magical, wonderful, that he'd captured her utterly with an old song and a designer scotch egg? The fool.

She put her hands on his chest. She looked to the uncharacteristically open sky. It was a perfect summer romcom sky. As clear and as blue as hope. She saw all the eager ducks gathering by the bank in case there might be bread. She could give them something better than bread.

She shoved him. Hard. He stumbled, almost fell, but stayed up. Tottered on the bank, arms windmilling. Several ducks show him how it should be done as they flap away.

'Hey,' he said. 'Hey.'

'Hey is for horses,' she said and pushed him again, even harder this time, and caught him flat-footed and unprepared and he went straight into the dirty water with a satisfying splash and a decent fanfare of spray. The ducks took off hooting with what sounded uncannily like human laughter. They're a very appreciative audience. Everyone likes to see a bloke fall over backwards into water. It never gets old. Not if you're a duck. Not if you're a kid. Not if you're Sarah Fisher.

And she picked up the gramophone and threw it in after him. And after that she threw the rolls, the pâté and the ham, the plates, the knives, the rucksack itself.

'Six hundred quid that gramophone cost me.'

It was later, back in her office, Russell's clothes on the radiator filling the room with the rich scent of warm river mud, and he was under a towel moaning. Sarah always kept a towel in her office just in case. It was part of being organised, a grown-up. Other just-in-case things she had in the office included dressmaking scissors, cotton, tights, an evening dress, posh shoes and a bottle of brandy. He was sipping at a small glass of it now.

She asked him how he'd thought she'd react. He gave a hostile look like a mutinous schoolboy caught writing rude words on the blackboard.

'I want you, Sarah. I need you. I do.'

'I'm pregnant, Russell. I'm married to your oldest friend. You were the fucking best man.'

'I know. But still . . .'

'But still? You are fucking insane.'

'That wedding made me sad, Sarah. Those dweebs in cheap suits. Those fat birds getting pissed on pinot noir.'

'My friends, my sisters . . .'

'You going back to that desperate hotel for your honeymoon.' He took a swig of his drink. Made a face. The big baby. 'I just think you are worth more. I could give you more. A lot more. And the baby.' He stopped, rubbed his hand through his hair. Looked sadly at the mud and slime that had transferred from his hair to his palm. 'All the time I was doing that speech, I kept thinking it should have been me not him.'

He told her how he'd gone back to the US after the wedding, how he'd tried to settle back into his life but how she was always with him. Haunting him. Stopping him sleeping. Stopping him focusing on his work, making him think about what was really important.

'And you decided that fucking up the lives of your friends was what was really important?'

'No, I decided that happiness was what was really important.'

She sighed. She made them both a cup of tea. He asked her not to tell Nicky. She refused. Said she was definitely going to tell him. It was the first thing she was going to do when she got home. 'You just hate him being happy,' she said. 'I bet you've always tried to take things off him.'

'That's bollocks.'

'You're jealous of him.'

'I am now, yes. And it's a weird feeling.'

'I bet you've always been jealous of him.'

The last thing he said was that he always got what he wanted in the end, and she should remember that. And he squelched off in his still damp clothes, his sodden brogues. He didn't look back.

And pretty soon it all felt like a daft dream. Like he'd never really been in her office at all. And that's probably why she didn't tell Nicky. Not that night. Or the next one, and then of course it was somehow too late to say anything at all. It would look weird that she'd held back. And when the year moved on until it was time for Russell's birthday again and the tickets didn't come for the flight to San Francisco like they usually did, she still didn't say anything.

And when she saw how puzzled Nicky was when his texts and emails weren't answered – how hurt he was – she still didn't say anything. And then two, three years go past until this year the invitation does come with the usual business-class air tickets, sent as an attachment to a cheery email, just as if nothing had changed. As if there had never been a break in the birthday tradition. Nicky is really made up and Sarah hasn't the heart to say she doesn't want to go. All she says is, 'But he's just such an *arse*.'

'I know,' says Nicky happily. 'I know.'

And so now it turns out that, weirdly, Russell does get what he wants. In a way. She's going to be Mrs Knox after all. If he'd had a sense of humour he might have laughed at how things have turned out.

Rich people don't laugh much though, do they? It's one of the things they trade for jet-set perks like being able to sit close to the action at ball games, or decorate offices with original pre-Raphaelite art. Sarah is inclined to think the price is too high.

Thirty

POLLY

'Completely irresponsible.' Irina is enjoying this, Polly can tell. Righteous anger has given her a glow, some new energy. She's feeling a bit alive right now. She looks quite pretty too, which Polly has never noticed before. She should get annoyed more often maybe. 'You know poor Mr Fisher was in the taxi for over an hour. He went all over town many, many times. It cost him over twenty pounds and by the time he found his way here, he was very distressed.' She pauses. 'And, also, when he came in he woke everyone up because he couldn't work his key. Poor Stanley had to spend ages making everyone calm down.' Stanley was the caretaker/handyman who sometimes acted as a kind of concierge during the nights at Sunny Bank.

There's silence. 'What have you to say, Polly?'

'Sorry, I guess.'

'Sorry, you guess? That's it? That's all?'

'What do you want me to say, Irina?'

'I want you to say a proper sorry. And then I want you to promise me that it will never ever happen again. Also, Polly, what the fuck was Mr Fisher doing at your house? Most unprofessional.'

This is too much. 'But I'm not a professional, Irina, I'm a volunteer, remember.'

Irina purses her lips. Her eyes narrow. She doesn't look pretty any more, Polly decides. 'That's irrelevant.'

But Polly hates rows, so she says, 'Irina. I messed up. I'm sorry. Can we put it behind us? Just, you know, move on?'

She sees Irina consider this. And then reject it. 'No. Sorry Polly, but I just can't let it go. I must make an official report.'

Polly almost laughs. Who will she make a report to?

'Well, this is so serious it is almost a matter for the police, I think. It's a kind of abuse, Polly.'

Really? What, going for a pint or three with an old geezer?

'He's a grown-up, Irina. He's not a child.' She makes an effort to keep her voice soft. She keeps her eyes fixed on the carpet. The worn, dirty, dingy carpet.

'He's ill, Polly. He has a serious disease. And you went drinking with him and then you left him to get home on his own.'

Polly thinks that if she had a serious disease she might want to go drinking all the time. If she had a serious disease, then she might chase any scrap of adventure going.

'Are we done now?' This is the rudest Polly has ever been to anyone. At school she never really got in trouble. Kept her head down, tried her best. With her friends, she's a listener not a talker, certainly not an arguer. Not a fighter.

Irina takes a deep and noisy breath. 'No, not quite Polly. I think you shouldn't spend so much time with Mr Fisher. In fact maybe you should deal more with our long-term patients.'

The cabbages, Polly thinks. She wants me to babysit the cabbages. 'And I want you to be more involved in the day-to-day running of Sunny Bank.'

'How do you mean?'

'I mean, taking a turn preparing food, serving food, cleaning up. The basic stuff.'

'I'm a volunteer, Irina.'

'But still . . . you are meant to be serving others. You're not meant to be here for your own self.'

Now Polly takes a breath. 'Fuck you, Irina.'

'Fuck you too, Polly.' And so at last they are saying the things they really want to say. And Polly says she's quitting and Irina says she isn't, she's being sacked. And Polly says how can she be sacked when she is A VOLUNTEER and can't Irina get that into her thick skull? And Irina says volunteers can still be sacked and Polly says no, they can't. They can quit but they can't be sacked. And Irina says that's crap. And this goes on for a while until they stand panting, looking at each other. And Irina says, 'You know, I really liked you, Polly. I even thought you might have a future in care management.'

And Polly thinks that's a shame because I never really liked you. And you can stuff your care management. But she doesn't say anything. And Irina says, 'I feel let down.'

And Polly knows she has to say something. 'There, there,' she says flatly, and Irina looks like she's had her face slapped and Polly thinks that's good. Serves her blinking well right. But on her way out of Sunny Bank she feels a bit shit. All the anger leaves her and she feels shaky. She feels like crying and she almost turns round to go back and beg Irina to keep her on when she bumps into Daniel. He's looking very smart in a blue suit she hasn't seen before.

'Oh, hello, you,' he says. 'I hoped you'd be in. I just wanted to say thank you. I had a brilliant time the other night. Haven't had a jolly up like that in ages.'

'Really? You had a good time?'

'Yes, of course. I had a great time. Didn't you?' He sounds surprised she should even ask.

'Well, I think I got a bit drunk.'

'My dear, you were maybe the teensiest bit squiffy.'

'Squiffy?'

'OK – you were completely and utterly trolleyed. But in the most charming and amusing way. And everyone needs to cut loose sometimes.'

'But Irina . . . she said – what about getting lost?'

'Oh, well it did take a while to get back, that's true – but Roger, the cabbie chap, he was very good about it. He didn't mind really, the meter was running. Easy money for him, especially with the tip I gave

211

him. And we got here eventually. Of course, old Stan made a bit of a song and dance about it. Until I stopped his mouth with gold as well.'

'What?'

'I slipped him a few quid. He shut up sharpish then. So no harm done. No, it was a thoroughly splendid night out and I was thinking we should do it again as soon as poss. What's wrong?' He's seen her stricken face. Polly explains. She's quit. She's fallen out with Irina, she won't be back. Daniel is silent for a moment. And then he asks her to come along with him to his room, he wants to show her something.

Daniel's room doesn't look like many others in Sunny Bank. Other rooms are cluttered with overlarge furniture, knick-knacks and momentos, glass snails, pottery animals, graduation photos. Daniel's room has a single bed against one wall, a small fold-out table against another with a solitary IKEA chair tucked under it's one extended leaf. He has a TV and a battered leather armchair and that's it. There are two pictures, both slightly wobbly watercolours. Pretty good. Really good actually, but not done by a professional. Polly doesn't know much about art, but she knows proper professionals don't really use watercolours any more.

One of the pictures is of a handsome middle-aged woman smiling but in a way that seems uncertain, as if she isn't sure what's going to happen next and whatever it is, she's not sure she's going to like it. Polly guesses that the woman is Susan. The other painting is of a particularly fine-looking horse, a sheer black Murgese stallion, Polly guesses, giving the painter a frank stare. I know you, he seems to say. I know all about you.

'Who's that?' she asks.

Daniel smiles. 'Ah, now that is Mr X. I know you shouldn't have favourites but of all the horses we had, he was a bit special.'

'I didn't know you had horses.'

Daniel's smile wavers a little. 'Really? I'm sure I said.'

'Maybe you did.'

In her time at Sunny Bank Polly has discovered that one of the things about dealing with people with chronic memory problems is that you assume that it's always them doing the forgetting and the getting things wrong, when quite often it's the staff or the volunteers. People forget stuff. All people. Particularly if they weren't listening to the stuff in the first place. But she'd have remembered about the horses, wouldn't she?

Daniel's room smelt different to other rooms too. It didn't really smell of old people. It didn't smell of boiled sweets, Shake N Vac and milk. Instead it smelt of freshly baked bread. Daniel liked to make his room welcoming and so often warmed rolls in the oven. Sometimes he even ate them when they'd done their main job. If he remembered.

There was fresh air in his room too. Daniel had the window open and that was unusual in itself in Sunny Bank. Most of the residents here liked to shut themselves in, to cocoon themselves in central heating.

Polly feels oddly uncomfortable. She's been in here many times. They've played draughts and cards. They've watched the Six Nations rugby in here together. Drunk beer from cans and yelled encouragement as big men crashed into each other. Daniel taught her what a knock-on was in this very room, but now it seems to have shrunk somehow.

'Yes, I've always loved riding. So did Susan. We were members of a polo club actually for a while. But Nicky didn't like horses, he was scared of them, and then Susan got ill and with my job taking me all over the place we just couldn't keep it up. They're a lot of work, horses.'

'Tell me about it.'

'Yes, of course. You've had horses too, haven't you?'

See, he's remembered her horse stuff and he's got a hole in his head. Polly is feeling tired now and wants to be at home. A bath, she thinks. Then some time on the internet, see what's out there. Write some reviews maybe. It would be brilliant to become a top-thousand reviewer on Amazon, wouldn't it? That would be a real achievement.

'You were going to show me something.'

'Oh, yes. But now I've got you here, I'm not sure . . .' He trails off and Polly is irritated, she can't actually be bothered with this right now. She hasn't got time to be coaxing anyone.

'Oh, come on, Daniel,' but then she thinks she's been too snappy, so she says, 'I'm all intrigued now.' And she puts her hand on his arm. He seems to start, as if he'd been thinking of something else entirely and she's tugged him back into the present.

'Er, yes, right, well,' and he goes into the little kitchenette and she can see him take down a piece of paper fastened to the fridge behind a little yellow sun. A magnet, Polly guesses.

He comes back out. It is a leaflet, one that is all words and no pictures. **THE HOMECARE OPTION**. That's the headline. Polly looks at him closely as she takes it.

'Probably not practical . . .' he starts.

'Shush, Daniel, let me read it properly . . .' and she sits down on the arm of the chair.

'Gosh, you are being forceful today.'

'Sorry,' she says but she doesn't lift her eyes from the paper.

'Oh, don't apologise. I like it,' he says.

The leaflet is all about how families can earn extra money taking an elderly person into their home. It's like fostering, adoption even, but for pensioners rather than for kids. She reads it carefully and then goes over it again.

'I just thought . . .' He breaks off.

Polly looks up at him, then down at the leaflet again. She doesn't know what to say.

'Like I say, probably out of the question, but I just thought that . . .' He stops again. He smiles. 'Gosh this is hard, like asking for a date.'

Bit more than a date, but she doesn't say anything. She's thinking *Come on, Daniel, spit it out*. But she says nothing.

'You're not making this easy.'

'I'm sick of making things easy, Daniel.' And, as she says it, she knows it's true. She's always made things easy. Easy for teachers, easy for friends, easy for boyfriends, easy for her mum. Easy for her managers. She even made it easy for her dad to sell most of the horses and then fuck off with Lavinia fucking Macleod. And Lavinia had been her babysitter when she was small. And she'd always made things easy for her then too. Didn't play up. Put on her jimjams, cleaned her teeth, took the wooden hill to Bedfordshire as soon as she was told to. Put the light out and everything. Lay there in the dark listening to Lavinia downstairs fix herself snacks and drinks and then snort at *Roseanne* on the telly. Maybe if she'd been a bit more of a brat then Lavinia would have thought twice about stealing her dad. It's a possibility anyway. Polly has always made things easy for other people, hard for herself. Well, it's going to stop now.

'Yes, well . . .' Daniel takes a breath, wanders back into the kitchenette. Mumbles something.

'I can't hear you, Daniel.'

'I just said that this place costs a fortune and I'd rather give my money to people I like, that's all. And I get on well with your mum.'

'I don't know, Daniel, I'll have to ask her. I think she'll be freaked out.'

'Well she sort of suggested it actually. She gave me the leaflet anyway.'

Polly stares at the carpet. It could do with a hoover, but so could everywhere at Sunny Bank. Not really the cleaners' fault, they're just a grubby lot, the old. Always shedding bits of food, hair, teeth.

She is certain that she has to say no. She even opens her mouth to say this when Irina bangs into the room without a by your leave.

She ignores Daniel, just stands there, hands on hips, lips curling, sneering, spitting nasty words in Polly's direction.

'You still here? Leave now please. Right this minute. Or I really will call the police.'

Polly sighs. But at least that's a decision made for her. 'Come on then, Daniel,' she says. 'Your stuff won't pack itself, will it?'

And so that's Irina nicely stubbed out.

Thirty-one

NICKY

We are lounging separately on our absurdly super-sized sofas, the pink one for Sarah, the electric-blue one for me, and we are watching sport. For those with time on their hands televised sport is a total boon. I never much liked sport as a kid. My dad did, so that might be why it never appealed to me. Rugby, that was his big thing.

I did get into Test cricket as a student. But that's not really sport as such. Five days of not very much ending in a draw. It's like contemporary experimental theatre more than anything. I've always been drawn to an absence of drama I think. Even in drama. Consider my favourite playwright after Shakespeare – Beckett. The man with the most inventive ways of saying and doing nothing. Only trouble with Beckett is that the plays aren't long enough. Test cricket at its best is five days of Endgame and what could be better than that? Russell liked sport. He liked it all. Motor racing that was his favourite. F1 on the muted telly. Punk rock on the stereo. Cider in his hand. Bilkofest still to come in the evening. Russell's perfect Sunday back in the day.

But now when I myself am running, jumping, skipping, jabbing, bobbing, weaving, squatting, pulling, pushing, pressing, lifting and stretching a lot of the time – and then resting – I find I'm becoming increasingly tolerant of sport. Especially American sport. Everything about sport here is such a big production. The plays, the uniforms, the commentary, the ad breaks. To watch American sport is to see the way the whole empire thinks and moves. Want to know about American morality? American politics? American business? Watch baseball.

Right now I'm not watching baseball. I'm half-watching the group stages of the Beach Volleyball World Cup but not thinking about sport, morality, politics or business. I'm thinking about love and I'm thinking about railways. They go together, don't they? Specifically, I'm thinking about InterRail and I'm thinking about my first big love. Unrequited naturally. I'm thinking about Caroline Dawson. Lorna's mum.

In 1985 a hundred quid would buy you a rail ticket that gave you a month's unlimited travel on Europe's rail network. It was the summer after our first year at the college, I had some money saved from the job at the card place, Russell had his student overdraft facility, and we both had a burning desire to be somewhere that wasn't Bedford. In particular I had a burning desire to be somewhere where my dad wasn't.

It would be fair to say that me and my father have never got on. I worshipped him as a kid, but he wasn't very good at hiding his disappointment in me. I was a shy and nervous child and my dad didn't really do shy or nervous. Didn't get it. My dad could get by in any of half a dozen different languages. See him in an Indian restaurant and he'd be doing banter with the waiters in confident Bengali. We were always getting extra side dishes.

He'd give it a go in Santanello's pizzeria too, serenading the harassed waitresses in booming sing-song cod-Italian. Like he was in an opera called Mr Fisher Orders A Margherita. Prepared to embarrass us all for extra garlic bread. The language of Shy, however, the dialect of Nervous, these were tongues he didn't speak and wasn't about to attempt.

So, yep, when I was a little boy he was away a lot and I used to miss him and then he'd come back and I used to get nostalgic for the ache of missing him. Of course I couldn't articulate it like this then. Then, I was just confused. And, later, when I was an adolescent, he wasn't away so much and he and his opinions took up every corner of the house. I kept bumping into his views on the EEC, or the miners. Tripping over his thoughts about Northern Ireland or lenient judges in the hallway. Squeezing past his position on the miners' strike or modern pop music on the stairs.

A very tidy man in most ways, he scattered his attitudes, positions and sentiments like a careless picnicker scatters crisp packets. And in the end all this litter spoilt the view.

So when Russell suggests going to Greece by way of Amsterdam, Munich, Vienna, Belgrade, and more or less every other major rail terminus in Europe, I jump at it. Of course, it isn't just about my dad, there is the hope of adventures too. I'm twenty after all. God knows I'm ready for some.

They don't even have to be big adventures. Athletic Swedish adventures. Severe German adventures. Moody French adventures. Breezy Australian adventures. Generous Dutch adventures. The pale fire of a Scottish adventure. Even a nerdy English adventure maybe. An adventure whose drama is hidden behind librarian specs and a liking for Virginia Woolf. That'll be OK. That'll be a big enough adventure for me. A sound return on my investment. And I'm hoping my own complete fluency in Shy will eventually count for something, somewhere. Get me into a tight spot or two. Perhaps abroad, talking books with serious girls, Shy could translate as Enigmatic.

And it is true that there are a lot of girl-shaped adventures. They just don't happen to me.

We could call that InterRail tour 'Confessions of a Wingman'. And I'm not even a wingman to a real, live flesh-and-blood human being. I'm wingman to a haircut. I get to watch as Russell's Duran Duran hair woos and wins backpacking girls in sad cafes right across Europe. My role turns out to be to make Russell and his hair seem less threatening, more normal. To sit and radiate comforting ordinariness, making small talk with the companions of the girls Russell's hair is doing its number on.

And it absolutely must be the hair that does the wooing because the 1985 vintage Russell Knox has a very limited supply of chat. Some very ropey material. In the shopping mall of banter Russell's is very definitely a Soviet-era store. Not much in the way of choice and all of it packaged in a stark, brutalistic style. All he stocks is heavy-handed piss-taking, mainly of me, but also of the accent and perceived national characteristics of whichever country the adventures come from. So the Scottish girls are miserly, the Australian girls are uncouth, the German girls are efficiently authoritarian, the Swedish girls are efficiently promiscuous and so on.

And yes, he gets told to fuck right off. Maybe twice this happens. He even gets laid out rather than laid by one Aussie girl rebutting her own resemblence to national stereotype in somewhat ambiguous style. But mostly it gets him where he wants to go.

And yes, I know it wasn't just the hair really. It was also the insanely unjustified self-confidence, though one of the girls did tell me it was also the dreamy curl of the eyelashes. But no one fucks someone just because they have nice eyelashes do they? Maybe they do. Or maybe they did then.

Lorna Dawson might not be the only child Russell has. There could be other kids from other girls seduced by peacocky hair, bad jokes, and those goddamn eyelashes. And if there are other progeny, there's a good chance they'll all be beautiful and all filled with the restless light of the driven and dissatisfied.

And I think about Lorna's mum. The quiet and lovely Caroline. The girl Russell's Casanova hair left behind on the platform at Bedford Midland.

I met her first. A course on the romantics. Blake, Keats, Byron, Coleridge, Wordsworth and the Shelleys – all of them recollecting experience in tranquillity, defecating into pure transparency. Generally laying down the blueprint for every scene that came after. All the white ones anyway.

The alliances, the betrayals, the grand statements and gestures. The adventurous, incestuous sex. You Young British Artists, you neo-folk kids, you Brit-poppers, you grungers, you punks, you angry young men, you Beatniks, you Bloomsburys, you pre-Raphaelites, all you brotherhoods, all you movements – you owe all your attitudes and ways of carrying on to the guys with the daffodils and the sick roses.

That was the sort of thing Caroline would say as we sat on plastic orange seats in the refectory after class. And then Russell would join us and she would shut up, stop being interesting and entertaining and knowledgeable and instead look at him – at his eyelashes and hair – while he spoke. And I would sit and say not very much and concentrate on watching her watching him. I would watch the truth behind the word 'crush'. A person bewitched in this kind of a way becomes so much less than they are, so much less than they could be. Flattened. Squashed. Crushed.

Caroline. She liked her beer in pints. She could play a mean game of pool. She could play piano. She could roll a fag with one hand. And her major was in modern languages – just think how huffy the Shelleys would have been if they'd known they were only a minor – and she would have been hugely helpful with the many *bitte, wo ist das bahnhof*-type situations we found ourselves in that summer.

Taking Caroline along might have negated the mesmerising effects of the hair I suppose. There was a chance those beguiling eyelashes would have had their style cramped. Even the Swedish girls don't usually like getting off with someone while their regular girlfriend is watching.

And when we come back for our final year Caroline has left. Dropped out to do some paralegal thing in London. She doesn't leave me her address.

I often wonder about her over the years, but Russell just shrugs when I mention her. Easy come, easy go he says, but he really liked her. I know he did. Everyone did. She was a bit like Sarah in that way actually. They looked a bit the same too. Pale, freckled, clear-eyed. Sometimes caught smiling at secret jokes that they won't ever tell.

Yes, Caroline Dawson, she would be the kind of girl to keep a pregnancy quiet. A good sport.

I'm trying to think if there was any time after that InterRail trip when I actually liked Russell. I'm thinking maybe there wasn't, not really.

And then I wonder if maybe I need an eyelash architect. I don't want to be undone by a detail like that. Tripped up at JFK because my eyes don't look sad and soulful enough. That would be shit.

A latte-coloured supermodel spikes the volleyball over the net and directly into the face of one of her opponents, who falls to the sand. The crowd roar approval.

'What are you thinking?'

Ah, Sarah's employing the four most loaded words you can have in a long-term relationship.

I counter them with the three most important.

'It doesn't matter.'

'No, really. What are you thinking.'

'No, it really doesn't matter.'

And on we go like that for quite an irritating while before I cobble something together that I can share.

'You really want to know? I'm thinking that we've all this money but we don't seem to be having much fun yet.'

On the screen the supermodel scores another devastating point and high fives various other beauties. This is Brazil versus Switzerland and the Swiss look dejected. Not much of the spirit of William Tell about them. But then they don't even have beaches. They're very much the underdogs here. They shouldn't feel bad. And the Brazilians own this sport. Brazil is on the way up generally. If you want to see what the new world order will look like don't watch baseball, watch beach volleyball. The girls are in, the men are out. The northern hemisphere is done: the south is rising.

There is a pause, and then Sarah says, 'No, we're not exactly having fun. We're not exactly happy, but at least we're miserable in comfort.'

I smile at this but tell her that I'm not all that comfortable actually. Not really. I hurt and I'm hungry.

'Well, maybe we should start the big trip,' she says. 'Maybe you've done enough. But I was thinking we might start in England, if you didn't mind.'

England? That grey and sodden place? That cantankerous old git that keeps moaning on about the good old days? Yes. Yes please. Let's go there.

Sarah says, 'I miss it. I miss my family. I miss our friends. Just a couple of days and then we'll go anywhere else you like. It's just that Mum worries about me. I'd like to reassure her.'

'All mums worry, don't they? If they're doing their job properly, I mean.'

'I guess. But she wants to see her granddaughter too.'

Yeah of course she does. And who are we to stop her?

It occurs to me that I should feel quintessentially Californian now, in a way. I've reinvented myself. Hell, I've even had work done. I push my hand through my hair. Feels good. More than this, it really does feel real. Even better than the real thing. I should love it here now, but I don't. I feel like I'm in a prison. A sunshiny prison and there's the Russell problem, the way he's in the walls somehow. In the very air con. But then maybe he'll always be with us now. Wherever we go.

The big problem is Scarlett. I know we're both worried about moving her.

I'm the one to actually say it. 'What about Scarlett?'

And Sarah says, 'I know. All this – it was for Scarlett. But . . .' She leaves the sentence hanging, she chews her lip.

'And it's sort of working, isn't it?' I say. 'I mean, look how happy she is. And she's speaking, Sarah. She's flipping well talking.'

'She's said the word badass.'

'And awesome. And oh my actual god. You can get a long way on that. Especially here. If she learns to say dude and what the fuck she'll have the entire vocabulary of a typical American teenager. She'll be a straight-A.'

Sarah doesn't laugh. Why should she? Because it's not really true, is it? In truth I find American youth incredibly articulate when they want to be, though I only have Mary to go on. Oh, and reruns of golden-age comedies like *Happy Days* and *Saved By The Bell*, both of which are secret pleasures when I come back knackered after a work-out and there's no decent sport on TV.

Now Sarah says, 'You don't worry that she's liking it a bit too much? That she's getting too attached to Mary and she won't be able to cope without her? You know when we move on, or when Mary does.'

And I have thought about this. Scarlett is growing obsessed with Mary. She wants to be her. Sarah has been buying her tons of new stuff, just as she said she would, and yet we find Scarlett shuffling around in Mary's cast-off pumps, carrying her old purse, cramming paperclips in her mouth to try and replicate her babysitter's dental scaffolding. Walking around with her ukulele the way she used to go around with Spot the Dog. Mary is Scarlett's role model. Her mentor.

'It's hard to know the best thing, isn't it?' I say. 'But you're sure leaving here is the best thing?'

'Of course I'm not sure,' Sarah says. 'Only idiots are sure and certain about things. Look at Russell.'

And it's true. Russell was always more or less doubt-free. It's one of the things people liked about him. And not just girls. It was how he got people to do stuff for him. He always seemed certain of the direction of travel. People crave certainty and love those who seem to have it. Surprising when you think how those people have screwed it up for the rest of us over the centuries. The history of certainty is the history of genocide. Doubt has, on the whole, been involved in far less mass murder. Far fewer pogroms. Doubt may not get you very far, but sometimes here is the best place to be anyway. I don't understand why more people don't embrace doubt, when it generally works so much better than the alternative.

And so many good things turn out to be the result of accidents or mistakes. Penicillin and Cadbury flakes. Kelloggs cornflakes and Post-it notes. America itself is an accident. The result of an idiot thinking he'd discovered a short cut to Samarkand. While nuclear weapons are the product of brainboxy doubt-free kids conducting successful science experiments.

Yes, fucking up often turns out to be the best thing long term. We should all of us be more relaxed about mistakes I think. Mistakes often save us from something worse. Often much, much worse.

The power of doubt and the virtue of fucking up. I can't believe no great religions have been founded on these precepts. If I wasn't minted already, maybe that's what I could have done. Started the Church of Self-Doubt and the Immaculate Mistake. Maybe I'd have got a little business start-up loan from the government.

So I have my doubts about going, and I have my doubts about staying, but I do know I want to get away from this house. This place that refuses to become a home, this building which I am convinced despises me.

My phone chirrups. These days I have the best phone money can buy. Sarah and Jesus took a long time choosing it. I'm told it does a lot of things. You could, if you wanted, make a blockbuster movie with it. Really. On this phone you could write it, shoot it, edit it, compose and record the score and finally project it in shinier than life widescreen gorgeousness at the nearest wall. You could dub it into any major language and several of the minor ones. You could work out the budgets on it. Draw up all the contracts on it, find the private cellphone numbers of your chosen Hollywood stars on it. People have.

And you could, if you wanted, snooze on your flight to the premiere at Cannes, knowing that the phone could land the plane should the pilot have a heart attack.

Everything is on your phone now. No need even for the ancient clutter of desktop or laptop. And this despite the fact that we all of us know that our hard drives aren't safe. That at some point in the near-ish future a hard, driven soldier in a crack Chinese Special Cyber-Ops Squad is going to stab a finger at his own Smartphone screen and wipe all our information about everything in less than a nanosecond.

Or the Taliban will shoot down a satellite with a well-directed beam from a laser-pen, causing a lot more havoc than 9/11. Planes into buildings? No, no my friend – so crass, so old, so vulgar, so noughties. Not like a nice clean utterly contemporary blue screen of death.

Or maybe it'll be an anti-climactic ending. Maybe it'll just be the bathos of Microsoft and Google finally overreaching themselves and everything from birth registration to death certificate via school reports, medical records, bank statements, payslips, driving licences, and criminal convictions will simply vanish. Not to mention books, plays, films, parish council minutes – the whole history of human record-keeping and communication will be deleted into nothingness. Upgraded into a black hole from where no amount of system restore will bring it back.

We all know this, which is why Parliament even now keeps a copy of all its laws on vellum. When it comes to the laws of the land not even paper is trusted to last long enough, but for everything else there is chip and there is pin. The handy little plastic smart thingamajigs with screens to touch and buttons to press. As a species we like pressing buttons. We like touching things. We're good at it.

But as a species we're also careless, sloppy.

So it might, in the end, be a pushed button that brings about the end of the world. Just as we knew it would be. But it turns out it won't be the big red one of cold-war nightmares – nothing as dramatic as that – instead it might be a chirpy wee graphic of a button that gets accidentally sat on in a works canteen in a light industrial unit somewhere on the edge of Shenzhen. It won't be Dr Strangelove that finishes us off, it'll be a sleepy, overworked geek trying to archive the history of porn on his new tablet during the long, lonely nightshift. We'll be undone by a pocket call.

My phone is so futureproof, so resolutely advanced that it seems almost quaint that you can also make calls and send texts should you be into that retro kind of caper.

This cheerful cheep-cheep turns out to be a text from Polly, the girl at Sunny Bank. It says: *Just thought I should say your friend's dad is now my lodger! How weird is that?*

'Very fucking weird,' I say to the phone.

'What?' says Sarah.

'It's my dad's care home,' I say, 'Sunny Bank. The old bugger's done it again. Got some bird to wipe his arse for him.' And I type '????'

'No kiss?' says Sarah. She's moved so she's looking over my shoulder.

'I don't put kisses. Not on texts to strangers.'

'If you don't put a kiss these days it looks rude. There's been rampant endearment inflation in the last few years you know. You should probably put two. Or three.'

Really? Sometimes I can't tell if Sarah is messing with me. She just laughs and then Mary is in, telling us that our gorgeous daughter is ready for her story.

Sarah and I take it in turns to read to Scarlett. It is the favourite time of day for both of us. Scarlett smelling deliciously of baby shampoo and talc, murmuring nonsense, her thumb snugly slotted into her mouth as though thumbs and mouths were designed to go together. Which maybe they were. Maybe thumb-sucking is a normal feature of human development which we, in our cruel and unnatural way, frown at and discourage. By 'we' I mean this cold, utilitarian world we live in, not we as in me and Sarah – because here in Nicky-and-Sarah World it is frowning that is frowned upon and discouragement that is discouraged.

And even though she's only three, even though she's more or less mute, she has taste. Our Scarlett is proper old school when it comes to literature. Scarlett likes verse. It is rhyme and it is iambic, or it is nothing. So she'll accept *The Gruffalo* naturally. She will sigh with appreciation at *The Snail and The Whale* too. But her favourites are darker hued than this. As long as there are pictures then she loves literary derring-do. Sabres gleaming. Cannons roaring. She loves flashes and bangs. Tennyson's gallant 600 charging the Russian guns. The Highwayman with his dash and his finery. The section where the highwayman comes across the moor using the road that's a ribbon of moonlit, tlot-tlot-tlotting on his horse. That, my friends, is our Scarlett's very favouritest line out of the whole history of literature. Sometimes I have to repeat all the tlot-tlots several times.

I like to think she doesn't quite get all the sexual heat of the girl with her finger on the trigger – the landlord's black-eyed daughter whose violent suicide warns her lover of the ambush of redcoats at the inn – but who knows? They grow up so fast these days.

And I'm here to tell you there is an advantage to reading to children who can't talk. There are no annoying questions to answer.

In 'The Highwayman' our tragic heroine is undone because she has spurned the love of the ugly old ostler, but I've never had to explain what an ostler is or how exactly you ostle, never mind why the landlord's black-eyed daughter is prepared to top herself for love of a car jacker – because that's what the highwayman is, no matter how fancy the clothes.

It's usually me that does the old-school stuff. Tonight I think Sarah's doing *The Hungry Hen*, a tragic morality piece where a fox watches and waits until the hen he's had his eye on is fat enough for him to eat. Only he waits too long, and by the time he makes his move the hen is not only strong enough to fight him off, she's big enough and ravenous enough to eat him up. In one gulp. A lesson in carping the bloody diem if ever there was one. Don't wait while your enemies prepare, strike while they're weak. Kick them when they're down. Kicking your enemies when they're down would seem to be the absolute optimum time to do it.

Another fragment of exotic birdsong. I read the message: *You should see how much better he's doing here xx.*

I bet. And she's right. I should see. England it is then. And then Everywhere. And then Anywhere, just as Russell planned.

And I notice that Polly's seen my one kiss and raised it another one. Maybe Sarah is right about the inflation in this area. So, while Sarah makes Scarlett giggle with her hen voices and her fox voices, I pop the question to Mary.

'Ah, Mary. How do you fancy seeing my sceptred isle?'

She looks at me, uncertainly, her innocent eyes looking troubled. She is perhaps wondering if I've made an indecent proposal.

'Do you want to have a butcher's at my other Eden, my demi-paradise? Take a wander around our precious stone set in a silver sea?'

'I'm sorry, what?'

'Do you fancy meeting up with that most happy breed of men?' I can't keep it up any longer. 'Do you want to come to England with us?'

'Get out of here! Russell, are you serious? England? Like the UK?'

'All expenses paid plus per diems. A per diem is—'

'I know what a per diem is.' She grins metallically. Her pigtails shake from side to side. She gives me the full radiance of her butter-milk face. 'Thing is, Russell, can Jesus come too?'

I think about this. And oh, what the fuck, why not?

'Of course.'

I've never seen a person look so delighted and she practically hurls herself into my arms. I'm distracted, attempting to reply to Polly's last text and she squeezes so hard that I lose my balance toppling back onto the sofa, she lands on top of me, perky all-American breasts in my face and we're all tangled up, but sorting ourselves out, laughing, embarrassed, when Sarah comes back in. She arches an eyebrow.

'Just told Mary the good news,' I say.

'And what good news is that?'

'About us all going to England.'

'Sarah, thank you like a million. It's just so, so awesome. I'm totally beyond thrilled and Jee is going to so freak!'

She calls him Jee? I wonder if the disciples did that to the original Jesus? Hey Jee, great work healing the old sick today. Hey Jee, the thing you did with that Lazarus guy, like totally awesome, man. Way to go.

Sarah submits to a more restrained hug from Mary – little in the way of squeezing and certainly no toppling her over, falling onto her, tits right in Sarah's face. None of that. But then mothers and child-minders always have an uneasy relationship, don't they?

And, later, when Mary is safe back home with Jee, Sarah and I have a tense tête-à-tête.

And I tell her what I think, which is that across the whole world everyone is living just slightly beyond their means – except us. Teachers, rock stars, yak herders, tea pickers, Apple assembly line operatives, High Court judges, policemen – everyone worrying. Everyone feeling that the last week before pay day lasts a whole lot longer than all the other weeks of the month put together. But not us. Not now.

We're not like the common herd. Our every step is feather-bedded, cushioned, smoothed and soothed. Or could be. Taking Jesus and Mary to England, putting them up, feeding them, clothing them, buying them tickets for the London Eye and *We Will Rock You* – how much is it going to cost really? We could buy them each a house and not notice. A nice house. A London house. A Hampstead house. Each.

'It's only money, love,' I say. 'And Scarlett'll be pleased. And it was you that wanted to go back to England anyway. What's the problem?'

'It's just too much, Nicky. Too complicated.'

'They're just employees, Sarah. Staff. All rich people have staff who look after their stuff. Nothing could be more ordinary or more normal than servants.'

'I'm not sure those particular servants are all that normal.'

'Oh look, it's done now. I can't uninvite them.'

'No you can't. I guess. But it worries me, Nicky. I've got a bad feeling about it.' And then she gives me the real reason. The obvious one. The one I should have guessed at.

'I was looking forward to being a proper mum again, Nicky. I was looking forward to it being me who did the worrying about Scarlett.'

And I get that. But it'll be fine. I'm sure it'll be fine.

And it'll be good to have Mary as back-up just in case Scarlett continues to favour the second best kind of love.

I go and check on our baby. I do this from time to time, just go and look at her sleeping. Wondering at a life that comes from nowhere and changes everything you think and everything you do.

Scarlett is not asleep, she's doing something complicated with two of her Sindys. Sindys, not Barbies note. This is a deliberate choice on my part. Sindy is British and much more demure and well brought up than Barbie, who seems like a brash, oversexualised gold-digger if you ask me. The sort of girl who would marry a minor Rolling Stone. Even in her air-hostess uniform she looks like a hard-eyed little pole dancer. And don't get me started on the Bratz. At least Sindy looks like she might have some GCSEs.

Scarlett glances up, puts the dollies down and holds out her arms. I give her a hug and then sit on the edge of her bed telling her that she ought to be asleep now, which is a bit rich I know, seeing as I've come in completely heedless of whether she was asleep or not. But I had a sudden urge to see her little face which, if you're a parent, you'll completely get.

I get up to go and Scarlett shakes her head. So I sit down and talk some more – just blether – and then I get up again. And she shakes her head again. And I sit down again and talk again. And on it goes. For about an hour. And when I do go, I leave her crying and Sarah goes in to comfort her, shooting me a frankly hostile look as she does so. And she's in there another hour. Then it's my turn again. And I'm about to phone Mary and fuck paying her the earth to come to England, I'll pay her a million bucks just to come over from Protrero Hill, when Scarlett suddenly collapses into sleep.

When I come back into the living room Sarah is watching women's tennis from Dubai or somewhere. She is also stuck into the fifty-year-old Scotch. Not her first glass by the looks of things.

'Job done,' I say. 'Finally.'

'It was a job we never needed to start,' she says, which is a fair point. I don't say anything, just head for the fridge because I've noticed that it is protein shake o'clock.

Then she says, 'You know that Jesus totally wants to shag me.'

Her eyes don't leave the screen. The grunts and gasps of the players sound oddly sexual now she's said that. What am I meant to say? I know I'm in a minefield here. She's already pissed off about my disturbing Scarlett. She's already pissed off about my asking Mary and Jesus to England. And she might be quite drunk. I'm not just in a minefield. I'm in a minefield while actually sitting on a ticking bomb wearing a suicide vest. Best go careful, but what can I say? And, of course, my nerves are also jangled from what we've gone through. I just wanted to watch my kid sleep for fuck's sake.

I say, 'That's nice, dear.' And tense myself for the bomb going off. Drunk, Sarah can produce a fully authenticated Celtic temper to go with the hair. But this bomb is a dud and fails to explode. She just sighs. And on the telly some Swedish teen prodigy explodes instead, rocked by an orgasmic spasm as she achieves an impossible cross-court volley.

And suddenly I find myself telling Sarah about being asked out by the jogger, Catherine. And I tell her about agreeing to go for coffee. And I tell her about phoning to cancel the date. And to all of this she says nothing. Which is not an especially good sign, though the game between the Swede and her Venezuelan opponent, a veteran of the tour at twenty-five, does seem to be a particularly prolonged and fascinating one – lots of deuces – so it might just be that.

'Do you want to have sex with Jesus?' I say eventually, a sentence that sounds wrong on so many levels.

She waits until the point is over and the crowd cover themselves in whooping and applause and the commentator declares it to have been the rally of the tournament, possibly of the year.

'Not really,' she says.

Not really is not no, is it? Not really sounds quite like yes.

And we sit in silence while the plucky Swede is now comprehensively demolished by the savvy veteran, that cross-court volley proving to be the very pinnacle of her game, a golden age at sixteen that lasted a microsecond and yet is now the place to which all her memories will return. She'll be watching holographic reruns of that shot over and over in her dotage, in whatever version of Sunny Bank lies awaiting her in her future.

And now the Venezuelan destroys her as though that volley was a grotesque personal insult that must be avenged. Our Swede doesn't win another point. Clearly, it is not a day for giant-killing. Not in the world of televised games anyway. In that world the giants can all sleep safe. And these are southern hemisphere giants too. Giants going places.

And I wonder how I feel about Jesus's designs on my almost-wife. Should I feel flattered? Should I feel enraged? Should I call the jogger and cancel my cancellation? Get my retaliation in first. It's surely what Brazilian beach-volleyball players would do. What champion tennis pros would do. What life's winners would do.

I'm at a loss here; before the money we never used to have this spiteful sort of interlude. Not even in the angry, grieving, sighing weeks after Scarlett was born. What to do? Should I reclaim my place in my almost-wife's heart by making furious love to her. Is that what I'm meant to do? I could try that. I'll try that.

I cough. 'So, Missus. Fancy having a bit of a cuddle? Celebrate going back to dear old Blighty?'

On the telly they're doing post-match analysis. That cross-court volley varispeeded and from all sorts of angles. And the girl crying at the end, suddenly looking six not sixteen, while the cruel Venezuelan punches the air from the other side of the net.

'Not really,' says Sarah. Which is a relief in a way, because it does mean that not really can still mean no.

At least it can sometimes.

Thirty-two

POLLY

It is a cool September afternoon and, on Daniel's orders, Polly is picking blackberries, so that he can make jam. It's chilly now but it's been a good summer generally and the bramble bushes along the lanes behind her house are groaning with fruit. It's hard work getting it all, but she's enjoying herself. She's already filled three old carrier bags and now she's on to her fourth and last. She's also eaten loads. She wants to get a wriggle on though, because it definitely looks like it's going to rain. She's just got her fingertips to a particularly dense clump of berries hidden deep in the midst of the brambles when her phone goes.

It takes her a while to answer, what with having to struggle out of the thorns, put her basket down, fumble with gloves and the zips on the pocket of her parka and the phone is never in the pocket you think it is, is it? And of course by the time she has located it and pressed the button, the music has stopped. She calls back though, and it's the man himself.

'Hello?' Daniel sounds cagey, suspicious. He also sounds oddly echoey.

'Daniel, it's me, Polly.'

'Oh hello, poppet. How are you?'

'I'm fine. I've picked loads.'

'Goodo. Loads of what?'

'Blackberries – for jam.'

'That's a good idea. I used to make blackberry jam you know. Every year.'

'I do know, Daniel. You said you were going to do it this year too. That's why I've been out picking the sodding things.'

'Well I will then. Yes, definitely. I'll do that. Jam. Yes.' There's a pause.

'Daniel. You know I'm returning your call, don't you?' Another pause.

'Yes. Absolutely, of course.' Another pause.

'So, er, why did you call me?'

A sigh. And a strange gurgle. Daniel trying to gulp a bit of brightness into his voice. She can hear him engage that gear.

'Well I guess it might be because I seem to have got myself into a bit of a jam myself actually. Or a pickle maybe. Yes, perhaps more of a pickle than a jam.' And he laughs, but not convincingly.

'Daniel, that's lame even for you.'

'Lame. Yes. And that's the thing. I've, er, I've been having a bath. Good long soak, you know and now, well . . .'

'Well, what Daniel?'

'Well,' a deep, deep sigh and then a rush. 'Thing is, I'm lying here in the bathroom, legs akimbo, just a little bit awash in my own blood I'm afraid.'

'Daniel!'

'I was getting out of the bath, and I seem to have slipped, cracked my head on the sink maybe. A bit.'

'Oh God. Where's Mum?'

'Out, I guess. Anyway I don't actually seem to be able to get up. It's lucky I left my trousers on the floor with my phone in the back pocket.'

'You can't get up?'

'Head's a bit bloody sore, you know. Hip's a bit bloody sore too, but I think I'll live. It's just the old standing up thing that is proving problematic.'

'You should call 999.'

'Good heavens, no need for that. I'll just get my breath back and have another go at this getting vertical malarky.'

235

'Daniel, stay where you are. I'll come straight back.'

'Good girl. And, Susan?'

'It's Polly, Daniel. Polly.'

'Of course. Absolutely, yes. But Polly, don't call an ambulance or anything mad like that.'

'OK, Daniel.'

'I just think that once I'm in hospital I won't be coming out.'

'I said OK, Daniel. See you in a minute.'

'Don't forget the blackberries.' She clicks off. Blow the blinking blackberries she thinks, and then finds she's staring straight at a naked man.

He's about three metres away and she recognises him immediately. The Naked Hiker. Or the Starkers Trekker depending on what paper you read.

Of course he's not entirely naked. He's wearing thick hiking socks and walking boots and his tanned and wiry chest is criss-crossed by the straps of his rucksack.

'Hello,' he says.

'Hello,' she replies and of course she can't help herself, her eye is drawn to the thick bush of hair at his crotch. She has time to notice that the hair there is flecked with grey. Who knew that you could get salt-and-pepper pubic hair? And she also notices that his penis is substantial. Flipping heck, it's like a baby's arm. And it's as tanned as the rest of him. Well, of course it would be. She jerks her eyes back up to his face. He's looking at her sadly, as if to say that he expected better of her.

She feels oddly ashamed.

'That's a lot of berries,' he says. And, suddenly shy, she just nods and then he asks if he can have some. He says that he's been picking his own but it's hard without clothes and he smiles and comes closer and shows her the long and vivid scratches on his arms. And now Polly can feel the first drops of rain on her face and she thinks that surely most things are harder without clothes, and maybe he

236

should have thought of this before. She picks up a full carrier and holds it out open in front of her and the naked hiker takes it, spends some time rummaging in it choosing the fattest and the ripest. Polly is a bit irritated by this. Surely, it's good manners just to take a handful, not ensure you get the pick of the crop? Plus he must be bruising and squishing the ones he doesn't pick. But then she thinks about what he's gone through and tries not to let it get to her.

After all, here is someone who has actually achieved something. Someone who has been more or less tortured in order to win rights for the rest of his fellow countrymen. Even if his fellow countrymen have shown little enthusiasm to exercise those rights, he's still kind of a hero.

For years the naked hiker had strolled around Britain dressed only in these stout walking boots, these socks and this rucksack, risking both chafing and mockery in his quest to make the nude human body acceptable in public.

At first the authorities had turned a blind eye. And then he trekked nakedly into a zealously buttoned-up part of Scotland and they'd taken to locking him away from view.

They'd arrest him, sentence him to a few days in jail, then release him. He'd walk out of the prison naked, so they'd arrest him again immediately and sentence him to a slightly longer term. All served in solitary of course, lest the other prisoners be upset by the sight of a free willy. He even had to go to the showers on his own.

It had become a battle of the kind she guessed parents got familiar with when dealing with a wilful toddler. It didn't matter how many times they took the naked hiker to the naughty step or how often they confiscated his toys, he was not going to give in. And in its quasi-parental role, once it had decided to notice, then the state couldn't give in either. What message would it send to the rest of the properly sensibly clothed population? He had to be grounded until he learned his lesson, however long that took.

He'd ended up serving several years hard time – longer than the average rapist – so missing the conjugal comforts of his wife – who eventually divorced him – the pleasures of shopping, of having friends over for supper, of going to the football, or a lads night out, of mini-breaks, of DIY. He exchanged all that normal stuff for the principle of being free to freeze his nads off in the British rain in a chilly September.

Bonkers in Polly's opinion, which is what the state tried to argue too, only he frustrated the court-appointed shrinks by being able to converse rationally, sensibly, even wittily about – well, everything.

And when it came down to it the state – like any parent – finally caved and went back to the blind-eye principle, wondering why they had ever tried anything different. Because it was clear that this tough-love approach had made this naughty, naughty boy into a hero. He was the man who flipped the finger at the government and won. The man who didn't back down. He wasn't quite Nelson Mandela, no one was saying that, but was maybe a John Peel, or a Joe Strummer. He was certainly up there with Red Rum or Desert Orchid. More or less untouchable.

Polly could remember the fuss when he was first released. He had been everywhere for a while. Profiles in all the papers. And he'd been on both *Newsnight* and on *Question Time* naked. Meanwhile, between media appearances, he'd been doing a kind of victory lap of honour, criss-crossing the country, tramping determinedly down the high streets of small-town Britain. Picnicking in the buff whenever he got a bit hungry.

In the first town he came to after his release there were maybe twelve hardy souls braving a stiff wind to show their support. But pretty soon this built up to hundreds, many of them naked in solidarity. And of course the police were there too, only now they were there to protect him in case his supporters got too enthusiastic. He was a proper celeb. There were offers of sponsorship from energy drinks companies.

The interesting thing was that he never really acknowledged the excitements around him – not the crowds, not the police – he just kept marching on to some hidden beat in his head. In the various interviews he was polite and firm but hardly controversial. In fact, as his naked *Question Time* appearance had proved, on everything except the right to take his clothes off, he was fairly conservative. A big fan of grammar schools, for example.

Eventually media interest waned. No one followed him now, no crowds turned out to see him. He wasn't cheered but neither was he banged up. He'd been downgraded. Found his level. He was neither a threat to public order nor a revolutionary hero. He was a curiosity, an eccentricity – as innocently English as Morris dancing or an unarmed police force. And now he is in front of her, unsheathed cock gently swaying in the late summer breeze, eating her blackberries and making small talk.

'Bit of a bugger all this rain, isn't it?' he says now and Polly feels a bit flustered, it is after all the closest she's been to a naked man in ages. She could, if she wanted, just reach out and give his thingy a good hard tug, like it was the rope on a church bell.

'Good for the garden though,' she says and then she remembers Daniel. 'Christ, I better go. There's a bit of a crisis at home.'

The naked hiker frowns his concern. 'Anything I can help with?'

Polly says no and starts to hurry away, but he calls after her that she's forgotten her blackberries. Polly turns and shouts that he can have them, but he runs after her and she's impressed how fast he can move with a rucksack on his back. Polly has already slowed to a walk. A brisk walk, but a walk nonetheless.

He asks her again what the emergency is and this time she tells him that her elderly lodger has fallen and can't get up, and the naked hiker is insistent that he comes back and help, and they arrive at the house at the same time as Polly's mum. Polly's mum is completely unfazed by the sight of the naked hiker.

'Hello, dear,' she says. 'You're a bit shorter than you are on the telly.'

'Everyone says that,' he replies and smiles crookedly.

'Slimmer though,' says Polly's mum. And at this the naked hiker's grin broadens and he does a little drum roll on his stomach. 'Think so?' he says, and he looks ridiculously pleased.

'Shall we go and deal with Daniel?' says Polly, and Polly's mum gets all worried as Polly explains about the fall.

When they get in and up the stairs, Daniel is in bed.

'If you can't walk you crawl,' he says when they ask how he'd managed to get from bathroom to bed.

'A good motto for life that is,' says the naked hiker. Daniel looks at him and does a double take. He is clearly only noticing him now.

'Good lord.' he says. 'You're—'

'I am indeed.' And he sounds smug, thinks Polly.

Polly wipes the blood off Daniel's face. He has a small cut on the fleshy bit just underneath the cheekbone. Could have been a lot worse. Still, a fall for a man Daniel's age is always serious.

'You need a doctor,' says Polly firmly.

'No doctors,' says Daniel just as firmly.

'I'm a doctor,' says the naked hiker, not firmly – softly.

And, yes, Polly remembers that before starting his hikes he had, famously, been a GP in Eastbourne. It's something everyone knows about him. A strategically placed old-fashioned doctor's bag, or a stethoscope, was a feature in most of the magazine photospreads on him.

'And I thought you were just the military wing of the Naturist Society,' says Daniel.

'Don't mention those puffs to me,' says the naked hiker. And he runs his hand over Daniel's head. And he murmurs hem, haw, hmm, just like a proper doctor would. And he lifts the duvet to look at Daniel's leg. He whistles through his teeth at the bruising that's already forming there. He feels around Daniel's limbs. Daniel grimaces and gasps, but otherwise submits pretty well. And then the naked hiker looks into Daniel's eyes with one of those little torch things and then riffles through his rucksack, emerging with a prescription pad.

'I'm still registered,' he says, though no one has suggested he isn't. 'Part of the GMC's protest against the fascist bully-boys who had me sent down.' And he scribbles something. 'He does need keeping an eye on though. That was some wallop on his skull.'

And pretty soon it's fixed, the naked hiker – who now reminds them that his real name is Mervyn – will stay overnight and check on Daniel's condition regularly. Concussion is the big worry and if Daniel really won't go to hospital, then a doctor on the premises is a good idea. He doesn't think the hip is broken though, and Daniel will probably be right as rain if he takes things steady.

'And it'll be a luxury for me to stay in a bed,' he says. 'Being outside all the time can send you a bit mad to be honest.'

And he says this like it's a profound revelation.

'I don't suppose you'll be wearing clothes at all while you're here?' says Polly's mum, mildly. The naked hiker – Mervyn – smiles and shakes his head.

'No can do I'm afraid.'

'Of course not, dear. Silly of me to ask.'

So Polly and the naked hiker make jam to Daniel's recipe while he dozes. And in the evening Polly, her mum and Mervyn watch *Notting Hill* on DVD with the hiker chuckling more or less all the way through.

In the morning Daniel seems bright enough and answers all the questions Mervyn asks about who the prime minister is and who was in the World Cup team of 1966. So Mervyn leaves a repeat prescription for heavy-duty pain killers, eats three bowls of Crunchy Nut cornflakes – leaving none for anyone else Polly notices, then he heaves his rucksack up around those narrow shoulders, thanks them all, kisses them all goodbye, even Daniel which startles him, though he doesn't say anything. And Mervyn, the naked hiker, assures them that he'll definitely keep in touch. And then he turns, flexes his taut little bottom, says, 'Nice firm buttocks,' just like Hugh Grant's idiot flatmate in the movie, and strides away whistling.

'Well, that was weird,' says Polly as they watch him disappear along the road to Harewater.

'He does have a nice bum though,' says Polly's mum. 'And he's quite big, isn't he? You know, downstairs.'

'I didn't really notice, Mother,' says Polly, exasperated, and goes to talk about everything to Daniel – only he's asleep.

And he's still asleep five hours later. And when he's still asleep five hours after that, Polly begins to panic.

Thirty-three

JESUS

At first Jesus tries saying it's just because he doesn't want to go to Europe. 'The old world,' he says, 'is a zombie world. Is full of people who haven't worked out they're dead yet. But they stink like corpses all the same.'

Then he says it's because his business negotiations are at a delicate stage and that he needs to be around to consult with potential investors. Then he says it's because he doesn't want to spend so much time with frigging Russell and Sarah, that they are making him feel like he is just some damn slave.

Which is when Mary says, 'You're illegal, aren't you?'

And he denies that for a hot minute or two, before he has to admit it. Yes, he is illegal and if he leaves the States, he might not ever get back in.

Mary is pissed. No point pretending she isn't. She had been looking forward to London, to seeing Buckingham Palace, and the Tate Modern and maybe taking a day trip out to places like Wales or Cornwall. She wanted to see quaint old cottages and village greens. She had also thought they might go to the Night Garden fetish club down in Dockland or whatever it was called. She had thought that might be kinda fun. And she was looking forward to going to the Plumstead district and checking out whether Jee's famous cousin Martina was as hot as he said. She'd bet her life she wasn't.

Yes, she's pissed but she gets over it.

Jesus has to work hard to bring her round though. He buys her things, flowers and chocolate don't impress but he does better with the jewellery and he cooks and takes her to the movies, and finally he even agrees to get a tattoo.

'But you got to let me choose the design. And it won't be small,' Mary says.

And then she reminds him of her other ideas about getting funding. And Jesus says OK, OK, whatever. One way or another, they have to get the money for the Company Barrios. He'll do anything.

'The what?' Mary asks.

Jesus explains that Barrios was a famous figure from Guatemalan history, a man who had wanted to unite all of Latin America, but who had been killed fighting for his dream in 1885. 'Imagine if he'd come through,' Jesus says. 'Man, what a country that would be.'

And Mary can see that it might have been pretty amazing.

'So Barrios for my corporation – as a tribute.'

'Yeah. That's awesome. But you got to listen to me now, and listen real good, hun,' she says. 'Because this is for real. I got it figured. All the details and everything.'

And together they examine the plan from every angle but they can't see any major stress points. It requires nerve, patience and a bit of poker-face, and these are things they do have. You don't need to go to a bank for those. They are just the basic building blocks of business.

And Jesus says if it all works out he will give Mary thirty per cent of the shares in Barrios.

And Mary laughs and kisses him and says that it will absolutely definitely work, he doesn't need to worry about that. And that he'll give her forty-nine per cent of the shares with no argument.

'Forty-nine? Really? Seriously? You kiddin' me?'

'Or fifty-one per cent even.'

And she laughs again at the dangerous golden fire that begins in his beautiful brown eyes, the way his weight shifts like he is getting ready to fight.

'Relax, Mister,' she says. 'I'm only funning with you.'

He smiles wide with relief. Jesus doesn't smile a lot and it's always like the sun coming out from behind a big ole cloud. She gets him to give her the list again.

It begins with Selma Hayek, and goes on with Arnold Schwarzenegger, Colonel Tom Parker, Michael J. Fox. All stars who were once undocumented. Famous illegals. Inspiring stories. Stars of the American dream. There are over a hundred other names on that list and Jesus knows them all. And new names are added every week, and he learns them too.

Thirty-four

LORNA

'Hey, Armitage, listen to this.' She clears her throat and reads aloud: 'The Linnaean taxonomy of smells was expanded by Zwaardemaker in the nineteenth century to include nine categories: ethereal, aromatic, fragrant, ambrosiac, alliaceous, empyreumatic, hircine, foul and nauseous.' Armitage Shanks looks unimpressed and she rubs his belly. 'Oh you're so hard to please. Those are great words. I want a lover who smells alliaceous or empyreumatic, don't you? In fact I wouldn't mind a lover called Zwaardemaker come to that.'

There is a knock at the door, a hard old-school rat-a-tat-tat and Armitage Shanks springs from her arms and hurries off to see what the commotion is all about. He really is a most inquisitive cat. 'You know what curiosity did, don't you?' she calls after him, puts down the book and hauls herself up, just as whoever it is knocks again, harder this time. Lorna is convinced it's the post, otherwise she might have been more cautious.

There at the door, hidden behind a vast and colourful bouquet, is Jez. She is obscurely disappointed. No one has ever brought her flowers, or sent her any, not even the poet at uni, and she has sometimes fantasised about it, but now she just feels let down. Let down and somehow bullied.

She'll have to spend some time with him now, talk with him, ask how he is. She might have to fend him off. She might find herself sleeping with him out of laziness or tiredness, or for old times' sake. Or because he does some little thing that makes her want him. Basically, her day – which she has set aside for reading old history books so she could feel more immersed in the nineteenth-century social context in which her coven of authors lived and worked, well that's all spoiled now.

Maybe they'd get drunk, Jez and her, in which case tomorrow is probably ruined too. All in all, it's a pisser. Armitage Shanks clearly feels the same. As soon as he sees it's the Fuckweasel on the doorstep he heads back up the stairs.

'Oh. Jez. Why are you here?'

'Well, that's nice.'

'Sorry.' And she is. Kind of. Sorry, because it isn't really Jez she's disappointed with. She is irritated at herself. Another girl, a differently wired girl, a girl like Megan in fact – well, she'd just send him away, wouldn't she? That girl would smile but she'd be firm, and in under a minute the Fuckweasel would know that he was the past. He'd be gone. But Lorna knows she isn't capable of that and it makes her a bit cross.

She takes the flowers. They are heavy as well as colourful – and they smell heady, almost ambrosiac even. She carefully places the bouquet in the hallway, turns and embraces him. All the times they'd been together he'd definitely been vaguely hircine, but now he smells of soap and apologies. And, also, rather too much Dior pour Homme. He's made way too much effort.

It feels good to be embraced though, Jez's wiry frame feeling strong through the battered leather jacket.

But that's enough of that.

'Let's go grab a coffee,' she says.

'Oh, right.'

And she knows he is disappointed not to be getting inside the flat, but she can't quite remember what she's left lying about. She doesn't think there is anything too incriminating, but it'd be demeaning to be running around collecting stray underwear from the sofa just because the Fuckweasel was in the building.

They walk in silence for a minute or two and then, of course, begin to speak at the same moment. They both stop. There is a good deal of after you-ing and you first-ing, and, again, Lorna feels irritated. The Jez she had first got to know in The Vesuvio all those months ago, well, he would have just talked over her, wouldn't he? What had happened to that bloke? She definitely preferred that bloke.

She stays quiet and lets him talk and he just asks how she's been, and of course she's been fine, just fine. He says he's been worried because she hasn't replied to his texts.

'And you moved,' he says accusingly.

'I did. How did you find where I lived?'

Jez shrugs. 'There's an app.'

'Of course, there's always an app.'

And as they walk, Jez fills the growing silence by pointing out all the more interesting plants and shrubs, including fruit trees.

'I've actually done a map, a trail that shows all the places where you can pick edible stuff in Berkeley. You know, so people can eat for free.'

Now, that is a surprisingly interesting and useful thing for him to have done. Oh God.

And then they are in the Guerrilla Cafe and he looks at her and she looks at him and they both smile and she feels some of the old chemistry mixing in the air around them. A sort of penumbra of sparkle. Anyone looking over might think what a good-looking couple, what a handsome pair. Her so blonde and him so dark, and both of them so raggedy-stylish. People might think they looked like a young Anita Pallenberg and a young Keith Richards. Or a young Courtney and Kurt. Doomed lovers in a moment of grace in a coffee shop.

So she smiles warmly at him now, and takes his hand and says, 'So tell me, what have you done with the body?'

And he starts. 'What?'

'I mean, where is the real Jez? Because you have to be some kind of replicant what with the flowers, the hunter-gatherer trail and all this polite enquiring after my health and everything.'

'Oh.' He relaxes and smiles again. Shit, that is one damn heart-breaking smile. They stir coffee in silence and if he had just sat there a bit longer, looking vulnerable and tired and in need of a good meal . . . If he had let the tension build and then finally just taken her hand and said, 'Let's get out of here,' then she might have gone with him back to the apartment and ignored the clothes and the mess. She might have shooed Armitage Shanks off the three-week-old sheets on her bed and done it with him. Yes, she might well have done that.

Only Jez blows it. Blows it by crying. No man ever got a woman to go to bed with him by crying.

It isn't a pretty thing to see. His face sort of melts and it is all very snotty and gulpy and really quite noisy too. Not Keith Richards now. Not Kurt Cobain.

He is trying to be quiet but not very successfully and Lorna has to ask a waitress for a hankie. The waitress looks at her like she's a cretin, and then takes in Jez's collapsing, waxy face and liquid breaths and looks her up and down, as if unbelieving that Lorna could be responsible for such distress, and she asks her if she means a Kleenex.

'Yes, a Kleenex. Whatever.'

It's probably less than a minute before Jez gets himself together. Fifty-five seconds or so, while she wishes she were somewhere – anywhere – else. Fifty-five seconds spent looking over his trembling head and shaking shoulders, staring out of the window of the cafe, at the people strolling in the sun. Students smiling, holding hands, dawdling, enjoying the fact that they are the beautiful, chosen ones. Except for the dude picking up soda cans and putting them in his trolley. He isn't beautiful, and he hasn't been chosen for anything good. He hasn't made the team. He has plastic bags for shoes. String for a belt. Maybe he was beautiful once. Maybe he was jogging along, keeping up with the pack in the fun run of life and he tripped and that was it. Couldn't get up and everyone else just kept right on going, right over the top of him.

And towards the end of those fifty-five seconds Lorna sees her dad.

Of course, she doesn't actually know it's her dad right away. For several of those long seconds it's just some guy, some reasonably handsome middle-aged guy, but while Jez wipes his eyes with his hands and blows his nose on the Kleenex, the conviction takes hold that it's him.

He is looking hard into the window of the Guerrilla Cafe. Staring right at her. And she meets his eye, wondering where she's seen this guy before. And then she remembers the photo her mum showed her, the one taken while her dad and his mate were travelling in Europe the year she was born. Two boys. Kids. Arms around one another's slim bodies, raggedy T-shirts, lean faces beneath spiky hair, laughing into the lens. Venice or Prague or Paris or somewhere behind them.

He hasn't even changed that much. Looks in great shape. Still slim, hair cropped but slightly spiky, quite funky for a fifty-year-old. A silver fox, like a proper dad. Like the ones you see in the soaps and the movies.

What she should have done was run outside and say, 'What are you staring at, buster?' and she'd have known for sure then, but she's paralysed, glued to her chair. And Jez is reaching for her hand and muttering that he is sorry, so, so sorry. And she mutters back, saying that he shouldn't worry, there is no need to be sorry, even while she's looking over his bowed head and defeated shoulders. And the bloke outside, her dad – her possible dad anyway – nods to her and turns away from the cafe window.

And now is the time. She stands up suddenly, upsetting her coffee and snatches her hand away from Jez's and moves to catch up with possible dad. Their table is quite near to the door, but she has to struggle past some chairs with purses hung over the backs of them, and it slows her up. Even so it can't be more than a few seconds until she is pulling open the door of the Guerrilla and looking down the street and shouting, 'Hey! Hey!' but he's gone already.

She runs a few yards down the way he went, but he could have ducked down a side street, he could be in any one of these little shops.

He could, in fact, have been a figment of an overheated imagination. Already she is embarrassed, wondering if he wasn't just some random dude. A mentally ill bloke maybe, though in her experience mentally ill blokes don't look like TV dads. Then again, neither did most dads. Most real dads looked too tired and sad to get anywhere near TV standard.

She heads back into the cafe. Chairs make an irritable scrape as they inch forward again. Girls with swishy, caramel hair and fresh butterscotch complexions purse their plump lips, annoyed, and suddenly look like their mothers.

Jez seems to have got himself together, but he's looked better. A red nose is not really a good look for him. Would Jack Kerouac have wept in public over a bird? Would Jim Morrison?

The waitress comes over with a rank cloth. 'Here, you'll need this,' she says. Lorna looks at her, looks at the cloth. Doesn't say anything.

'I'll do it,' says Jez and he takes the rag. The waitress swivels on her Converses. Lorna remains standing while Jez gets on his knees and mops up the spilt coffee. And then he wipes the table with the same filthy cloth.

And finally they sit again and she has to listen while he tells her how he can't sleep, can't eat, how he thinks about her all the time, how every song he listens to now seems to be about her, how he realises that she is the one, that he has just been scared of the strength of his own feelings, that he hasn't felt this way since . . . well, for a long time, and that he has actually started writing poetry about her. Of course it's probably not very good. And he tries to smile, but it doesn't quite work. This smile doesn't come anywhere near breaking her heart.

And when he's finished, Lorna tells him that he is very sweet and everything but that she thinks they should probably just drift.

Which is when Jez stands and throws his coffee in her face. It isn't quite a full cup and it's cold anyway, but still a shock.

'You fucking heartless bitch,' says Jez. 'But don't worry, Lorna, you'll get yours.' And he spits out her name – like it's a mortal insult.

251

Like it's something rotten in his mouth. He looks at her for a hard moment. His face slightly pink, that ruby nose dripping. His mouth twisted. She can't think of anything to say. He turns to leave.

And he then has to do the negotiation past the other customers and their purses, and they tut and look like their mothers again, and the chairs squawk and it all spoils the effect of his storming out somewhat.

Now the waitress comes over with another Kleenex and says that's seven dollars ninety. Eight dollars nearly for two cups of coffee, one of which went on the floor and the other in her face.

Lorna leaves a twenty-dollar tip on her table, even though she doubts the waitress will pick up on the sarcasm. Those were, thinks Lorna, bloody expensive tissues in the end.

When she gets home Armitage Shanks is waiting for her just inside the door. First thing she does is toss the flowers out onto the sidewalk.

'Sometimes, Armitage my boy, ambrosiac can still be foul, can still be nauseous. Mr Zwaardemaker didn't think of that, did he?' And she thinks that if, God forbid, Armitage Shanks is ever knocked down by a motor, then her next cat might be called Zwaardemaker.

And even though things have been a bit weird between them recently, she wishes Megan was home. She could do with some of her funny little ways right now.

Thirty-five

CATHERINE

If you asked her when and where she was happiest, she would think for a while and then she would probably say the time they went to Grettislaug, Iceland in 2004. In other words the day she spent with Tough in a natural hot tub in the first weeks of this job.

No one knew about Iceland then, how the economy was going to go down the toilet. Except Tough. He explained it as they sat naked in the volcanic hot spring looking beyond the snow-covered turf huts to the Arctic Ocean as it fizzed and foamed against the frigid scorn of the wind.

It wasn't just greed, he said. And it wasn't just about Iceland – it was the same with all these small countries on the edge of things, places where for a thousand years it has been a struggle just to get enough to eat. Thing is, now, somehow, they feel rich. Iceland, Ireland, Greece. They are like neglected, deprived foster kids who have found a bag of used twenties. They are going straight to the sweetie shop to spend it all on dolly mixtures and Mars bars. Of course they are. And they are not really caring too much whose twenties they are, who the bag really belongs to.

'And it turns out it's our bag,' Tough said, stretching so she could see all the long muscles of his arms, 'and it contains all our food money, all our mortgage money, the money that was going to put our kids through college.'

'So that's what we're here for? To get our bag back?'

'After a fashion,' said Tough.

And they stayed like that for a while. Just sitting there, not saying anything. It was hard to get your head round the fact that the water, as hot as a hotel bath, never ever cooled while all around a thin layer of snow lay over everything, making everything look pristine like the old Norse Gods have got out the tablecloth they reserve for best.

And Tough told her the story of Grettir, an Icelandic warrior who got into scrapes. Occasionally he was heroic, defeating the undead for example. The original zombie slayer. Or he was saving villages from weird and gruesome monsters, Beowulf style. At other times he was just a yob. His temper getting him into serious bother with the authorities. He was always going too far in bar fights, that kind of thing. Glasses got smashed, pubs got trashed, innocent bystanders ended up a tiny bit dead. He got a bit wasted on super-strength mead and took an axe to people he thought were looking at him a bit funny. Or he burned down the houses of people who disrespected him – while the owners were inside. With their children.

Catherine knew the type. She was always having to pepper spray them in her time in the military police.

'Eventually they declare him an outlaw, which means anyone can kill him without legal penalty.'

Anyway, there are various adventures and then, after twenty years, he's chased to Drangey. 'Which you can just see today.' Tough pointed at a clenched fist of black rock punching its way out of the water on the horizon. 'And his enemies think he'll die there because he's wounded and there is nothing to give him comfort – no food, no shelter. Only, being actually, you know, a hero, he swims the whole nine-mile stretch between there and here and – nearly dead – manages to revive himself in this very pool.'

Catherine raised herself up a little on the stone bench that ran around the edge of the pool, a bench worn smooth by centuries of bums. It made her smile. She felt the exhilarating tattoo of fresh Arctic air on her bare shoulders.

Such a strange country, Iceland. She wondered if she could live here. Not in Reykjavik, that reminded her too much of Ipswich oddly, but out here where it looked like the surface of the moon, where the wind still sang of trolls and the bad-tempered heroes that fought them. And where you could sit in the exact same place where generations of Vikings had sat, looking at the exact same lunatic landscape they saw.

And Tough and Catherine stayed there in that water that didn't cool, under the sky that didn't darken and talked of their childhoods and the different ways in which their fathers and mothers are mad – because all fathers and mothers are mad in their own way. They talked of the blind, unthinking cruelties of school, because all schools are cruel. And when they did finally get out of the pool, unselfconsciously naked with each other as they towelled down briskly, they shared strong black coffee from Tough's flask – the one that had survived the bullets and the shrapnel of every peace-keeping mission from the Lebanon to Sarajevo.

And late that night, they drove through dusk back into Saudarkrokur. This was Iceland's eleventh biggest town and basically a single street of punch-drunk houses, homes bullied the year round by weather but refusing to ever quite give up or give in. Refusing to go down.

They walked into the bar like characters from a bad old joke, where Tough ordered two Irish whiskies. It took minutes for the word to spread that there were Irish in town and it did no good for Tough and Catherine to protest that they were from Kent and Suffolk respectively. The people in the Sportbar just wouldn't hear it. They wanted them to be properly Irish. They wanted craic and they wanted it immediately. The people of Saudarkrokur wanted storytellers and poets in their bar. They wanted singers and fighters and wisecracking charmers, and Catherine watched as Tough gave them all that. He told jokes, he bought drinks, he beat the locals at pool, he flirted with their girlfriends, he got into a ruck, then accepted a drink from the guy he laid flat out on the floor.

He got up and sang a beautiful lament for the auld country. A song in the ancient tongue of the Celts that filled the whole bar with an ache for the things that they have loved and lost and will never see again. Tough made sure no one in the Sportsbar would forget them.

All Catherine had to do was drink and laugh and slap the face of a twat that groped her arse. And then accept another drink off him. 'No hard feelings?' he said anxiously. He must be six foot six, with a massive nose and a funny eye. Catherine felt sorry for him.

And in the early hours of the morning with the party still going on, and with no sleep and with Tough surely many times over the limit, they started back through dusk towards Reykjavik.

Catherine asked how he knew Irish and Tough looked at her and said, 'You mean the song? That was Georgian. Who was going to know though, eh?'

And they drove through the Elvish mists and whispers of Iceland, the rumours of ancient steam, listening to disco hits of the seventies because, bizarrely, that is what Tough insisted on. That landscape, that music, it was an unsettling clash, but it worked somehow.

Catherine dozed and, as they approached the city, Tough ran through it all again.

They were going to do a piece of work on a guy who had four daughters aged between eight and eighteen. He wasn't a bad man either. He'd done nothing illegal. He was kind. Everyone said so. He was a good dad. He was a senior guy at a bank. Had worked there twenty years. He was a governor at the local elementary school, he was in the amateur dramatic group, the men's choir.

But if they didn't do this work then hundreds of thousands of British jobs would go, children would go hungry, or be forced to eat supermarket ready-meals made of donkey eyelids. Transplant operations would be postponed or cancelled.

And the effects would hit the Third World too. No one would be buying trinkets from India or Africa, no one would be going on holiday, the international development budget would have to be cut. And if that happened babies would sicken and die. Millions of them maybe. All those potential doctors, lawyers, teachers, actors, pop stars. All those possible Mandelas, all those tiny Gandhis. All of them starving to death. Flies crawling on their eyeballs. We've all seen the pictures.

This was the hard choice. One wife, four crying children, versus suffering and misery for millions. No choice at all really.

'I know, Tough, I know. I'm OK.'

''Course you are. Maybe I'm just reassuring myself.'

They made it look like a freak accident. Einar Jonsson went out for his regular early morning jog, when he stumbled over a fallen power line that was still live. At least the police were able to tell his brave and dignified wife that he died instantly and painlessly.

'He wouldn't have known a thing,' one of them said.

It didn't really comfort his wife. Didn't really stop the tears of his girls.

The deeper sadness was that it didn't work. There were the four crying daughters, the one crying wife, but there was still the misery for millions. Still all the dead Gandhis and all the dead Mandelas. But not every plan comes off and you couldn't know how much worse things would have been without this action. You have to take risks in this life. The biggest mistake is to be scared to make a mistake.

Yes Grettislaug, Iceland. A top day.

But that was then, this is now. That was all in the old days, before they got the new stuff. At least it's all much simpler now, or should be. No pissing about with cables. And they have better intelligence these days. But here, in the now, the place where Catherine acknowledges to herself that she is not quite so happy, it has already been over a week and still this Knox is doing his thing. Getting on with living. Fucking things up for her with his tiresome propensity to keep breathing.

Catherine is back from her run and warming down. She does some slow press-ups, and then some stretches while her bath is running. She does her meditation and then flicks through the web, still no news of any sudden deaths of multi-billionaires in Russian Hill.

And then there is a soft knock at the door.

In Catherine's business this is never good news. You never have anyone come to your room. You never order anything from room service, like you never pick someone up in a hotel bar. Like you always sleep on a mat next to the bed, rather than in it. This is all basic stuff.

The knock comes again. Soft but insistent. A professional knock.

Catherine unfolds herself from the floor, stands up and keeps her eyes on the handle. The most likely thing is that it is the hotel staff here to do something with the air con or the shower. The second most likely thing is that it is the hotel staff come to rob the room.

Yep, the door is opening inwards quietly. Catherine moves in one silent stride until she is standing behind it. She's not afraid, she's confident she can deal with whoever it is. She is curious and excited. This is action of a kind even if it just ends with her yelling, 'What the hell do you think you're doing?' and a terrified bellboy mumbling some excuse as he backs away.

The door pauses a few inches in. And then swings wide, meaning that Catherine is hidden in a triangular hiding space watching as a thin man steps into the room. Narrow shoulders, a slight stoop, an old man in a cheap suit. Balding head. Not maintenance and no bellboy. Senior staff then. Management. All of this taken on board in less than a split second.

'What the hell?' she begins, as she pushes the door closed. She stops.

The old man turns. 'Catherine?'

'Tough?' It is Tough – only old and shrunken, his face scored by a network of lines as close together as those on an ordnance survey map, his neck sagging like the slack rigging of an old sailboat. He looks like a reptile. Like a tortoise. They look at each other for a long moment.

'You wouldn't have any booze in the place would you, old girl?'

'There's the minibar.'

258

'Of course, which means we can each have a snack pack of Pringles too. Oh joy. I get these salt cravings. Now, aren't you going to hug me?' And he smiles and it is the old Tough again for a moment. The Tough she knows from Iraq. From Grettislaug.

She finds she can't smile, but she moves forward obediently into his arms. He seems frail and he smells funny. Expensive scent of course but there is something sour beneath that.

'That my dear is rot.'

'What?' She pulls back to look at him properly, putting her hands either side of his head. He twinkles, the old Tough is living in the eyes and in the smile even if he is horribly absent from everywhere else.

'That whiff. I can't smell it myself but I see it in the slight but emphatic recoiling of others. Rot. Corruption. Death. Nothing to be done about that ugly little trio is there? They come for us all. Will come to you too, Catherine my love. Though not for a good long while yet we hope.'

He goes to the small fridge and fixes the drinks. Two vodkas and tonic. He hands one to her with tremulous hands. His sniping days are long gone. She snatches it. She can't bear to see that shake in her old mate. Tough must notice her reaction, but he doesn't comment. Instead he says, 'You get a taste for voddy living out in what I still think of as the USSR.' They clink glasses. He sits down on the bed, Catherine sits next to him. 'It's not AIDS or anything like that by the way. Though that's probably what I deserve, the way I carried on in the glory years. No, this is just a nasty group of ordinary plebby cancers giving me grief. I'm dying, Catherine. Got a few weeks left, few months if I'm lucky. But hey-ho, I do intend to be lucky.' He swallows half the vodka. She opens her mouth. He holds up the thin quivering bones of his hand. 'Don't worry. There's nothing to be said. It's shit but there it is. And in my own way I am raging at the dying of the light.'

She can't get her head round any of it – Tough in her room in San Francisco. Tough sick. 'But I'm due to see you. I'm going to finish up here and then come to Abkhazia.'

''Fraid I couldn't wait. Shall we go out? This room is very claustrophobic.'

Tough watches crap TV while she bathes and changes. She can hear him chuckling as she soaps and rinses.

'All right?' she says when she's done. She's wearing jeans and blue pumps and a pink Superdry sweatshirt. Tough smiles. She decides to keep him smiling, if she can. It is the only time he looks like himself.

'Perfect. You look both feminine and sensible. You'll look like a dutiful, unmarried daughter taking out her doddery old dad for pizza.'

There is some small talk about the weather in the corridors and in the lift. Catherine wonders if anyone has ever said anything worth hearing in a hotel lift. Have there ever been marriage proposals or break-ups in a lift? Has anyone ever had the temerity to have a heart attack in a lift?

And when they are settled in the nearest pizza joint Tough says, 'How's the firm?'

And Catherine shrugs and says, 'We're having to refresh our priorities. We're having to chunk up.'

And Tough smiles. Result, thinks Catherine. She tries to make it happen again. 'And we're all going to go through a competitive migration process. Because there's going to be less jobs.'

It works. He smiles again. 'Where do they get these phrases?' he says. He snorts. 'Chunk up indeed. Oh, but it's fewer jobs by the way. Not less. No reason for us to forget our grammar just because the barbarians are at the gates.' And then they choose pizzas and drinks and help themselves to salads.

When they are sitting back down Catherine asks, 'Do you remember Grettislaug?'

'The day we had to be Irish? Of course. What a bloody brilliant day that was.'

And Catherine feels like kissing him. Kissing him and crying, and they relive the whole day – and then some other highlights

260

from the years they've known each other and, just as Catherine is wondering if she will ever find out why he is in California, Tough tells Catherine two things. He tells her that he has decided to believe in God. And he tells her that everything that she knows about her life is a lie.

Thirty-six

POLLY

The minute they decide to call the ambulance Daniel wakes and says he feels fine, that he obviously just needed the kip. Nevertheless, he's not right – Polly can tell. For one thing he keeps getting her name wrong. He keeps calling her Susan. Or Sarah. Or Jean. Or Nicholas even, all of which is understandable if annoying. But she begins to wonder if he's doing it on purpose.

'A cup of tea would be lovely, Irina,' he says at one point.

'Fuck off,' she says, and then regrets it because he looks so hurt. 'Sorry, Daniel, call me any name you like except that one.'

'What did I call you?'

'Irina.'

'No way!' He sounds like a teenager. Polly smiles. It's hard to stay mad at Daniel for long.

'Yes way. Now I'll get you a cup of tea if you get dressed. We're going for a walk.'

'Not with the naked hiker?'

'No, he's gone, Daniel.'

And the picture of Mervyn's sturdy cock forms in her mind. She's shakes her head to clear it as if it was an Etch-A-Sketch drawing. It doesn't work. She has definitely seen horses with smaller dongs.

She wants Daniel up and moving because she's worried that he won't sleep tonight and then they'll be in a disastrous pattern where he becomes nocturnal and she's not having that. Tired and grumpy during the day and agitated at night, she's seen that happen with the cabbages at Sunny Bank and she's not having that in her own home. She needs to wear him out.

When he's up and dressed, they walk into the village. It's slow going – Daniel is definitely finding it a struggle, but he doesn't moan. Just keeps on going, one foot in front of the other. They do all the sights of the village. That is, they go down to the shop, they go past the pub, they do a circuit of the village green with its tired see-saw and creaking roundabout on which three teenage girls sit smoking and passing a bottle back and forth between them.

'Ah, what it is to be young and carefree,' sighs Daniel, and Polly feels a pang because she never did this. Never sat in the park drinking cider and smoking and she feels like she probably missed out.

As the sun begins to set, the sky turning an astonishing euphoric pink, they wander the graveyard and Daniel is delighted at some of the graves they find. And this makes Polly a bit sad too, not because of all the dead people and their lives that have gone, but because it's another thing she's never done before.

Daniel finds a grave that reads 'Foolish enough to have been a poet' and one that says 'To my royal male'.'

'Clearly a much-loved postman,' says Daniel.

Set apart from all the other graves in a corner of the churchyard is the gravestone of a Deborah Ann Burgess that reads 'In hope of Forgiveness' and they stand in front of it, speculating on what she might need forgiveness for.

'Could be anything round here,' says Polly. 'Being too gobby. Having opinions. Wanting to be listened to. Standing up to blokes.'

'Or it could be robbery, murder . . .' says Daniel.

'Nothing that exciting has happened round here.'

'I think you might be surprised,' says Daniel. 'My money's on infanticide.'

'That's the same as murder, isn't it?'

'Not really,' says Daniel, and then they move on to what they'd have on their own graves and Polly says, 'When I die, I just want them to dig a hole and sling me in.'

And Daniel says, 'Well, that's OK then because that is more or less exactly what happens anyway. Unless they burn you and tip your ashes into a jar.' And then he says he admires those Victorians who built massive monuments to themselves and their families. And he points to a few mossy examples dotted around the churchyard.

And on their way out they pass a grave that says 'An honest man is worth numbers'. And Daniel reads it out approvingly. 'It's a quote from Oliver Cromwell.'

'I'm not sure what it even means.'

'It just means that one honest man is worth loads of ordinary men. That they are rare and valuable.'

'Well, that's true enough.'

And Daniel laughs and says, 'You're being very Women's Lib today, Susan.'

And Polly doesn't bother correcting him and reads the next grave.

'Look at this. This bloke 'Fell Asleep on July ninth in the year of our Lord 1856'. Fell asleep and they buried him. You should think about that next time you sleep the clock around.'

And Daniel laughs and says, 'I wonder what the pub's like.'

'Crap. And full of idiots. But it does have bar billiards.'

'Sounds perfect.'

And in the pub he tells her that he's made a will. He's downloaded a form off the internet and filled it out and sent it away to his solicitors and it's all legal and everything. He says he's never bothered making a will before, which is crazy he knows. 'Guess I thought I was going to live for ever.'

He tells her he's left everything to her and holds up his hand when she tries to argue. 'Who else am I going to leave it to? And it isn't as though there's millions anyway. And the bastards will steal a lot of it in inheritance tax.' He takes a deep pull of his beer, chucks down a handful of peanuts. 'And you'll need money if you ever do have a baby. They ain't cheap, you know. Clothes and shoes and school dinners and Game Boys or what have you. All adds up. Anyway, if you do have a baby maybe just think about calling the little one Daniel. All I ask – just that you think about it.'

'Right. Yes. Daniel. It's a good name.' Though actually she's been thinking of Steig, or Lars maybe. She's finally decided on Norwegian sperm after all and has been thinking that the babe should maybe have a name that reflects his heritage. But Daniel Simmonds works all right, and is the least she can do in the circumstances.

He smiles. 'Thank you.'

'Or Danielle.'

He looks confused.

'It might be a girl, you know.'

He smiles again. 'Oh gosh, yes, right. Of course. Danielle.'

There's a pause. 'Thank you, Daniel.'

'No worries. And in any case, I've got plenty of miles left on the old clock yet. Plenty of gas in the tank.'

'Of course you have.' Something occurs to her.

'Daniel, you did put the right name on the will didn't you? You know, Polly, not Sarah or Susan, or anyone else?'

He frowns. 'Botheration,' he says. 'I might not have done.'

'Never mind,' she says. 'I'm sure it's easy enough to fix.' Though she's not really sure.

There's another short pause before Daniel says, 'One more for the road?' and, without waiting for an answer he picks up both their glasses and shuffles off towards the bar. He's looking very, very tired now. Polly thinks that she doesn't have to worry about him sleeping. That won't be a problem.

Thirty-seven

LORNA

'Look, she never stays away overnight and she never would without telling me where and why. It is absolutely inconceivable.'

'Lady, I appreciate your concern and I've logged the details and we'll sure keep an eye out, but right now that's all we can do. If she's still missing tomorrow then we'll step things up a gear, OK?'

It isn't OK, but she has already been on the phone twenty-five minutes, being passed from pillar to post and this has the sound of an absolute final offer. There is some steel in this police voice. 'Right. But could you repeat the details back to me, just so I know you've got them down properly.'

The officer tries hard to keep from sighing as he repeats her description of Megan and all her personal info, but he doesn't quite manage it. She can practically hear him rolling his eyes at the other end of the line. Finally, with exaggerated patience, he says, 'Your friend is nearly thirty. She sounds like a sensible, capable woman. I'm sure she's fine.'

'Well, let's hope so.'

'Oh, one more thing, Miss Dawson.'

'Yes?'

'I've been wondering the whole time we've been talking. Where is it you're from?'

'I beg your pardon?'

'Your accent. I can't place it.'

She hangs up. Cheeky fuck. And as she does so she hears keys in the lock downstairs. She hears the semi-trot of Megan's footsteps down the hall. The soft patter her sneakers make. Sometimes it's hard to tell whether it's her coming home or Armitage Shanks. She always steps light along the hall, before attacking the stairs at a sprint, as if running up the stairs was some kind of Olympic event.

There is the click and creak of the door to the apartment itself being opened. Lorna takes a breath. Things have to be said.

'Where the fuck have you been?'

Megan laughs, but nervously. 'Are you mad?'

'As hell. Of course I am. I'm livid. You couldn't call? You couldn't let me know where you were?'

'OK, Grandma. Keep your hair on.'

'It's not actually funny, Megan.'

'Lorna. I'm twenty-nine.'

'Inconsiderate is inconsiderate at any age.' She stops. She sounds like her mother. And it is also annoying that the lazy-fuck cop turns out to be right on the button.

'I was worried sick.'

'We pulled a late one at work is all. Way too late to get back home so we kipped at the Days Inn across the road.'

'There was a marketing emergency?'

Megan smiles briefly. 'It does happen.'

'You could still have called.'

'I know. I was just – I was beat is all. I was done, you know? And I will call next time. I promise. And right now I'll make some coffee.'

Lorna follows Megan into the kitchen. She's not going to let it lie. Not yet. 'So there's going to be a next time is there?'

Megan turns round, slow and deliberate. She looks Lorna right in the eyes. Lorna is shocked by how tired she looks. There are shadows beneath her eyes, and her peachy skin looks smeary somehow. Like a glass that has been breathed on. She looks ill.

'I don't know Lorna. I just don't know. But back off 'kay?' She spins back round and starts rinsing cups. Her shoulders tense. Her whole posture a kind of force field. Lorna leaves her to it. One thing is certain: it was no work crisis that kept her out. Lorna feels hollow. Megan and her, they don't tell each other fibs.

She goes back into the living room, calls the direct number the cop had given her.

'She's back.'

'Who is this?'

For fuck's sake, it had only been a minute ago. 'Lorna Dawson. I called a few moments ago? About my missing flatmate?' She's aware that she's speaking way more loudly than usual, and that Megan is smart enough to know that she is doing this just so that she'll hear her, but she's still bloody angry. Relieved obviously, but angry too.

She explains that Megan has just walked through the door exactly as he had predicted she would. To his credit the cop doesn't sound amused or smug. Just says that it is good news.

'Yorkshire. By the way.'

'Sorry, Ma'am?'

'You asked where I was from. It's West Yorkshire, England. Near Bradford.'

'OK, right. Thank you.'

'So that's two mysteries sorted. The SFPD clear-up rate is really picking up today, isn't it?'

The cop laughs good-naturedly. She carries on, 'If only everything could be resolved that easily, huh?'

'You got that right, Ma'am. I'm pleased your friend is safe home.' A pause. He seems to be on the brink of saying something else. But whatever it is, he doesn't pursue it. Tells her to have a good day now.

'You too.'

As she replaces the phone in its cradle, Megan hands her a cup of coffee. She sips it. It's good. Megs is much, much better than Lorna at coffee.

'You called the cops?'

'Yeah, well. I didn't know what else to do.'

'I should have called you.'

'No. Like you said, you're a big girl now. None of my beeswax.'

They sit and drink coffee for a while. Then Lorna tells Megan about seeing Jez. Megan's nose wrinkles comically. And she tells her about thinking she'd seen her dad or certainly someone who really looked like him. So maybe he's back from his travels.

'OK, let me get changed and we'll go to the city and see if he's home.'

'Just like that?'

'Why not?'

'You don't have to go to work?'

'I'm taking some time off.'

'Because of yesterday's late one.'

'You got it.'

Lorna thinks Megan looks shifty, but she also knows that her own reaction to her friend staying out was over the top, and she's embarrassed. She isn't going to start quizzing her about stuff now. If Megan has things to say she'll tell her when she's good and ready.

Megan picks up their cups and goes back to the kitchen. Lorna calls out over the sound of the taps.

'Megan, my love?'

'Yes, Lorna?'

'Am I still your best girl?'

Megan reappears in the doorway, broad athletic shoulders filling the whole frame. She is smiling, but a little sadly Lorna thinks. Or maybe she is just being hypersensitive.

'You will always be my best girl, Lorna. You know that.'

'Just checking. It's good to know.'

Thirty-eight

NICKY

The bobby-dazzler suit is almost ready and I go for my final fitting feeling cheerier than I have in days.

I'm reconciled to going back to our soggy little island now. Actually I've moved a bit beyond reconciled, maybe I'm even quite looking forward to it. When I was last in England I was a balding, greying, pudgy council drone with dodgy teeth. Now I'm a rascal, a rogue, a rapscallion. A master criminal. Rich and fit, my sharp cheekbones set off by my artfully mussed-up hair. My teeth – they gleam, they spar- kle. I could be a kind of dandy highwayman myself, tlot-tlotting my gangster glamour through the damp suburban streets in my eye- catching whistle. I'm so different from the anonymous little man who left from Gatwick three months ago that it's hard to believe that I won't see the place differently too. Maybe I should make a documen- tary on my phone. Capture all the oddities and absurdities of the English.

Another thing that has made me realise it's time to go. San Francisco is shrinking, the way all places do when you get to know them too well. The other day, for example, glancing into a coffee shop and seeing Lorna Dawson sitting right there holding hands with her boyfriend, that had given me a bit of a turn. Time to go.

England, my England. It is a bit frustrating that the one place I won't be able to wander is the place where I lived. Even with the new hair, the new teeth, the new threads, and without the twenty pounds of flab I used to haul around with me everywhere – we've decided that there's still a risk I'll be recognised. So when we're in Southwood I'll be in the Manton Grange Spa and Golf complex – Southwood's premier hotel – watching sport on Sky. But that won't be for long. Sarah has promised she'll see her mum and her sister. Maybe a girls' night out with her mates, and then we're off. We're friends again now, by the way. In the morning, Scarlett wriggling and gurgling between us, our snarkiness seemed pointless and stupid. And Mary and Jesus aren't coming with us anyway, they tell us. But sssh, don't tell our kid.

We'll do London – I suspect that London might be the best place in the world to be rich – and then who knows? New York, Paris, Istanbul. Check out some of Russell's other pieds in other terres.

And even if I'm stuck indoors watching crown-green bowls on a hotel telly, then I may well be wearing this suit. It is truly a thing of rare beauty. A fully hand-sewn summer kid mohair three-piece in the kind of subtle purple the classier kind of Roman emperor might have appreciated. Mother of pearl buttons to add a bit of bling. A bobby dazzler indeed. Jimmy's not happy though, and even through his mouthful of pins he still manages to articulate the cause of his disapproval.

'I do wish you'd stop losing weight,' he says, sulkily. 'There's another hour's work here now.'

'It's OK,' I say. 'I have nothing important to do. I'll just, you know, mooch about a bit. Come back in an hour or so.'

And now Jimmy manages to convey what he thinks of those of us who have nothing to do in the middle of the day except mooch. A shoulder twitches dismissively. It's obvious that he thinks we're all a symptom of something profoundly wrong with the state of things. All of us, his clients, we're unworthy of him – that's what that shoulder twitch says. And it's true too. Jimmy after all is a man made stooped and grey and squinty with work. He's more or less bald apart from the twin feathery tufts of white hair above each ear. He stares anxiously at the world through thick-lensed glasses held together with Sellotape. He doesn't even wear a suit himself, preferring to work in a vest and old jeans that look a size too big. He shuffles, sighing, around his

271

workshop, crooked with pronounced scoliosis. He looks like a man expecting to be foreclosed at any minute, though Jesus assures me that he is a man of immense personal wealth.

Work is maybe not a choice for this man, it is a weird compulsion.

And so I head off out into the streets around the shop and am startled to come face-to-face with Catherine, the woman who asked me out while running. She looks nervous, agitated. I can't think what I saw in her.

'We need to talk,' she says, and she sounds like she means it.

And so we go to a coffee shop where she has a double expresso and then reveals herself to be completely off her nut.

One of the jobs I had before the cultural services billet came up was working with the long-term mentally ill. The people who were being moved from asylums into 'the community', whatever the hell that is. And among that bunch of elderly schizos we had Walter who, he said, drove buses in the spirit world. And I remember thinking then, if you're going to have a fantasy life that involves you journeying between here and the astral plane, don't be a bleeding bus driver. It's your world and you can be anything, so be a king. Be supreme overlord of the Galaxy. Be God. Be Lord of everything. Aim high. Have some ambition, man.

And there was another old man – Doug – whose big thing was that he had come up with the idea of Interpol, but that our dear Queen Elizabeth had infringed his intellectual copyright, and then had him locked up to prevent him gaining the vast riches that would obviously accrue from being the inventor of international cooperation between police forces. Apparently, at some point in the 1940s, he'd tried filing his brainwave with the patent office and the very next day he was in Broadmoor.

Walter and Doug. I'd liked them. As delusional schizos went they were very engaging.

This Catherine is less engaging, her fantasy less compelling and her whole manner less convincing too.

When we're sitting down, I can see that she's close to tears.

'What is it?' I say. 'What's the matter?' And to be honest I'm expecting a tale of woe involving a lost passport maybe or possibly sudden redundancy. Perhaps a text arriving from England saying that due to the economic situation etc. etc. Or maybe a sick family member. And that seeing me by chance, she's taken it as a sign that maybe rescue is at hand. Something like that. Maybe not rescue even, but just a supportive shoulder to lean on in a place where she is foreign and alone.

I'm emphatically not expecting her to tell me that I have days to live, that apparently I have a lethal, incurable virus travelling around my bloodstream. That she herself is actually a kind of James Bond figure, licensed to kill and all that, but has been duped into bumping off Western venture capitalists on behalf of shadowy forces operating out of Asia or Moscow. She does tell me the precise details, but to be honest it's so convoluted and confused that I struggle to keep up. You know when someone's trying to explain the plot of a movie to you, one that you have no wish to see. Or when someone is trying to tell you about this really amazing dream they had last night? Well, that basically. Give me the simple clarity of a Walter or a Doug any day.

Anyway, less than two minutes in I'm thinking of how best I can escape this psycho nutjob and thanking my lucky stars I never ever got myself properly entangled with her. So, what with one thing and another, I'm not really listening.

'Russell. You're not really listening.'

'I am. You're a government assassin.'

'I hate that word.'

'A foreign agent then, and you shot me with some kind of poisoned dart when we were out running, because her Britannic Majesty's enemies want to manipulate the international money markets. You've been working, without your knowledge, for an organisation which is dedicated to the eradication of usurers.'

'You think I'm mad.'

'No, no, no. 'Course not.'

'I wouldn't really blame you. Sometimes I think I'm mad.' Which is good because it does suggest the possibility of some kind of self-awareness, so perhaps some kind of redemption is also possible. I read somewhere that way more people than you think have psychotic episodes in their life. Mental illness is one of the great hidden epidemics.

I decide to humour her. Play along. It seems safest given that we're in a place full of knives and forks. 'But what can I do, Catherine? You tell me there's no cure for this poison. Seems to me like I just have to accept things.'

'You *do* think I'm mad.' Her eyes fill up again. I wonder what we look like to the other customers in the cafe. Maybe we look like a couple breaking up. A good-looking middle-aged couple who have come to the end of their rainbow. I wonder if they think I'm the chucker or the chuckee.

'You can . . . I don't know . . .' She takes a deep breath. 'Look, I'm telling you so you can get your affairs in order.' Very kind of her I'm sure. 'And it's not really much use, but I know the people responsible. And I will get them for you, Russell. You can be sure about that.'

My phone breaks into its polyphonic dawn chorus. Its avian aria. Mary. Hurrah. Saved. Whatever she's calling about it's going to necessitate my getting a fast exit out of here. It'll be something that needs dealing with that can't be put off. It'll be *sorry Catherine, thanks for the warning* and then *see ya (don't wanna be ya)*.

Mary is hysterical. I can hardly make out a word she's saying. I make her slow down and start again, take her time. But I can feel my heart start pounding, a sickness rising in my throat. Not Scarlett. Not our gorgeous little girl. Our defenceless angel.

'They've taken her.'

'What? Who's taken her?'

'I don't know. I only left her for a minute, she was playing with her dolls and I was stacking the dishwasher and I came back in and she was gone.'

'Where has she gone?'

'I don't freaking know, Russell! But someone has taken her. They've left a note.'

'You saying she's been kidnapped?'

'I don't know! Yes, I guess. There's a note.'

'A note?'

'Yes, a freaking note. Jeez. I told you already.'

'What does it say?' She starts wailing again. 'Come on, Mary get it together. What does it say?'

'It just says . . .' I hear her gulping for air. 'It just says, "The kid will be fine as long as you're smart. Wait for our call. Don't call the cops." That's all it says.'

Fuck's sake. It's like something from a shit no-budget made-for-TV movie.

I repeat it back to her. '"Kid will be fine as long as you're smart. Don't call the cops." That's really what it says?'

'Yes, and it says to wait for their call. I'm really sorry, Russell. I was only out of the room a minute—'

I cut her off. 'I'm coming back. I'll get a cab. Where's Sarah?'

'I don't know. I've left a message.'

'Keep trying her. And Mary – if something happens to that little girl I'll . . .' I'll what? What will I do? I can't finish the sentence. I just click off.

I'm already on my feet and I throw a note on the table. I don't even see what denomination it is. I look at Catherine, the woman who has been wasting my time with her stupid mad shit. But I'm taken aback by how she's looking at me. Just for a second I am shaken out of my rising panic. She's looking shrewd, alert, focused. She looks fucking sharp. Entirely fucking sane is what she looks like.

'I have a car,' she says. 'I'll drive you home.'

I hesitate. 'Come on,' she says. 'Take you ages to get a cab.' And she's right. She might be nuts but she's right there and she's got a vehicle.

'OK,' I say. 'But don't talk please. Just drive me where I say. And don't say a fucking word.'

'Deal,' she says. And then she moves from her seat fast so she's in front of me and she pulls me into a powerful hug.

'What the fuck are you doing?' I say. 'We've got to go.'

'Of course,' she says meekly, and she shrugs. 'I was just—'

'Forget it. Let's go now. Please.'

Thirty-nine

CATHERINE

If her passenger had been taking in anything of his surroundings he might have been impressed with how she handled the car. She certainly doesn't drive like a mental case. Catherine drives that Toyota Camry – the middle-aged female jogger of cars – as all cars should be driven, with an unhurried deliberation but still with an eye for gaps in the lines, opportunities to bob and weave to shave minutes off the journey time as estimated by the satnav. No over-fussy traffic cop would have found anything to pull her over for, and yet they are in Russian Hill way quicker than your average chump commuter could ever manage it.

Yes, if Russell Knox was in any state to think clearly about things he would applaud. That's what Catherine thinks anyway as she watches him swipe his card at the gate of this mansion block and dive inside.

Catherine puts the Camry into drive and moves off. As soon as she is out of sight of the house, round the corner in Jackson, she stops and pulls Nicky's phone out from her pocket. It takes her twenty seconds to find Mary's number and another twenty to scan that number with Ariadne. How, she wonders, had they managed to operate before that neat little app had been developed?

But anyhoo, less than two minutes after delivering Russell Knox back to his house of tears she has Mary's address and is heading there. One thing she knows about child abductions – whether by perves or ordinary decent thieves – is that they are usually an inside job. Want to find that paedo child killer? Start with the uncles, the stepbrothers, the neighbours. And the father, of course. Don't forget him. That ransom note? Usually dictated by a trusted retainer. Except where it is dictated by the uncles, the stepbrothers, the neighbours or the father.

Even driving the way Catherine does, it's going to take her twenty-five minutes to get to Potrero so she has plenty of time to think.

She's confident that if the kid is still alive, then she can get her out, that won't be too much of a problem. It's what she's going to do afterwards that's the concern. She should, actually, be pretty pissed off with Tough because he's put her right in the shit.

As soon as Madam knows that she knows what the firm is really about, then it'll be goodnight sodding Vienna. So her only option really is to disappear. Drop off the radar, like Tough did himself. Not Abkhazia necessarily, though Tough has offered her his place there, but somewhere like it. Somewhere out of the way, some failed state without much likelihood of rejoining the civilised family of nations any time soon. And somewhere where her skill-set might be valued and rewarded.

And there's always Mossad, of course. There's always them. They take anyone. They're always hiring.

Yeah, she should be pissed off with Tough, but she isn't. Always worth knowing the truth, even if it complicates your life.

And there is the question of vengeance. Madam, and the others like her and above her, they should answer for what they've done somehow.

Catherine shifts in her seat, the air con is a bit buggered and she feels sticky, clammy. She tries to put her mind into neutral the way she does before any gig, even a small one like this. She flicks on the stereo. Fleetwood Mac's Greatest Hits. Perfect.

The drive takes her all the way from 'Don't Stop' to 'Tusk'. 'Tusk' makes her wonder about going back to Africa, even despite that close call in Sierra Leone.

Then it is time for action.

* * *

The apartment is above a florist. She presses the button. A wary Latin voice answers.

'Yo?'

'I got the money.'

'What the fuck? You don't bring it here!'

Bingo.

'New plan.'

'Fucking A.' The buzzer sounds angrily and Catherine pushes her way in and along the narrow hall that smells of flowers. Gardenias. The smell follows her as she goes up the stairs. That must be nice to wake to every morning, she thinks. Or maybe you don't notice after a while.

The door to the apartment is open and she walks straight into the living room. A tall, handsome Latino is standing in the centre of the room, biting his thumb. He looks like a villain in a Western. Drooping moustache and everything. Long black hair slicked back. Maybe he could do with losing a few pounds, but he carries it well. The room is cheaply furnished but immaculate. On the foam cushion of a pale, oatmeal Naugahyde sofa sits a small girl, her eyes intent on some kind of DS. She doesn't even look up.

The Latino guy faces Catherine, puts his hands on his hips. It makes him look even more like a gunslinger.

'Hey,' he says. 'You a friend of Mary's?'

'Yeah.'

'And it's safe, right? I mean no one knows you're here?' He pulls at his moustache. 'You want a drink or something? Water? Coke? Beer?' He's panicky, gabbling, absolutely not a pro.

'Just water. Thanks.'

He goes to the kitchenette. While he's gone, Catherine takes a proper gander round the room. Your typical hutch really. Everything very Sears and Roebuck. Nothing of value, no weapons.

And when the Latino comes back he says, 'We only got con gas unless you want it from the faucet.' And then he notices she's got a

279

gun pointing straight at him. Always surprises Catherine how long it takes people to register a gun in the room. And in this case it's not just any gun, it's her favourite gun, the one she hardly ever uses – a Smith and Wesson 38 special, Model 36, five-shot revolver J-frame, blued finish with Dymondwood grips. It was a present from Tough. He'd got it for her after the Iceland trip. Seems appropriate to use it for her last job.

Then she thinks maybe she could go back there. To Saudarkrokur. Disappear there. Live in a cabin miles from anyone, work in the Sportsbar maybe, write her kids' books.

'What the fuck?'

'This is how it goes. I'm going to take the kid home. You try and stop me, I will take you out.'

The Latino is silent. Pondering his options. Catherine makes things easy for him. 'You actually don't have any options here,' she says.

'What about Mary?'

'As I drive the kid home, you call and explain things to her. If she's still at the house when I get there I'll incapacitate her. Probably with lethal force. Depends how polite she is. How cooperative.'

'You ain't the police.'

'No. I'm what the police should be.'

And then the kid looks up from her toy and says, clear as a bell in beautiful unaccented English, 'I like it here. Don't want to go home.'

Forty

LORNA

One of the English habits Megan has adopted is that of the lingering bath, which is why she is still in the tub when Amelia calls round.

Lorna is puzzled, people don't just call round any more, they just don't. And now it's happened twice in two days. First Jez. Now Amelia. Conscious of the marketing emergency situation – whatever that could be – Lorna buzzes her up. So, maybe her and Megs won't drive out to Russian Hill today after all, maybe she'll catch up with her buddies from the nineteenth century instead. See if Mr Zwaademaker has anything else to teach her. That won't be so bad.

She goes and calls through the bathroom door. 'Hey, marine girl. Your boss is here.'

There are paroxysms of splashing behind the door, which opens suddenly. Megan appears – flushed, wet and naked – without so much as a towel. Clothed only in steam and panic. 'God girl, you are magnificent,' says Lorna, because her room-mate does look amazing, like some warrior lioness woman. Like Xena only hotter. Only she isn't exactly acting much like a warrior. She's jumpy, twitchy.

'Shush, Lorna. Amelia's here? Now?'

'Yep, she's on her way up.'

'You haven't buzzed her in?'

''Course I have. Why not?'

'Shit.'

Megan disappears behind a closed door again and Lorna goes to answer the knock on the door to the flat.

Amelia is wearing Roman sandals, a white shirt drawn tight on a blue skirt, her lips smiling, too red. And she is wearing too much blusher. She looks like she has got dressed in a hurry or with her mind on other things.

'Hey, Lorna.'

'Hey, Amelia.'

Lorna wonders if they are meant to kiss hello, but Amelia doesn't seem inclined to go for one. 'Come in, take the weight off your feet. Megs is in the bath. You were lucky to catch her in. We're off out in a bit,' which is a dig about not phoning first like normal fucking twenty-first-century people. But Amelia just nods.

'She's taking a bath?'

'Yeah.'

'Figures.'

A weird thing to say, and in fact the whole atmosphere is becoming so deeply odd that Lorna can feel her mouth going dry and her hands getting sweaty. 'Can I get you anything? A cup of tea?'

'Yes. OK.'

Yes. OK? One of the things Lorna has struggled to get used to over here is the lack of eagerness when offered tea. In England if you are offered a cuppa you seize on it with the enthusiasm of a dry man in a desert. 'Oh yes!' you say. 'That would be lovely! I'd love one! A cup of tea! Yes, please!' Cheap and easy to make it may be, but you celebrate each and every cup like it is a rare and exquisite spice brought back from Samarkand at great peril.

Not here. Here tea is just one more beverage option in a land full of them.

'Right. How do you have it?'

'Just black.'

And drinking it without milk is wrong, and not saying please or thank you is an absolute diabolical liberty.

She goes to boil the kettle and get out the cups. To make a point she's going to do it all properly with a teapot, a milk jug – who cares if the

282

Melster doesn't take it – and those pretty little cups and saucers that they hardly ever use. She is going to use the loose Yorkshire tea bought on a whim in the English deli when she was downtown one day. She is going to use a strainer. *Be the change you want to see.* You want people to take tea-drinking properly, then you have to set an example.

Biscuits. Where are they? She hopes she didn't eat them all last night while she was wondering where Megs was.

She didn't. There are six left. Hobnobs. Another English product taking the States by storm. Perfect.

And now she hears a violent sneeze from the living room. And so she guesses that Amelia is being ostentatiously allergic to poor old Armitage Shanks. She hopes that Megs will be able to get rid of her pretty soon, though this work crisis is clearly bad enough to make everyone behave like freaks. Maybe the firm is going bust, which will be shit but at least they might be able to finally get to go on that Yosemite trip. And Megan will get another job. She's skilled, talented, sorted. Anyone can tell that just by looking at her. She radiates competent good sense. Megan is the most employable woman she's ever known. And, in any case, they are loaded now. Lorna has to keep reminding herself about that.

She carries the tray with all the necessary into the living room just as Megan walks in from the bathroom. She's dressed carefully, Lorna can see that. Her super-skinny claret Hudson jeans. The ones that make her legs even longer. Her black Wildfox sweater. Her Porselli pumps.

Lorna pretends not to notice the heavy weight of the silence as she sets the tea things down.

'Shall I be mother?' she says and pours three cups, adding milk and sugar to hers even though she doesn't usually take sugar, but it allows her to use the nifty little tongs she's got from that vintage shop for three dollars. She knows Megan will notice this affectation and smile inside but that is all good, she wants Megan to smile because things are a bit too bloody serious at the minute.

She's just about to say she'll leave them to talk business strategies and audience segmentation or whatever when Amelia speaks.

'He won't leave me.' Her voice is dangerously even.

'I know that,' says Megan. 'I don't want him to. In fact I don't want to see him again.'

'Well that's good, honey. Because you won't.'

Lorna stirs her tea, takes a sip and leaves the room. This is clearly not the right place for her to be, but fucking hell – Megan and John? Jesus. This is huge.

Music would be good, but there's nothing that fits. It needs to be loud so she won't be tempted to try and overhear whatever is happening in the living room. Something loud. Something angry. Something from her loud and angry teens. Opeth.

She lies on her bed and looks at the ceiling. Megan and John? She doesn't really know her room-mate at all obviously. How have they even managed it? And the whole dinner-party thing takes on a whole new colour. She decides that she is pretty pissed off about that.

Would they be able to say friends after this? Of course they would. Better friends. Or would they? Oh, it's all a bit of a head-fuck.

Opeth do their madly angry shouty thing and she lets herself think of Megs and her down the line. Five years' time? Ten? Maybe not room-mates any more, but living near each other in their own places.

And she thinks about the magnificence of Megan. Not just her body, but the all-round brilliance of her. And she wonders what it would be like if she found she actually did have a Sapphic bone or two somewhere in her body.

Maybe one night after too much drink and too many good songs and with the realisation that all men are wankers and that they are both gorgeous – both absolutely smoking fucking hot in fact – they'll just start snogging and one thing might lead to another, and it's common knowledge that sex with another girl is actually amazing. And she wonders which of them would be the mum if they decide to have kids. Maybe they both would. Maybe they would have a kid each. At the same time. That would shake up the NCT group. She wonders whether they'd be in the USA or the UK. Certainly be a whole lot cheaper to have their babies in England.

Then again, common knowledge is often wrong. For example, it is common knowledge that dope is a good thing but in Lorna's experience stoners are very boring people. Give her a conversation with an insurance agent over one with a stoner any day. Which brings her back to John and Amelia.

She presses the remote, stops the album. It's actually too, too loud, too, too angry. God, her teenage self was a state. Needed help. How come no one saw that back then?

In the sudden silence she wonders if maybe she's overthinking things. It's Megs she should be thinking about, because clearly things are fucked up for her right now, this minute. And of course, it's now that Megs opens the door.

Lorna doesn't look round. Keeps her eyes on the ceiling.

'She gone?' she says.

'Yeah.' A pause. 'Pretty messy, huh?' Megan says.

'Just a bit.'

'You got some questions?'

'A few.'

'Fire away.'

Lorna makes a big show of thinking. Puts her hand on her forehead. Then flips around on her bed so she can see Megan hovering sheepishly in the doorway. Sheepish doesn't really suit Megan, Lorna thinks. Megan should be a beautiful she-wolf in beautiful she-wolves clothing at all times.

'Question one: did you leave any biscuits? Question two: shall I make a fresh pot of tea? Question three ... Question three is ... Dear heart, what the fuck were you thinking?'

There's a pause, then Megan tries to laugh but it comes out all wrong and suddenly she's in tears. Lorna can't feel pissed off any more. It's not like when Jez was crying. Jez crying just got on her tits. Megan crying tugs at her heart.

She gets up off the bed. Crosses to her roomie and hugs her. 'It's OK, hon. If you've eaten all the biscuits we can get some more.'

Megan hiccups into Lorna's hair. 'It's fine. There are still biscuits.'

'That's all right then,' says Lorna.

And later, after more tea, after all the biscuits, after some chat about nothing that really matters because they agreed they'd talk about all of that other stuff some other time – maybe over a pool game ('Like lads would,' says Lorna, 'they're better than us like that.') . . .

After all that, they finally go outside to drive to the city, like they'd planned, but they can't get very far because the tyres on Megan's Focus are flat. Slashed in fact. They won't be going to Russian Hill today.

'Bit petty?' says Lorna. 'Or fair enough?'

'Fair enough, I guess,' says Megan.

'Can we start drinking now, do you think?'

'I think that yes, yes we can.'

'And I think that tonight we should aim for more than a pitiful thirty-two units, don't you?'

'Hell, yeah.'

Forty-one

NICKY

The first thing is to calm Mary, who is weeping noisily on the sofa. I can't think with that racket. I put my arms around her and say the right things – not to worry, not her fault, they won't harm Scarlett because then how would they get their money? I say all that but it's hard because I absolutely hate her right now. I can't help it. Logically, it's probably really not her fault but it doesn't matter – she was in charge and now our baby's gone. She's our irresponsible first babysitter, Noel, times a million.

When the tears have subsided a bit, I get her to show me the note. It's a classic pantomime ransom note. You know, letters cut from newspapers and stuck onto card, the thing we're all familiar with from childhood comics. I'm thinking the police would probably unravel this in minutes. They'd find out which editions of which papers the letters came from. Which shops they were bought from too probably. There'll be DNA all over the letters, the card, the glue. There's bound to be fingerprints. Maybe even the grammar of the note has a distinctive hallmark which would point to known suspects. But the police are never going to be in a position to see this note. We absolutely can't take that risk.

My biggest fear is that whoever did this simply kills Scarlett once we've paid the money. She's the only thing that can give them away. Why take the risk of looking after a kid who might attract attention? We're clearly going to pay anyway, aren't we? It's not like dealing with Amazon or eBay is it? We can't just ring a helpdesk and complain that we've paid but that our goods haven't arrived.

I say this to Mary. I shouldn't. I mean, Christ, she obviously feels guilty enough already. I shouldn't even really acknowledge it to myself. Sometimes articulating things kind of makes them happen. Like you hear about people worrying out loud about their aches and pains being cancer and then that worry actually gives them the disease. I think what I'm probably hoping is that Mary will reassure me by explaining exactly why my fears are groundless, that of course they won't do that and explaining scientifically why it would be crazy for these bastards to even think of that, how it would fuck up their whole game plan. How history and psychology and plain good sense mean that won't happen, but of course she can't do much in the way of reassurance right now. She's in no fit state to.

But I tell her anyway – the thoughts have to go somewhere – and she looks shocked. 'Fuck,' she whispers, wide-eyed. 'Fuck.' And she looks so sick that I end up reassuring her. 'It won't happen. They won't do that. These are businessmen. It's just a transaction to them,' I say. But of course businessmen will want to maximise profit and minimise risk. Getting rid of Scarlett removes risk entirely, without affecting their potential profit at all.

We could demand proof she's alive before we pay I suppose, but what proof could we ask for? A photo of Scarlett next to the front page of the paper? A video with date and time along the bottom? That would only prove she was alive up to the moment the picture or the video was taken.

Mary's phone goes and she leaves the room to take the call. I remind her not to tell anyone about our situation and she snaps at me.

'I'm not a retard,' she says and tosses her pigtails from side to side. She is not one of those women who looks at their most beautiful when angry. She looks quite ugly in fact. But she's under intolerable pressure here, I know. What if something does happen to Scarlett? How will she live with that? How can she go on?

Though people do. They have to.

Christ, I wish Sarah was here.

And I reach in my pocket to get my phone to call her, even though Mary says she's called her plenty of times already. And that's when I realise that I've left my phone in that psycho Catherine's car, or the cafe or somewhere. It's not here anyway. I haven't got it. This makes me panic more than anything. Not having a phone makes me feel blind and helpless.

Less than two minutes later Mary's back and scooping up her tote bag. The one that says 'My bag. My rules' in zany pink on the rustic hemp cloth. And she's gone.

'Got to go,' is all she says.

I'm shocked. 'Now?' I say. 'In the middle of all this?'

'It's all such fucking bullshit,' she says and there are angry tears in her eyes. 'Everyone lets you down. Everyone. In the end.'

And I say, 'Look, Mary, there's bigger things to worry about right now than your boyfriend troubles.'

She gives me a long, hard look. It's chilling actually.

'Fuck you, Russell,' she says at last. 'Fuck you. Fuck Sarah. Fuck the brat. Fuck your money. And fuck England too.'

On another day I'd probably laugh, but now, with my kid missing, possibly dead, with all the rage and fear I have dammed up inside me, I raise my hand. She stops me with a look. 'Don't even think about it,' she says. It's enough. What am I doing? She's just a kid herself. An angry kid full of guilt and fear. Just like me. Just like all of us. At moments of great stress we all become furious toddlers.

She heads for the door. Then spins back. 'Land of Hope and Fucking Glory,' she says. 'Big joke.' And then she really is gone, banging out of the doors, crunching down the gravel and power-walking away. I've never seen Mary at anything above languid before. She's pretty speedy when she wants to be.

There's something I have to say, despite everything.

I run to the street. She's already a hundred yards away and she's actually broken into an awkward half-jog. I call after her: 'Thank you, Mary. For what you've done with Scarlett. Thank you.' I'm not

289

even sure she hears. And if she does, I hope she doesn't think it's sarcasm, because I really am grateful. Whatever happens, Scarlett has been happy with Mary. She's made real progress. Mary brought us all hope, and that's a great gift. I'm still grateful for that, even now. The second-best kind of love is still a good kind of love.

On my own now I feel sick, literally sick, with dread. There's a sour taste in my mouth and my stomach spasms painfully. I want to scream and shout and break things. I want to rage and howl and strangle someone. But I also feel so tired, I could sleep for ever. And I want to somehow relieve the volcanic pressure in my head. But there's nothing to be done except wait for a new note and that might not be for hours or days.

And where the fuck is Sarah?

In the end it's the money that's done all this and I get the notion that if I do some immediate good with the money, then maybe some good will flow back my way. So I go into the downstairs toilet, the place where just a few weeks ago I had discovered Russell stiff and cold and gone. I go in there and pick up one of the *Private Eye*s stacked in a pile next to the pan and go through to Russell's office with it.

I flip the lid on Russell's iThing and there, under the tubercular gaze of those pre-Raphaelite girls, I start shoving wads of electronic tenners into electronic begging bowls.

You know *Private Eye*, right? It's this magazine that attempts to keep the ruling class in line with satirical jokes and, also, by revealing the stuff they'd rather keep hidden. It has some very good political cartoons. At the back it has a classified section, one column of which is called EYE NEED. It's where people beg basically. They stick in one line about their particular misfortune and also put their bank details in the hope that people will be moved to donate. Does it work? I guess that sometimes it must because people wouldn't do it, but it seems unlikely.

Anyway, this copy of *Private Eye* is three months old so the philosophy student who wants to do a PhD, the newly divorced mum who wants to keep her kids at private school, the wine merchant about to go bankrupt because of late payments from his suppliers, the guy who wants to buy some land and build a straw-bale house, the Surrey roofer who needs to buy a kidney, all of these are going to find ridiculously pleasant surprises in their bank accounts. Surely they've given up all hope by now?

Of course it might be too late for the roofer.

I also send money to all the charities advertising through the mag, so Save The Children, WaterAid, Oxfam, Help The Aged, Shelter, they all get a million. And Scope, the cerebral palsy people, they get five million on the grounds that they help people like Scarlett.

Right from the start of this whole thing we'd talked about which charities we'd support, but hadn't actually quite got around to doing it. I'd bought new suits and new hair, Sarah had bought new frocks, but we'd not actually done much concrete good with the money. Though I have given money to Russell's daughter. But I should give more, it is all her money after all. So I transfer a million across to her. And then another million.

Giving all this cash away has taken a while and has kept the sickness at bay just a little – at least I'm doing something – and I come off the bank site and sit back and stretch. My neck clicks uncomfortably. I glance at all the short cuts on the screen and click on one more or less at random, which is how I find out something that any other time would be kind of fucking hilarious.

Forty-two

CATHERINE

After the kid announces that she doesn't want to go home, she starts screaming. Catherine has heard this kind of desperate noise from children before, several times. She's heard it in Mostar, in Fallujah, in Helmand, in Sierra Leone. And the children screaming then had something to bloody well scream about. This kid is being rescued. Catherine is this kid's Queen bloody Arthur. Her Galahad.

Catherine can't allow this racket. Not here. Not now. She can't. It isn't just the fact that the noise might bring the neighbours round, or have staff and customers from the shop downstairs investigating. It isn't just the fact that someone might phone the police. All of these scenarios could be dealt with. It's more that it threatens her sanity. It's doing her head in. Catherine feels her whole body begin to go rigid. She clenches her teeth. She wants to throw that child out the window.

There is lots of advice for dealing with major tantrums out there on the net. Top tips include holding the child really tightly; making eye contact while you say – calmly but firmly – 'I'm here, I won't let you hurt yourself.' Some experts advise a time-out strategy. This means you put your child somewhere safe but boring, like a playpen, and let them rage for a while on their own.

Some people think that a silly song or a tickling game will change a kid's mood sufficiently that they forget about screaming and yelling.

These days very few recommend a sharp slap on the leg and almost none suggest telling the kid that you have a gun and you will use it if you have to. But then Catherine has never wanted kids and has always thought that ninety per cent of them seem to be horribly spoilt. Take her sister's kids, for example, with their incessant demands for stuff. Demands that are always met too. In the end.

No wonder the Western world is so messed up. Little children are not democrats. Discussion, debate, reasoned argument – all of these are wasted on them. Might is right, however, and the ankle-biters, they get that. Violence, blackmail, extortion and bribery. Kids understand how all of that works more or less from birth. Kids are born terrorists.

It's one reason Catherine wants to write children's books. She wants to show a world that children will recognise rather than this baffling make-believe adult place where things can be talked through and resolved with love and magic. That's all horseshit and children aren't fooled by it. They know the world is a war of all against all and that you use every weapon you have. Being cute, that's just another tool kids have, and when that doesn't work, they try something else. You can't blame them – it's nature – but that doesn't mean you give in to them.

Keeping a steady bead on Jesus she crosses over to where the brat is now thrashing around on the sofa barking and yelling. She looks like a thirsty seal stranded on dry land. A seal having an eppy.

With her right hand keeping the gun on Jesus, she wallops Scarlett hard on the back of her thigh with her left. The noise stops. See, Catherine thinks, see. You just need to have clear boundaries.

The screaming stops for about five seconds. If that. And then starts up again louder than before.

And that's when Catherine says that she will use the gun if she has to and, to be fair, she does say it calmly and firmly just as they recommend on Mumsnet. And she does get eye contact. The screaming stops again. The child looks back at her just as calmly. And then slowly, deliberately, purposefully, the kid opens her mouth, fills her lungs and lets rip twice as loud, the child's hot, fierce eyes never leaving Catherine's. Catherine feels panicked. Trapped, What to do now?

Across the room, the Latino closes his eyes. He swallows and shows his palms to Catherine as if to say kids eh, what can you do?

And then he takes a step forward.

Catherine hates have-a-go heroes, they fuck it up for everyone. Her finger tightens on the trigger.

Latino stops.

'The baby?' he says, and so Catherine understands that he is offering to comfort the child, and so she nods and lets him cross the room where he sits on the sofa and murmurs and croons and babbles and strokes the kid's hair and whispers in Spanish. Catherine thinks she'll give him one minute. And that is almost exactly how long it takes before the kid is snuffling rather than wailing.

'Be good now, you hear?' says Jesus in English and the kid hugs him and then stands unsteadily on thin, crooked baby foal legs. Very solemnly he takes off his necklace and places it around the kid's neck. She giggles and limps over to Catherine and holds out both arms.

Catherine has to admit that as teary, snot-streaked faces go, this is quite a bearable one. Or maybe that is relief at the cessation of that excruciating shrieking. She squats down and scoops the kid up. One arm is tight around her neck. The other one squashed against her chest. She is warm and she smells soapy. She weighs almost nothing.

Catherine tells the Latino to go to the bathroom and to stay there for five minutes. 'Use the time to call your girlfriend,' she says. 'Remember – lethal force. Anything happens to her, it's your bad.'

He goes meekly enough. 'Nice work with the brat though.' Catherine says this to his retreating back.

'Fuck you,' he says, without looking round. He sounds tired. He sounds like the weariest man on the planet.

Forty-three

POLLY

She is standing with her mother, with the package in her hand, listening to Daniel's breathing. It sounds like water on stones, like the tide coming in fast on a shingle beach.

'Mervyn will be here soon,' her mother says, and squeezes her arm. 'I'll make some tea.'

Polly looks at Daniel, and wonders. She wonders if he can still hear anything, hear his own breathing maybe. You know, with hearing being the last thing to go and everything. She wonders if he knows he might be dying.

He's 77 she thinks, he's had a good life, an interesting life. He's lived in India. He's made things, big things that have lasted and that have improved lives. The world is a better place than it was when he came into it, and that's all you can hope for really.

And he might still wake up of course. He might suddenly sit up, announce that he fancies a fry-up, or that he wants to go to the beach, or up in a hot-air balloon. Or that he's going to sort out the garden, or paint the kitchen, or write a song. You don't ever really know with Daniel.

Still, this feels like the end coming. And she thinks Daniel knew it was on its way.

Last night he'd asked her what she would do if she knew the end of the world was tomorrow. And got a bit cross when she replied that there were probably lots of people she should say sorry to.

'Why?' he'd said. 'What's the point of that?' And he had explained that it was actually pretty damn rude of her, because if it was the last day on Earth did she really think people would want to have any of their final precious minutes wasted listening to her apologies?

And she'd felt like she'd been tricked somehow and was annoyed at herself. And she'd asked him what he would do and he'd obviously been giving it a lot of thought because he had the whole day planned.

He would get up early before the dawn so that he could see the last sunrise come up and hear the last dawn chorus. He would watch the birds at the feeder for a while.

And then he would have a bucks fizz like it was Christmas Day, or a wedding breakfast. Then he would have toast made from home-made bread with home-made bramble jelly.

And while he ate his breakfast he would listen to Samuel Barber's 'Adagio For Strings', the 2001 performance with Leonard Slatkin and the BBC Orchestra. And then he'd go for a long walk somewhere he'd never been before, maybe even get lost.

'What if the weather is bad?'

'No such thing as bad weather,' said Daniel. 'There is only inappropriate clothing.'

Polly wasn't so sure about that.

'Anyway, ' said Daniel, 'I shall want some rain, if that's what you mean.'

In Daniel's perfect final day it would just so happen that as he was growing tired from his walk, he would stumble across a lovely little pub that is, somehow, still serving and he'd sit near a fire, drinking and thinking – maybe doing the crossword – listening to the rain as it hammered down outside.

'A place can only be truly cosy if it's wild outside,' he said.

And then the pub would fill up and there'd be good conversation and songs and stories, and then somehow there'd just be him and the landlady with her twinkling black gypsy eyes and an easy smile. And she'd ask him if he has anyone to be with on this last night and he'd say no and she'd say that she was also alone. And so there would be a moment of silence and thought and after this she would smile and say, 'No sad stories, not tonight.'

And she would get a bottle of the finest Islay malt, the kind that costs hundreds of pounds a glass, and she'd pour them a generous measure, and they'd go upstairs to a room that smelled faintly of oranges and they would undress each other by candlelight.

Polly stopped him there. She couldn't hear any more.

'Maybe I could say sorry to everyone by text. That wouldn't take up so much of everyone's precious time,' she said.

And Daniel had laughed and asked if he was making her uncomfortable, and she said no and then she laughed as well. And she'd admitted then that, yes, of course he was making her uncomfortable. And that's when he'd told her that he was going to stop taking his pills.

'What? All of them?'

'All nineteen of them, yes.'

'What will happen?'

'Well, I hope I'll feel better. I hope I'll have more energy. I hope I won't be quite as dozy. And then I hope that one morning quite soon I'll drop down dead. Possibly while mowing the lawn, or maybe while listening to music or watching a film. Or maybe I just won't wake up. That would be the dream scenario.'

And now it looks like he might have got his dream ending, even if it's come rushing up a bit quicker than they'd imagined.

Looking at the rise and fall of his chest beneath the covers she wants to tell the daft old bugger that his fantasy last day is way too easy. What about the children? The babies? What about the pregnant women? What about all the people who have just got started. Easy for him to imagine it all lovely with candles and posh whisky and conversation and crosswords. She can't help thinking of all the people who would be in bits. She could just hear all the angry tears. All the shouting.

She goes to the kitchen and has a cup of tea with her mum. Her mum who is pointedly not asking what the package is. Who doesn't even ask about the package when Polly is taking the ice cream out to make room for it in the freezer.

'That'll melt,' she says.

'Oh well, there's not much left anyway. Maybe I'll have some now.'

'Ice cream in the morning?'

Yes, why not ice cream in the morning? Let's go crazy. Let's imagine it really is our last day on Earth. And actually, Polly can easily imagine her mum using her last day trying to use everything up, to make sure there was no waste. Spending her last hours making a casserole out of leftovers for a dinner no one would ever eat. How sad is that?

Polly goes to her room and lies on her bed and watches *Cash In The Attic* and *Wife Swap* and wonders where they find these people prepared to humiliate themselves on national TV. But she's glad these shows are on now. Much easier to let your mind wander with the telly on.

If you can imagine it then someone somewhere has actually done it, that's what he'd said to her once. When? When she was speculating about killing Irina, probably fantasising about cutting her up and using her to thicken the lunchtime soup. But if it's true that a thing imagined is a thing that has been done somewhere or other, then it means someone somewhere has really spent their last day on earth using up leftovers, even when they knew it was the final act of their life. Someone has made radish pancakes or something because that was what was left in the fridge.

And it also means that a lady somewhere has actually gone into the bedroom of a dying old man and put her hand around him – around his thing – and has massaged him gently till he's hard – or hard enough anyway – and then that lady has straddled him, guided him into her and moved up and down on him until he's come. And that lady has gone on to have his baby, so that his fantastic genes carry on. Maybe the old guy's only son is dead and this lady, whoever she is, maybe she thinks that's a shame, what with him being so clever and so talented and such an interesting old man and everything. And still quite hand-some even though he's 77 and ill.

Someone, somewhere, hasn't just thought about this. Someone, somewhere, has done it.

There's a knock at the door. She jumps. It's like someone has been reading her thoughts and is so disgusted that they've come to stop her thinking any more of them. And it's not her mum's knock, her mum doesn't knock. This is a man's knock. A confident man's knock.

The door opens and she sees Mervyn's face. He looks serious.

'Came as soon as I could. Got a lift most of the way. Cabbie who'd seen me on *Newsnight*. Wouldn't take a fare.' A pause, then, 'I've had a look at Daniel. I think he's had a big stroke. If he really won't go to hospital then it's probably just a case of waiting now. And keeping him comfortable.'

Polly is suddenly really glad he's here.

'Come in, Mervyn. Come and talk to me. And close the door.'

She can always eBay the package.

Forty-four

SARAH

A homeless guy. Nothing remarkable about him. Another motionless kid in the stained pupa of his sleeping bag, lying by an ATM on California Street. Next to him is a takeaway coffee mug. Starbucks. Trente-sized, though it looks like someone has actually bitten a lump out of the rim, there are jagged edges that are definitely suggestive of teeth marks. Nevertheless it's half full of nickels and dimes. And Sarah bends down and stuffs in her own five-dollar bill. There's no acknowledgement. The sleeping bag doesn't stir. If the body inside was dead, how long before anyone noticed? And how long after that before someone removed the corpse? The money would definitely go first.

And, as she stands looking down, there is a spastic wriggle deep in the depths of the bag. A rustle that tells her there's life here. And relief pulses through her, she can feel it moving through her body just like blood.

And then she thinks sod it, and stuffs all the cash in her purse into the mug. A couple more fives, a twenty. A fifty. A lot of change. She fills the trente and hugs herself as she walks on. Nice to be nice. And it's only money.

Sarah remembers a live art project the council had funded back when she was with Cultural Services, and back when local councils still had money for art.

A local performance artist sat next to an ATM in the town centre, styrofoam cup in front of him – not a trente – filthy sleeping bag over his knees, looking every inch the woebegone beggar. Looking exactly like this guy here in California Street. And every time someone approached he would mutter, 'Want any change, mate?' and try and give them handfuls of silver. Properly freaked people out. Not children. Children happily took the cash, but adults didn't know how to respond. Some couldn't hear what he was really saying and ignored him as effectively as if he'd been a real beggar, some got quite annoyed. One or two got violent and had to be restrained by council security. Because of course the change the artist was giving away was taxpayers money, part of a grant that she'd approved, so a health and safety assessment ensured that burly men were on hand to prevent trouble.

It was a piece she'd always liked, and one of the few arts projects Nicky had ever supported with enthusiasm.

Sarah goes to the ATM. She takes out her daily limit. Five hundred dollars. Twenty-five brand-new flat notes that smell of sophisticated inks and mischief.

It takes her an hour to find twenty-five can collectors and convince them to take her money. Even the homeless are suspicious of free cash. And who can blame them? The homeless know the dangers of money better than anyone.

She gives out her last note outside Grace Cathedral.

Behind the hunched shoulders and haunted face of her last beggar she reads a sign that says 'What they're all talking about – Fifty shades of Grace'. It makes her stop and smile. And then she finds she's actually inside the body of the church. On a pew. She isn't really praying in here exactly, but she is thinking hard about things. And maybe that is all praying is.

When her phone goes off she is mortified. There's only one old guy in the pews near her but he gives her such a beady look that she turns her phone off without even looking at who the call is from. It only rang for a second, but the cheery ghostly echo of her ringtone seems to continue to reverberate around the vaulted Gothic space. Queen. 'Crazy Little Thing Called Love'.

She shuts her eyes.

When she opens them again, it is to find that the old guy next to her, a bum she guesses at first, has scooted along the pew so that he is pretty close. Not offensively close, but right on the edge of her personal space. She can sense him staring at her. Staring and smiling. This is always happening to her. She's the one the nutters warm to, the person they feel confident enough to approach.

She looks down at the floor for as long as she can, tries to pick up her train of thought, but it's too late – gone. Between her phone going and this old guy watching her, her concentration has dissolved.

She's thinking that she might as well go now, the cathedral clearly isn't going to give her the peace she needs. She puts her hands on her bags and it's then that the old guy speaks.

'Interesting choice of tune.'

'Excuse me?'

'On your phone.'

She's made a mistake, she's engaged with him. He scoots just a little closer. And as he moves up she thinks she can detect a sweetish smell, like sandwiches left too long in their Tupperware box on a long coach trip.

'Beautiful place this, isn't it?'

He's English she realises. So a tourist not a bum, and now that she gets a proper look at him she can see that he's decently clad. Perhaps a little overdressed for San Francisco in late summer, especially with that tweedy jacket. And he's very thin. But neat and conservative. She wonders if he's with a group and looks around.

'I'm here on my own. Don't worry, there's not a whole coach-load of coffin dodgers about to pounce.' She hears the chuckle in his voice and relaxes a bit.

'Yes, it's beautiful in here.' And she looks around and realises that she hasn't really taken it in at all before now. She'd just come in, found a pew, dumped her bags and started thinking about whatever it was she had been thinking about. Money. The homeless. Life. Scarlett. Work. Nicky. Family. What they'd done and where they were going.

302

How it might all end. But there was no coherence to her thinking. It was all discordant and nonsensical, and it makes her panicky to be all over the place like this because planning and order are key parts of her skill-set. Only now, with this nice old English gent taking her out of the spinning waltzer of her own thoughts, she does start to breathe a bit. So at first she's grateful to him for lassooing her back to the real and manageable world.

She looks around now and admires the ambition of this place. Grace Cathedral was built in 1844 – she'd read that on the notice-board as she'd come in – and what was San Francisco then? An outlaw town. Not even American then really – still Mexican – and a town about to explode with the gold rush and the railroad. But they didn't know that was down the line when they built this. This was a state-ment of intent. It said: We are going to be somebody. It was like an intern spending her first month's salary on a pair of Jimmy Choos and then living on lentils for weeks to pay for them. It said: I'm going places. Just watch me.

'Have you been saved?' The old guy says it conversationally, in the same way you might say, 'Is it raining out?'

Bloody hell. Turns out he's a nutter after all. Shame, he seemed so normal at first. A nice old man. 'No. No, I haven't.'

The old man nods, chuckles wheezily. 'I was like you once. There wasn't a bigger atheist than me. I was famous for it. Militant about it in actual fact. I used to say God was an imaginary friend for grown-ups. Someone we'd made up out of words just so we wouldn't be lonely or sad.'

'I'm sorry, I've got to be somewhere.'

He puts his skinny hand on her arm. Grips it. Christ, the strength that is in that feeble-looking claw. Like being grabbed by a belligerent lobster.

'I won't be long.' He is smiling as he says this, showing his teeth. There's some menace there. Some sense of threat. Sarah looks around for a vicar or a nun or someone obviously connected with the proper

303

authorities, but there's no one who looks like that. Just curious architecture fans, daydreaming day trippers, the prayerful, and her and this nutty evangelical with the ridiculously strong lobster-grip.

'OK,' she mutters, 'five minutes then I have to go.'

'Good girl,' he says, and releases her arm. Pats it gently. The complete avuncular Werther's Original OAP again.

He pauses to gather his thoughts and she thinks bugger him, because she means it. She is only going to give him five minutes, if he wants to waste it in staging meaningful pauses let him. She glances at him, and too late realises that this is what he is waiting for – the chance for eye contact. He fixes her with his kindly eyes, and his thin, impossibly wrinkled face splinters in a broad warm grin. And he begins.

'When you finally begin to see the end of the road, the tunnel at the end of the light, as it were – well, it's natural to question things, and I just kept thinking – what if I'm wrong. What if, by some billion to one, impossible fluke there is a God?'

'A white man with a flowing white beard, sitting on a cloud?'

The old guy frowns, holds up a finger for silence. Clearly this is more a tutorial than a debate. 'Sorry,' says Sarah, and is immediately disgusted at herself. Put out because he's the rude one here. He is the one intruding on her privacy.

'And if there is a God, well, then the signs are that he is, as the ancient books tell us, a vengeful God. A God who sent his only son as a sacrifice to us. A sacrifice that we have pretty much ignored. And I thought, well if there is a Day of Judgement my defence of "Oh well, it just seemed so unlikely, m'lud" is going to look weak. I could easily imagine this particular God – this capricious, jealous God – getting pretty furious. I could imagine him asking, hadn't he shown me? Hadn't thousands of years of art and literature and theology and philosophy, hadn't that been enough in the way of proof of his existence and a guide to his personality? And the simple faith of countless ordinary people? Was that all out the window because of Darwin and

304

his turtles? I imagined that scene and thought that would be pretty embarrassing, wouldn't it? I mean if my first thoughts – my atheistic thoughts – were correct and there was no God well, fair enough, I'll just be an unlikely collection of proteins returning to the earth. But if that position was wrong, well, I'd have to live with an eternity of hell-fire. Because the books are pretty clear on this. Unless we accept God's love we are going to have a pretty bad time of it. For ever. And I don't know about you, but I don't really fancy that.'

She knows about all this.

'Pascal's wager,' she says.

'You know about Pascal?'

'Yes, yes. Yes I do!' She is aware of how excited she sounds, like the girl in the class whose hand stretches high to the ceiling, the girl who is desperate to be asked for the answer. She hates the way that girl is still there inside her, waiting for a chance to get a gold star and a smiley face. She hates this tendency towards swottiness.

She makes the effort to slow herself down, to dial down the enthusiasm in her voice. 'Yeah, Pascal said you might as well bet on the existence of God because you'll only know about it if you win. It's the exact point you've just made. That's my uni first year Introduction to Philosophy unit that is.' She actually thinks it might have once been a question on *University Challenge*. Most of the cleverest stuff she knows comes from that show.

'Yes it is, and he's right, isn't he?'

'Well, no actually. It's like kids and Santa Claus. At first they believe completely and then, round about seven or eight, they start to wonder, but they can't afford to really question Santa's existence in case it's true that he only brings presents to believers, so they are trapped in this kind of psychological limbo for a while. Blinded to the truth by the desire for presents. They have to believe and not believe simultaneously. It can't be good for them.'

'And what happens when they finally admit that there isn't a Santa Claus?'

'Well, the presents don't stop coming, do they?'

'No, but the children are never quite as excited about Christmas again. They have been robbed of something. And they never trust their parents again, which is probably why the younger generation are so ready to put their faith in material things rather than things of the spirit.'

Sarah frowns and stretches her back, hears it click. Maybe she should treat herself to a massage later. Maybe Jesus would do it?

Sarah blows a raspberry. Yes, she's blown a raspberry. A loud and long one. In church. If there's a hell she's going there for sure now. But she couldn't help herself. This funny old bloke doesn't seem bothered. He does his wheezy chuckle again.

'Not much longer, my dear.' He makes a show of looking around him, his loose skin tightening on his face and neck, and she gets a sense of what a handsome man he might have been once. 'Look at this place. Or, better, think about the medieval cathedrals in England. Think about the people who built them. Poor people using block and tackle to haul stone hewn and shaped at huge effort. No plans. Taking scores of years to do it. No one has built an atheist cathedral, have they?'

It's out before she can stop herself.

'The Twin Towers.' Shit. She groans inside. She knows it is the worst thing to say. It's a gift to this annoying old git, an open goal. The Twin Towers are never the answer to any question worth asking.

He twinkles. 'Well, yes, the Twin Towers. The World Trade Centre. And what happened to them again? Without God – without the idea of God – human beings are always at Ground Zero scrabbling around for something more important than themselves.'

'What about all the wars in the name of religion?'

He waves a hand as if to say, not that old chestnut. Have you nothing better to offer than that? Is that really all you've got? Dear, oh, dear.

'Well, now, war is something I know about. You might say war is my specialist subject. And I can tell you no war in history has ever actually been about God. For the people that start wars they're about money and power. And for the poor sods that actually fight them it's about the chance to ride around in a truck with a big gun making some exciting bangs. Never underestimate the appeal of fireworks. I'll agree that religion has quite often been used as an excuse. A fig leaf if you will. And it's one of the things He might be extremely annoyed about actually.'

'But say there is a God. If you've lived a good life don't you think He will let you into heaven anyway? Even if you didn't believe.'

'Oh, sweetheart. No, I absolutely don't think that. I would say that from what has been written about God through the ages, He is very unlikely to react like that. That would be the reaction of a *Guardian*-reading God. A PBS God. And that particular God definitely doesn't exist. And in any case' – he looks away now, his skin loose and reptilian again, his voice dropping to an unnerving whisper – 'I haven't lived a good life. I have done terrible things. Terrible, terrible things.'

He's grave now. Still and silent. And, despite herself, she's intrigued.

'Really? Like what?'

'Everything. I've done everything. I've done the very worst things you can think of.' He shakes his head and it's obvious he means it. Sarah tries not to wonder what the worst might mean. Rape? Murder? Child murder? Child rape? This harmless old guy? She remembers the extraordinary power in his fingers and shivers.

He stands. 'Well, it's been lovely to talk to you. But that's our five minutes up and I must tootle along. I'm sure I haven't convinced you or converted you. But maybe I've planted a seed.'

Good heavens, he's ending the conversation first. It's him dreaming up an excuse to leave. She's surprised by that. And oddly offended, like it was a date with some hopeless geek and then he's the one to say it's never going to happen between them. She wonders for a minute how her life might have turned out if Nicky had said no to going for a drink after his annual review. Not that there was ever any chance of that. She'd known right from the off that he would fall in love with her.

307

The old man puts out his hand. She stands to take it. Shy. Not wanting to be rude, but not really wanting to touch him. He looks her in the eyes again as if searching for something. She thinks that he doesn't find it, whatever it is, because he frowns, his whole lizardy face scrunching up like an empty crisp packet. She catches a whiff of that hot, sweet, sweaty-sandwich smell again.

'Jack Tough,' he says. Good name. Can't be real though, can it?

'Sarah,' she says. 'Sarah Fisher.'

'And don't worry,' he says, as he shuffles along the pew away from her. 'You've probably got time to put everything right.'

'What? Time to put what right?'

He looks back at her. 'Whatever it is you've done or left undone.'

She watches him as he leaves the church. He walks with a martial briskness. It's surely true that he's been a soldier.

And she sits there for a while. Could have been a long time, could have been a short time. She just sits there not really thinking of anything. And then she wonders how to put things right in her life. Scarlett, she thinks. Scarlett's life will be my defence. If there really is a fierce old judge with a beard she will be able to say, Here my Lord, here is something good. And if it's not enough. Well, fuck him.

And now, finally, here's a vicar. A woman. Pretty, spiky-haired and pixie-faced. Her dog collar giving her the look of a singer in a punk band. She has kind eyes and a collection plate.

'Hope you don't mind . . .' she says and waits. Expectant. And of course Sarah has no money. Not a dime.

'I'm sorry . . .' she begins and the elfin punky vicar just shakes her head, puts her hand on Sarah's shoulder. 'It's OK. Really, it's OK.' She moves down the pew.

Sarah gets up to go. She checks she has everything. Bag. Empty wallet. Keys. She switches her phone on and instantly the jokey bounce of her ringtone insults the cool ecumenical air. Heads turn her way. An Asian tourist with a heavy camera gives her a thumbs up.

She is giving him a thumbs up back as she clicks Answer.

'Nicky,' she whispers, 'I'm in church. What is it?'

And then she's running. Sprinting from cool gloom to the bright light outside. The light that hurts and leaves her blinking and disorientated. She has to stop. Shield her eyes, gather herself. And then she's running again.

Forty-five

NICKY

I hear her coming before she reaches the house. Even though I am inside and on the landline phone raging to Sarah, I still hear that distinctive tlot-tlot crunching unevenly over our gated gravel.

I stop whatever it is I'm yelling, and am at the door in a stride yanking it open. Scarlett is smiling, face all pinked up in the September sun, curls the colour of vanilla ice cream swaying gently in the breeze, looking like a poster child for hemiplegia. Looking like the kind of HD snap that brings in millions from soppy-hearted rich guys, or unlocks the dosh from those frightened billionaires trying to manipulate the karmic stock exchange before they snuff it.

Scarlett sees my face and her smile wobbles and she looks behind her. Which is when I see the psycho nutjob. Catherine. She's standing near the gate, also smiling – though thinly. Hands on hips. I'm gobsmacked and my first thought is a furious one. Did she have something to do with this whole abduction thing? I step forward and scoop Scarlett up. Hold her fierce against me.

This Catherine woman speaks.

'The babysitter and her boyfriend.'

'Mary? Bollocks.'

'Daddy.' A small, disapproving voice. I can't believe it. What did she just say? What did my beautiful, clever girl say?

'Daddy don' swear,' she says now, and I find I'm crying. This is all too much. I put my hand to my eyes. 'Daddy sad,' she says now.

'No,' I say. 'Daddy not sad. Daddy happy.' And I bury my face in her neck. She smells of leather and amber. Paco Rabanne. Jesus's aftershave.

'I doubt they'll try it again. It was all very G4S.'

'Very what?'

'Sorry, work slang. I mean the work was shoddy, not very robust. DIY in the extreme. Unprofessional.'

'Oh.'

'And I think I scared the poo out of them.'

'Bad word.' This is Scarlett again. I laugh. And then I start crying again. I have to take several deep, deep breaths.

'Not really, sweetheart. Poo is not really a bad word.' And then I can't speak any more. No matter how many deep breaths I take. I'm all tears and snot. Scarlett uses her good arm to stroke my hair.

This Catherine woman sighs. I guess I might have to stop thinking of her as a mentalist. 'Thank you.' I cough out eventually. 'Thank you.'

'No problem. But, sir, the other things I've told you, you need to act on them.' Her voice is urgent. For a moment my mind is blank and then I remember. Oh yes, right, the other things, like dropping down dead at any moment.

'And that's all certain is it? Definite?'

She shrugs. 'I've never known it not work.' She pauses and then says doubtfully, 'We could have got a duff batch, I suppose. We might have switched suppliers. Everyone is trying to make savings these days. Does usually work before this, to be honest.'

'Or maybe I'm super-strong, super-immune, super-resilient.' I'm sure that to Catherine it sounds flippant. But my baby's back. And she's talking, so I don't really give too much of a shit about anything else.

'Hungry,' Scarlett says now.

'Of course, darling. I'll get you something. What would you like?'

'What you got?'

'You'll have trouble there.' This Catherine is not smiling, not joking, clearly. Telling us our little princess might be a bit spoilt. And

311

she's probably right. But who the fuck cares if she is? My feeling is that spoilt people often get on. It gives them a high opinion of themselves and means they attempt things others wouldn't because they think they can do anything. Get anything. And I would say that if you're a wonky-bodied kid, then you need that self-belief. That sense that the world actually does owe you a living.

But Catherine's got something else to say, anyway. She is trying to make sure I understand her properly. She walks over to where we are. It's only fifteen metres or so and she walks them deliberately and I am reminded of old Sunday afternoon westerns. The slow walk of a righteous gunslinger.

'You need to assume it will happen. You need to make plans. I'm sorry. I wish it was different. I really do.' And if I retained any thoughts that she might still be a nutter, I shed them now. I've never seen anyone radiate such certainty, such clear-eyed common sense.

'OK,' I say. 'OK.'

She puts her hand on my shoulder. She ruffles Scarlett's hair. I wouldn't say she was a natural hair ruffler.

'Bye-bye,' says Scarlett.

'Ooh, you chatterbox,' I say to her, and then I am startled as this Catherine leans in very close to my ear almost as though she were going to kiss me. She doesn't though, instead she whispers hard and low and fast, 'Also, you do need to get out of here. Do it as soon as you can. Tonight. And do it discreetly and don't tell anyone where you're going.'

'Jesus and Mary?' I whisper back.

She wraps her arms around me and Scarlett. A big hug as if she can't bear to be parted from us, and under cover of this she breathes, 'No, I think you're safe from them – but there are people watching the house. Not amateurs. Pros. Or more or less.'

'What do they want?'

I feel her cheek against my face, her breath warm against my ear. She smells sharp, clean. Fresh earth.

'Who knows? Be as low profile as you can. Go as soon as you can.'
And then she releases us. 'I'm sorry,' she says again. And she does look it. In fact now she looks like she's about to cry. There's a lot of it about today. I try for a cheery grin.

'Hey, like you say – maybe a dodgy batch . . .' She looks at me seriously, and seems to come to a sudden decision.

'OK look,' she sighs. 'Go and pack – I'll try and sort something out.'

I'm in the house stuffing pants and socks into a large Adidas holdall with one hand, while holding Scarlett with the other – I'm not putting her down, not just yet, she can wriggle and squirm all she likes – when I remember a case in the papers from years back. A bloke had convinced his best mate and his best mate's girlfriend that they were wanted by the IRA or someone, and managed to keep them prisoner in his flat because they were too shit scared to go outside. He'd also managed to con them out of hundreds of thousands of pounds along the way, though I can't quite remember the details of how he'd done it.

I wonder if something similar is going on here, because it all seems so mad. But then I think, what if it is? I hate this house. I hate everything about how we've been living our lives. So, if this Catherine is some kind of master con artist, with some plan that doesn't make sense yet, well, who cares? Who gives a shit? Let's just go along with it, see where it leads.

And that's when Sarah comes in, so red in the face and breathless that I almost laugh. Grace Cathedral isn't that far away. She needs to let Linwood get her on a programme.

She sees Scarlett, who just holds out her good arm. Sarah crosses the room and takes her from me.

'What happened?' she says. 'I thought she'd been taken.'

'Well.' And I can't face going through it all.

'Well, what?'

'Well, I think we just had a bit of a Noel situation. Mary let Scarlett wander off and it was panic stations for a while, but a nice neighbour found her.'

'She got a gun.'

This is Scarlett, and Sarah's mouth forms a perfect O.

'Yeah, apparently our baby can speak now. I sacked Mary by the way. And we're going away – all of us, right now.'

'Are we?'

'Yes, we are. No arguing. We're going to England, but we're going via Las Vegas.'

'Vegas? And why would we do such a thing?'

'So that we can get married in the Church of Elvis or somewhere.'

'Really?'

'Really. And because marriage is so good, we're going to do it twice. One time we're going to come out Mr and Mrs Knox and second time – in a different church – we're going to come out Mr and Mrs Fisher. We're going to cover all bases.'

'Is this a proposal?' she says, but she's smiling and I think the whole Scarlett being kidnapped hysteria has been safely buried under this avalanche of new information. I have no doubt it'll work itself to the surface again in time. She's a smart cookie, Sarah, she doesn't really forget anything.

'No, it's an order,' I say.

And I'm about to show her the amazing thing I found on Russell's computer, when Catherine comes back and drives it out of my head.

'I reckon you got an hour,' she says.

Forty-six

LORNA

'We could never be a proper couple.'

It's deep into the afternoon and they are drinking tea and eating toast in Lorna's bed. Lorna feels that she is in better shape than Megan, and she's meant to be the finest female white-collar boxer in Alameda County or whatever. She doesn't look like such an athlete now. At least Lorna can sit up, at least she can talk – Megan just groans, puts a pillow over her head and pulls the duvet tighter around her.

'No, you're pretty fine and everything when we're out, but get you home and into bed and you fall straight asleep, start snoring, farting, and stealing all the covers. It would never work. Frankly, you're too like a man.'

Well, that gets her going. Megan groans again and coughs like an expiring heroine in one of Lorna's novels, the ones she reads for her course where conspicuous consumption means something very different from what it does now. And then, ever so slowly, ever so carefully, Megs sits up, scratches her head. Gets ready to fight back.

'And you, missy, you drop crumbs in the bed. And you reek of marmite. And I do not snore. Or fart.'

'You did last night. And this morning.'

It has to be said though, they did have a right laugh. They'd been in the Bison first for noodles and honey-basil ale, and they would have stayed but there was a band on and everyone knows that a bar band kills the buzz pretty effectively, so then it was on to the Albatross where they'd played skinny-hipster boys at pool and darts and drunk

315

good Guinness. And Lorna had been reminded just how much fun Megan was.

It was Megan who'd suggested Brennan's. And done it at a perfect moment, when they were both pretty wasted, but still had just enough sense left to know that they needed to get out of the pub before something embarrassing happened with a couple of the skinny-hipster boys.

Megs had found a cab and got them to 4th and Uni where they had sat over cold ones with the beer-bellied truckers and talked about guns. At least that's what Lorna had thought they'd talked about, though it seemed unlikely. She did remember that a big bearded biker-type had asked Megan for a kiss and she'd told him to 'swivel, asshole', and the whole pub had choked on its cheap suds because big biker guy was meant to be such a hotshot hood, but he had just blushed and left. And they hadn't had to pay for any more beers. Or the Jägerbombs. Lorna had been shocked to find that they didn't really do Jägerbombs in the States so she taught J-bombing to the blue-collar barflies in Brennan's. They were enthusiastic students.

And then they were somehow back at home, and they'd just crawled into Lorna's bed. And it didn't need talking about, they'd just stripped to knickers and T-shirts, cleaned their teeth and got into bed. Though she did remember Megan insisting they each drank a pint of water first. Good old Megan, always sensible even when wankered. And then she thought they'd laughed about nothing for quite a while, before she'd noticed that Megan was noisily asleep. Lorna had been genuinely put out by the racket, but before she'd had time to get properly cross, she'd obviously dropped off too.

And then it was daylight but there had been a long, long period of really quite effective denial about that. They'd both got up for a piss but got back into bed and dozed and moaned and sipped at new pints of water until just a few minutes ago when Lorna had made them toast. Marmite for her, peanut butter for Megan, only Megs hasn't touched hers yet, said there's fire behind her eyeballs.

'And you kept fiddling with me,' says Lorna.

'I so did not,' says Megan.

'So did. Rubbing up against me and everything.'

'In your dreams, honey.'

'It's OK, I quite liked it.'

'You're such a liar.'

'You don't think I liked it?'

'I know I didn't do it. If I'd done it, you'd have liked it a lot.'

'Ooh, such confidence. Well, I suppose it could have been Armitage Shanks. Come here, boy, come have your belly rubbed.'

'It was probably him snoring and farting too,' says Megs.

And they watch as the fat cat stirs himself from his position on Lorna's feet and tries to sashay up to her waiting, waggling fingers. Only it is hard to sashay across bobbly knees, and bony shins, so it's probably not the big lion strut old Armitage has intended. Lorna laughs. 'You silly sausage,' she says. She tickles him. 'Were you touching me up in the night? Were you? You big old randy thing, you.'

And Lorna can tell that it's probably going to be a good day. Maybe they'll watch an old movie, something romantic but with a strong female lead. Maybe they'll have a hair of the dog around six.

And then they finally start the glacially incremental process of getting up and getting dressed. There are interruptions like American *Come Dine With Me*, and lots more tea to be drunk and quite a lot of sitting down holding their heads, and problems with finding clean clothes, and texts to be answered including some shyly pleading ones from numbers she doesn't recognise. She guesses these are from the skinny-hipster boys they'd met in the Albatross. She won't go there. It could be fun, but she's probably still too young to start getting all Cougaresque just yet. They'd been mostly Jezes in the making anyway. Baby Fuckweasels. She wonders briefly what he's up to. I wonder how jolly old Jez is doing, she thinks, but she has no urge to call him or text him or anything.

And then she checks her emails.

*　　*　　*

She goes into the kitchenette, where Megan is making a smoothie.

'Russian Hill then.'

'What?'

'That's where we're going today.'

'Oh, babes. Does it have to be today? We both look like crap.'

'Cheers, mate. Thanks for that. As if I wasn't paranoid enough already.'

'It's true.'

'Well, anyway, *babes,* we do have to go today, because there is the small matter of a coupla million bucks that has appeared in my account, courtesy of Daddy dearest's factotum.'

'His what?'

'His factotum. Anyway, apparently I'm a millionaire which is a bit of a brainfuck actually.'

A long pause while Megan looks at her with eyes the colour of cigarette ash. Ash sunsplashed with blood.

'And you want to go and say thank you?'

'I want to go and say something. I'm not sure what exactly.'

'I'd sure start with thank you.'

'So you'll come with me?'

'Of course I'll come with you. Old buddy. Old pal.'

'Oh, all nice to me now I'm loaded.' At which point Armitage Shanks comes into the kitchenette and begins rubbing himself against her legs.

'Oh, not you as well,' Lorna says, as she picks him up. 'I can't believe it. I'm surrounded by whores.'

Forty-seven

CATHERINE

Chunking up, that's all she's doing really. Preparing herself for life as a freelancer, where everyone is your boss and you have to say yes to every job you're offered. That's what Catherine tells herself as she gets what she needs from the boot of the Camry. It's just a tiny bit of extra pro-bono work. And the least she can do, considering. As she slips the aerosols into the pockets of her jogging bottoms she thinks again about the advances in technology that make her job so much easier these days.

Minutes earlier she'd come out and jogged sedately around the block and concluded that the couple in the car were the only people watching the Knox house. This is not really much of a stake-out. Sortable.

And now, as she trots towards their Subaru, she can see that the man looks like a classic grade C government worker. Cheap suit, limp hair boringly cut. He could be one of the more slovenly missionaries for the Mormons. The old lady is more interesting. She is kitted out as an ordinary pensioner in her grubby pink jogging suit and the rigid steel-grey helmet of hair. Either she's pretty senior in the organisation, or she just didn't save enough for her pension and can't afford to retire. Maybe she didn't ever expect to get to retirement age. Interesting that she's in the driver's seat.

Catherine knocks on the passenger-side window. Resting on the dashboard of the car there are large Starbucks styrofoam mugs. Old newspapers are coming apart on the back seat. Sweet wrappers. It's sloppy and self-indulgent. Not as Group 4 as the kidnapper's' operation but

319

getting that way. The demoralising effects of cuts to public services no doubt.

As the window slowly eases its way down she can see the bloke has been reading *The Economist*, which he now chucks into the footwell of the car. She draws the can from her pocket. Gives it a gentle shake.

'Can I help you?' he says, and she lets him have it – a long squirt that envelops him in brackish-smelling vapour. He coughs once and goes quiet.

The woman is slow to react. Reflexes are gone. Dead wood. They should have retired her anyway, pension or no. She just about manages to reach across the slumped body of her partner. She is clearly going for the glovebox and some kind of weapon she has in there, but she's nowhere near sharp enough. Catherine leans into the car, and then she gives the old lady the second can full in the face. She can see the woman holding her breath, but there is forty-five seconds' worth of gas in the can and the woman looks like she won't last out for half that time.

Sure enough, twenty-five seconds later the woman's fingers stop scrabbling at the glovebox and she is quiet too, lying across the lap of her partner in a way that might be mildly embarrassing for them when they come round. Catherine gives her the final seconds of the can anyway, just in case the woman is faking.

Then she uses the phone she'd nicked from Russell Knox to take photos of them both. She has to admit this kit is impressive on lots of levels, but to carry something like this around is to have a tracker device round your neck. Send even one text from a piece of hardware like this and almost anyone could find you, almost instantly.

She'll show Russell the pictures of who is watching the house, then she'll make sure this gadget is destroyed in the approved manner.

She goes to the boot of the Subaru and flicks it up. Nothing. That's annoying. She thought it was standard equipment these days. So it's back to her own car for the rope and gaffer tape. It is Catherine's opinion that everyone should have rope and gaffer tape in the car, like they should have a spare tyre, a flashlight and some barley sugars. Basic common sense.

She ties the feet and hands of the operatives. Tight enough, but not too tight, she isn't wanting to properly hurt anyone. She isn't doing real work on these nobodies. Not taking any major action. She's just napping them. Giving them their own little daytime slumber party.

She does all she needs to and then she has a quick look for some ID. She finds it in the glovebox and she guesses it was actually these plastic oblongs that the woman had been fighting for. Certainly there are no angel-makers in there, no armoury. A notepad, some pens – and these ID cards on their tangled lanyards. She makes a quick mental note of the names and numbers on the cards and then puts them back in the compartment and jogs back to the Knox house.

She has a brief moment of concern when she sees the front door is open, but it's OK. She walks into the nearest reception room and she can see it's all happy families. Russell Knox, his partner and his little girl, all smiling, all laughing.

She tells them she thinks they have an hour. Really, she thinks they probably have two but if you want people to do things by a deadline it's always best if they think they have less time than they do.

And Sarah raises an eyebrow and Russell just says that he'll explain later. And then Catherine shows them the pictures of the people watching the house and sees them both switch on frowns of wonder and concern.

'Hey, it's the honorary consultant, Mr Jones. The computers and fruit guy.'

'And Dorito woman.'

And they both look a bit lost. Like they paid to come into some kind of hall of mirrors and it stopped being fun a while back. Now they just keep banging their heads as they try and find the exit.

And then Russell says, 'Hey, is that my phone?'

And Catherine says no, it's hers and he looks doubtful but he doesn't challenge her.

And Sarah asks her who she is again exactly, and Catherine looks at Russell and he tells her that she is the woman who found Scarlett, and brought her back to the house, and Sarah hugs her and thanks her and then says, 'You're a neighbour?'

And Catherine says, 'That's what the man said.'

Which, after all, is not yes and so is not a lie. Catherine hopes she has maybe told her last ever lie.

And there is a silence. Time for her to go. Time for them all to go.

She says, 'Well, there's nothing more I can do so this time I really am gone. Take it easy. And sorry again.'

And Sarah's puzzled frown deepens a little.

And Russell walks her to the door and she tells him who the people watching the house had been working for. And he does something surprising. He laughs. And they shake hands. Funny, people don't often find it amusing that the IRS and HMRC are both chasing them.

And just before the door closes behind her she hears Scarlett shout, 'Bang. Bang. Bang.'

And she hears Sarah coo, 'Oh, my clever darling. My beautiful baby.'

And as she makes her way down the driveway Catherine thinks – not for the first time – that parenthood clearly turns your brains to mush.

Forty-eight

NICKY

There's no doubt that Sarah likes me being in charge. A bit freaked out naturally, but delighted. I also seem to have got a bit of credit for the fact that Scarlet is speaking now. It's nothing to do with me, it's just happened, but I was around when she started and Sarah wasn't, so I'm getting some extra warmth because of that.

Anyway, it's me who decides what we're packing. Me who orders that one of Russell's RVs be brought round from the garage who are storing it. And me who, when she attempts to ask some questions about all the shit that's happened while she's been out, tells her to shut up and drive. Really, I'd like to be doing the driving and it's a ten-hour trip to Vegas, so I'll probably have to at some point, but if I really am going to drop dead at any moment, I don't want to be behind the wheel of a 44 feet long, 380 horse power, 42,000 pound Fleetwood Providence 3000 when it happens.

It's the perfect machine for me. More my style than Jesus's limo was. This is like the best appointed mobile library you've ever seen. Sarah's nervous about driving at first, and we crawl out of the city with me shouting directions.

We make a slight detour because I want to pick up my suits from Jimmy. I want to get married, and die if I absolutely have to, in a beautiful bespoke suit. A bobby dazzler.

Jimmy is shutting up shop when we get there. The Providence waits in the road holding up traffic while I sprint in. He seems unsurprised both by my appearance several hours after I'd said I'd be back and by

323

the fact that I've arrived in the kind of luxury camper van that is the sort of thing Cirque Du Soleil might travel in.

I was hoping for a surgical strike: In. Pick up suits. Out. Go go go. But Jimmy doesn't work like that. He's a real artist. One of the few I've known to be honest, despite all my years in cultural services. He insists I try the bobby dazzler on again.

'You've lost two pounds since this morning,' he huffs. 'There's another hour's work there.'

For all I know I don't have another hour.

'You know what Apollinaire said?' I say.

He just looks at me, his mouth full of pins. I carry on, '"A poem is never finished, it's abandoned." I think the same is true of all works of art, don't you?'

Jimmy carefully spits the pins into his hand. 'A poem is just words,' he says. 'Words that anyone can read. One size fits all. This, my friend, this is a suit. A suit just for you. That only you can wear.'

I tell him that I like my suits a little loose. 'Growing room,' I say, then feel foolish as he gazes seriously from behind the bottle-thick lenses in his ruined specs. In the end he shrugs. He has little tufts of coarse maran-grass-type hair on his shoulders. His vest is stained. Odd that this tailor cares so little for how he looks himself.

'If that's what you want.'

'The customer is always right,' I say, and he laughs loudly. Too loudly. Two quick dry mirthless barks. Ha. Ha. And then another two. Ha. Ha. I feel his contempt following me like a foot pushing me out of his shop as I leave wearing the very slightly baggy but absolutely beautiful work of art that is the bobby dazzler.

And speaking of art, the road outside Jimmy's place is now a modernist symphony for car horns. In California patience is not a virtue. In California patience is a pathology.

'Nice suit,' says Sarah as I clamber back aboard. 'Is that for our wedding? Or are you going into the pimping business?'

'You know in less than twenty-four hours' time you're going to promise to obey me, don't you? Twice. In front of witnesses.'

She laughs good naturedly as she puts the Providence into drive. Just as we leave the city and hit the freeway, I remember something else that will make her laugh. It's a good moment to tell her about the file I opened on Russell's iThing.

'Hey, Sarah, you want to hear something really funny?'

'That would be nice,' she says.

'You have to promise not to crash the bus.'

'Just tell me. I'm used to shocks by now.'

'OK. So I found Russell's will. All notorised and authorised and legally attested. Guess who he left his money to?'

Her eyes don't leave the road, but her skin seems to pale and tighten. And then flush. This must be an illusion, but it definitely looks that way.

'Don't tell me.'

'Me. He left everything to me. Ain't that a kick in the head?'

'I said, don't tell me.'

'And I said don't crash the bus.'

I say this because we have drifted dangerously and are straddling two lanes of the freeway. We are half over the FARE lane – the more or less empty lane you pay to use – and half over the ordinary plebs lane where we could tailgate a jalopy at any time – Sarah overcompensates and now we wobble into the FARE lane in a way that's properly frightening. I think about suggesting that I take over for a while, but can't of course.

'I need to think, Nicky.'

'Yes, that's a thing – maybe I can return to being Nicky again,' and I go on to say it'll make an interesting case if we ever do get to court. We might turn out not to have committed any major crimes at all. And I find myself talking about other people who have faked their deaths. There was that MP. And there was that guy who ran from his creditors and hid out with his wife in Panama until they were

325

photographed proudly accepting the keys to their new house, and then that happy snap ends up on the estate agent's website.

But the MP was wanted for other crimes. And the Panama twerps cashed in the life insurance fraudulently. And I like to think that they really went to prison for their stupidity rather than their veniality. Of course, we've also cashed in the life insurance but it's different for us, surely? I mean we could pay it back many times over.

Sarah stays quiet and lets me ramble on like this, while the Providence swallows miles like a great whale hoovering up plankton.

Takes me a while to realise that she's crying.

And there's me thinking it was all actually kind of funny.

'I'll be OK. I won't crash the bus. I really do need to think, that's all.'

'OK. OK.'

I make my way into the back of the bus to watch some sport with Scarlett on the forty-eight-inch plasma screen set into the wall. I don't need to say anything to her, she's giggling the moment she sees me. This suit seems to have turned me into a right comedian. As long as I keep away from the beneficiary of the will material, I go down a storm with everyone.

'What you watching, kid?' I say.

'Field hockey,' she says. And I'm floored again by this talking version of our baby. How would she even know what the game is called? But anyway, I explain that in England, back home, this is just hockey, no field attached, but she doesn't seem very interested to be honest.

'You'll be playing that one day, girl,' I say, and it makes me smile to think how the sport considered most suitable for schoolgirls is the one where you give the players weapons. Curved wooden clubs that are perfect for stoving in skulls and smashing up teeth and noses. And of course, Scarlett will be waving hers one-handed. I bet she causes havoc. I bet she turns out to be a right Boudicca wielding her stick like a battleaxe. I hope so anyway.

And when Scarlett changes the channel to the one that seems to show twenty-four-hours-a-day Spongebob, possibly the creepiest cartoon hero yet, I get out the iThing and check emails. Which is how I learn that my father is dead.

And my first thought is what great mitigation it'll be if whatever crime I turn out to have committed does ever come to court.

I can hear my barrister now. I imagine a northern woman. Well groomed, glamorous but down-to-earth, still with a touch of the mills in her voice, seducing the jury with a playful hint of BDSM in the eyes, telling them of the great sorrows of my life. Disabled daughter, dead dad. Ladies and gentlemen of the jury, hasn't this man suffered enough? And when you think how generous he's been – and with what turns out to have been his own money all along too . . . Who, exactly, is the victim here? Who indeed?

Reading on, I find Polly tells me all the details of the funeral. Apparently they're cremating him in her village and we can come if we like. Afterwards, they're all going to fly kites while the ashes are scattered. Turns out that dad has made kites with his own hands for all those who he especially hopes will be there. So there is one for Sarah, one for Scarlett. None for me of course – why would he make one for Russell Knox? She says how fitting it is with Daniel being a master of the Punjabi fighting kites and all that.

The way she tells it my dad was the kite king. The kite guru. The man whose creations ruled the skies like so many trained golden eagles. I remember reading about a golden eagle in Canada that swooped on a four-year-old kid and bashed his head against a cliff to open him up so he could get to the juicy brains inside. My dad would be impressed by that. The single-mindedness, the ambition, the invention. The ruthlessness. Yeah, the complete lack of ruth.

Polly says how she's hoping for a good turnout from the village. Dad was only there a few days but apparently he had a fan club. The pub quiz team, the darts team, the pool team – they'll all be there, as will the bar staff and all his friends from Sunny Bank. It will be quite an occasion. I can picture it, dozens of kites dancing in the sky. A weird pre-migration ritual of exotic birds that don't really belong in the Bedfordshire countryside.

I thank her for telling me. I think for a moment. Then go on to express my regret that I won't make the event, that pressing commitments over here make it impossible. That I think it all sounds beautiful. It's what the old man would have wanted and what a shame that his son couldn't be there to see it either.

And I am impressed with myself for refraining from telling her that the Punjabi fighting-kite guru thing is a crock of shit. Or, even if it isn't, my dad certainly never made a kite for me before, never flew one either. Of course, I know the dead always have secrets. All of them are conjurers of a kind. There's always a final ta-dah and a cymbal crash and a big reveal. But kites? Kites? Really?

Forty-nine

LORNA

It's almost dark when they reach the house in Russian Hill. In the dusk it looks especially daunting, especially grand. And the fact that there are no lights anywhere and yet the imposing front door is obviously open, well, that's all sinister too.

Lorna and Megan stand on the sidewalk for a while, pretending to ponder their next move. It's a no-brainer really. They press the buzzer on the door several times, but no salivating dogs appear. Likewise no uni-browed goons with big hairy hands and too-shiny shoes. So they walk in. They pause in the hallway for a moment. It isn't really a moment of doubt, more a chance to savour the shivery deliciousness of going somewhere forbidden. And even in the dark they can sense the hallway has some grandeur. The ceiling, so high there's a faint echo.

'It's like when I played on building sites as a kid,' whispers Lorna as they walk the absurd length of the hallway. Jesus, you could play ten-pin bowling in here.

'You played on construction sites? Why would you do such a thing?'

Lorna shrugs. 'I was just a naughty girl, I guess. If I was told not to go somewhere, well, that's where I went.'

They creep forward, still half-expecting sirens and tannoyed voices telling them to remain exactly where they are.

'I was always a good girl.' Megan sounds sad.

'Well you know what they say. Good girls go to heaven . . .'

'And bad girls go everywhere. Yes, I've heard that.'

'Anyway,' says Lorna. 'You're not a good girl any more. Sleeping with the boss's husband, breaking and entering . . .'

They are just into the kitchen when they are blinded by all the lighting coming on. Lorna freezes as if the music has stopped in a game of musical statues.

'What are you doing here?'

The voice behind them is deep but mild enough, and it's Megan who recovers first and whirls around to face the threat.

'Linwood!'

'Hey, Megs.'

The trainer's hard black shape lounges against the handmade oak kitchen cupboards. A solemn presence, his eyes questioning.

'Linwood, this is too fucking weird. What the fuck are you doing here?'

'No need to curse,' sniffs Linwood. 'I came to give Russell Knox his workout, you know, Russell – the guy that lives here?'

Lorna gradually turns too. Her eyes are hurting. This sudden light is too much. 'You're my father's personal trainer?'

'Russell is your dad? Gee. Lucky girl.'

'That's woman, Linwood. Lucky woman.' Then a pause. 'Why am I lucky exactly?'

Linwood spreads his arms as if to say, just look at this world, and despite herself Lorna looks about and sees the wardrobe-sized SMEG fridge-freezer, the straw-coloured Tuscan tiles, the gleaming monster range, the hard black marble work surfaces, the languid curves of the S-shaped island in the middle of the room. She could practically see the brochure where the designer claims to have been influenced by the ripples left by the tide on the black sands of the volcanic beaches of Martinique.

Linwood has followed her gaze.

'And I don't just mean this house and everything. I mean he's actually an amazing guy.'

'How so?'

Linwood thinks for a moment and Lorna has a chance to take in the whole room. From the kitchen part where they are, you can move straight into a huge living space. Three enormous sofas and at the far end an impossibly wide staircase without banisters. The sort of staircase you'd see Fred and Ginger kicking their way down in a romantic movie musical about showgirls. Geometric art on the walls. Real art too, made with real paint, no Rothko prints here.

But mainly what freaks her out is the size of the place. You could hold a college graduation in her. A movie awards ceremony. And there's the strange acoustics. The fact that walls seem to be rustling with the rumours of voices. She shivers though it's not cold.

'He just doesn't act like a big shot. Always tries hard. Even though he's actually a klutz. Nerdy and really not that into sports. Zero talent. But even so he's been making real good progress. I think that's outstanding. To work hard at things you fail at.'

Lorna feels rebuked somehow.

Linwood continues, 'And rich guys are normally somewhat cunts you know.'

'Linwood!' This is Megan.

The big man smiles now, shows that great wall of teeth. 'Oh, I can cuss sometimes. When it's called for.'

'And it was called for just then?'

But of course it was. He has used this swearing to surprise his audience, to make them laugh, to catch them out, to make them see him in a bit of a new light. It's a neat bit of emotional theatre. He has in fact used the word cunt flirtatiously, and that is a difficult trick to manage. Nice one, Linwood. Kudos.

The odd tension between them all is fading now and, without anyone suggesting it, they begin to wander around the room, looking in the fridge and the cupboards, moving into the living-room area to sprawl on the huge sofas. It feels a little like being on a stage or movie set which is maybe why the normal rules about privacy seem forgotten for the moment.

Linwood is the most concerned about where Russell might be.

'It's not like him,' he keeps saying, 'not like him at all.'

'You think we should call the cops?'

'I'm not saying that.' Linwood's experience of rich people, though largely confined to listening to them talk about business while on treadmills and on rowing machines, is enough for him to know that they don't really like the police involved in anything much. Rich people see cops as being like valets or bellboys. OK to park your car and open doors, and of course you tip them generously if you want good service, but you don't want them in your house.

Nevertheless, there is something dangerously odd about the door of this mansion left open and the whole house has the eerie feel of an abandoned ship waiting to sink. It feels like it's listing somehow. And maybe that's another reason why it makes the pulse quicken to be there. Lorna suggests that they all have a beer. She's seen some in the fridge. Good beer too.

'We could just wait half an hour. See if anyone turns up. They're lucky it was us who walked in. After all, it could have been axe murderers.'

And so she liberates two cold bottles of Pyramid ale and a Pepsi Max for Linwood, turns off the blinding main lights, turns on the art-deco lamps, and they sit in their buttercup glow, just chatting about this and that for a while. None of it is important. Nobody says anything profound, but the weirdness of the house fades a little. All the talk is friendly and happy and inconsequential. The best kind of talk. As gentle and as warm as the lamplight. They could be in a quiet bar, the kind where grown-up men and women might go.

Lorna listens more than she speaks, and indulges herself in a detailed reverie where she and Megs and Linwood all live together. They have healthy breakfasts together. Smoothies and muesli or egg-white omelettes and wholemeal toast. Then they go off to their separate places of work and, later, when it gets dark there'll be music or films and sometimes Linwood goes to bed with Megs because they clearly fancy each other – look how her knees point to him, look how animated they are with one another. And sometimes he would go to bed with Lorna. And sometimes Linwood might not even come home because he'd been invited back to a house like this by one of his middle-aged women clients, one who'd had an especially successful divorce. But whenever that happened, Lorna and Megs wouldn't mind.

Because, after all, Megs would sometimes stay in Lorna's bed, though Megs maybe also had another lover – a serious, thoughtful grown-up, high-achieving lover – in Castro or somewhere, and she'd spend occasional nights there, planning Democrat fundraisers or whatever.

And every now and then Lorna might find herself waking up in the self-consciously artistic studio apartment of some poet or film-maker or theatre director. Some good-looking Fuckweasel anyway. Maybe even a baby Fuckweasel. Only every now and again though. Not too often.

And on Sundays maybe Linwood would go to church and Lorna and Megs would lie together in the big bed they'd had commissioned, and they'd read the Sunday papers. When Linwood came back he'd carefully hang up his church suit and he'd climb between them and love them, and then read the sports pages. And then maybe they wouldn't get up again until it got dark when Lorna would go and make toast.

We couldn't be a proper couple, thought Lorna. But maybe Megan and me, maybe we could be two thirds of a proper trio. We could be part of the polyandrous future of love.

And of course, the whole set-up couldn't last for ever, maybe just a year or two, but it would be a time they would all look back on with fondness. When each of them had been reeled back into the safe, quiet horrors of coupledom, as they would be, maybe they would also, in their separate places, sometimes mourn their own lost private triangular Eden.

And if it did happen, she wondered who would crack first. Who would run back to the regular two-by-two world. Her money would be on Linwood. Men are so conservative when it comes to sex and relationships.

She wonders if he likes cats, because if he can't cope with Armitage Shanks then it's all off anyway. Shanksy is her one true love after all.

Megan has just asked her what she is smiling about, and is looking at her so shrewdly that Lorna is blushing – maybe she really is a witch that girl – when a couple begin to descend the absurdly grand stairs, like low rent stand-ins for movie leads. These two have been upstairs the whole time.

One is a tired, white middle-aged man. The very definition of pale, male and stale with his thin, tired hair and a thin, tired suit. With him is a cross-looking old lady in a grubby pink jogging suit. He looks like the deputy head teacher of a failing school, two years off retirement. His companion, the lady, looks like a regular at bingo games and church jumbles.

Only neither of them are these things.

When they reach the floor, they stand awkwardly in front of them. The man twists his fingers. The lady glares at them each in turn from behind her cheap plasticky brown glasses. They are, they say, just the tax people, one from the UK, one from the US – so don't be alarmed, but could they please ask a favour?

Fifty

CATHERINE

So this is the famous Blue Lagoon. She is lying, covered in wellness-promoting mud, amid 5,000 square metres of geothermal seawater, in the shadow of a power station. It is meant to be good for the skin. Good for the soul too.

Place is pretty packed. Not many Icelanders, not many Brits either, but lots of Russians, Chinese, and Americans judging by the voices around her. And that is fitting in its way. According to the blurb, those trying to rebalance mind, body and spirit at the Blue Lagoon are lying between continents. This hugely overgrown outdoor hot tub is exactly where the Euro-Asian and the American tectonic plates meet.

As the minerals, silica and algae do whatever it is they are supposed to do, Catherine is thinking of a story where Grettir finds himself in the modern world. It's a bit like her King Arthur story, but there is no Heidi/Harriet-type character in this one. In this tale Grettir flees all the ninth-century bounty hunters through a crack in the time-space continuum – she'll work out the details later – and he'd be here, disgusted at the way people happily pay nearly a hundred pounds to bathe in this one when the whole country is full of wellness-promoting pools that are free.

Maybe he will, all unknowing, somehow allow the bad guys to track him to the twenty-first century and there'll be a massive battle scene set right here in the Blue Lagoon. Blood and guts and gore mixed with the water and the mud. Very visual. Kids'll like that. Bearded men in horned helmets causing mayhem with axes and swords, scaring the shit out of all the women who just moments before have been pampering themselves and trying to hold back time.

It isn't all women here though. There are some family groups. Children shrieking as they throw handfuls of grey-blue sulphurous gunk at each other. There are plump, middle-class men in baggy shorts looking anywhere except at the women. Here and there you also see a self-confident jock with a V-shaped torso and Speedos.

She wonders what it would all look like if you could see a bird's-eye view, if you were in a chopper maybe. All these people, herself included, they'd look like so many strange hairless water rats. Except with less purpose. Rats are always doing something, going somewhere. A rat is always on a mission, they don't do downtime. A rat isn't fat. Human beings? Well, downtime is mostly all we do. Rest and relaxation are mankind's big achievements as far as she can see.

A rat isn't fat. She likes that. That could be the title of a good kids' book. One for younger readers.

Catherine has at least earned her R and R. One of the things she's been doing while lying here, is trying to tot up her missions over the last ten years. She thinks it's thirty-two, but there's always the possibility she's forgotten one or two. Nevertheless, she's definitely completed more actions than she's had lovers. Killed more people than she's had sex with, and she can't decide whether this is a good thing or not. Does it mean she is particularly choosy when it comes to sex, or does it mean something else, something much worse?

And here, now, in this packed spa full of people with too much money, too much flesh and too much time, all caked in clay, she can't feel that she's done too much harm. Not even if every job has been done under false pretences. What does it matter in the end? The human race keeps on going, keeps on doing its ridiculous stuff. Keeps striving for new ways to do nothing that matters.

And there are always more people. Thirty-two, thirty-three ... Not much in a world of seven billion, most of whom are only dreaming of one day being able to take a spa break like this themselves, where they

336

too can have a seventy-five-quid foot massage. She thinks about China. At one time the Chinese just wanted rice and bicycles. These days they want ... well, they want everything. And who can blame them?

She wishes now that she hadn't come here. The Blue Lagoon isn't blue and it isn't a lagoon. It's a super-sized paddling pool. In taupe. Yes, it's probably a design triumph, but really it's just another municipal lido with added mud. Though she's prepared to accept that wouldn't sound quite so good on the promo leaflets. And since the fish started dying, and the money turned to shit, the Blue Lagoon is probably the country's biggest hard-currency earner.

She closes her eyes. She finds that with a bit of effort she can imagine that she's not here, that she can tune out the hundreds of face-packed spa-breakers and can instead put herself back at Grettislaug, enjoying a companionable silence with Tough.

And it's now that she feels the sharp, sudden pain just behind her left knee. It's like a jellyfish sting. Or like someone poking her in the leg hard with a sharp stick. But she knows what it is really. Shit.

She opens her eyes and looks around for a likely culprit, but it could be anyone. There are about a dozen people in her little section of the pool, none of them looking her way. That flabby bald man with the ginger chest hair and the matching bushy beard? That petite Indian-looking lady with the two small children? The skinny, tanned teen in the mirrored sunnies? That fat lady in the absurdly cheerful yellow bikini? Really it could be anyone. Nemesis could easily be wearing a mudpack, or a yellow bikini, or have a bushy red beard.

Catherine swears softly to herself, and closes her eyes again.

She never finished writing her kids' book. Come to that she never finished the last few book-club reads either. But she's always done her best.

She spreads her arms and legs out so that she is floating in a star-shape. She looks at the roiling columns of steam from the pool. The fat seagulls. The closed sky.

The soreness behind her knee is already fading. She feels a strange relief. This moment was always going to come and now that it has, she realises how tense worry about it has been making her.

She thinks about how she might use the week or so she has left. No point in hospitals or doctors. She wonders if she still has enough time to get to Madam.

She looks again at the people around her. It could even be one of the kids. Probably was. Kids will do anything for sweeties. Cheap, easy to train, remorseless. Savage. Better than a machine in some ways. Real-live terminators. One day all the big outfits will use kids. Firms like hers, they'll be like factories were in the nineteenth century. Women and children doing all the dangerous work.

A week. Maybe ten days.

But it turns out that Catherine has less than ten minutes. She has time to feel the sudden irregularity of her heartbeat, the weird flush of heat down her left side. Time to cry out at the sudden cramping in her legs, time to register some strange, high-pitched keening. She has time to notice the final lie, the one about it being painless. Because this hurts. Really hurts. A diamond-tipped corkscrew deep in her guts.

And that's it. She's gone. She doesn't hear the screaming that starts up somewhere suddenly. She doesn't see the panicked rush to clear the pool. She doesn't feel the strong arms that carry her to the side and pump her chest. She doesn't even feel the soft lips of the Malaysian dentist Dr Ng, who tries to keep her lungs inflated with the kiss of life. Dr Ng who only stops trying to save her when Catherine's blood rushes into her mouth and so into his too.

Two people die every second in the world. Most of them not as lucky as Catherine. Most of them are poor, young, frightened, sick, alone. A lot of them are babies.

And far away in Suffolk at that moment, an elderly lady shivers while chopping onions and her knife slices deep into the pulp of her thumb, not that she cares. She doesn't even worry about the blood that pulses from the cut and begins to pool on her chopping board.

338

As she reaches for the kitchen roll and begins to wrap a thick wedge around the wound, she is already hurrying to the phone. She feels certain that something awful has happened to one of her children, or to one of her grandchildren maybe.

And mothers are never wrong about these things.

Fifty-one

JESUS

Jesus is blindfolded, lying face down with his hands cuffed around the bench he's lying on. His legs are tied together. He is drunk and he is naked apart from his jockey shorts, and he's also crying. He's babbling in Spanish and English but not making any sense in either language. It should be pathetic, but it isn't. It's actually kind of hot. He's so vulnerable, so scared.

She'd been pretty pissed at him at first, the way the knucklehead wetback had been taken in by that bitch, but he'd been so sorry, so willing to do anything to make it up to her. How could she stay sore at him? Guys aren't as tough as chicks. They aren't as smart either. She knows that. You want something doing, you don't get a guy to do it. Unless you have to. Like she has to get Jeremy to do this; she doesn't know anyone else who could. Or would.

She wishes now she'd made Jesus take the jockeys off too.

'Hey, Jeremy, you got any sharp scissors?'

They are in Ink, the new tattooists in Buena Vista Park. Jeremy was her true love in high school, but he'd left town after their thing had ended. Had to really. Moved to the city and now six years later, he runs this place. Or he does at weekends when the boss isn't around. It was Jeremy who'd done Mary's first tattoo, back when it was still a hobby for him. When he was still learning. He did that first little baby owl on her right breast. A big day that was. Her fifteenth birthday. Her first tat. And the first time a man had gone down on her. Not to mention the first – and only – time her mom had walked in on her while a man was going down on her. Not just any man, the teacher of

340

Horticulture 101, her favourite subject in high school. Mr Peress. Jeremy.

It had taken everyone a while to be cool after that. Even though Jeremy had moved on pretty quick. Fact her pop would still shoot him if he saw him again.

'Sure. I have scissors. What for?'

She has to give him credit, Jeremy is being very chilled considering he hasn't seen her for like nearly a year. Considering he always says she destroyed his life. Every year she gets a Valentine that says exactly that. It's like a tradition.

'I'm going to cut those jockeys off.'

And Jeremy sighs and goes and fetches the scissors from the drawer. Mary looks around approvingly. This is a well-run place, you can see that. Everything is sterile, clean. And the designs Jeremy has had blown up and put up around the main workspace are stunning. He is too good for a place like Ink, like he was too good to be part of a high-school faculty. He should be in LA doing work for the movie stars. She wonders if he has a regular date these days.

When Jeremy comes back he says, 'You've changed so much since high school.'

And Mary says, 'Really?' and frowns. She doesn't think she's changed at all. Except maybe she knows how to get what she wants these days.

Now to Jesus she says, 'Keep still and quit bawling,' but she says it quietly, tenderly even. And she sits on the very edge of the bench next to where Jesus thrashes and moans, and she snips up each leg of the jockeys. She pulls the material away. Jesus yells something. Her Spanish is pretty good, but this she can't make out. She looks at Jay who shakes his head.

'Aw, the poor kid,' says Jeremy. She can't tell if he means it.

Jesus is squirming on the bench. Mary puts a hand on the soft fuzz of his ass. A big naked man tied up and at her mercy. She tries an experimental slap. Jesus hollers again. She laughs. She does it again, a

341

bit harder. And then remembers Jeremy is in the room. She looks at him and smirks. Jeremy's eyes are wide, he licks his lips.

'Hot, huh?' says Mary. Jeremy nods. Mary turns back to Jesus. His shoulders are shaking. She kisses his neck.

'Hey, hey,' she soothes. 'You gotta keep still. All be over soon.'

'Well, about eight hours actually,' says Jeremy.

'Really, that long?'

'Pretty much. With breaks.'

'He won't want many breaks.'

'No, but I will. This is a big assignment.'

'We better get started then.'

But Jeremy still has one more thing to make sure of. One more piece of prep to do.

'You're gonna pay me right? One hundred dollars. That's friends' rates.'

Which is when Mary knows Jeremy isn't really a friend, because a friend charges nothing, but she nods and says, 'Sure. I'm good for it,' and wonders what the hell he'll do when he discovers she has no money at all. It isn't like he can repossess the tattoo. He can't exactly impound it, can he?

And Jeremy turns on his machine and approaches Jesus's broad back with his needle. The needle that seems to Mary to be buzzing with a special eagerness. Jesus is very, very still now.

'Hey,' she says. 'You can relax a bit. It's going to be all right you know. Jeremy knows what he's doing.'

'I'm the best,' says Jeremy. 'The best in Buena Vista anyway. And, Mary, you know most people here don't call me Jeremy any more. Here I'm Jez.'

'Boss name.'

'Just wanted to be a bit, you know, less uptown.'

There's a pause, then Mary asks, 'You got a girl, uh, Jez?'

'No,' says Jez. 'No girl.' He's telling no one about Lorna. The girl he murders nightly before he drinks himself to sleep. The girl who makes him cry when he hears sad songs on the goddamn radio.

'I spoil you for anyone else, huh?' Mary's golden pigtails quiver. She likes this idea. Jez doesn't say anything. He lets her know that the talking is over because the work is starting. The business.

He begins. Jesus gasps and moans and the blood begins to appear on his back, a thin trail of dots and dashes as the needle makes its careful, steady, repeated loops and curls. Its graceful swoops and dips. Its figure-skater's dance. Jesus murmurs softly. Still, she can't make out what he's saying.

'See,' says Mary. 'See. It's not that bad.'

Jez pauses a moment. Looks up at Mary's sweatshirt.

'What?' says Mary.

'Just getting it all fixed in my mind.'

He bends to his task again.

In eight hours' time Jesus's back will be covered in the same shouting red swirling Superdry logo as is on the faded purple of Mary's cheap cotton top. A punishment and an inspiration all at the same time. She hopes it will spur him on. Jesus has greatness in him somewhere, she knows that. All she has to do is find the way to bring it out. As she looks at his ass, she wonders about pegging. She's never done that. She wonders how it would feel. If Jesus would be game for that. She could talk him into it anyway. Easy.

Jesus is still murmuring, but louder now.

'What? What is it?'

'He's saying he loves you,' says Jeremy. Jez. He says it deadpan, without pausing in his task, without taking his eyes from Jesus's back with its flexing muscle, with its vivid quivering spots of blood. Like ladybugs, thinks Mary. Like especially bright and beautiful ladybugs. She puts her thumb on one swelling scarlet oval. Presses firmly. Imagines the bug squished.

'He's saying that he loves you, over and over and over.'

'Of course he loves me,' says Mary. 'Why wouldn't he?'

'Crybaby though, ain't he?' says Jez.

And it's true, Jesus is crying. He's crying not just from the pain of the tattoo or because he is breaking his momma's heart by getting

Fifty-two

LORNA

'The cheek of you people,' says Lorna. It turns out the favour the tax guys want is for Lorna, Megan and Linwood to ignore the fact that the two of them have broken into a house without a warrant. They are, they say, in the middle of an important investigation and yes, they've had to cut corners and should have applied for the necessary permissions from judges – which they would have got – but they are convinced that major crimes are being committed and, in the aftermath of a serious act of violence carried out against them personally, have simply tried to expedite proceedings.

Lorna tells them to fuck right off. She tells them she'll be making a complaint to all the relevant authorities.

The anxious-looking English tax guy shakes his head sadly, while the bright-eyed American pensioner-lady tax woman tries to explain that this'll be unfortunate because it will certainly mean the end of the case and that will mean a person of interest, someone who they believed might be a major player in various international frauds, escaping justice.

Megan asks what their evidence is. The lady says she can't say. Megan says well, they can't help then, and the woman actually growls.

'Look at this place,' she says. 'No one who can buy a place like this has gotten their money honestly.'

'So that's your evidence? He lives in a big house. He must be a crook.'

The Johnny English speaks up in his soft, tired voice. 'We can tell you there have been a number of recent unusual patterns of funds transfers from Mr Knox's accounts. Large sums given to charities, as well as private individuals. In our experience philanthropy on this scale is most often associated with criminal endeavours.'

'Money laundering,' says the old lady, just in case they hadn't got it.

There is a sudden flash. Linwood has taken a picture of the tax people on his phone. The tax people blink.

'I am right now sending this photo to my website. I have eleven thousand followers there. I get twelve thousand hits a day. If you proceed with this investigation, this picture of government agents violating the basic right to privacy of a citizen will be filed as part of a suit against you personally and against the organisations you represent. Mr Knox's lawyers – and I am sure they will be good ones – are bound to sue for punitive damages that could run into the tens of millions of dollars. So I would get along if I were you and count yourselves fortunate that you don't get a fistfulla hot lead in yo lilywhite punk asses.'

The tax people say nothing else, they simply leave.

'And please close the door on your way out,' calls Linwood as they disappear down the long furlong of the hallway.

'Go screw yourself,' calls back the old lady, but seconds later they hear the door slam anyway.

Megan says, 'Go Linwood! Go Linwood!'

Lorna says, 'Did you actually say a fistfulla hot lead in yo lilywhite punk asses? Please.'

Linwood shrugs. 'Sounds better when I say it. But I was just giving 'em what they expect from a big black dude. And I hate those guys. You know, a citizen has the right to get rich without the Feds getting all forensic on him.'

Megan says, 'Funny, but Lorna doesn't actually believe that. Lorna thinks that everyone should be paid the same. Rock stars and movie stars and sports stars should be on the government pay roll and paid a wage like teachers or nurses.'

'No, that's not right,' says Lorna. Megan and Linwood look at her expectantly. 'No. In Lornaworld, parasites like rock stars and movie stars would get far, far less than nurses.'

'And Lorna has actually said, and I quote, "all really nice houses are monuments to thieves". Which is pretty much what the IRS lady said, isn't it?'

'When did I say that?'

'When we had John and Amelia round for dinner.'

'Really? Well, I'm sure it's a line I nicked from somewhere. Sounds too clever for me. It's true though.'

Linwood stands up. He looks genuinely angry. 'Commie bullshit is what that is.'

Lorna thinks her imagined three-way idyll is probably not a goer now. Sounds like Linwood wouldn't fuck a Red.

'And what's wrong with communism?' she says, and it's worth it just to see the way Linwood's eyes almost bug right out of his head.

Megan laughs. 'OK, Ms Trotsky, so what's with stopping this federal investigation?'

Lorna grins. 'He's my dad. Family. Plus, all coppers are bastards. Even the tax police. Plus, some of the unusual patterns of funds transfers were to me. And I have plans for that money.'

'Oh yeah?' says Megan.

'Yeah,' says Lorna, though she hadn't yet, but she soon would have. Spending money isn't hard.

She stands up, stretches. She feels good, fit. She feels like dancing. She catches sight of herself in the mirror above the fireplace. In this gentle lamplight, she looks kind of amazing actually. Really alive. She feels great, looks great. This is clearly one of those moments to savour. She sort of wishes Jez could see her now. She winks at herself. She is a bad, bad girl. And she is, she decides, going to get badder. She hears Megan cough, and so she turns and pokes her tongue out at her. She doesn't let you get away with anything that lass. Thank fuck.

'Who's for a nice cup of tea?' she says.

'Ooh, lovely,' says Megan. 'That would be absolutely fantastic.' And they smile at each other.

Fifty-three

NICKY

I still don't know what to think about Catherine and her insane James Bond, licensed to kill-type stories.

But I do know that this Catherine has the ability to assassinate sleep. I wonder if maybe I will never sleep again. Not properly. No one under sentence of death sleeps easily.

For something to do I get up, put the Providence into drive and get it to eat up the remaining miles to Vegas. And as we steadily chew those miles we pass a couple sweating away on a tandem. I envy them. The harmony you need in your relationship to take a long distance nighttime tandem ride through the desert. I wonder if we, Sarah and I, own one – and if we do where it's kept – and from there it's quite natural to find myself thinking again about cycling proficiency.

That course a lifetime ago ran every Tuesday lunchtime for twelve whole weeks and it was run by real policemen. Two of them. Two coppers who, instead of catching rapists, burglars and murderers, were teaching the highway code and bicycle etiquette to ten year olds. That's not a proper job for a grown-up is it? Not for any grown-up never mind a copper. Would Soraya or Claudette have been fobbed off with being put on cycling-proficiency detail? I think we all know the answer to that. The kindest explanation is that the policemen were recovering from nervous breakdowns. Another, somewhat less kind, is that they were under suspicion for corruption or incompetence.

And I suddenly realise why I failed. It was because I'd had a Raleigh Chopper, bought for me by my dad who always loved novelty, and the very look of it annoyed these policemen who must have been looking for ways to make themselves feel like men again.

It was nothing to do with my lack of finesse with the hand signals. It was the spite of men in authority. So many of the world's problems come down to that.

And then I spend the rest of the night heading towards the future. And out of the steady lulling thrum of the engine a new plan comes to me. A great plan actually. But then it is morning. Viva Las Vegas. Hurray for the meadows. The communities of Paradise and Enterprise. A kind of heaven. A haven anyway. The Strip.

The Strip where, in the nervy, giddy afternoon, we win a fortune on the slot machines. Really. Thousands of dollars. Funny, huh?

Playing the machines is not something Sarah or I would do normally, but we are light-hearted because we have been officially and properly married. Twice. And our unions have been blessed by no lesser authorities than both Elvis Presley and James Brown. The first pastor urged us not to be cruel to a heart that's true, and the second urged us to get on the scene, like a sex machine – and both of these are probably good pieces of advice for newlyweds.

Our rings are from Sterlings. The American H. Samuel. And our witnesses at both weddings are a couple of guys collecting soda cans for recycling. You could say it's not a big affair. It is not a fairy tale. But better than our first wedding.

And afterwards we win the cash. Actually it is Scarlett who wins the money. I lift up our own sweet little one-arm bandit and she pulls the fateful lever that sends a tsunami of cash spilling out of the tray and onto the floor. It's not one of the really, really big jackpots. It's just one of the modest ten thousand dollar wins, but it's still enough to have the manager beetle over to have his photo taken presenting us with a bottle of bubbly.

And Sarah tells me about giving cash away to the homeless.

'Five hundred dollars.' There's wonder in her voice and I think about the hundreds of thousands I was giving away at the same time.

The evidence from our little experiment is that it works. Giving money away works. Or maybe it's just another form of shopping. Retail therapy. Buying stuff to make yourself feel good. I hope the Surrey roofer is still around to get his kidney.

I have an idea.

'Sarah, let's leave this money on a street corner. And then let's go and find somewhere that will let us dance.'

'That is a brilliant idea, Nicky. Let's do that.'

And I raise my eyebrows and Sarah laughs and says, 'Don't I always say yes?'

And this is true. And it's only occurring to me now that with every idea I've ever had, Sarah has said yes to it. And not just to the good ones. She's pointed out practical problems, but then she's suggested solutions. She's made good ideas better ones. She's made bad ideas feasible ones. She's always up for stuff, and I think I'd forgotten that somehow.

And I feel a sudden flush of shame, because when Sarah suggests something I think my instinctive reaction is to say no, to put roadblocks and barricades in the way.

And in her arms Scarlett pipes up, 'Yay! Dancing!'

'We have to do something about Scarlett,' I say suddenly, because the moment is right.

She's ahead of me, of course. 'Are you suggesting we try rules, boundaries, bedtimes, saying no, and things like that?'

'Yes. Yes. I think I am.'

'It'll be hard work, after all this time.'

'She deserves the best though, doesn't she? She deserves the best kind of love.'

'Even though she seemed to do so well on the second-best kind?'

And I wonder for a moment where Mary is, whether she's still with Jesus. Maybe her braces and her ukuleles have ended up looking after the little emperors of the Chinese ambassador, the princelings of a Saudi sheikh, the czars and czarinas of Russian oligarchs. Good luck to her, good luck to them. I can't bring myself to hate her.

But we agree. Sarah says yes to saying no. And then, because in Vegas you can find anything as long as it's not real, we find a hotel where not only Elvis, not only James Brown, but Michael Jackson, Dolly Parton, Tina Turner, The Beatles and The Stones are all playing. It's like a tribute Live Aid. A tribute Woodstock. And they're all good. All better than the real thing, or very nearly, because they are all young and enthusiastic and hungry. And the real thing is so rarely this.

Scarlett shows us just how dynamic her equinus can be. She wears us both out with full-on boogaloo bopping. She's the dancing queen.

And when, later, we tell our sleepy girl about a new world of bedtimes and earning screen time and the rationing of that crazy evil bastard Spongebob, she seems relieved. At least, that's my interpretation. Sarah thinks she's just puzzled.

'And Sarah, if anything happens to me, you've got to promise to carry on with this little experiment in child rearing. As a tribute to me. A memorial thingy.'

'Nothing's going to happen to you.'

'No, but if it does. You got to promise.'

'OK.'

'Really. Promise.'

'Blimey.' She's on the verge of getting irritated now, I can tell. 'I promise that I will raise our precious daughter Scarlett according to the principles laid down by Mr Knox né Fisher. There will be regular healthy meals, plenty of exercise, and screen time and sweets will be kept to a minimum. There will be cabbage. And she'll go to bed early and get up early. And her homework will be closely monitored. Also, I won't encourage the taking of crystal meth. Not on school nights anyway.'

I make the effort to grin. But the important thing is she's done it now. If, or when, Catherine's ridiculous 007 death-dart thing kicks in, Sarah will remember this conversation and she keeps her promises. Sarah always, always, does what she says she'll do. It's why employers love her, it's why people love her.

And we talk about our first wedding. The real wedding if you like, and we agree that it was fine. Good, if not outstanding. Nothing wrong with it – we don't mention the sadness of it – but we agree that we prefer this one. And I tell Sarah something I've actually been too ashamed to mention until now. Something about my stag night.

'Go on. I'm not easily shocked,' she says. I can tell from the way she's biting her lip that she thinks this is going to be a tawdry story of strippers and lap dances and a last night of freedom flings. And it's much worse than that.

I take a breath and I tell her about Russell and I burning a fifty-pound note apiece in front of a *Big Issue* seller. And how we would have burned more if a passing hen party hadn't threatened to put us both in hospital. And, now that I think about it, it wasn't even Russell's money. My money and I think it might have been my idea. What a wanker, eh?

'I think you're in the clear now, Pog,' she says. 'You've paid your debt. Done your time.'

And we put Scarlett to bed at eight – she's confused but compliant – and we pop in when she cries for us the first time. And the second time we leave her yelling for five minutes and then pop into her room, grin and say hi and then leave again. And then we leave her yelling for ten minutes. And then pop in again. We don't switch the light on, we don't pick her up, we don't sing to her, or read to her. We don't beg her. We don't threaten to throw her out of the window.

And then, according to our new routine, we have to leave her yelling for twenty minutes. Have you ever tried to listen to a child screaming for twenty minutes and not done anything about it? We turn the telly up – live wheelchair basketball from Kiev – but it's obviously not loud enough to drown her out. You'd need a major PA system to do that.

After seventeen minutes Sarah cracks.

'I can't do this.' And she gets up, which is when Scarlett stops screaming suddenly. So suddenly, that we both think something terrible has happened and we are both up and across to her room and yanking open the door. It's an ecstasy of fluster. I snap on the light. She raises her head from the pillow. She's red-faced, her eyes raw with tears. Blistered with ignored sorrows. But she's also quite clearly just been woken up. She hasn't swallowed her tongue, or screamed herself into a stroke or a coma. She hasn't been stolen by Guatemalan black-mailers. Or whatever it was we thought might have happened.

'Sleeping,' she says.

'I know honey. Sorry we woke you.' And Sarah goes to the bed and does some vital cover straightening.

'Sleeping,' Scarlett says again, louder this time. And we know a dismissal when we hear one, and we back out apologetically, as though from the throne room of some capricious queen renowned for her beheading parties. We switch the light off, half close the door and stand outside listening. All we can hear now is her breathing. Deep, slow, confident breaths.

I don't know how long we stand there for, but it's a while anyway. And then we're kissing. I don't know who initiates it, but somehow our hands find each other and then lips and then mouths and it's not quite like we've just met. Not quite like the very first time. It's much, much better than that, but there's some of that same urgency. When we surface, she pulls my hair.

'One day, when we can, we're getting rid of this.'

'Oh, why?'

'It unnerves me. Makes you look all rock starry. A bit too beautiful. I'll put up with it for now though.'

She touches my face. Runs her palm over my cheeks, my nose, my lips. It's like she's assuring herself I'm real. That I'm really here. That I'm not already a ghost.

She slips the bobby dazzler jacket off, unbuttons my waistcoat and my shirt. Runs her hands over my chest and down over the new six-pack.

'Now this – this you can keep.'

And her hands are on the belt of my bobby-dazzler trousers.

'Time for bed, Mrs Fisher. Mrs Knox. Mrs Fisher-Knox,' I say.

'I think I'll keep my own name, thank you very much.'

'Time for bed, whoever you are.'

She has dealt with the belt, and now her hand is unbuttoning the fly of the suit.

I can imagine Jimmy's pain if he knew that in seconds this suit is going to lie crumpled and discarded on the floor of an RV.

And we begin to do all the things we've learned to do with each other. The things we can all learn, rich and poor, old and young, beautiful or not. The things we should have done in the back of that limo when we had the chance. We touch and stroke and kiss and whisper filthy instructions in the warm dark. We are dancing and wrestling and calling out in a fierce strange tongue that no one speaks. That everyone speaks. And yes, if you could see us or hear us it would be ridiculous. Laughable. We storm, we form, we norm. We reach all our short-term objectives.

And you'd envy us. You wouldn't be able to tear your eyes away.

But no one can see us.

And here tonight there are no wars or murders. No babies crying for milk or for their mothers. No poisons swimming patiently through the blood to the heart. There is only this. And for now it's enough. And it didn't take ten thousand hours to get good at this. Afterwards there is toast and we get crumbs in the bed as I start to tell my love about my new plan. About Knoxville. My dream city. What it could be like, the colour of the postboxes, the perfect houses. The parks. The pubs. The easy-going, child-friendly cafes where the poets cry over girls and the young philosophers punch each other. The wide open spaces to fly kites.

She's up for it. Pretty soon she's joining in. She talks about the schools we'll build where the only compulsory subjects are art, music, drama, dance and languages. Where the kids elect the faculty. She talks about the retirement homes the seniors queue to join. Where the care assistants have PhDs. Where they have to pass exams in kindness. Reach proper established benchmarks in love.

And I talk about the sports stadium. The field-hockey squads, the rugby team. The cricket pavilion. The beach-volleyball centre, because Knoxville will be by the sea. Of course it will. Who wouldn't live by the sea if they could? I talk about the fact we'll only need the Knoxville police to teach cycling proficiency. There'll be no proper crime, we won't allow it.

'What do you think?' I say.

'You know what I think, Nicky. I think yes. Yes to all of it. Yes, yes, yes. Knoxville. Absolutely. Knoxville. Perfect. We can be the punk-rock town planners.' And she laughs and wraps her gluey self around me. 'But now my dearest love, my own Pog, please, please, please let me get some fucking sleep.'

And she's off in seconds while I listen to the gentle music of her breath and pulse, remembering her dancing in the kitchen to Jefferson Starship that day a few short weeks ago – a million years ago – thinking about the world our daughter will grow up in, and if anything should keep me awake, that should. But it doesn't because now I have this new dream to keep me going. To take my mind off death and poisoned darts. Toxins and taxes.

Next thing I know there's a small child telling me to carpe diem. Telling me this through the powerful modern medium of bouncing on my head.

'Daddy.' Bounce. 'Wake up. Daddy.' Bounce. 'Wake up.'

'I am awake.'

'Daddy.' Bounce. 'Wake up. Daddy.' Bounce. 'Be happy.'

'I am happy.'

And I am. Kind of.

And then she says, 'Mary. Want Mary.'

'Mary's gone,' I say. And wait. Scarlett opens her mouth, fills her lungs. I raise an eyebrow. Scarlett stops and thinks hard and very visibly about the advisability of yelling. I see a resigned look pass over her face. An oh-well-it-was-worth-a-shot kind of look and I suddenly remember this game my father used to play with me when I was small. It might distract her.

'Hey, let's play bucking bronco,' I say. She gives me a puzzled frown. In my best cowboy voice, my Woody from *Toy Story* voice, I go, 'Well, howdy there, pardner, what's your name?'

Scarlett just looks at me with those serious eyes. There is no one as serious as a child in a game. I say it all again. Exact same words, exact same intonation, like I was some kind of fairground ride, just programmed with a few short sentences. 'Well, howdy there, pardner, what's your name?'

And her eyes are wide as she whispers, 'Scarlett. My name is Scarlett,' and my eyes are hot and wet – sometime I might get used to her speaking, but not yet.

I keep my voice bright and metallic and machine-like. 'Scarlett. That's a purty name. Let's play bucking bronco!' And holding her round her waist I buck and thrash and generally act like I'm a horse trying to throw her off; she grips my ribs hard with her knees. It is actually quite hard to tip her over, maybe she'd be good with real horses. Maybe that could be her thing.

After a minute or so this rodeo horse tips her to the side, holding her firmly as she crashes next to me on the bed.

'Again!' she says. 'Again!'

'Well, howdy there, pardner,' I say again as I lift her back into position on my stomach. She weighs almost nothing at all. 'What's your name?'

'Scarlett,' she says, more firmly this time. 'My name is Scarlett. And I am awesome.'

356

ACKNOWLEDGEMENTS

Thanks to my editor Helen Garnons-Williams for her usual patience, good humour, sound judgement and unshakeable tolerance. Thanks also to the rest of the team at Bloomsbury especially Oliver Holden-Rea, Jude Drake, Amanda Shipp, Xa Shaw Stewart, Ianthe Cox-Willmott, Holly Fordham, Alice Shortland, Trâm-Anh Doan, Elizabeth Woabank and Imogen Corke, as well as Lea Beresford in the USA.

Thanks to the famously hawk-eyed Gabriella Nemeth for sensible and sensitive copy-editing.

For having the grown-up conversations I'm not equipped to have, I'd like to thank my agent David Smith at Annette Green Agency.

This book also owes something to the inspirational life of my old Colchester housemate Nick Crawshaw 1963–2005.

I'd like to thank Lucy Conroy – Lucy And The Caterpillar – for allowing me to quote from her song 'Bumble Bee'.

Also owed thanks are Arts Council England, Joe Compton, Jacqui Corcoran, Jan and Tony Cropper, Jodie Daber, Ralph Dartford, Joanna Dennis, Lizzie Enfield, Jim English, Denise Fahmy, Emma Forster, Sadie Hassell, Mark Illis, Duncan May, Herbie May, Carole Ockelford, Hannah Procter, Anthony Roberts, Ruth Scobie, Jim Tough and Richard Whiteley who all contributed to this book. Usually without knowing it.

All these thanks are heartfelt but the most heartfelt of all go, as ever, to Caron who has to live with these characters (and me) through their most turbulent, most dangerous, most annoyingly formative times.

A NOTE ON THE TYPE

The text of this book is set in Linotype Sabon, named after the type founder, Jacques Sabon. It was designed by Jan Tschichold and jointly developed by Linotype, Monotype and Stempel in response to a need for a typeface to be available in identical form for mechanical hot metal composition and hand composition using foundry type.

Tschichold based his design for Sabon roman on a font engraved by Garamond and Sabon italic on a font by Granjon. It was first used in 1966 and has proved an enduring modern classic.

ALSO AVAILABLE BY STEPHEN MAY

LIFE! DEATH! PRIZES!

Shortlisted for the 2012 COSTA Novel Award

Billy's Mum is dead. He knows – because he reads about it in magazines – that people die every day in ways that are more random and tragic and stupid than hers, but for nineteen-year-old Billy and his little brother, Oscar, their mother's death in a bungled street robbery is the most random and tragic and stupid thing that could possibly have happened to them.

Now Billy must be both mother and father to Oscar, and despite what his well-meaning aunt, the PTA mothers, the social services and Oscar's own prodigal father all think, he knows he is more than up to the job, thank you very much.

The boys' new world, where bedtimes are arbitrary, tidiness is optional and healthy home-cooked meals pile up uneaten in the freezer, is built out of chaos and fierce love, but it's also a world that teeters perilously on its axis. And as Billy's obsession with his mother's missing killer grows, he risks losing sight of the one thing that really matters . . .

Funny, bittersweet and unforgettable, *Life! Death! Prizes!* is a story of grief, resilience and brotherly love.

'If you're in the mood for a good bout of sobbing and your own life is just too nice to make you cry, this will definitely do it . . . A warm novel, written with a wry wit, and the end is as uplifting as a good bra' **THE TIMES**

'Stephen May's rites-of-passage novel is a painfully raw examination of the effects of loss and grief, and the confusion and difficulty of trying to be a male role model when you've never had a proper one yourself' **DAILY MAIL**

'A raw, funny and heartfelt book, full of surprising tenderness and hope – a fine achievement' A. L. **KENNEDY**

B L O O M S B U R Y